THE
FISHERMAN

THE
FISHERMAN

A THRILLER

VAUGHN C. HARDACKER

Skyhorse Publishing

Skyhorse Publishing books may be purchased in bulk at special discounts for sales promotion, corporate gifts, fund-raising, or educational purposes. Special editions can also be created to specifications. For details, contact the Special Sales Department, Skyhorse Publishing, 307 West 36th Street, 11th Floor, New York, NY 10018 or info@skyhorsepublishing.com.

Skyhorse® and Skyhorse Publishing® are registered trademarks of Skyhorse Publishing, Inc.®, a Delaware corporation.

Visit our website at www.skyhorsepublishing.com.

10 9 8 7 6 5 4 3 2 1

Library of Congress Cataloging-in-Publication Data is available on file.

ISBN: 978-1-63220-479-0
Ebook ISBN: 978-1-63220-852-1

Printed in the United States of America

To my wife, Connie, whose idea this was.

1

Cheryl Guerette stood on the pedestrian bridge, staring at the swan boats as they passed. Her face twisted, and she wrapped her arms tightly around her stomach as another wave of pain raced through her. She gripped the railing to keep from falling and stared at the strange face that looked back at her. Her blond hair was disheveled, and her blue eyes were ringed with dark circles; she was as pale as a sheet of paper. She was coming down and edgy, her body supersensitive. Anything touching her skin—even the gentle touch of the summer breeze—felt like a million daggers slicing flesh. She knew she was within an hour or two of coming down hard. She breathed deeply, too strung out to enjoy the warm evening. Exiting the Public Garden, Cheri—as she was known on the streets—walked to Charles Street. Turning toward Chinatown, she staggered down the sidewalk oblivious to passersby and the steady flow of late rush hour traffic.

Cheryl wandered aimlessly, waiting for the sun to go down. She glanced at her watch. It would be at least an hour before normal people went home, leaving the streets to the denizens of the night: drug dealers, pimps, hookers, and johns. It was going to be a slow night, but then Mondays always were. She should do the smart thing and return to her shabby room and take the night off. Mel always said that hookers were like preachers and should take Mondays off. That was, Cheryl knew, not an option open to her. She scratched at her arms, clenching her teeth as jagged, rough fingernails threatened to slice her open. It wouldn't be long before she was out of her mind with need—on the ground thrashing and screaming.

Cheryl reversed direction and returned to Boston Common and the Public Garden. She walked the nearly empty sidewalks until her withdrawal symptoms lessened and she could think straight. At the Public Garden, she roamed the paths, searching for Chigger. He would fix her up; he knew she was good for the money.

She had blown all of her weekend earnings on heroin. No matter how many times she vowed to keep a reserve to get her through the slow nights, she gave in and used it to buy more. She passed by a homeless man frantically searching for food in a trash bin. If he hadn't kicked her leg while digging to the bottom of the receptacle, she would've walked by as if he didn't exist. She rubbed the spot on her calf that his filthy, torn sneaker had hit and hurried past him. Under normal conditions, she would have stopped and ripped into the bum, but this was not a routine situation.

As if withdrawal wasn't enough, Mel would come around later wanting his money, and he wasn't going to be happy when she told him she had none. It wouldn't matter what line of bullshit she made up, Mel would know where the money had gone. Failing to locate Chigger, Cheryl left the Common and headed toward the theater district.

Cheryl glanced at her watch: 11 p.m. In spite of her condition, she knew it was time to get to work. She walked slowly, swinging her hips at every vehicle that passed. A couple of cars stopped, and she smiled and bent toward them, allowing each car's occupant to look her over. Each time the vehicle's driver pulled away. Anyone else would have known it was the wild junkie look in her eyes that turned them away.

Cheryl turned the corner and walked along Mass Ave and Tremont Street, through the theater district. Most times she would have paused to read the marquees for each show while longing for her name to be on one of them, but not on this night. Even in her current state, she knew her dream of an acting career was gone—lost forever in the kiss of a needle followed by the bliss of hot smack racing through her veins.

A strange-looking truck stopped beside her. Cheryl had never seen anything quite like it. It was the tractor of an eighteen-wheeler; only instead of pulling a trailer, someone had built a refrigerated box on the frame over the rear wheels. She thought it was strange that the blue commercial truck was devoid of signage; however, like everything else, her defenses were down. The driver rolled down his window, and hoping to score a trick, Cheryl went into her act. She stood beside the truck and purred, "Hey."

The driver stared at her but said nothing.

"You looking for some action?" Cheryl asked, hoping her tremors were not too obvious.

He motioned for her to get in the truck.

Suddenly, in spite of being close to crashing, Cheryl had misgivings; something about this john was not right. Still, she needed dope, so she got over her reservations and got in the truck, pulling the door closed behind her.

A strong fish smell filled the cabin, and involuntarily Cheryl slapped a hand over her mouth and nose. "Hi, I'm Cheri."

The driver stared at her. His head was misshapen—flat on one side, as if someone had smashed it with a beam. As he looked at her, his slightly crossed, pale-blue eyes flickered from side to side for a few seconds and then seemed to focus on her and cease moving.

"What are you, the strong silent type?"

No response.

Even her need for dope could not quell the alarm bells that sounded in her head—this john was whacked out.

"Look, maybe this isn't such a good idea." Cheryl reached for the door handle. It was missing.

2

M ike Houston saw the cloud of dust from the corner of his eye and buried the bit of his ax in the middle of the stump he used as a chopping block. He watched the plume of brown as it raced up the dirt road that led to the log cabin he and Anne Bouchard called home.

In a few moments, he saw the unmistakable fire engine red of Anne's Ginetta G33 two-seater flash through an opening in the trees. He took a handkerchief from his back pocket and wiped sweat from his forehead, then turned to the enticing shade of the porch that spanned the width of the structure. He sat in an Adirondack chair and reached into the plastic insulated cooler to extract a can of beer. He popped the top and took a long drink, savoring the cool liquid as it chilled his parched throat.

The car pulled into the yard and stopped within ten feet of the house. Houston walked off the porch, met her at her car, and opened her door. Anne smiled at him. "Is sitting there drinking beer all you've done today?"

"Hey, it's a tough job, but someone has to do it."

She hopped out of the sports car and landed in front of him, then raised up on her tip-toes, kissed him on the forehead, and smacked her lips. "Salty. Houston, you're the only guy I know who can sweat drinking beer in the shade."

"Not much cooler inside. How was your day?"

"Great, I went to Kittery and hit the outlet stores." She returned his embrace.

He shifted and held her at arm's length. "So what did you get me?"

She grinned. "I was going to get something sheer, slinky, and tantalizing for you."

Houston grinned. "Show it to me. Better yet, model it for me."

She laughed. "I said I *was* going to get it for you. Then I realized that it was a waste of money, because within minutes you'd rip it off me. So why waste the money when I already have all we need?"

He pretended to look crestfallen. "You mean you didn't buy it?"

"I mean I didn't buy it."

He gave a lecherous grin. "You'd rather run naked through the woods with me."

"Too many bugs. We can run naked through the house, though."

She stepped out of his arms and onto the porch. She sat in the chair he had vacated and opened the cooler. She stared inside for a second, pulled a beer from the cooler, and popped the top. She sat back, enjoying the respite from the late summer sun's heat and said, "I got to hand it to you, though. At first I wasn't sure I'd like living here, but it isn't half bad . . . ."

Houston sat beside her and drank his beer. "It does grow on you, doesn't it?"

They sat in silence for several minutes, enjoying each other's company. One of the secrets to their success as partners was their ability to accept each other's privacy and go long periods without talking.

"Something's on your mind, woman. What is it?"

"I want you to help me do something."

"Okay . . ."

"I met an elderly couple. A fisherman and his wife. They live in Kittery. Their granddaughter has gone missing."

"How'd you meet this elderly couple, hon?" Houston doubted that it was a chance meeting.

She smiled, and he knew that he was right; there was more to this than she'd let on.

"Well, I've been seeing posters about a missing woman. They said she was from Kittery but last seen in Boston. Naturally, I thought, 'Who would be better than Mike and me to look into this?' We got good connections in the city—on both sides of the fence."

"The police would be better. We're not cops anymore."

"The authorities have been notified. Besides, you have one thing that the cops don't."

"And what might that be?"

"Jimmy O and his organization. And that's not to mention contacts within the BPD."

"You have as many department contacts as I do. And ever since the Rosa incident, you can connect with Jimmy."

"I just thought that this could be something we can do together. It'd be like we're partners again."

"We are partners—in a much more meaningful way."

"I know that," Bouchard hesitated and then added, "I never thought I'd say this, but it'll be like the old days."

"Those *old* days were barely over a year ago."

"There's more to it—a lot more to it. I'd like you to talk to the Guerettes."

"You sound as if you've already met with them." Houston studied her and saw that she was deeply concerned. He also knew that until injury in the line of duty forced her to take a medical retirement, Anne was one of the most perceptive and intuitive cops he'd ever known. "Okay, we'll drive to Kittery in the morning."

She stood up from her chair and sat in his lap. She kissed him. "You always were a hard sell, Houston."

He laughed. "Why pretend I can resist you? Once you got me in bed, you knew you'd get whatever you wanted anyway."

"Aw, but when you give in so easy, it takes all the fun out of the sale."

3

A predawn fog rolled off the polluted water, obscuring the view of Chelsea and holding the composite stench of diesel fuel, rotting fish, and garbage close to the surface. Jimmy O'Leary walked along the pier while feeling his way along the wet planking. He hated boats almost as much as he did airplanes. *If God wanted men to fly and sail,* he thought, *he would have given us wings and webbed feet.* "You sure about this?"

"Yeah, boss, I'm sure," Gordon Winter answered. "This guy got in and out without coughing up on his last trip. He unloaded and was out to sea before we knew it." Winter saw the question on O'Leary's face. "Yeah, we dealt with the foreman of the longshoreman crew. He won't make that mistake again."

"We cover the hospital bills?"

"They were mostly dental." In many ways, O'Leary baffled Winter. He would have a man beaten and then cover his related medical bills. He knew better than to waste a lot of energy arguing over it; it was Jimmy O'Leary's way—given the opportunity, he could be a benevolent dictator.

"I want to put an end to this, Gordon. I can't have these idiots making stupid mistakes. It ain't respectful."

"Neither are we."

"What?"

"Sorry, boss, I thought you said *respectable*."

"There's an old Chinese proverb, Gordon. Everybody likes a little ass, but nobody likes a smartass."

They reached the end of the pier, and Winter stopped beside a small gangplank leading to a rusty-hulled tramp steamer. He heard O'Leary curse. "I hate the fucking docks—so goddamned damp you can't even light a smoke."

A shadow appeared at the top of the gangway. "What you want?" the voice was heavily accented—Slavic, O'Leary thought.

"We're here to see your captain."

"He know you're coming?"

O'Leary's stomach had had about all he could handle of the kelp and brine-laden foul air. He was sure he could smell every bit of offal, chemical waste, and dead body that had ever floated in the murky water of the Mystic River. "Listen, shit-for-brains. Get your ass inside that ship and tell your useless fucking captain that Jimmy O'Leary is here—and you better goddamned hurry up."

The seaman darted away, and Winter smiled. "Boss, you got to learn to be patient."

"I am patient—at least I'm as patient as I'm gonna be with this asshole."

The shadowy figure reappeared at the head of the ladder and motioned them up.

"About fucking time," O'Leary muttered. As he climbed the gangplank, he gripped the rope handrails so tight that he resembled an acrophobic walking on an icy tightrope. At the top, the vessel was no more impressive than it had been from below. Everything was in need of paint, and rust was evident in every corner. "Now I know where the expression tramp steamer comes from," O'Leary said to Winter.

They followed a long narrow passageway and ascended several metal stairways until they were deep inside the bowels of the ship. The air was rank and smelled of diesel fuel and stale cigarette smoke. The passageways were so narrow that Winter's broad shoulders barely cleared the walls as he walked.

"Ever been on a ship before?" O'Leary asked.

"A couple of times. Those ships were nothing like this though."

"Bigger?"

"A bit, but mostly they were cleaner and better kept."

The passageway ended in the galley, where the sole occupant sat at a table with a steaming mug in front of him. He wore a grimy captain's hat and a white T-shirt with black grease and oil stains on it.

"Not exactly a slave to fashion, is he?" Jimmy said.

"Yeah, but you got to admit, the grungy hat goes well with the grubby T-shirt."

The man glared at them and inhaled, illuminating the tip of the cigarette that dangled from his lips.

"Must be European registry," Winter remarked. "If it were American, there'd be a smoking ban."

"Well, that's one thing in its favor."

The seaman stepped aside and pointed to the man at the table. "Captain Gorky."

"Must have named him after the park," Winter commented.

"What park is that?" O'Leary asked.

"Gorky Park. Like the book."

"What book?"

"Forget it, boss. I doubt you read it."

"Remember what I said about wise asses, Gordon?"

"How could I ever forget such words of wisdom?"

O'Leary chuckled. "I saw the movie."

"*Gorky Park*?"

"No, Central fucking Park—of course it was *Gorky Park*. I'm not ignorant. It starred that guy that screwed Kathleen Turner in the movie where they killed her husband and then she framed the idiot for it." O'Leary shook his head. "Guy was one dumb shit to let a broad set him up that way."

Winter had no clue who or what his boss was alluding to but knew better than to pursue the subject. He followed O'Leary and crossed the room to the captain's table.

O'Leary pulled out a chair across from the captain, sat down, and lit a cigarette. "Captain Yuri Gorky, how was the voyage?"

"Was . . . how you Americans say . . . a piece of cake?"

"Well, we got a bit of a problem. Seems last time in you didn't follow the rules."

The captain glared at O'Leary through a cloud of heavy cigarette smoke. "Maybe I don't like rules."

"Maybe I need to have ol' Gordon here teach you the consequences of fucking with me."

Gorky's eyes narrowed. It was obvious to O'Leary that he did not like anyone threatening him, especially on board his own ship. However, Gorky was not foolish enough to voice his outrage. Gorky had most likely dealt with people like him in most of the ports around the world.

On the other hand, O'Leary knew that if he allowed one ship to unload without paying the fees, they would all stop paying. Control of the wharves was a significant moneymaking proposition, and O'Leary would do whatever he deemed necessary to ensure he didn't lose it.

As soon as he sensed the sea captain's hostility and arrogance, O'Leary nodded at Winter, who circled the table and stood behind Captain Gorky.

"Say the word, boss."

O'Leary held up a hand, signaling him to stop. "I don't think our friend Yuri will be a problem in the future. Am I right, Yuri?"

The sailor did not miss Winter's threat and smiled. "Jimmy, mistakes happen, no?"

"Not anymore they won't."

The captain nodded toward the galley's door, and in walked a seaman holding a revolver in his right hand and carrying a briefcase in his left. Gorky smiled at O'Leary. "Maybe you don't leave my ship alive?"

Winter pressed the muzzle of his 9 mm pistol against Gorky's neck. "Maybe when we leave your ship you ain't alive," he said. His voice was unemotional, which made the threat seem more real.

Gorky laughed. He motioned for the crewmember to put his handgun away. When the revolver disappeared, Winter removed the semi-automatic from Gorky's neck.

O'Leary saw sweat on Gorky's brow and knew he had won this battle. He swiveled around in his seat and said, "That case better have my money in it."

The seaman placed the briefcase on the table and stepped back.

O'Leary looked over his shoulder and stared at the goon. "Move out of my fucking space. Other than Gordon, I don't like people behind me."

Gorky motioned again, and O'Leary kept his eyes fixed on the captain's, listening to the sound of the sailor walking away. He sat still until he heard the metal door slam. He nodded to Winter, who stepped to the side so that he was in Gorky's line of sight.

"You can count it if you would like," Gorky said.

"No need for that. But just to be sure there are no little surprises in that case, open it."

Once again, Gorky laughed. "Jimmy, Jimmy, you show so little faith."

"That's why I'm still alive—open it. If that fucking thing is rigged and I go, you're coming with me."

Gorky opened the briefcase and turned it so O'Leary could see it contained money. If there was anything else in the briefcase, it was under the cash. Winter removed a pack of bills and riffled through each one, ensuring the stacks were not all one dollar bills with a single hundred on top to mislead them.

O'Leary tossed a cloth laundry sack on the table. "Put the money in this. I wouldn't want to take such a fine briefcase." Gorky laughed again and did as asked. As Winter had, Gorky flipped the end of each stack so Jimmy could see there was no filler in them before placing them in the sack. When he finished transferring the cash, he slid the sack across the table.

"I like doing business with a cautious man," Gorky said.

"Like I said, it keeps me alive."

"Would you like to see the cargo?"

"Sure, why not."

Gorky stood and motioned for O'Leary to precede him. O'Leary smiled and deferred.

"Always the careful man." Gorky laughed again.

"Yuri, you laugh too fucking much. It makes me wonder what you're planning."

"Jimmy, think how dreadful life would be if we could not laugh."

Winter picked up the sack, and they followed Gorky out of the galley. They descended more metal stairs, working their way deeper into the bowels of the ship, where they again followed a series of passageways so narrow that Winter's shoulders brushed the walls.

O'Leary soon lost his sense of where they were. He knew it would take him hours to find his way out of the labyrinth. He looked at Winter, who sensed his boss's unease and smiled back. "Don't worry, boss. I'll get us out of here," he said.

Gorky led them past several small doors with bars in the windows.

O'Leary glanced into one and saw several soiled mattresses and nothing else. "Who uses these?" he asked.

Gorky stammered when he answered, "W-we also carry passengers occasionally."

"It doesn't seem very luxurious to me." O'Leary was skeptical. Why would anyone pay for such a crappy room?

"This is a freighter," Gorky said, "not a luxury liner."

"Must be a cheap ticket," O'Leary commented as he walked away from the tiny cell.

They came to a small door and Gorky opened it, stepping through in front of O'Leary.

"What's your cargo?"

"This trip I carry bananas and fruit from Mexico."

O'Leary cast a wary glance at the hold full of hanging bundles of yellow-green fruit. "Wonderful. There's probably a million spiders and shit in here."

"It's not so bad. Although from time to time we do see tarantulas. . . ."

"Gordon, if a goddamned hairy spider comes for me, kill it. Then kill Yuri for keeping such a filthy ship." O'Leary turned to Gorky. "We'll have a crew here first thing in the morning to off-load."

————————

Jimmy O'Leary and Gordon Winter walked across the parking lot. "Something ain't right on that boat," O'Leary said.

"He's carrying more than fruit," Winter replied.

"Do those compartments have you wondering, too?"

"If that Russian prick is carrying passengers," Winter said, "they ain't willing ones. Those rooms looked more like jail cells than passenger berths. I wouldn't put it past these slimy bastards to be smuggling in women."

"That's quite a leap, Gord."

"Maybe not. There's been talk of Konovalov bringing in women from Eastern Europe and Russia. The sons of bitches promise them jobs and a better life. Of course, they got to pay off their passage first."

O'Leary stared back at the rusty hull of the tramp freighter. "Whatever it is, it's a hell of a lot more profitable than South American bananas. Find out who his broker is. Before I accuse the sonuvabitch of trafficking in white slaves, I want some answers." O'Leary spat and gave the ship another hard look.

"Don't hold back, boss," Winter quipped. "Tell us how you really feel."

O'Leary spun on Winter—something he rarely did. "Forcing young women and kids to be whores ain't a jokin' matter, Gord."

Winter realized that he'd crossed the line. Jimmy O'Leary had been known to kill pedophiles without reservation. It was not a subject that he took lightly. "Sorry, boss."

4

The stench enclosed Willard Fischer like a putrid cocoon, a homing signal for flies. Hundreds of them buzzed around and landed on his face and sweaty, naked torso. He ignored them and trudged along the dock, barely noticing the weight of the buckets he carried. With each step, the sticky pink swill splashed and slopped over the sides of the pails and stuck to his bare legs. Fischer ignored the itching as the foul-smelling feast attracted more of the voracious flies.

Fishing, both commercial and charter, was hard work, but it was all he knew. He had never done anything different, nor worked anywhere else, either before or after inheriting the business. His chaotic thought process switched, jumping from one subject to another. All thoughts of the hardships of fishing dissolved into an image of the stern visage of his father. The old bastard had only done one decent thing in his life: he'd died. Fischer knew without a doubt that before dying the old sonuvabitch was pissed because he knew that, of his two sons, the *imbecile* would inherit the business. Somewhere in the depths of hell, the miserable shit was ranting and raving, giving a new meaning to eternal damnation and making hell an even more miserable place for everyone there—even Satan. For the thousandth time that month, Fischer ground his teeth and swore he would show the rotten son of a whore that he was worthy, and in turn, he would leave it to his son—when he finally got a woman who could give him one.

When he thought of his heir, he stopped on the pier, set the slop buckets down, and turned to stare at the house. His eyes settled on the upstairs windows. Hers was the middle of the three. He hoped this one would finally give him the heir he desperately needed. If not, he would have to make yet another trip into Boston. With a violent shake of his head, he dismissed the thought. Frustrated by his three-year search for a satisfactory mate, he muttered, "This has to be the one."

He turned away from the house, picked up the buckets, and trudged toward the boat. Without pausing, he walked up the wooden gangplank. Similar to a tightrope walker, he extended his arms out to his sides. Using the buckets for balance as the ramp bent, he bounced with each step he took. Placing the pails on the deck, he opened the bait well. He pushed the first of the metal pails aside and poured the contents of the second into the small compartment. A stiff breeze blew in from the Gulf of Maine, cooling his sweaty chest and coating it and his face with the fine mist that blew back from the compartment.

Fischer watched the bucket's contents splash against the walls, coating the interior like thick pink paint. He straightened and noticed that some of the chum had missed the opening and landed on the deck. Mindlessly, he picked up the bit of meat and threw it into the well.

He set the empty pail down, picked up the second container, and poured it in. Fischer set the bucket beside the first and reached inside the bait well, stirring the mixture of ground bone, meaty tissue, and blood until it was the desired texture. He stood and used his hand to squeegee the pink stew from his arm, chest, and face.

He stared across the empty quay, admiring the cove's sparkling water. Turning his eyes downward, he saw his image reflected from the water's mirror-like smoothness. Most people thought that the face staring back at him was ugly. The nose was bent and misshapen from being broken several times. The old bastard had never spanked his son—punching him in the face was more his style. Once he'd done it in front of a couple of other fishermen, and they'd told him to go easy on the kid. The old man had said,

"The Bible says if you spare the rod, you spoil the kid." He'd laughed and added, "Leastways, I ain't never beat the bastard with no rod."

Turning his head slightly revealed what Fischer believed was the one thing that made everyone call him ugly. Rather than the round contour most people had, the right side of his skull was so flat as to appear concave. He barely remembered the day when the mast's block and tackle had let go and whipped across the deck. The windlass had hit him so hard that it knocked him to the deck, fracturing his skull and bursting his right eardrum. Even though he could not remember the rest of that day, he did recall the old bastard screaming for him to stop malingering and to get to work. The old man had refused to take him to a doctor—said he needed him on the boat and if it still bothered him in a week or so, he would do something. His mother had tried to make him feel better and said he was like a puppy that was so ugly it was cute. He wished that his right eye didn't turn inward—maybe then he'd be handsome. He studied himself for several seconds, admiring the left side of his face, which he believed was his best.

A brittle female voice admonished him, "*Vanity is a great sin!*"

He looked about, seeking his mother. As usual, she was out of sight, probably hiding somewhere in the woods along the shore.

"*Stop your fooling around and get to work!*" He turned his head ninety degrees, so with his good ear he could hear his father's voice better.

"Ain't fooling around, old man," he muttered.

He put his hands on his back just above his narrow hips and stretched. Vertebrae snapped loudly as he stressed them into place. He slammed the well's lid shut, shook off the residual bits of flesh that clung to his arm, gathered the buckets, and left the boat. He still had at least fifty pounds to grind before his job would be finished. As he walked down the pier toward the ramshackle workshop, he swung the sticky pails, looking as carefree as a child.

"*Goddamn it, boy, get a move on!*"

"*Hallet, don't you use the Lord's name in vain again!*"

———

He entered the woman's room. An acidic stench met him at the threshold; he knew immediately that she had puked again. He turned on the ceiling light.

The naked woman lay on the bed, hardened vomit and waste caked on the mattress, and a fresh patch of spew lay near her head. Seemingly unaware of his presence, her legs kicked and her body thrashed about like a dinghy in thirty-foot swells. When she heard him enter and close the door, her bloodshot eyes turned to him.

"Please," she begged, "I need a fix."

He looked at her with a scowl bordering on contempt. He knew that she was in excruciating discomfort but had no sympathy; drug addicts didn't rate it. He had gone through this with several of the others, and he knew that the worst of the withdrawal symptoms had passed. The bouts of vomiting and diarrhea had become fewer and farther between; however, the kicking and thrashing body movements were still evident, only not as severe as they had been during the first seventy-two hours. He was unmoved by her pleas. "No, it will be over in a few more days. You're young and still healthy, so I don't think you'll die." He refrained from adding that either way, he could not care less . . . there were plenty more women like her out there.

His words angered her, and she leaped forward, stopping abruptly when she reached the limits of the chains that bound her. The woman fought against her bonds, eyes flashing with hatred, and spittle flew from her lips as she lurched toward him and screamed, "I'm dying, you fucking pervert!" Her strength seemed to give out, and she slid back on the fouled mattress and folded her legs into the fetal position. The chains he used to restrain her rattled when she wrapped her arms around her torso. He knew that her nervous system was hyperactive, and like the others had, she complained about muscle and bone pain. Each time her hands touched her feverish flesh she recoiled, and he knew that it felt like she was covered in third-degree burns.

"I won't have a junkie as my wife," he said.

"Wife? What woman would marry you, you ugly freak?"

He ignored her taunts. He knew she didn't mean what she'd said; it was just a ploy to goad him into giving her drugs.

"That stuff you been shooting into your body is poison," he said. "But in a few days it'll get better, you'll see."

"I'd rather die from poison than spend another minute here!"

"Give it time—you'll learn to like it."

He walked to the bed and looked at the mess that covered it. He debated whether to clean it and her or to let her lie in it. His nostrils flared when he breathed in the rancid air. To leave the room in this state was dangerous; if Mum smelled the foulness, she would never accept this woman. He left the room and gathered a basin of fresh warm water, soap, and a clean washcloth and towel.

Even though the room was hot, goosebumps covered her flesh, and she screamed when he touched her. He ignored her ranting and cursing as he cleaned her body; then he picked her up, ignoring her cries of agony, and placed her on the chair beside the bed. He removed the fouled sheets and flipped the mattress over, ignoring the fact that the newly exposed side was no cleaner than the other. He put dingy, yellowed sheets on the bed and once again paid no attention to her rants and curses when he picked her up and placed her on the bed.

"Can't have Mum seeing you like this. She's a good Christian woman and don't like people who consume strong drink and do drugs."

She glared at him.

"The last thing I want to do is meet your mother, you stupid son of a whore."

His face reddened, and he slapped her.

"Don't you ever call my mother a *whore!*"

Cheryl woke up and stared through the gloom at the ceiling. A light tapping came from someplace but from where she was uncertain. She was soaked with sweat, still dealing with delirium tremors, and was possibly hallucinating and hearing things. Still the incessant tapping continued, and she realized that it came from the adjacent room. Cheryl struggled to her knees and placed her ear against the wall. The tapping seemed to be coming from some point below her bed. She rolled off the bed and onto her hands and knees. Seeking the point of origin, she trailed her fingers along the wall. Several times, she stopped searching and raised her head to ensure that he wasn't in the room. Once she knew she was alone, Cheryl resumed her quest. After several tense moments, her fingers detected an irregularity near the leg of the bed.

She lowered her face until she was able to see that there was a hole in the wall. She placed her mouth by it and whispered, "Hello?"

She replaced her mouth with her ear, and a voice said, "Help me."

"Who are you?"

"Monique . . ."

Cheryl inhaled sharply and caught her breath. She believed she knew this woman. Monique had disappeared from the area around Arlington Street several weeks ago. "Monique, it's Cheri."

"Oh my God, Cheri! We have to get out of here!"

"How? He keeps me shackled to a beam in the ceiling."

There was no immediate response from Monique. Then Cheryl heard her crying. "Are you alright?"

"Now that he has you, he'll take me to the factory."

"The factory?"

"It's where he takes the women he's done with."

There was a loud bang from Monique's room, and Cheryl heard him shout. "What are you doing down there?" There was the sound of a scuffle followed by the loud reports of someone being slapped and beaten. Cheryl leaped into bed and curled up, trying to ignore the sounds coming from Monique's room.

She had no idea how long it was from the time she returned to her bed until she heard the lock on her door rattling. The door opened, and she opened her eyes enough to see while at the same time hoping he would assume that she was asleep. He stood framed in the door—a black demon silhouetted against the hall light. Behind him, lying on the floor, was the unmistakable figure of a human body. He stood there for several moments and then closed the door.

Cheryl heard the rattle of the lock being engaged and then the sound of something being dragged. It took several seconds for her to realize that the figure on the floor was in all likelihood Monique.

She started to drift off to sleep when she heard the whine of some sort of machinery. She lay in the darkness listening.

The next morning he appeared in her room and made her stand against the opposite wall. He searched around her bed and then stood up. He smiled at her but said nothing. He left the room and returned in minutes, carrying a flat-bladed putty knife and a small plastic container. He squatted beside her bed and filled the hole in the wall, using the knife to smooth the Spackle. "That'll put an end to that," he said as he left the room and once again locked her in.

5

Anne Bouchard placed her empty coffee cup on the table and smiled at Houston. His black hair was still messed from sleep, and he needed a shave and shower after the Olympian effort he had put forth the previous night. His hazel eyes were bloodshot, and he yawned.

"What's the matter, Mike? You out of shape or something?" She suppressed a laugh. The truth was that she, too, felt the effects of the previous night's activity and wanted a hot shower to revive her.

"Well, it's been a long time since we went to bed that early and went to sleep that late . . ."

"Take a hot shower—that'll wake you up," she said. "Better yet, I'll go first."

"Don't you think we should shower together to conserve water?"

"Are you up to it?"

Houston thought for a moment then said, "Probably not. . . . You wore me out, woman."

Bouchard stood and, as she walked to the bathroom, said, "I'm starting to think you're too old for me, Houston."

"Too old for you? I'm only four years older—"

She smiled and with an exaggerated sway of her hips turned toward the bathroom. "Age is only one way to measure how old a man is. I'll only be a few minutes."

———————

Once showered, Houston made a fresh pot of coffee and took two mugs out to the porch. He sat in one of the Adirondack chairs beside Bouchard, who said, "You were right about one thing, Mike. This life grows on a person."

"And I thought you'd go nuts up here. It's a long way from here to Newbury Street and Quincy Market."

"Oh, I knew I could adjust."

"Maybe so, babe. But a part of you will always be a city girl."

"You're probably right. Let's get down to business, okay?"

"Sure, I'm all ears." He sat back and listened. When he and Anne had been partners on the BPD, he had always deferred to her when it came time to make a presentation or to present the facts of an investigation to their superiors. They had both been born and raised around Boston—he in Irish South Boston and she in affluent Newton. However, it was she, not Houston, who had the gift of blarney.

"An old couple, Betty and Archie Guerette, have been hounding every law enforcement agency between Portland and Boston. Their granddaughter, one Cheryl Guerette, was a student in Boston, and she's disappeared."

"Well, college kids are an impulsive bunch. She probably took off to the Cape or some romantic getaway with her latest boyfriend."

"Maybe, but I got a bad taste about this."

"Anne, I don't have a clue as to what I'll be able to do in regards to this."

"I've arranged for us to meet with the Guerettes at their home in Kittery. That should give us a starting point."

"If," he added, "I decide to take this on."

"When," she countered, "you take it on."

"That sure of me, are you?"

She smiled at him. "After five years as your partner and over a year of living as your *significant other*, I know you better than you know yourself."

"I still don't know if I want to do this. We've been off the job for over a year."

"Mike, you were the best when it came to closing cases. Like I said, you have a couple of resources that make you uniquely qualified for this."

"I think you overestimate how much influence I have in Boston." He took a sip of his coffee and placed the mug on the small table beside his chair.

"Twenty years as a cop, fifteen as a detective, and being a lifelong friend of Jimmy O'Leary's gives you more influence than even you realize."

"How does Jimmy fit into this?"

Houston and Jimmy O'Leary had grown up together in South Boston. They'd separated when Jimmy dropped out of school, and the rift had widened when Houston joined the Marines. Later, when Houston became a cop, the relationship became adversarial and remained so until a deranged sniper killed Houston's ex-wife, Pamela—Jimmy O's sister.

Bouchard pressed on. "Even though you chose to walk a different path, he'll still do anything he can for you. He'll still help you. He never stopped thinking of you as his brother-in-law, even after the divorce."

Houston's face turned pallid. "Pam's been dead for over a year . . ."

"Yes, she has, and Jimmy helped us bring Rosa down."

"I didn't promise anything other than I'd go talk to the girl's grandparents. I'm not committing to anything yet . . ."

"I know you will . . ." She leaned over and kissed him on the cheek. "And you know it, too."

6

Houston stepped from his pickup and waited for Bouchard to touch up her makeup before following him. He spent several moments observing the small cape house and the commercial fishing boat moored at the dock behind it. The yard was neat and showed the results of hours of loving care. Someone put in a great many years planting, pruning, and nurturing the flowerbeds. He sensed rather than saw Bouchard beside him. "Nice house."

"Betty must really love working in her garden. I like the farmer's porch."

Houston looked at his partner. "If you ever stop finding cases for us, I'll put a farmer's porch on the cabin."

She said, "Mike, if all I did was work around the house all day, I'd go bonkers." Bouchard pushed open the gate of the small white picket fence and stepped aside for him to precede her in. He placed his hand on the gate and said, "Humor me . . ."

She stepped through the portal and gave him a look that was somewhere between a smirk and a smile. "He suffers from latent gentlemanly tendencies . . . who would have thought?"

"Five minutes from now you'll be calling me a chauvinist."

"Well, it is a woman's prerogative to change her mind."

"Depending upon her mood and the situation."

"Ah, Michael Houston, you're not as slow as you look."

A diminutive woman, who Houston thought to be in her mid- to late sixties, appeared on the porch, interrupting their never-ending battle of quips. She stood in the shade, her nervousness evident by the creases along the side of her eyes and the way she twisted a towel in her hands.

"Be nice." Anne warned him in a hushed voice. "Don't even bring up the possibility that the girl may be dead . . . these people still have hope that their granddaughter is alive."

"And you don't?"

"We both know there's little chance of that . . ." Bouchard escalated the volume of her voice. "Good afternoon, Betty. This is my partner."

The elderly woman nodded and said, "Please, come inside." She stepped aside, allowing them entrance to her home. Once inside, Houston found himself standing in an immaculate though small living room. The furniture was not new but showed no signs of wear. It was either of good quality or hardly used. Either way, Houston knew it was the result of a New Englander's desire to get the most for their dollar. He thought of his maternal grandfather, Chester Mahan. A Scotsman by heredity and frugal by virtue of being raised in Maine, Chester was tight, but when he did open his wallet he would purchase something once. Houston recalled him saying that you might as well spend two-thirds more and get quality rather than pay one-third less for something of dubious quality, only to have to pay it three times. When asked what he meant, the wily Scot merely said, "Think about it."

Bouchard took control. "Betty Guerette, this is Michael Houston. Mike, meet Elizabeth Guerette."

The petite woman held out a tiny hand and said, "Pleased to meet you. Please call me Betty." She pronounced her name in two syllables: Bet-tee. Her accent was that of down east Maine.

A door slammed in the rear of the house, and someone called, "Where are yuh, woman?"

"That'd be Archie." Again, Houston thought the accented Ahh-chie had an almost lyrical ring to it. A small man—barely an inch taller than his wife and who had a barrel chest and heavily muscled arms that made him look like a beer keg with arms and legs—entered the room. Still, in a tussle, Houston, who was six-two and 220 pounds, would be careful not to let the older, smaller man get his hands and arms around him.

Archie wore a plaid shirt with the sleeves rolled up and a green and yellow John Deere cap. "Archie, deah, this is Mr. Houston. He's the private detective Anne told us about."

Archie held out a hand so huge that it seemed oversized for his body. "Pleased ta meet cha." That deep timbre coming from such a small man surprised Houston.

"Can I get you something to drink?" Betty asked. "Maybe some tea or coffee? If you'd prefer something cold, I have iced tea and lemonade."

"A glass of cold water would be fine," Houston said.

When Betty returned carrying a pitcher of ice water and four tumblers, Archie said, "Why don't we set out on the porch? They's usually a nice breeze this time of day."

Once they were seated, Houston said, "Anne told me some of your problem. Still, I'd like to hear what you have to say."

Betty sipped some water and placed the glass on the small table between her and her husband. She sucked in air in a manner that said *let's get this over with* and said, "It's about our granddaughter. She's missing."

Houston decided to conduct the interview tabula rasa—a blank slate. "How old is your granddaughter?"

"She just turned twenty the fifth of this month."

"Mrs. Guerette, the police are truly your best option here. They have a much better chance of finding her than Anne and I would."

"Anne has already told us that. We have already notified them, but they haven't been able to find her."

"Well, these things can take time."

"It's been two weeks," Archie said.

"The police don't seem to care," Betty said. "It wouldn't surprise me if a bunch of people in Boston think that they have better things to do than worry about a girl from up here. That's why Archie and I thought that maybe if we hired a . . ." She hesitated as if she were trying to find the correct word. ". . . private eye, they might be able to go down there."

"Well," Anne said, "Mike and I have licenses to conduct investigations in Maine, New Hampshire, Vermont, Rhode Island, and Massachusetts. We have more freedom to go between states than members of police departments do."

Betty pressed on. Her eyes bored into him, and Houston saw a steely resolve in her. "I want to know if our Cheryl is alright. We'll pay you for it even if we have to mortgage the boat."

Archie nodded his agreement.

Houston thought that her inner strength was reminiscent of a she-bear protecting her cubs. "Well, Mrs. Guerette, I feel it's only fair to advise you that it can be expensive."

A bright-red hue crept upward from the collar of Archie's shirt. He took a weathered leather wallet out of his hip pocket. "We ain't looking for charity." He counted six one hundred dollar bills and placed them on the table near Houston's leg. He held the money in place with a strong, gnarled index finger and said, "Here's six hundred dollars. Take it and go to that school. All we want is for you to find out why she hasn't called or written us."

For the second time that afternoon, the old fisherman reminded Houston of his grandfather. Like Archie, Chester would have slid down a banister made by Gillette before he took anything that remotely resembled charity. Houston's reservations as to whether or not he would help were swept away. When Houston took the money, Archie removed his hand. Houston shifted in his seat and held the money toward Betty. "Tell you what. If we think we can help you, and then, if we find your granddaughter, we'll talk about compensation. Okay?" He saw Bouchard's questioning look and knew he'd have to explain why he refused to take the money.

Betty and Archie looked at each other for a few seconds. "I suppose that would be alright," Archie said.

"You must also keep in mind that we may not learn anything—and if we do find her, she's twenty and we can't make her return home if she doesn't want to."

Betty took the six bills from Houston and handed two of them back, saying, "For your expenses." She passed the remaining four to Archie. She settled back in her seat and studied Houston as if she were unsure of him.

Houston saw her skepticism and realized that for some reason he was compelled to overcome it. "Okay, tell me everything—from the beginning."

Archie glanced at Betty, waiting for her to decide which of them would tell the tale. She nodded; it was all the affirmation he needed, and he settled back.

"Cheryl—that's her name," Betty said, "has lived with us since she was a baby. Her father, our son, died young, and her mother left." When she spoke of her departed daughter-in-law, her gentle, grandmotherly demeanor disappeared, and her eyes turned cold. "That one was not made from good stock. Had a problem with . . . drugs."

"Was she an addict?" Houston asked.

Archie nodded. Betty's cheeks flushed, and she looked away from Houston and stared at the porch decking. When she regained her composure, she began to speak, accenting her words by tapping the arm of the chair with a crooked finger as she spoke. "Last year Cheryl left home and went to school down in Boston. She wanted more out of life than what being the granddaughter of a fisherman could give her. But we told her it was nothing to be ashamed of . . . it's what we do." She straightened up when she spoke; her posture was all the evidence Houston needed to know that she was a strong, proud woman.

Houston rarely interrupted people when they were telling their story. He knew that once they began talking, momentum would loosen their tongues, and they would reveal even more than they had intended, but when she paused, he realized she wanted some form of affirmation. He gave it to her. "What type of school?" In spite of Archie's ability to have six hundred dollar bills in his wallet, these people did not strike him as having enough money to pay for their granddaughter to attend Harvard, Radcliffe, or MIT.

"She goes to the Suffolk College of Acting and Modeling," she said. "Cheryl is such a lovely child."

Houston smiled at her and said, "I can see where she gets it."

Betty blushed. Houston knew it had probably been years since anyone had told her she was pretty. Nevertheless, she was an attractive woman. She must have been a beauty in her youth. "I have a picture," she said. She fumbled inside her purse for several seconds and then produced a small photograph. She leaned forward and handed it to him.

It was a photograph of a gorgeous young woman; the resemblance to the woman sitting across from Houston was close enough that there could be no doubt they were from the same gene pool. The young woman leaned against a late-model SUV, her arms draped around a swarthy man. When Houston looked at him, one word came to mind: pimp. The man wore a shirt open to the middle of his chest and had more gold chains around his neck than a character in a 1970s disco movie. Houston thought, *If he's trying to look like Travolta in* Saturday Night Fever, *it's not working. He looks like Travolta in* Pulp Fiction. "Who's the guy?"

"Melvin Del Vecchio."

"What's his relationship with Cheryl?" Houston asked.

"Cheryl has been doing some modeling already," Betty said. "He's her agent and business manager."

Houston did not want to tell them what type of business the grease-ball in the photo most likely managed. However, he knew it was not smart to make quick judgments. Over the years, Houston had learned a few basic rules about life. One of them was that things were usually the way they looked; for instance, if the animal in your backyard was black with a white stripe down its back and smelled like a skunk, there was little probability that it was a cat on its way to a masquerade. Houston spent a couple of seconds committing Del Vecchio's face to memory. He had a premonition—one he hoped would remain hidden from the Guerettes.

He shifted his attention to Cheryl's image and looked closer at it. Her eyes had a faraway look to them. Back in the day when he was a cop, he had seen eyes like that a thousand times—usually on drug addicts. He suddenly had second thoughts about taking the case. Something told him that the outcome might not be one the Guerettes were going to like. It would not be the first time a big city predator hooked an attractive young girl from the sticks.

7

Houston and Bouchard exited the highway at Mystic Avenue to avoid the traffic backup on the lower deck. Interstate 93 piggy-backed into upper and lower decks from Sullivan Square to the TD Bank Garden, where it joined US Routes 1 and 3 and disappeared under the old Southeast Expressway in the O'Neil Tunnel—usually a driver's most horrific nightmare.

They cut through Somerville and Cambridge and entered Boston via the Boston University Bridge. Once across the Charles River, Bouchard turned onto Commonwealth Avenue, following it through Kenmore Square. Houston studied the familiar shape of Fenway Park as they passed.

Cheryl Guerette studied art at the Suffolk College of Acting and Modeling on Fairfield Street. Houston remembered the area from his days on the BPD—a neighborhood comprised of Victorian brownstones and narrow cross streets between Back Street and Boylston Street. Houston thought it a strange place for a school. He cursed the weather—it was not even nine o'clock in the morning, and the temperature and humidity index were the same: eighty-eight. When Boston gets that hot and humid, a deep breath puts you at risk of drowning.

As they strolled along the street, Houston realized that Boston was a part of him, and although he had left the city, it had never left him. He also knew that the city was not a big enough part to lure him back except to visit.

They had no trouble finding the Suffolk College of Acting and Modeling. Inside the main entrance was an open door. The school was, like most small for-profit proprietary colleges, extremely money conscious and hadn't spent a lot on decorating when they opened. It appeared as if they had just removed the doors from a set of apartments and converted them into office suites. It didn't surprise him. Boston was a college town and full of places like this. Cambridge was even worse; as Harvard University had grown, the school bought up blocks of old brownstones and triple-deckers and turned them into offices.

The school was easy to identify; every glass door in the campus had the SCAM logo stenciled on it. Bouchard chuckled and said, "I wonder if the logo is indicative of the quality of the education?" Knowing that many of these so-called vocational colleges were nothing more than diploma mills, Houston, too, wondered just how appropriate the acronym was.

A number of students walked out of the building, and Bouchard commented, "Seems to be a large summer contingent."

"Most of these for-profit vocational schools offer two-year associate degrees and are in session year-round. A friend of mine has a kid attending one, she's studying to be a medical assistant."

"Must be tough going all year," Bouchard commented.

"Well, in a way it's not such a bad thing. They get vocational training, and besides, once they get a job it's gonna be year-round anyway."

They walked inside the building and entered a door that had REGISTRAR painted on the glass. He thought the overweight elderly woman behind the desk that fronted the door leered at him. Whether her attitude was caused by their interrupting her or because she might have to move, he wasn't sure. "May I help you?" Her tone sounded as cold as the blue tint in her hair.

"My name is Mike Houston, and this is my partner, Anne Bouchard. Mr. and Mrs. Archie Guerette—they're grandparents of one of your students, Cheryl Guerette—and they have . . ." The woman became attentive when he mentioned Cheryl—she obviously knew her by name. ". . . asked us to check on Cheryl. Is there someone I can speak to?"

"That would be the Registrar, Ms. Cooper. Please, have a seat. I'll tell her you're here." She grunted as she got up, muttering under her breath that the school needed an intercom. She ran her hands over her imposing derrière, trying to smooth out the wrinkles in the fifty yards of material that had been used to make her dress, and walked deeper into the suite. She stopped before a closed door, knocked, and waited a few seconds. A muffled voice summoned her into the inner sanctum. After a few moments, she waddled back out. Houston noted the exertion of walking thirty or forty feet had left her breathing hard, and her forehead shone with perspiration. Her struggle reminded him of an aunt who suffered from a glandular imbalance and became so large that she was unable to climb the stairs to her second floor. The woman inhaled deeply, trying to catch her breath, and said, "You can go in now."

He thanked her and stepped aside to allow Bouchard to precede him into the Registrar's office. As large as the receptionist was, Ms. Cooper was the opposite. She was so skinny that Houston thought she would make most supermodels turn green with envy. Her office was small and immaculate, which, based on his experience, was unusual for college administrators. After his discharge from the Marines, he'd taken a number of night courses at Northeastern University, and his deans and professors had worked in a pile of books and papers, the flotsam and jetsam of university life.

Ms. Cooper stood and offered her hand. Houston took it and gently shook it a single time; her hand was thin, skeletal, and so pallid that blue veins were visible through the skin. She seemed so frail that he was fearful of crushing her hand, and he made a point of gripping it lightly.

"How may I help you, Mr. Houston?" The pitch of her voice was so high that he was certain that when she spoke the head of every dog in the neighborhood popped up.

"I'm here about a student. Cheryl Guerette."

"I'm not at liberty to discuss our students. I'm sure you're familiar with privacy laws."

Houston had anticipated that, and after he had agreed to help, he had Archie take them to his bank, where they got a notarized letter authorizing them access to any information pertaining to Cheryl Guerette. Bouchard reached inside her bag and handed it to the Registrar. "We have authorization," she said.

Ms. Cooper read the letter and inspected the notary's seal like a bank teller inspecting a hundred dollar bill suspected of being counterfeit. "How do I know you're the people authorized in this letter? Do you have ID?"

Houston took out his Maine driver's license and handed it to her. "Will this suffice?"

She compared him to the picture and handed the license back. She picked up the letter and said, "Can I have this?"

"We'll let you have a photocopy, but we always keep the originals in our files," Houston said. "Should an auditor or anyone else want to see it, you can refer them to us."

Cooper motioned for them to sit in the straight-backed wooden chairs that fronted her desk. Before she could say anything, Houston said, "Cheryl's grandparents have retained my partner and me to look into her whereabouts. They haven't heard from her in several weeks."

"I'm not surprised."

Something set off alarm bells in his head. Similar to the obese secretary, Ms. Cooper knew Cheryl without checking a file. Her coldness indicated there was history between Cooper and Cheryl. "You seem familiar with Cheryl."

"Unfortunately, most of the staff and faculty are familiar with her. Suffolk is a small school. We own the two buildings on either side of this one and only enroll about a hundred students per semester."

"Tuition must be astronomical," Bouchard said.

"Actually, it's quite affordable. We get a number of grants through the National Endowment for the Arts. Regardless, one of the positive aspects to our small size is that it allows us to be close to our students. Ms. Guerette was particularly troublesome."

"Troublesome . . . how so?" Houston asked.

"All I can tell you is that she is no longer a student here. Anything else I might say on the matter would be hearsay and rumor."

I'll bet you know every word of it, Houston thought. Instead he asked, "So she's been suspended?"

"No. She was expelled for violating our Student Code of Conduct. Her behavior forced us to dismiss her permanently. Are you satisfied? Now, I'm really quite busy. Is there anything else?"

Houston surmised that Cheryl must have done something unusually severe. Schools such as this one only worried about two things: student retention and the dollars associated with it. Administrators and faculty only had one duty: keep the students in class and the revenue flowing. "Ms. Cooper, there must have been something more than *hearsay and rumor* for such a severe action."

"All I'll say is there were a number of incidents, all in violation of the student code of conduct."

"Ms. Cooper," Houston said, "we are here to find Cheryl, not place any responsibility or blame on your school. We represent her family."

"I'm sorry, due to the possibility of . . . well, if you require more, I'll need some sort of legal documentation from—" Cooper hesitated and then said, "I'm sorry, but that is all I am going to say on the subject. Now, can I do anything else for you?"

"There is one other thing," Bouchard said. "Cheryl's grandmother told us that she had a friend—Sarah Wilson. Can you tell us how we might get in touch with her? Maybe you could give us a number where we might call her?"

Cooper pondered the question for a few seconds, and then she removed her glasses; unconsciously, she chewed one of the plastic earpieces. "Law prohibits me from giving the number to you—unless you have another letter pertaining to information about Sarah."

"I understand," Bouchard replied. "She and Cheryl were roommates, were they not?"

"Yes, that much I can tell you."

They thanked Cooper and made their way out of her office.

———

They found the apartment where Cheryl and Sarah Wilson lived three blocks from the school. Houston was thankful the young women lived so close. Apartments near college campuses usually charged higher-than-average rent, and many students lived in Boston's less affluent neighborhoods, relying on mass transit to travel back and forth. This was especially true in late August when the heat and humidity made walking very far out of the question. They checked the mailboxes in the foyer and found Sarah's name on the box labeled 2A. Bouchard tried the door leading to the inner stairs and was surprised when it opened. "Lousy security," she commented.

"Unfortunately, most of these converted single-family homes don't install security systems."

"They should." Bouchard entered the building first, and Houston followed her up the stairs to the second floor. She knocked on the door and for several moments stood to the side and listened for sounds from within. There was no sign of occupancy; Sarah was obviously not at home. On either side of the door were windows that overlooked the street, and Houston walked over to one. He peered outside, looking for a place where they could keep an eye on the apartment and smiled when he saw a coffee shop across the street.

The investigators left the building and crossed the thoroughfare. They entered the coffee shop, bought iced tea, and sat at one of three small tables the shop owner kept on the sidewalk. Bouchard selected a table, and they settled back to wait.

Houston sipped his drink and looked at Bouchard. She caught his look and asked, "What?"

"Nothing, this is just so . . . so like when we were on the force."

"I know," she said. "There are times when I miss being a police officer."

"There's one thing I don't miss about it."

"Which is?"

"We no longer have to hide our feelings from everyone. I can come right out and tell you that I love you whenever I want to."

She smiled. "Be careful, Houston. You're starting to sound romantic rather than like a big bad Marine sniper."

He grinned. "You know better than anyone a lot of that is just an act. Besides, you bring out the touchy-feely side of me."

She laughed. "Where is this coming from?"

"Oh, it's always been there, I just keep it hidden from most of the world."

"I know one other person that you need to show it to more often."

Houston bent forward. "If you say something absurd like Jimmy O, I'll never show you this side of me again."

"No, I was *not* alluding to Jimmy. I was talking about your daughter, Susie."

"What? She knows that I care for her and love her."

Bouchard reached across the table and tapped him on the forehead. "It doesn't hurt to tell her once in a while, you dolt."

He grew pensive.

"What's wrong?" she asked.

"Susie scares me."

Bouchard leaned back. "Now who's being absurd? How can a man be scared of his own daughter?"

"When he suddenly realizes she's no longer the little girl who idolizes him but is an intelligent young woman who sees him as he really is."

"Maybe," Bouchard said, "you need to try something different with her."

"Like what?" He took a drink of his iced tea.

"Like stop being the all-powerful father and become a friend and mentor to her."

He placed his drink on the table and said, "That's another reason that I love you. You always know what to say to me when I need my eyes opened."

Bouchard placed her hand on his. "Mike, you can be so strong in many ways yet so weak in so many others."

"That," he said, "is why we make such an ass-kicking team, hon—we complement each other."

Bouchard suddenly became alert. "I think she's here," she said, watching a young woman enter the apartment building.

A few minutes later, one of the windows opened. Houston threw their empty cups into a nearby trashcan, and he and Bouchard crossed the street.

Bouchard said, "Let me lead. She'll be more likely to open the door for a woman than a strange man."

They climbed the stairs, and Houston knocked on the door and stepped aside so Bouchard was in front when it opened as far as the security chain would allow. He hated those stupid chains. As a security device they were only as good as a swift kick against the door; a buzzer on the entrance door was a much more secure device.

"Yes?"

"Sarah? Sarah Wilson?" Bouchard asked.

"Do I know you?"

"No, but Cheryl's grandparents do. They've asked us to find her. They're worried and want to know if she's all right. I wonder if you might talk with us for a few minutes."

It became obvious that Sarah Wilson was smarter than most people her age when she said, "How do I know you're who you say you are?"

"Do you know the names of Cheryl's grandparents?" Bouchard asked. She nodded.

Houston passed the notarized letter through the door. "Her grandfather gave us this so we could look at her school records."

Wilson read the letter, then handed it back and said, "Just a moment."

The door closed, and Houston heard the chain slide. It opened, and Sarah stepped aside. "Come in."

They walked into a typical scantily furnished student apartment. Houston waited until Sarah took a seat on a ratty easy chair before sitting on an old couch that felt as if it had ten or more broken springs. Houston studied her for a couple of seconds. She was girl-next-door pretty. If Hollywood ever decided to remake a 1960s teen-queen movie, she would be perfect for the title role. She curled her legs under her, ensuring that her skirt covered them, and tried to cover the holes that years of use had worn into the arms of the chair. Her fingers tapped as she fidgeted in the seat.

She returned Houston's intense scrutiny, obviously wondering if she had made a mistake by allowing these people into her home. Wilson finally broke the silence. "Is Cheri all right?" she asked.

"That's what we hope to find out. You called her Cheri," Houston said. "Is Cheri her street—" He quickly changed the phrase he almost said, replacing it with: "stage name?" Street or stage, he was not surprised the girl had assumed one; knowing what it was would make tracing her much easier. It would be easier to find a streetwalker named Cheri the same way it would be easier to trace John Wayne than Marion Mitchell Morrison.

"Yeah, she felt Cheryl was too plain. An artist and model needs a name that will stand out, and she figured a French name would make her more memorable. Is she in trouble or something?" She stopped tapping her fingers and placed her hands in her lap, clenching them together.

"We don't know—that's the problem," Bouchard answered. "Cheryl hasn't contacted her family in several weeks, but what bothers us most is nobody seems to know where she might be."

"She might have gone to New York City."

"Why there?"

"She always talked about going there." She gave each of them an intent look. "How much do you know about acting?"

"On a scale of one to ten, I'd rate my knowledge at minus five," Houston answered.

"Well, it's common knowledge in the industry that Hollywood or Broadway are where you have to be if you're serious about making it." The solemn timbre of her voice and the intensity of Sarah's gaze proved how strongly she believed what she said.

"When did you see her last?"

"It was in early July." Wilson looked away, and Houston knew she sought a way to avoid saying anything that might harm her friend.

"Sarah, we know Cheryl was kicked out of school," Bouchard said. "If you hide anything from us, it could hurt her much more than if you tell me what you know."

Wilson turned to face them. For several seconds her look reminded him of the sixties mantra, "Never trust anyone over thirty." It was obvious that Wilson was trying to decide how much trust she could place in these older strangers. Finally, she came to a conclusion and said, "Early in the year, Cheri was a model student. You wouldn't believe how talented she is, and with her looks, she could go to the top. But something changed her—she started going wild."

"Wild, like in—?" Bouchard probed.

"Partying and staying out until all hours of the night. Cheri got heavily into drugs and alcohol . . . and not party stuff like grass and coke. She was doing heroin. I could have lived with that. But when she started bringing *that* man around . . ."

"What man?" Bouchard countered.

"She said he was her agent. I didn't buy it for one minute." She turned away, breaking eye contact, and began picking at the frayed fabric on her chair. Houston knew she was holding something back.

"Do you have any idea where Cheryl might be living now?" Houston asked.

"She didn't say anything to me. She knew I disapproved of what she was doing." She paused for a second. "Don't get me wrong, I'm not a prude or anything. I like to have a good time just like all the other kids, but Cheryl just went over the edge. I can't prove anything, but some of my stuff started disappearing—I know she stole it and sold it for drugs. I confronted her, and we argued. Then I went home for the weekend, and when I got back, she was gone along with all her things. If she didn't go to New York, you might look in Roslindale—that's where he lives."

"By 'he,' do you mean the guy she brought around?" Houston inquired.

"Yeah, I think his name was Mel."

"What do you know about him?" Bouchard asked.

"Not a lot. But I didn't trust him. He was creepy. It didn't surprise me one bit when I learned he was a drug dealer."

Houston offered her the picture Betty Guerette had provided. "Do you recognize this man with Cheryl?"

She took the photo, and after a cursory look, she nodded. "That's Mel. He used her—got her hooked on drugs and used her."

"You know that for a fact?" Bouchard asked.

"Yeah, Cheri told me that she met him at a party, and he fixed her up with some crack. A couple of times, she tried to get me to go with her.".

"But you didn't."

Sarah responded to the concern in Bouchard's voice. "Lord, no. I want a modeling career as much as anyone, but I'm not going to do it by smoking crack and sleeping with every asshole who says he has connections."

"How did Cheryl support herself? She had to be getting money from someplace," Bouchard asked.

Wilson unclenched her hands and leaned toward Bouchard. The girl was obviously more at ease talking to her. Houston remained silent and let Anne carry on the interview. Once again, Wilson blushed and stared past them. When she spoke again, her voice was soft, barely audible. "She was . . ." Sarah looked like she had just swallowed something soft and hairy. "She was selling herself."

"She was a prostitute?" Bouchard inquired.

"Yes." Wilson exhaled as if they had lifted a great burden from her.

8

He balanced the tray with one hand, unlocked the door, and pushed it open with his foot. He walked into the room and ignored the caustic odor of feces and stale urine. He stopped at the foot of the bed and studied the emaciated old woman, who lay immobile staring off at nothing. The large down-filled pillows on which her head rested made her look frail and childlike. He waited for her to acknowledge his presence. When she did not, and he realized she was not going to, he said, "Good morning, Mum. I got your tea and oatmeal."

"When am I going to meet this new girlfriend?"

"Soon, but first I got to get you cleaned up."

He placed the tray on a small table and then left the room. A few minutes later, he returned carrying a washcloth, a towel, and a basin of warm water.

He sat on the bed and used a lightly scented soap to clean his mother. Once he finished bathing her, he pulled her forward and put a fresh nightgown on her, pulling it over her bony shoulders and lifting her until it fell down, covering her lower body. He kept his head averted during the entire process—looking at her only when he had to. It would be sinful for a son to see his mother unclothed. He placed her in an old Boston rocker and then changed the linen on her bed. Once the bed was in order, he placed her in it, fluffed her pillows, and propped her against them.

"That should make you feel better. Here's your breakfast." He placed the tray on her lap and stood before her. When she ignored the food for several minutes, he sighed in frustration and squatted beside the bed, picked up the spoon, and began to feed her. "Come on, Mum, you got to eat. I made the maple flavored oatmeal you like so much."

He held the spoon under her nose, and when her mouth opened, he slipped it in. Her loose lips smacked, oatmeal and saliva dripped from the corner of her mouth, dribbling down her chin. He skillfully caught the gruel with a paper napkin before it fell on her gown. He held the cup of tea to her mouth, waited until the slurping sound of her drinking stopped, and then dabbed her chin clean. He repeated the process until she consumed half the bowl of mush and most of the tea and refused to open her mouth for him.

The morning meal completed, he stood back and smiled at her. "It's going to be a wonderful day, Mum. You sit here in the warm morning sunshine. I have to get to work now, but I'll check back in a bit."

———————

Cheryl woke up. It took several seconds for her to remember where she was, but that was about all she knew. She had no idea how long she had been under his control; the days were a blur of agony and relentless nausea. Her body's violent and painful reaction to going cold turkey had become bearable, but she still wanted a fix. Her skin was hypersensitive, and while her pain had lessened, the feel of the bedding touching her skin irritated her. Cheryl turned her head so she could see out the window and lay quiet, trying to figure a way out of her dilemma.

She heard him enter a room other than hers and listened. He was talking, probably to the bitch that spawned him, but she was unable to make out his words. After a few minutes, she heard a key in her door, and she feigned sleep.

As he crossed the room, the old hardwood floor creaked under his weight. The sound of his walking ceased, and Cheryl lay still, fighting the urge to sneak a look at what he was doing. Finally, he spoke to her. "I know you're awake. So stop fucking around and get up."

Cheryl opened her eyes and raised her shackled right hand. "With this on?"

"There's enough slack for you to stand up."

He threw a pair of jeans, a belt, and a shirt on the bed. "Put these on."

She studied the man's shirt, long-sleeved and made of plaid flannel; it was too hot for the weather. "Don't you have anything a bit more seasonal? Where are my things?"

"Gone. I burned them. You ain't going to meet Mum looking like a harlot."

She raised her shackled hand and shook the chain that held her secure to the beam. "It's hot today—short sleeves would be much more comfortable. Not to mention that it isn't going to be easy putting that shirt on over this."

"And have your arms show? They will be hidden from sight until the bruises and needle marks fade." He stepped forward and removed a key from his pocket. He grabbed her wrist and unlocked the shackle. "I don't have to tell you what will happen if you get out of line, do I?"

Cheryl almost shrieked when he touched her. She clenched her teeth, glared at him, and then shook her head.

"Good, now get dressed."

She stared at him, determined to be defiant to the end. "Some privacy would be nice."

He laughed. "Why? Ain't like I haven't seen all you got." His eyelids narrowed and a menacing sneer came over his face. "Now put the fucking clothes on."

He stood back and watched her, his arms folded across his chest. When she was dressed he said, "A word to the wise. You better be on your best behavior because if Mum doesn't approve of you . . . I'll have to get rid of you."

Suddenly, Cheryl felt a wave of nausea, and her legs seemed to lose strength. Meeting Mum took on an ominous importance.

She turned her back to him and slowly picked up the jeans he had thrown on the bed. Before pulling them over her hips, she noted they were women's, size fourteen, and she wondered where they had come from. The floor creaked each time he shifted his weight, and she sensed his impatience. She stepped into the pants and buttoned them and then slid the belt through the loops, pulling it tight. The jeans were too loose for her size-six frame, and when she tightened the belt, the waist doubled over in several places. When she felt certain the jeans would not drop, she picked up the shirt and slipped her arms into the sleeves, which were too large for her slight frame. She rolled the cuffs until her hands were free of the material.

She turned to him and said, "I need a mirror."

"What for?"

"I don't want to meet your mother looking like a street person."

"Isn't that what you are?"

Her head snapped up, and without thinking of the potential consequences, she snapped at him. "I said *person*, not *walker*."

He hesitated for a few seconds, and she realized he was debating within himself. Finally, he said, "Come on. But don't get any funny ideas."

He took her by the arm. When he touched her, pain shot up Cheryl's arm, and she pulled away. He snarled at her and tightened his grip, multiplying her agony. "You're hurting me," she protested.

"Then stop struggling. Don't think you can get away—you can't." He guided her to the door, where she hesitated. Not having been out of the room since her abduction, she was unfamiliar with the layout of the house, and she had no idea which way to turn. He shoved her into the half-light, and she found herself in a corridor. He pushed her back down the hallway. They stopped before the second door on the left, and he pushed it open.

Cheryl stepped into the bathroom, and when she attempted to close the door, he placed his foot between it and the frame. "The door stays open."

"What if I have to pee?"

"Then you do it."

The cold look in his eyes told her that the issue was not open for debate, so she turned to the sink. She stared into the mirrored medicine cabinet door and gasped when she saw the woman who stared back at her. Her hair was snarled, matted, and greasy with sweat. Dark circles enclosed her eyes, and the only words she could think of to describe the look on her face were fear and exhaustion. The woman who stared back at her from the mirror looked as if she had been battered and beaten to near-death.

Suddenly, his malformed face appeared in the mirror. He looked over her shoulder, and she started with surprise. "See," he said, "I told you that dope was no good for you."

"I'm hurting," she said.

"Do what you got to do and come on." He stepped away and stood by the door.

Cheryl turned on the water and waited until the pipes stopped banging as they purged air and rust before spitting hot water into her cupped hands. Then she rinsed her face. "You own a bar of soap?"

He stepped past her, opened a mildewed shower curtain, and grabbed a green bar of soap.

Cheryl became angry and found a small reserve of strength in it. She said, "I don't suppose this is a beauty bar?"

He ignored her sarcasm and thrust the soap into her hand. "If you're going to wash, then wash. If not, shut up and let's go."

Once she had finished washing her hands and face, she turned to him. "A comb and some makeup would be nice."

He opened the medicine cabinet and removed a comb. "Mum says only homely girls need makeup . . . and you ain't that."

She combed several snarls out of her hair, wincing in pain whenever the comb found a snag and pulled the hair from her scalp. When she decided she had done all she could with it, she tried to pull it back into a ponytail. She thought about the repercussions of not meeting Mum's approval and added, "I need something to tie my hair with. I want to look my best when I meet your mother."

He exhaled sharply, and she tensed, expecting him to hit her. Instead, he took her by the arm, ignoring her involuntary attempt to pull free from his grip, and guided her out of the bathroom. They followed the corridor to a flight of stairs, and he motioned for her to proceed ahead of him.

When they reached the bottom of the stairs, Cheryl was appalled at the conditions she saw. They were in what she assumed was the living room. The couch and chairs had to be at least fifty years old and were so badly worn that the fabric was torn in several places and the padding visible. Discarded newspapers and magazines covered the floor, and the air smelled musty, as if the windows had been sealed shut years ago, trapping the stale air inside. Beside the couch and each of the chairs were lamps, all without shades; two were missing light bulbs. He cut her survey short when he said, "Over there." Cheryl looked at him and saw he pointed to a door in the far corner. "I might have something in the kitchen." Cheryl stared at the condition of the living room, and the thought of what the kitchen might contain made her shudder.

When she walked into the kitchen, Cheryl stopped short and clamped a hand over her mouth and nose. The kitchen was ten times filthier than the rest of the house. She looked at the work area and thought that the countertops were moving. She looked closer and realized the movement was from hundreds, if not thousands, of cockroaches scrambling to safety. The sink overflowed with unwashed dishes—some of which had been there so long she figured a hammer and chisel would be the only way to remove the remnants of food that had hardened on their surfaces. Nobody had taken the garbage out for weeks, maybe months, and the room smelled like the dumpster behind a fish market on a hot day. He pulled her toward the sink and opened a drawer. He rummaged around for a few seconds and then showed several rubber bands to her. "One of these will have to do."

Cheryl, reluctant to take her hand from her face, ignored the proffered rubber bands and in a muffled voice said, "You cook *my* food in here?" She became determined not to eat another bite as long as he held her in this pigsty.

He yanked her arm, and she almost dropped to one knee as agonizing pain raced through her. "Take your fucking hand away from your face and talk to me." He snarled like a rabid dog when he spoke.

She dropped her hand and said, "How do you stand living in this filth?"

He paused and looked as if he didn't have a clue what she was saying. Instead, he placed the elastic bands in her free hand. "Take these—Mum's waiting." He waited as she tied her hair into a ponytail and then led her out of the kitchen and back up the stairs. As he led her down the hall, Cheryl noted that there was another door past hers, and this one, too, was secured with a heavy-duty padlock. She wondered, *Is he holding other women?* He stopped beside the door directly across from hers, and when he opened the door, she saw a Victorian-era bedchamber. Through the open door, she studied the room. It could have been a queen's chambers but for the distinct smells of old woman and human waste. A huge canopied bed dominated the room, flanked by stained glass lamps, and a large dresser covered most of one wall. In a corner beside the bed sat an elegant rocking chair, large enough to be a throne. In the middle of the chair, surrounded by frilly pillows, sat a frail old woman.

Her captor gripped Cheryl's arm, and she automatically pulled away, which resulted in him tightening his grip. He pulled her through the door and across the room. He stopped in front of the old woman, who stared into a place only she could see. Her thin arms looked skeletal and rested on the chair's arms. The crone said nothing and did not acknowledge Cheryl. She sat with her head tilted toward her left shoulder with her mouth open. A thin line of drool trickled down her chin.

"Mum," he said, "this is Cheryl."

Cheryl was surprised to hear him use her name; then she realized that he must have her bag somewhere and had searched it. She stood statuesque, uncertain how to proceed. He turned to her and said, "Don't be bashful, dear. Say hello to Mum."

"H-how do you do?"

The old woman showed no sign of having heard a word.

"Cheryl is from Kittery," he said. "Her family is fishers, too."

Inadvertently, Cheryl's head snapped toward him. *How did he know how her family made their living?* She decided that he must have made it up, hoping to appease the incoherent woman whom only he could hear.

He paused as if listening. "Oh, yes, they're a very well-positioned family. They own their own boat."

Another pause.

"Yes, she's a church-going girl—not at all like the other girls that I brought home. Cheryl, tell Mum about your beliefs."

Suddenly it came to her that he expected her to talk to the old woman, who was clearly in a vegetative state. She looked at him and was amazed to see him urging her as if they were a couple of teenagers on a first date. She turned back to the old woman and said, "I'm a—" Not sure what to say, she glanced at him from the corner of her eye and saw him mouth the word Methodist. "—Methodist."

"Of course," he said, "Cheryl would love to have afternoon tea with you, wouldn't you, Cheryl?"

Cheryl stared at him. Her knees weakened, and she knew she was in danger of falling. Not only was her captor brutal and violent—he was insane.

———

He came to her in the middle of the night.

Cheryl felt someone grab her breasts, and she started from a deep sleep. She shouted, "Stop it!" and he covered her mouth with a hard calloused hand that felt like sandpaper against her sensitive skin.

She kicked at him, and he snarled, "Shut your fucking mouth."

Cheryl twisted her torso, trying to buck him off, but all it did was enrage him, and he slapped her. To her still hyper-sensitive body, each blow felt as if she'd been slammed into by an overweight truck. When he reached down to spread her legs, she resisted by tensing her thigh muscles. His nails ripped at her flesh, and she cried out in agony.

"Shut the fuck up—you'll wake Mum." Although he muted his voice to a soft whisper, the malice in the warning was evident.

"Get off me," she said.

He answered with yet another slap. The coppery taste of blood filled her mouth, and she realized that to resist him would only lead to more punishment and pain. Cheryl resolved to let him have his way with her . . . hopefully it would be over quickly.

He grabbed her breasts and began kneading them like they were bread dough. Cheryl decided to act as a willing partner. "Easy," she said. "They aren't made of clay."

He spread her legs apart, and she realized that he wasn't erect. Willard continued with his ministration, and his penis remained limp. Cheryl turned her head away and hoped that he couldn't see the smile on her face. There was justice in the world after all—the son of a bitch was impotent.

9

Houston and Bouchard were at Andy's, one of their favorite restaurants from their time as cops. They sat by the window and hunched over the table, as Houston drank his second cup of coffee. He had been smoke-free for more than five years, but caffeine still made him crave nicotine. At that moment, he would have killed for a cigarette. He turned his attention to Anne. "This case bothers me."

"It isn't going to be easy telling Betty and Archie their granddaughter is a hooker."

"And who knows what else."

Houston glanced at his watch, 9:45 in the morning; he had always been an early riser, and while he didn't like food when he first arose, around this time of day he was ready for breakfast. He had ordered coffee, ham, and eggs.

A black Lincoln Navigator pulled alongside the curb, and a skinny man of average height with an acne-scarred complexion stepped out of the vehicle. Houston immediately recognized Jimmy O'Leary. He was as dapper as Houston remembered him. Even when they were kids, O'Leary had been a slave to fashion. It hadn't been a surprise to Houston when he returned from the Marines and learned that his childhood friend had become one of the leading mobsters in Boston. O'Leary walked through the door and stopped while searching the room for something or someone. He saw Houston and took the seat beside Bouchard.

"Mike, how are you?"

"Great. You're looking good, Jimmy."

He turned to Bouchard. "You still hanging around with this burnout?" His acne-scarred skin seemed to crease when he smiled.

She kissed him on the cheek. "And you still smell like an ashtray."

Jimmy O laughed. "Trust her to put me in my place. I almost had a heart attack when you guys called. We ain't talked since that situation in Maine last year."

Houston smiled. "That's bound to happen when people are on opposite ends of the same business."

"Yeah, I guess that makes sense. I hear you're lookin' for Mel Del Vecchio."

"We need to ask him some questions."

"Want me to come along?"

"I think I can handle him," Houston said.

"Never said you couldn't, but Mel sees me, he'll shit a soft stool. It may get you your answers a bit faster."

The server warmed Houston's coffee and gave O'Leary an approving look.

"What you having?" she asked.

O'Leary studied her tight-fitting uniform and leered. "For now, coffee would be nice," he grinned. "Later we can discuss other options."

Houston knew that she was an experienced waitress when she played along without a second's hesitation. Her smile could have lit up the room when she said, "How you want your coffee—in you or on you?" Before he could reply, she spun around and walked toward the kitchen.

"God, I love a feisty woman," O'Leary said.

"I'm going to take a pass on this one," Bouchard said. "While you talk with the bottom-feeders, I'll run over to police headquarters and see what I can dig up. Spending a morning with a pimp isn't my idea of a fun time."

"Say hello to Bill Dysart for me," Houston said.

"When you want to go?" O'Leary asked Houston.

"As soon as I finish eating."

The waitress returned and placed a mug of coffee in front of O'Leary. She scribbled something on the back of an unused order slip and placed it with the written side down in front of him. When she was gone, he turned the slip over and smiled at Houston. "Her phone number . . ."

Anne Bouchard walked to the new Boston Police Department headquarters in Roxbury Crossing; it was the first time she'd visited the BPD since her medical retirement. The officer at the desk immediately recognized her and greeted her with a smile. She placed her bag on the table beside the metal detector and said, "It's been a long time, Harry."

"Not all that long, Anne."

"There's no piece in the bag."

The officer nodded and motioned for her to enter the detection gate. As she passed through, Bouchard asked, "Is Captain Dysart in?"

"He came in a couple of hours ago."

Bouchard retrieved her bag and said, "Would you call ahead and announce me?"

"You betcha. It's good seeing you."

"You too." Bouchard waved as she walked to the elevator.

When the elevator door opened, Captain Bill Dysart was waiting with a big smile on his face. "Anne, you look terrific!"

She returned his smile and followed him to his office. "Nice place," she commented. "It's much nicer than the old building."

"Yeah, but the old building had its niceties. Like windows that opened."

Bouchard laughed as she recalled his habit of opening his office window, taking one or two drags off a cigarette, and throwing it out. She noted that the windows in his new office were hermetically sealed. "These windows must really cramp your style."

"Well, I've cut back on my smoking, and now that I'm not tossing three quarters of a cigarette away, it's cheaper, too."

He guided her to a chair and then sat behind his desk. "How's Mike? I haven't seen nor heard from him in almost a year."

"Mike's Mike. We're doing some private work now."

"You and Mike gone private? I never would have thought you'd do that."

"Well, we're selective about the cases we take on, which brings me to why we're back in Boston."

"You mean this isn't a social visit?" Dysart grinned. "How can I help you?"

"We're looking for a missing girl—woman is more accurate. We know she was attending a local diploma mill and started partying and may have started hooking. What do you know about a pimp named Mel Del Vecchio?"

"Let me bring in one of my detectives. She knows the vice scene more than I do." He opened the door and called, "Tracy, you want to come in here for a minute?"

A young woman entered the office, and Dysart introduced her to Bouchard as Detective Nancy Tracy. After a brief description of Bouchard's background, he sat back and let the two women carry on the discussion.

"My partner and I are looking for a missing young woman," Bouchard said. "We believe that she's been hooking for a pimp named Del Vecchio."

Tracy was all business when she spoke without referring to any notes. "Melvin Del Vecchio is what you'd expect to find on the bottom of your shoe after walking through a dog kennel in the dark, but he's an open book. Like all pimps, he preys on young women." For a brief second her face lost its professional stoicism and her distaste showed. "He lives in Roslindale. His girls work what's left of the Combat Zone near Chinatown."

"I guess it could be worse," Bouchard commented, "there are worse areas in the city."

"Doesn't matter which neighborhood it is . . . he's still a bottom-feeder who runs a stable of alley-creepers."

"You seem to know a lot about him considering he's a small-timer," Bouchard interjected.

"I've interacted with Del Vecchio on several occasions. My sources tell me the only reason he's still in business is that his girls are loyal to him. They love the pus-bag."

"You got anything on Cheryl Guerette, the girl we're looking for?" Bouchard asked.

"Give me a minute." Tracy walked out of the office, leaving Bouchard and Dysart alone.

"She seems to be good," Anne said.

"Not as good as you," Dysart replied. "But she's new, and she's a quick learner—like you were."

Tracy returned with a handful of printed sheets. "We don't know much more about her than what you already know. Del Vecchio turned in a missing persons report on July eighth." She flipped through the stack, stopping when she found the sheet she wanted. "The investigating officer got a call from the Maine State Police about a week later and was told that an Archie Guerette filed a report, too."

"Archie is her grandfather," Bouchard said.

"I don't know what to tell you. I mean, hell, you been around the block a time or two more than me. By now, I'm sure you've found out that she was a streetwalker, probably a junkie, too. . . . She probably took a powder, maybe got a jump on the cold and headed south."

"I don't know. Something about this smells sour. I'm afraid there's more to it—something has happened to that girl," Bouchard said.

"I'll see if anything new has popped up." Tracy took a cell phone out of her pocket and hit a speed-dial number. "Sergeant Weaver, please. . . . thanks." She waited for a second and then said, "Charley? Nancy, how you doing? Me too. Listen were you able to find out anything on that missing person I asked about?"

She listened for a moment and thanked Weaver, then put the cell back in her pocket. "They have nothing."

"Do you know if she was ever busted?"

"Who knows? You know as well as I do none of those girls use their real names."

"Her street name may be Cheri," Bouchard said.

"Her and fifty million others; these women change names as often as most people change socks. You got a picture? I'll show it around, see if anyone knows her by another name."

Bouchard and Houston had had several prints made of the picture Betty had given them, and she handed one to Tracy, who studied it for a few seconds. Her reaction was the same as Bouchard's initial one. "She's pretty. What in heaven's name is she doing with a hairball like Mel Del Vecchio?"

"That's an answer we hope to have by the end of the day. My partner is probably talking to Del Vecchio about it now."

10

It was past eleven in the morning when Houston and O'Leary arrived at Del Vecchio's apartment building, a paint-deprived triple-decker on a narrow street. Houston studied the less-than-impressive neighborhood for several seconds and said, "Looks like the economy is affecting the prostitution business, too."

O'Leary snickered. "Del Vecchio ain't exactly an astute businessman, that's for certain."

They entered the building through a pair of warped doors. To the right stood a bank of mail boxes; Houston studied the names and quickly found Del Vecchio's. He lived on the third floor. They climbed the dark stairs, staying off to one side to lessen the creaking of the aged wood. Del Vecchio's apartment was on the left at the top landing. Houston knocked on the door.

Nobody answered.

He knocked harder—pimps work nights and usually went to sleep after the sun came up. O'Leary reached over Houston's shoulder and banged on the door so hard it rattled.

Houston heard a door behind them creak. He turned and saw an old woman peeping out through a partially opened door. She said, "Jesus, you trying to knock the door down or what?"

A cigarette hung from her mouth, and at least an inch of ash dangled from the burning end. Through the narrow opening, Houston saw that she wore a tattered chenille robe and worn pink slippers, on which the fuzz had turned to snarls. "Do you know if Mr. Del Vecchio is at home?" he asked.

"*Mr.* Del Vecchio!" She laughed. Air passing through her rheumy, phlegm-coated windpipe made a popping sound. "You mean Mel? He's most likely sleeping. He works nights."

O'Leary banged on the door again, this time using the palm of his hand. Inside the apartment, someone started cursing.

"You a bill collector?" the old crone asked.

"Nope."

"Cop?"

O'Leary turned away from Del Vecchio's door, stepped across the narrow hall and pushed his face close to her ear. He whispered, "Mafia."

Her eyes widened, and she darted inside the apartment like a hermit crab fleeing a gull's beak. When she slammed her door, the loud bang echoed through the building. They turned back to the pimp's apartment, and O'Leary hammered on the door again.

"Who's there?"

"Mel Del Vecchio?" Houston asked.

"Who's asking?"

"My name is Mike Houston."

"That supposed to mean something to me?"

"I need to ask you some questions."

"You a cop?"

"Nope."

"Del Vecchio, it's Jimmy O. If you don't open this fucking door, I'm going to bust it down and then kick your ass so hard you'll be strangled by your own asshole!"

"Jesus, Jimmy, why didn't you say it was you?"

As soon as the door opened, O'Leary bulled his way in, shoved Del Vecchio aside, and pulled out a pistol.

Houston followed and studied Del Vecchio. What he saw was radically different from the man in the picture Betty Guerette had given him. Either Del Vecchio had hit on hard times, or he was a lot older than he looked in that picture. His oily hair hung down over his ears exposing a growing bald spot, which he probably hid with a comb-over when in public. He was missing a couple of his front teeth: an upper and a lower. He wore a dirty sleeveless undershirt, the type Houston and his friends called "guinea tuxedos" when they were kids. The shirt barely covered his bulging gut, and gray hair protruded above its plunging neckline. He wore a pair of wrinkled boxer shorts—once white but now beige from too much wear and not enough washing.

Houston turned his eye to the room. It looked like a bomb had gone off. The sink could have used sideboards to contain the dirty dishes piled in it. The tabletop was invisible through the empty beer cans that covered it. Ants and some type of larger insect scrambled across its surface seeking the sticky, sweet treasures that coated it. He concealed his contempt for Del Vecchio's housekeeping skills and, without waiting for an invitation, entered the living room. When he was a cop, he had learned when someone lets you in, you go all the way in.

The living room was no more sanitary than the kitchen. The whole place smelled sour—a nasty combination of stale alcohol, cigarette smoke, and unwashed bodies. Overall, Houston thought it smelled as if someone had fried roadkill. Across the room, he saw the door of the apartment's single bedroom open, and a naked woman appeared in the threshold. She stood with one arm against the doorjamb and glared at the intruders. She was obviously one of Del Vecchio's stable; her face was young, but her eyes were old, and her body already showed signs of wear. It was the way a woman aged when she had seen too much and done even more in too short a time.

Del Vecchio walked into the room. He seemed to have recovered from the shock of having two men barge past him into his home. He saw the nude woman and said, "Ronnie, either put some fucking clothes on, or go into the bedroom and shut the door." He faced Houston. "You got some kind of nerve, buddy."

Ronnie ignored Del Vecchio's order to dress or close the door and walked further into the room. She flopped down in a chair and crossed her legs like a man, resting her left ankle on her right knee. Houston could not help but notice that she'd groomed her pubic hair, shaving it into the shape of a heart. A mocking smile spread across her face. Houston looked her in the eye, refusing to rise to her bait. She lit a cigarette and raised an eyebrow, daring him to look away. They remained like that for several seconds, engaged in a perverse version of a Mexican standoff.

"Jesus Christ, woman!" Del Vecchio stomped into the bedroom and, in seconds, returned with a bedspread. He threw it at her and said, "Cover your ass, will you?"

"It ain't my ass that's showing." Ronnie gave him a scathing look and covered her gaunt frame with the worn bed cover.

"Cheryl Guerette's family asked me to find her," Houston said.

Ronnie's actions seemed to irritate Del Vecchio, and he turned his wrath on Houston. "Mister, you got bigger balls than King Kong to come in here like this."

"Who the hell are you?" Ronnie challenged.

O'Leary walked into the room, and as soon as she recognized the mobster, the attitude left her, replaced by visible fear. "Oh shit," she said.

"Someone who wants to talk to Mel," O'Leary said.

Ronnie rebounded quickly, and when she realized neither of the men were paying attention to her lack of attire, her attitude morphed yet again. She became aggressive. "What's wrong?" she challenged. "Don't like what you see?"

Del Vecchio was as pallid as a newly laundered sheet. "Ronnie, watch your mouth."

O'Leary walked to the window and looked outside. "You should listen to Mel. Is it Ronnie? Ain't that a man's name?"

"It's short for Veronica." Her indignation at his obvious insult turned to anger. "What are you, queer? A couple of gay boys?"

"Just selective," O'Leary said. "I got this thing about hitting women. I think it's something only cowards do. But if you don't shut your fucking mouth, I'll make you an exception to the rule."

She started to retort but thought better of it and sat with her mouth open.

Houston added, "You can go back into the bedroom—unless you know something about Cheryl Guerette. You probably know her as Cheri."

Ronnie's eyes narrowed. "*That* snotty bitch, I thought she was gone."

"She is. That's why we're here."

"Sit down and shut up," O'Leary said. "You two answer a few questions, and we'll be out of your hair. Play games, and we'll be here all afternoon—we got lots of time."

Houston looked for a clean chair to sit in. He decided to stand.

Del Vecchio sat on the arm of Ronnie's chair in an obvious attempt to keep her under control.

"All right," Houston said. "Let's start with Cheryl." He directed his first question to Ronnie. "I get the impression you know her personally."

"Oh, I know her all right. She's a snotty bitch from the *right* side of the tracks who thinks she's better than the rest of us."

"Really? And just who are the rest of us?"

"The rest of the girls."

"The girls?" Houston asked. "What do you *girls* do? Were you in the same sorority? You work together? What could you and Cheryl Guerette have in common?"

Ronnie laughed, "The only fucking sorority she was in was *I Amma Whore* or *Getta Lotta Bangin'*, the same one I'm in. In spite of her uppity ways, she was just another hooker."

Houston turned to Del Vecchio. "What you got to add?"

"Get to the point, Mel," O'Leary said. "I'm more than a little tired of playing sixty-four questions with a whore."

"When I met her, she was out of money and screwing pimple-faced college boys for nose-candy money. Before long, she was on H. She had just started working the streets full time. I tried to pull her in, give her some protection. The street can be a bad place for a freelancer. Ain't that right, babe?"

Ronnie nodded.

"Did she let you *protect* her?"

"What?" Del Vecchio asked.

O'Leary walked over and clenched his fist with the middle knuckle slightly extended. With a quick snapping action, he popped Del Vecchio on the top of his head.

"Holy Jay-sus," Del Vecchio said as he rubbed the painful knot on his skull.

"Just answer the goddamned questions," O'Leary said.

"Did she let you take her under your so-called wing?" Houston repeated.

"Oh. Yeah, but she was something else." Del Vecchio looked at O'Leary while he rubbed his head in a circular motion. "That fucking hurt."

O'Leary smiled. "Just answer our questions, or you'll see just how much I can hurt you."

"How so?" Houston asked.

Del Vecchio stared at him as if he did not understand the question.

"What, you got ADD or some shit?" O'Leary asked. "How was she *something else?*"

"That's one headstrong kid. She wanted to choose who she'd go with, shit like that. Once she gave up the cocaine and began mainlining scag, she became a handful. You can't trust them once they start shooting heroin."

"So you had to show her the error of her ways?"

Del Vecchio looked at Houston, his head rolled a bit to the side. After a few seconds, he figured out what Houston meant. "Hey! It wasn't like that. No way! I don't beat on my girls. Do I, baby?"

"Naw," Ronnie said. "Mel's the salt of the fucking earth. Hell, he loves his fellow man so much he registered Democrat."

Houston glared at the two of them. "Yeah, I'll just bet he takes real good care of you girls, and all he asks is for you to turn over eighty percent of your take." Ronnie's smile told him he was close to the truth if not right on the money.

"So where is she?"

"Beats the fuck out of me," Del Vecchio said. "She might have gone to New York."

Ronnie nodded her head.

"Did she talk about New York a lot?" Houston asked her.

"All the goddamned time. It was her favorite subject," Ronnie said. "She was going to be a *big-time* actress or model—some stupid shit like that. She said from now on the only people she was going to spread for would have endorsement contracts on their desks."

"You have no idea where she went?" Houston turned his attention back to Melvin.

"Not a goddamned clue. After all I done for her. She never said a fucking word to me about leaving or anything—just took off owing me a bundle. Her habit got to the point where her earnings couldn't cover her daily overhead, you know what I mean?"

The comment amazed Houston. What did he expect her to do, give him two weeks' notice?

Del Vecchio looked uncomfortable. "Hey, I got to take a leak, okay?"

"Go for it."

When he bolted from the room at a half-run, Houston thought, *Old age is tough on the bladder.*

"He ain't bullshitting you," Ronnie said.

"Oh?"

"Yeah, Mel has his faults, but he don't make a girl work if she wants out—which is probably why he ain't so successful. He acts tough, but," she patted her chest, "in here, where it counts, he's soft as shit."

A toilet flushed, and Del Vecchio walked back into the room too soon to have washed his hands. Houston thought that although Del Vecchio might be a feeling, twenty-first century pimp, he had the hygiene of a pig. Houston retracted the thought. He knew a hog farmer in Maine; comparing his animals to Del Vecchio did a grave disservice to the pigs.

Del Vecchio returned to his seat on the arm of the chair. "What else you want to know? We ain't had much sleep."

"We heard she worked the Combat Zone. There isn't much left of the Zone."

"There are still parts of it around. My girls work the Public Garden. Occasionally in cold weather, they'll work some of the strip joints in

Chelsea and Revere or up north on the New Hampshire border but mostly we operate right here in the city."

"Did she mention any names—maybe someone in New York, a friend or a business acquaintance?"

"Nope, she never mentioned anything to me. She ever say anything to you, Ronnie?"

"Nah, she and I didn't talk much. We didn't hit it off—must have been one of them personality conflicts."

Houston believed her. He had only known Ronnie for fifteen minutes, and he disliked her.

"Who was Cheryl close to?" Houston asked.

"Shit, that bitch wasn't close to anyone," Ronnie answered. "But she would talk to Candy."

"Candy?"

"She ain't one of mine," Melvin said.

"She ain't nobody's. A real crazy bitch," Ronnie said. "She's a walking epidemic. She's loaded, got HIV, probably gonorrhea and syphilis, too. She says some john gave the shit to her, and she's going to pass it on to as many horny bastards as she can before she dies. She calls herself the Toxic Avenger like she's some kind of a fucking superhero, can you believe it?"

"And Cheryl was close to her?"

"No, Cheryl was too damned high and mighty to get close to anyone. I said she *talked* with Candy."

"Did she talk with anyone else?"

"Yeah," Del Vecchio said, "Patty, but she doesn't do tricks. She thinks that she can be a manager—you know, like a madam. I tried to talk her into getting out of this business while she could. The kid didn't listen. She has some crazy fucking idea that sex can be a real business. She's going to get herself and some others killed."

"What makes you say that?" Houston asked.

"She keeps talking about them starting their own service—no more pimps to pay. They'll share the expenses and the profits. She ain't had any luck though. Everyone she's talked to knows their pimps would fucking kill them if they got wind of it."

Houston wrote Candy's and Patty's names in his notebook. "These names real or are they street names?"

"You got me."

"Do they work Arlington Street, too?"

"Usually," Del Vecchio answered. "Sometimes they hang out on Traveler Street by the Herald building."

Ronnie spoke up, as if she had just remembered something. "There's one other person you should talk to."

Del Vecchio turned to her and gave her a dirty look, as if she were telling tales out of school.

Houston did not want him to cut her off, so he asked, "Who's that?"

"Lisa Enright."

"Who's Lisa Enright?"

"A reporter for one of them newspapers that the yuppies in the city read—I think it's called the *Progressive*. She was doing a series of articles on the trade."

Del Vecchio scowled at the mention of the reporter's name. "Nosy bitch," he said. "She thinks that the business should be legalized and run by the government. Can you imagine that? Fucking people can't run Medicare and Social Security, but they think they can run a private industry? As if the streets aren't bad enough, she expects a bunch of crooked politicians to clean it up."

Houston was familiar with the *Progressive*. It was very popular with young left-leaning intellectuals. As liberal as the *Globe* was, the *Progressive* made it look right wing. However, if Lisa Enright had been talking with the women who worked the streets, she was definitely someone to whom Houston wanted to talk. He added her name to his notes.

"You going to be around if I need any more help?" Houston asked Del Vecchio.

"Sure. I want to know that she's okay, too."

Houston thought Cheryl Guerette had been anything but okay since the minute Del Vecchio had latched onto her.

"You have a current address for her?"

"Hell, she's missing. As far as I know, she ain't got no address."

"Mel," O'Leary said, "if you don't give me the fucking address of the last place you know of her living, I'm going to pound the shit out of you."

Del Vecchio opened a drawer of a small table that stood beside Ronnie's chair. He removed a pad and pencil and wrote something. He tore off the page and handed it to Houston. "This is where she was staying. I hope . . ." He looked worried.

"You hope what?" Houston asked.

"I hope you don't find her dead of an overdose."

Del Vecchio peered at Houston and then O'Leary, looking for reassurance. His voice was subdued when he said, "Really guys, I care for my girls. Cheryl was a pain in the ass, but she wouldn't have taken off without a word. I think something's happened to her."

"Mel, you may a pimp with a heart of gold," O'Leary said, "but if I find out you're stringing us along, I'm going to come back here and break both your arms and both your legs—then I'm going to hurt you."

11

When Houston and Bouchard opened the door and stepped into the vestibule, they were immediately confronted by a stern, elderly woman. "I don't rent to couples or men . . . single women only."

"I'm sorry?" Houston asked.

"If you're not looking to rent, what are you doing here?" the woman asked.

"This is official," Bouchard said, flashing her identification.

The woman's posture was such that Houston knew she would not accept anything he told her; still he tried to explain their presence. "We've been asked by Cheryl's grandparents to find her."

"Who is Cheryl?"

Houston was taken aback. "Isn't this where Cheryl Guerette lives?"

"No, it isn't."

He presented her with the picture of Cheryl and Del Vecchio. "Is she the woman you rented to?"

"Yes. Only she told me that her name was Alana Turner."

"Well, that is Cheryl Guerette from Kittery, Maine. When did you see her last?"

The woman's attitude changed. "It's been a couple of weeks now. I thought she was avoiding me . . . she's going on two months without paying her rent."

"She didn't tell you anything?"

"Well, we weren't exactly friendly. But she was always on time with her rent until the last couple of months."

Houston put the picture back in his pocket. "Could you show us her room, please?"

"I'm not sure I should do that."

"We're trying to find Cheryl," Bouchard interjected. "She has disappeared, and we're trying to find out what has happened to her. Whether you like it or not, we're going in." She handed the landlady a white business envelope.

"What's this?"

"It's a search warrant. Now step aside, please."

The woman vacillated for a few moments, handed the unopened envelope back to Bouchard, and then said, "All right. Her room is upstairs." She reached into her pocket and removed a ring of keys. As she started climbing, she said, "This way."

At the top of the stairs, the landlady led them down a short hall and stopped at the third door on the left. She opened it and stood back. Houston stood in the threshold of the door. He studied the small one-room efficiency apartment. To call this twelve-by-ten room an apartment was a stretch. It was a major step down from the apartment Cheryl had shared with Sarah Wilson. There was barely enough room in this place for a bed, single wooden chair, and small dresser. He thanked the landlady for her help, ushered her from the room, and closed the door.

The only illumination was from a single bare bulb in the center of the ceiling, and it struggled to provide enough light to navigate the room. He turned to Bouchard and said, "What ID did you show her?"

Bouchard smiled. "A badge I ordered online. It says concealed carry permit."

"And the *search warrant*?"

"Archie's letter authorizing us to see her school files."

Houston grinned. "I knew that getting you involved with Jimmy might lead to this . . . he's taught you a lot in a short time." He opened the dresser's top drawer and searched for anything that might give him a lead to her whereabouts. "If she left for New York, she couldn't have taken much more than the clothes she was wearing." He turned back to his search; the warped drawer revealed an assortment of cheap makeup and hair products—nothing to give any indication of where their owner had disappeared to. The remaining drawers were half-filled with neatly folded underwear—none of which you'd expect to see on a prostitute—a few shirts, and several pairs of jeans. None of the clothing looked new but neither did it look excessively worn or frayed.

The bed was unmade, and Houston lifted the mattress, finding several letters from Betty Guerette—all unopened and addressed to the apartment that she shared with Wilson. He handed the letters to Bouchard. "Obviously, the Guerettes had no idea where their granddaughter was living."

He dropped the mattress and opened the door to the miniscule closet. The only clothes he found there were typical of what you would expect a streetwalker to wear. He did not know exactly how petite Cheryl was, but the dresses would be tight on a skinny thirteen-year-old. He checked the rest of the closet, finding a small carry-on type suitcase but nothing of interest. There was not a single indication that she had been a student anywhere in the room . . . no books, notes, or class schedules. He also was unable to find anything to indicate that she had left town of her own will.

He opened the door, and the landlady jumped backward, hitting the wall.

Bouchard walked out of the room, looked at the obviously flustered woman, and said, "Did you get an earful?"

The older woman regained her composure and ignored Bouchard's slight. "I'm glad she hasn't been avoiding me. But all things considered, I'm not surprised that she's missing."

"Oh?"

"I think she was into drugs." She suddenly became defensive. "Not that I ever saw her do anything . . . she just seemed out of it a lot."

"Well, we'll keep looking," he said.

"I hope nothing has happened to her," the woman said. "But if you find her, remind her about the rent . . ."

Once they were back on the street, Bouchard said, "Well, that told us exactly nothing, other than that Cheryl wasn't communicating with her grandparents."

"I think it told us something very important. No one willingly leaves a place and doesn't take any of their belongings. Her suitcase was still in the closet."

"So," Bouchard stated the obvious, "she didn't leave of her own accord."

"I think it's time for me to interview some of Cheryl's coworkers."

"That's something you'll have to do without me," Bouchard said.

12

There was a time when the section of Boston that lay between the Boston Common, the Theater District, and Chinatown was called the Combat Zone. Then-mayor Kevin White declared it the city's unofficial red-light zone. It was allowed to exist in the hope that the "adult entertainment" business would stay within geographical confines rather than spread throughout the city. It was a magnet that attracted off-duty soldiers, sailors, airmen, and Marines from the five military bases that were around the city. It thrived until 1978, when a Harvard University football player was murdered in an altercation over a missing wallet, and the Police Chief realized that the Zone as a social experiment was not viable and started a crackdown. In the years since then, a number of factors led to the demise of the red-light district. The demand for high-priced condominiums made the real estate desirable, and developers bought up many of the old strip clubs; as a result, the prostitution trade was forced to move. It relocated to Arlington Street, near the Common and Public Garden.

Houston took his time and strolled through the Public Garden. He stopped on the footbridge and watched the swans drift on the calm water. The light from streetlamps reflecting off their white feathers made them seem whiter than they actually were. It was not long before he saw a woman studying him.

She stood some ten feet away, and it did not take a degree in sociology to know her occupation. Her tank top barely covered her ample breasts, and her leather mini was so short that if she bent over, all her "wares" would be on display. A small purse with a long strap hung from her shoulder, and she blew smoke from a cigarette as she appraised Houston.

Houston looked around, trying to act surprised like a tourist who could not believe his luck. "Hello."

She took a tentative step toward him and then stopped, uncertain. She reminded him of the feral cat he'd found living under their cabin in Maine. He'd tried to befriend it by offering food. The cat wanted the morsel he offered, but did not know whether to trust him or not. Finally, Houston just dropped the food and stepped back. He fed that cat for two months before it let him get within five feet of it. Houston decided to play this woman just as he had the cat—no sudden moves. He did not want her to run off.

"Are you from around here?" Houston stepped toward her.

Suddenly suspicious, she stopped in her tracks, "Are you the cops?"

"No, I'm not looking for a good time either. I'm looking for Cheri."

The woman looked past him. Houston glanced back expecting someone to be behind him. Except for a large unmarked truck parked on the corner, the street was empty. He turned his attention back to the streetwalker. She was backing up, fumbling her purse open. He heard her mumble, "Fisherman . . ."

Houston slowed his approach. "I'm not going to hurt you or do anything. Cheri's family asked me to find her."

The prostitute spun away from him, walking rapidly in the direction of Boylston Street. He started after her. "Hey, wait! I just want to talk—"

She pulled a cell phone from her purse and hit a speed dial as she walked. Her pace quickened until she was almost running. Houston heard her speaking into the phone and then saw her shove it in her purse.

He gained on her, reached out, and grasped her shoulder. "Miss—"

She spun around to face him. When her hand reappeared from the bag, it held a black can.

"Listen, I only want to talk to you . . ."

A stream shot out of the can, hitting him in the face. Pepper spray. His eyes burned, and he gasped for air but could not get enough. Houston stumbled back, fell to the sidewalk, and threw up.

Once he stopped vomiting, Houston crawled along the pavement on his hands and knees, hurting too bad to curse. His left hand slipped when it landed in his vomit. Blinded and helpless, he sat on the cement and listened to the clicking of her high heels as she hurried away.

———————

Houston was unsure of how long he had been on the ground. The effects of pepper spray could last anywhere from ten minutes to an hour—a long time to be lying helpless on a city street in the middle of the night. His eyes had cleared enough to be able to discern light from dark, but individual items were still indiscernible.

He heard a car pull up. The doors slammed and suddenly there were people standing beside him. A rough voice said, "Is this the asshole?"

Houston tried to talk, to explain what he wanted but was unable to speak. Rough hands yanked him to his feet and spun him around, then slammed him against a wall. "Who the fuck you think you are scaring my woman like that?" Callous hands pawed him, and he was not so far gone that he did not know the man was searching him for weapons. He felt his wallet being removed from his pocket. "He's clean." It was a different voice.

The first man spoke again, "Asshole, you be either a cop, a pervert, or a do-gooder. That what you are, some kind of fucking missionary?"

Houston tried to answer. His throat and nasal passages were still on fire, and he was unable to speak. He knew he needed to answer somehow, so he shook his head.

"What you asking 'bout Cheri for?"

Houston gasped, sucking in a deep breath of air. It seemed an eternity before he was able to say, "Family . . . asked me . . . find her." The words sounded high pitched and squeaky to him.

Houston felt his captors shove his wallet back in his pocket. "Cheri gone, you better be gone, too. I catch you round here again, we gonna fuck you up good. You understand?"

The voice then addressed someone else—the hooker who had used the pepper spray on him. "What you doing spraying that shit on people? This asshole could have been looking to do some business." Houston heard the sharp sound of a slap.

"I seen one of them trucks and thought he was that fisherman asshole." She sounded defiant.

Another slap. "You stupid, bitch? I told you that bullshit about a whacked-out, psycho fisherman nothin' but street talk. Now you get your bony ass movin'. You ain't made nothing this past week, and I'm running out of patience. Where's your partner?"

"She's late again."

"Oh yeah? Well I be looking into that."

The pimp turned his attention back to Houston, who felt helpless as a newborn. When the man said, "You get my message, *white meat?*" Houston could only nod and mumble, "Yeah."

"This so you remember not to go fucking around on my turf again . . ."

Huge hands grabbed his lapels and lifted Houston off his feet, then a heavy fist slammed into his stomach, driving precious air from his diaphragm. He felt the big hands loosen their grip, dropping him to the sidewalk. Still defenseless, Houston curled into the fetal position. Heavy shoes kicked him in the back, and he rolled against the wall. He struggled to remain conscious as he heard them get into a car. The motor started, and a blast of rap music at 150 decibels ripped apart the quiet night. As the music faded, he spiraled down into the abyss.

Houston sat on the curb, his vision about fifty percent of normal. A police car pulled up within five feet of him. Two uniformed officers got out. One remained by the car while the other approached him. "What's wrong, fella? You have one or two too many?"

Houston did not trust his voice yet and merely shook his head. The cop knelt down on one knee and looked into his eyes. Houston realized that he was acting erratically and his eyes were probably bloodshot—all the cop needed to arrest him. Houston stood when the cop pulled him up by the arm. "Come on, buddy. Let's get you off the street and sobered up."

"I'm not drunk."

"Sure you aren't. That's why you're sitting here next to a puddle of puke at one in the morning. We'll take you out of here to keep you safe. Come on."

Houston knew that for him to protest would be futile, and in seconds, he was in the police car and on his way to the police station. He rested his head on the back of the seat and thought, *At least I won't get the shit beat out of me in a cell.*

Willard tossed and turned until he wrapped the sheets around him like a shroud. Grunting, the Fisherman sat up in his bed and rested his pounding head in his hands. He stared at the floor, his mind unable to function with the battle of the drums that took place just behind his eyes. Finally, he got up and staggered into the hall.

He stopped beside his mother's room. The throbbing pressure in his skull was so intense he saw white spots. He cautiously opened the door and stepped inside. She looked tiny and frail, like a small child alone in a king-size bed. Her eyes shone in the moonlight filtering through her window. She was awake. He sighed in relief.

"Ma, I got a headache."

He slid into bed beside her and rolled over. The warmth of her feeble body comforted him, and he nestled back against her. Within moments, he was asleep.

Houston perched on the edge of the narrow cot, his head in his hands. His explanation of how he had come to be sitting on a curb in the middle of the night had not gone well. In fact, as he related the story to the cops, even he had a hard time believing it. They interrogated him for two hours before letting him make his phone call. He called Anne Bouchard.

He heard the cell door open and looked into the bright light. A familiar silhouette stood beside a police officer. Houston thought the black figure looked like the Grim Reaper. "Jesus Christ, Mike, you look like shit," Bouchard said. "Do you have any idea what time it is?"

"Yeah, time for me to get out of here."

"What's this crap about some hooker spraying you with Mace?" A smile lurked behind her stern look.

"It's not crap—it happened."

"What did you do to her?"

"Hell if I know, Anne. She was nervous, probably scared out of her mind. I told her I wanted to talk to her about Cheryl, and *bang*, she blasted me with a dose of cayenne pepper. In all my years, I've never seen a hooker that nervous."

"Well, you are looking a little scurvy tonight."

"When can I get out of here?"

"You can leave whenever you like. I called Bill Dysart, and when he told the arresting officers that you were former PD, they dropped all charges." She grinned. "Besides, Bill told me that they don't usually bust drunks anymore; they got bigger fish to fry. They would have let you go in the morning."

"Life is just full of small miracles, isn't it?"

Bouchard said, "You know, you might show a little gratitude. I could have left you in here all night."

"I know. I'm just feeling more than a little stupid right now. She took me out like I was a rookie. One good thing did come out of this, though."

"And what might that be?"

"The hooker mentioned that she saw a truck and panicked. She also said something about a fisherman."

"You're damned lucky those pimps didn't take a notion to really mess you up."

"I think they intended to and then decided I was telling them the truth."

"I warned you about what might happen when you concocted this cockamamie plan . . . you could have gotten yourself killed or beaten a hell of a lot worse than you were." She held out a hand and when he took it, said, "Come on, let's go back to the hotel and get some sleep." She smiled at him. "Not to mention that you need a shower and a change of clothes."

13

Houston and Bouchard walked into the restaurant and looked for Tracy. They saw her sitting with a woman dressed in a flowered dress that went to her ankles. "That one looks as if she's lost in the sixties," he said to Bouchard. Tracy waved to them.

When Houston sat down, Tracy looked at the bruises and abrasions on his face. "What happened to you?"

"It's a long story . . . I'll tell you about it later."

Tracy shrugged, as if to say that if he didn't want to tell them what happened, that was his business. Rather than belabor the subject, she made introductions. "Lisa Enright, meet Mike Houston and Anne Bouchard."

Enright reached over and offered her hand to each of them. It was easy to commit her face to memory. Lisa Enright was not an attractive woman. Her sandy-brown hair was long, although he could not tell how long because she was sitting. Houston thought it ended at the small of her back. The hair's oily sheen gave the impression she had better things to do with her time than to mess with shampoo and conditioner on a daily basis. She reminded him of Mama Cass Elliott, only slimmer and less well kempt. Houston did not think he and Enright were going to be close friends.

Tracy led into the conversation saying, "Mike and Anne are trying to find a missing woman. They think she's been working as a prostitute."

Houston said, "Her grandparents asked us to look into her disappearance."

Enright said, "I've been waiting a long time for someone to blow the lid off this."

"Blow the lid off what?" Houston asked.

She gave him a quizzical look, as if he were a naïve child. "The missing prostitutes. . . . I believe that over the past four years more than fifty women have vanished from the streets of Boston."

Bouchard looked at Tracy in disbelief. "*Fifty* women!"

Enright said, "The Boston cops don't give a damn."

"That's a bit harsh, Lisa," Tracy said, sounding defensive.

Houston stared at Enright while still struggling to grasp what she had told him.

"You believe that more than fifty women have disappeared?" Houston asserted.

"That I'm sure of. There may be more. It's hard to get the women to talk."

"I know that for a fact," Houston grumbled.

Enright gave him a quizzical look.

"I approached a hooker by the Public Garden last night. She maced me."

"They've become pretty selective. In fact, they won't let a john approach them—they instigate the transaction, or it doesn't happen."

"I got the impression that things are more serious than a lot of people think. She called her pimp and one of his cronies."

"You're lucky to be alive," Enright said. "If the streets were business as usual, the pimps would be going crazy and taking it out on their women, but with this guy . . ."

"What did you say?" Bouchard interrupted her.

"I'm sorry?"

"Just now, you said *this guy*. Has someone seen something?" Bouchard inquired.

"It seems that there has been a truck seen in the area whenever a woman disappears. After all, their customers are almost exclusively men."

Once again, she gave them a strange look—this time as if they were from another universe.

Bouchard chose to ignore her condescending attitude. "So you don't know if there is any particular man involved."

"A single man? Lord, no. How could a single man kidnap over fifty women?"

"How many victims did Bundy have?" Houston interjected.

Enright paused and then said, "I believe in his trial he confessed to thirty."

"But the investigators believe it could very well be more than one hundred," he said.

"I see your point."

Tracy put down her coffee cup and said, "Lisa, maybe you'd better tell us what you've got."

"I've been doing a series of articles on prostitution in Boston concentrating on what's left of the Combat Zone. The first missing woman that I know of was a streetwalker named Victoria. Four years ago, her pimp was Shiloh Baines. I can't tell you if that's his legal or street name. Vickie talked with me on several occasions but blew off the last interview. At the time, I thought nothing of it because it was a particularly cold winter and on the day that she missed our meeting there was a blizzard. I tried for a couple of weeks to locate her but no luck. I even went so far as to call Shiloh. You can imagine how far that got me."

"I'm sure it wasn't far," Houston commented, "The last thing most pimps want is their picture on the front page."

Enright continued her story. "I asked around, but nobody has seen her since, at least not in Boston. Since then a woman has disappeared about every month—some months two or three will vanish. I'm not saying all of them have been harmed, but there's too many of them for this to be coincidence. When Nancy told me that you guys were looking for a missing woman, I knew I needed to talk to you. I want you guys to talk to one of the women," Enright said.

Tracy chuckled softly. "Sounds like Mike already tried that.... It didn't work out too good."

"I've had better nights," Houston said.

Enright showed no surprise. "As I said, you're lucky that's all that happened. I can put you in contact with a woman who has seen something. She may have seen our killer . . . and he may have your woman."

Houston turned to Tracy. "Are you in?"

Tracy nodded. "Try and keep me out of it."

"We're going to visit a prostitute using the name of Candy." Enright sat back and added, "There is a problem though. I don't think she'll open up to a man—and I know she won't to a cop. I think . . ." she looked directly at Bouchard, " . . . Anne and I should go alone."

Houston looked at Bouchard. "I don't have a problem with that. I've had more than enough discussions with pimps and hookers."

Bouchard glanced at her watch. "If we're going to get anything done today, we better run."

14

"Who the fuck is Cheryl?"

You would think Candy was sitting on a throne uphol-stered in the finest silk instead of a stained and tattered chair, Bouchard thought as she studied the emaciated prostitute. Her slouched shoulders did not go with her straight back. Something else was incongruous—the necklace gleaming on Candy's thin and wrinkled neck. The expensive, understated design spoke of good taste—not what you would expect on a woman who sold herself for drug money. Bouchard wondered what the story was behind this woman and her current lifestyle.

Candy stared back at her, eyes blank, and Bouchard answered the dull gaze with a soft smile. "When was the last time you saw Cheryl?" She shifted slightly on the worn sofa's edge to avoid contact with fabric so stained it was reminiscent of blood splatter at a crime scene. Her first reaction was alarm, then she pushed her revulsion away. She had been educated enough to know the blemishes on the couch presented no threat. Still she wondered what other contaminants the fabric might harbor.

Candy pounded her hand on the chair's arm. "Are both of you deaf or something? I told you I don't know who the hell she is." Candy blew a cloud of smoke directly at them. She tugged at the sleeve of her sweater—it was inappropriate attire for such a warm day. She was most likely trying to hide track marks on her arms. On the other hand, she might be a cutter, which is common for women with borderline personality disorder or some form of it.

Bouchard shuddered. Her best friend in college had been a cutter, and no matter how hot the day, she wore long sleeves to hide the pale scars on her arms.

Bouchard quietly studied Candy. The prostitute looked as if she were hours away from a rendezvous with the local undertaker. She pushed these thoughts aside, leaned forward, and thrust a snapshot inches from Candy's eyes. Candy nonchalantly exhaled smoke into her face, further irritating her dry and itchy eyes. Bouchard held her ground; the photo remained poised before Candy.

Candy took the photo.

Bouchard noted Candy's fingers shook as she struggled to grip the photo. *She is strung out—probably needs a fix.*

Candy ignored the attention Bouchard gave to her trembling hands and glanced at the photo, giving it no more attention than she might a spider. Then, almost as nonchalantly, she tossed it onto the nearby coffee table. The picture fell in the middle of one of the dishes coated with dried, smelly food. "Oh, her . . ."

"So you *do* know her. When was the last time you saw her?" Bouchard fought to quell her impatience. She was determined not to let her irritation show; she needed what this woman knew. Bouchard reached out and touched Candy's bony hand.

Suspicious of Bouchard's gesture of support, Candy snatched her hand away and blew more smoke into Bouchard's face.

Bouchard refused to react to the rebuke and reached for the photograph. She placed it back in Candy's hand.

Like a recalcitrant child, Candy bent her head to study the photo. Bouchard watched her face closely, ignoring the sores and ruined skin. Candy's jaw tightened before she spoke. After several tension-filled moments, Candy finally said in a muted voice, "That's Cheri."

"And do you know the man?" Bouchard asked.

"Melvin Del Vecchio," Candy seemed to spit rather than speak his name.

Bouchard sat backward, her clothing stuck as she slid across the surface of the couch. She decided she was going to have to buy new pants after this visit. Then her police training took command of her.

"What can you tell us about him?" Bouchard realized that she was falling into interrogator mode and came across as if she were interviewing a suspected murderer. Enright nudged her and flashed a look, warning her to soften up. Bouchard quickly returned her focus to Candy and decided to try another approach. While Candy's language might be coarse, she might respond to softness and sensitivity. Anne believed that no woman started out to be a hooker. Turning to the streets was usually their only recourse in dealing with circumstances beyond their control. She would love to know what event or events had propelled Candy into a lifestyle that was obviously killing her. However, she knew this was not the time to answer those questions. She forced herself to stay on task, hoping to find the answers she needed. She did, however, pledge not to forget one lesson she had learned, though not as a member of the BPD: no matter what Candy did for a livelihood, she was still a person with a heart and feelings. All she had to do was find a way to reach them.

Candy picked the picture up again, gave it another cursory glance, and then flipped it onto the coffee table and placed a nicotine-stained finger on Del Vecchio's image. "Now there's one useless piece of shit if ever there was one." She shook her head, paused, and then shook it again.

"Okay, all that aside," Enright interrupted, in a soft, compassionate tone, "when was the last time you saw Cheri?"

"Must be a month or more," Candy said. "Say, did she finally get the balls to go to the Big Apple? I've heard you can make some real money working Times Square."

"We don't know exactly where she went," Bouchard answered.

Candy got up from the chair and stumbled across the room. She opened the top drawer of a scarred oak dresser and took out a bottle of wine. She turned, waved it in the air, and asked, "Anyone care for a drink?" When no one responded, she staggered back to her seat, tripped over the edge of the torn rug and fell into the chair.

"Candy, you need to get some help," Enright said.

Candy snorted, the bottle of cheap wine poised before her lips. "What should I do—check into the fucking morgue early? Sweetie, I'm the walking dead. The only fun I get out of life anymore is when some horny idiot loses control and doesn't wear a rubber . . ."

Bouchard was shocked, and it showed when she said, "Surely, you're not working in your condition?"

Candy pulled the bottle away from her lips and glared back at Bouchard. "Why shouldn't I? Some lowlife with a hard-on gave this to me. I'm just giving it back. As they say in AA: 'It works; pass it on'. Well, it works for me, and that's what I'm doing—just passing it on."

Bouchard studied Candy as she tipped her head back and gulped down a long drink of wine. Even while drinking cheap wine like a homeless wino, Candy was, to a certain degree, poised.

Candy set the bottle aside and looked into Bouchard's eyes. When she said, "Honey, I'm a walking one-woman AIDS epidemic," her voice was as hard as the burn at the bottom of a pot of sauce that had been left overnight on a hot burner.

Bouchard met her challenge and stared back. She made a silent vow to call the Massachusetts Board of Health as soon as she left the apartment. The authorities had to intervene and take this bitter woman out of circulation before she could jeopardize more lives. Bouchard leaned in Candy's direction. "Tell me about Cheri."

Candy let out a hoarse laugh. "That kid was greener than a Granny Smith apple—a real fish."

"What do you mean exactly?" Bouchard asked.

"She didn't know shit—and even if she had, she'd've probably screwed it up."

"Okay, I know that fish is prison slang for a new inmate. But I'm surprised you'd use that phrase, Candy, considering . . ."

"Considering the weirdo in the truck?" Candy stared back at Bouchard with wide eyes.

Bouchard was immediately struck by this turn in the conversation. She recalled Houston mentioning a truck when he told her about the incident with the paranoid hooker. She leaned forward. "Weirdo?" she repeated.

Bouchard felt Enright shift on the couch but ignored her. Bouchard was now completely engrossed with Candy's story.

Candy pulled at a strand of her stringy hair. "Yeah, that fucking lunatic—women on the street call him the Fisherman."

A fisherman had also come up last night; now Bouchard was really interested. She leaned yet closer to Candy without caring if her attentiveness was obvious. "Have you seen him?"

"I saw him once," Candy picked up the wine bottle and placed it against her lips.

"What can you tell us about him?" Enright asked.

Candy swallowed and then set the bottle back down on the coffee table. "Not much. Hell, I'm not dumb enough to go with a sick bastard like that."

"There must be something you can tell us about him, right?"

Candy shrugged her shoulders. "He drives a big truck—a refrigerator unit. He hauls fish. Obviously he lives somewhere along the shore. What the hell else am I supposed to say?"

"When did you see him, Candy?" Bouchard asked.

She shrugged and her eyes drifted up to the right. "Maybe six months ago—I don't recall exactly. I have a hard time remembering dates, but I do remember it was cold."

Bouchard took note of how Candy unconsciously wrapped her arms about her chest before continuing, "It was one of those nights when the wind comes off the harbor and quick-freezes everything it touches. Frankly, I'd given up on getting any action, and I'd started home. What little business there was went to the young chicks." She suddenly stopped, seemingly lost in memories.

Bouchard lowered her voice and softly asked, "Where were you, Candy?"

"What?" A startled look came to her face, as if she had just woken up in a hospital.

"Where were you when you first saw this . . . fisherman?"

She sighed. "I can't remember."

Bouchard reached over and patted Candy's hand. "Take your time, the memory will be there."

"Shit, I know that." Candy's face flushed with anger. "That's the fucking problem, isn't it?"

Bouchard pulled back her hand and slid back onto the sofa. Enright followed her lead.

Bouchard continued to watch Candy.

Candy blurted out, "I was just past the Public Garden when this truck pulled up beside me."

Bouchard took note of the inadvertent wrinkling of her nose. "What happened then?"

"The passenger door opened, and I looked inside."

"But you didn't get in?" Enright asked.

Candy's upper body shook. "The smell was awful." She paused and then muttered. "When I saw there was no handle on the inside of the door, I got suspicious. But that isn't what really turned me off."

"No? Then what did?" Bouchard asked.

"It was his eyes," Candy murmured.

"His eyes . . . what about his eyes?"

"He isn't right." She tapped her head with a finger as she spoke.

"What was it about his eyes, Candy?" Bouchard repeated her question.

Candy lowered her voice and bent forward. "Have you ever seen the wild look a cornered lab rat gets?"

"I don't think I have," Bouchard replied. From the corner of her eye she saw Enright nod in agreement; she hadn't either.

"Well, they flash as if there's an insane fire in them." Candy hesitated, a dramatic pause that drove home her point. Bouchard thought it was the practice of a skilled lecturer. "That's how he looked."

"I see."

Candy shook her head. "He'd have been ugly even if his head wasn't misshapen."

"Misshapen?" Bouchard repeated. The word surprised her. She thought that it was a word not usually in a prostitute's vocabulary; *fucked up* would have been more likely.

Candy fished out another cigarette and fumbled with her lighter. Her head bobbed as she struggled to align it with her wobbly hand. Bouchard studied her, wondering if her hands shook from the chemicals in her system or if there was something particularly troubling about recalling this incident.

Bouchard was just about to ask Candy another question when Enright piped in, "How was his head misshapen? What did it look like?"

Candy turned and this time, she blew the smoke away from them. She coughed, and phlegm popped in her throat. She coughed a second time, trying to clear the obstruction, and then spat into a soiled handkerchief. She looked at her visitors, seemed embarrassed for a second, and then said, "He has a spot on the side of his head that looked like someone had smacked it with a flat object when he was a baby."

"I see," Bouchard said.

Candy stretched forward, and as if she were consulting with a couple of coconspirators said, "Nothing in the world could have made me get into that truck. Believe me—" She closed her eyes and leaned back in her chair. She sat with her eyes shut for several moments. When she finally opened her eyelids, she had let down the veil that kept her secure in a secret world of her own. Tears glistened in Candy's eyes.

What is happening here? Bouchard held back, deciding it was best to let Candy offer her own explanation.

Candy shook her head, as though she tried to clear away the alcoholic fog that clouded her mind. "I understand psychopaths, sociopaths, or antisocial personalities—use whichever term you like. They're all the same. Although, on a professional level, I think that for this one, psychopath is most appropriate."

Bouchard's back stiffened. Had Candy actually spoken those words in that professional tone?

Candy ground her cigarette on one of the dirty plates that covered the end table and sprang from her chair. When she crossed the room, she walked steadier—seemed to glide rather than stumble. She stopped in front of a windowsill, leaned against it, and stared at the street.

Bouchard thought she looked as if something were sucking life from her. She also noted how thin Candy's arms were, even though they were covered by the cylinders of faded wool that hung at either side of her shapeless body. A metamorphosis was happening—one Anne considered positive. There was a new softness and vulnerability in Candy's sunken face.

Candy turned to her visitors and whispered in a weak and hoarse voice, "Now, I've got things to do." Suddenly, the softness dropped from her face like shattered glass, and the hardness returned. As quickly as she had changed mere moments before, Candy reverted to the street-smart hooker. "There are johns to fuck—in more ways than one." Candy let out a short laugh. To Bouchard, it did not ring true.

Candy walked to the door and opened it. Bouchard nudged Enright and slid off the couch; the interview was over. Before Bouchard could step through the open door, Candy grabbed her forearm. "There's one other thing. I think the guy's from Maine."

"You're certain?" Bouchard asked.

Candy moved her head up and down slowly. "I saw his license plate. It was a commercial plate, but it definitely said Maine."

"Thank you," Bouchard said. It was like she was staring at the ghost of a woman who had once been vibrant and strong.

Within seconds, Bouchard and Enright were in the hall and staring at the closed door.

"That was bizarre," Bouchard said. "What just happened in there? I feel like I just interviewed two people."

"You did."

Bouchard stared at her. "Is there something you know that you haven't told me?"

Enright looked sheepish. "Yes."

"Out with it."

"I didn't say anything because I wanted you to talk with her without any preconceived biases."

"Such as?"

"Pity, maybe even revulsion . . . I don't know."

"I was a cop for a long time. Believe me when I say I know better than to do that."

"I didn't know who was walking in here with me . . . a woman or a cop."

Bouchard hesitated. "All right, I understand. Now tell me what you held back."

"You met Candy the hardened, bitter prostitute, and for a moment, ever so briefly, her former self appeared."

"What do you mean 'her former self'?"

"*Doctor* Candace Littleton, professor of psychology."

Bouchard stared at the door for a moment before she and Enright turned to go. "I'll be damned . . ."

They sat in Enright's car; neither seemed willing to speak. The interview with Candy still bothered Bouchard. "What could possibly happen to turn a woman with a PhD into that?"

"Love."

"Love? Lisa, please, this is serious, and you know that sounds ridiculous."

"Ever been in true love, Anne? The kind of love where being with someone consumes your every thought, your every action? Where you wake up thinking about that person, drift through your day lost in thoughts of him, and then in bed you stare at the empty pillow beside you and wonder why his head isn't on it? Then, when you finally go to sleep, you dream of him."

Bouchard thought about her relationship with Houston. They were as close as she had ever been with any man, but as much as they loved each other, their relationship certainly did not fit that description. "No, I haven't . . ."

Enright smiled. "Well, if it helps alleviate your guilt, neither have I. However, Candace has. He was a professor, too. Unfortunately, he had a darker side. He was a very self-assured man, dominant in his field and in his personal life. When Candace fell for him, she gave over control of everything. Jeremy was not the sort to live in the shadow of a successful woman. He controlled every aspect of her life, and at first, she happily let him."

Bouchard shook her head. She had known many women who put their lives, careers, and dreams aside for husband and family; still the concept was anathema to her. She realized how lucky she was; Houston had always treated her as equal, and in some areas—those in which he knew she excelled—acquiesced to her. "So where is this guy now?"

"He was physically abusive. Over time, he demolished Candace. She lost her self-esteem and became a shadow of what she had been."

"You seem to know a lot about her."

"I've been interested in how and why women turn to prostitution for years now. Ten years ago, when I first got out of college, she was helping me write my articles on the prostitution trade. I was looking into the psychology of the women who worked the streets. Candace really got into it. She developed a fascination with the women . . . looking back, her interest became more than just professional. It could have been a fantasy thing between her and Jeremy."

"It sounds to me like she became a dominant man's dream—by day a professor and by night his personal whore."

"Something like that. I wouldn't want to say anything definite, though. I often feel guilty for introducing her to that world."

The afternoon had turned hot and oppressively humid; Bouchard stared out the window and watched an advancing thunderhead. "It sounds to me as if there's more to her story. However, you still haven't answered my question. Where is this guy now?"

"One night she realized what Jeremy was doing to her. During one of his sexual fantasies, Candace killed him."

"Now I remember the case. I was a rookie on the force when it happened."

"The courts absolved her by ruling the death as an accident during the throes of passion, but it was the beginning of the end for Candace. She started drinking heavily, then drugs. Eventually she lost her job and no university would consider her . . . which finally led her to the streets."

Thunder boomed, and it began to pour. Bouchard suppressed a desire to step out into the deluge and let the rain wash away the filth of the world she lived in.

15

It was hot. So humid that the air felt as heavy as an anvil. He sat on the porch, sweat dripping from his chin, falling onto his already soaked dingy T-shirt as he watched the horizon, waiting for the cooling relief of darkness to creep across the gulf. He saw a harbor seal break the surface and cursed. He grabbed his .30-06 rifle, and in a single motion locked it into his shoulder.

The rifle barked.

The seal rolled over, diving below the surface. Several seconds later, he spied it swimming away toward the middle of the Gulf. He fired again and grunted with pleasure when he saw the seal jump in the water then roll over. "That'll teach the goddamned thief not to eat my fish."

He propped the rifle against the wall and picked up his beer. He glanced over his shoulder into the dark sweltering interior of the house. *Must be over a hundred upstairs*, he thought. *Maybe I'll go see if the little woman's calmed down now. I might even let her come out and watch the water for a spell.*

He got up and stretched. He looked at the seal's floating corpse, smiled, and spit. *Yup*, he thought, *it's going to be a hot, muggy night— makes a man a bit randy.*

Cheryl lay in the oppressive heat. She reached for the dipper and ladled out some of the tepid water. If she did not drink, dehydration was inevitable. On the other hand, if she did drink she would need to use the foul bucket in the far corner. She hated that thing. To compound matters, he had not emptied it in three days, and although she had become immune to it, she knew its odor permeated the room.

She sat on the edge of the bed, sweat running down her torso in rivulets. Even though she was past the agonies of physical withdrawal from the heroin that had ravaged her body, she no longer felt human. Cheri was gone, and the Cheryl that remained was no longer a woman and aspiring actress—she was a woman fighting for survival, and survive she would. She was not going to be like Monique and the others who had occupied the next room over. *Lord,* she wondered, *how long ago was it? A day—a week—two weeks even?* She tensed when she heard his heavy tread on the stairs. Suddenly the door opened, and he was there.

He walked to the foot of the bed and stared at her for a moment. "You alright?"

Afraid to talk because she never knew what would trigger his insane rages, she nodded, keeping her eyes averted.

He reached over and picked up the slop bucket and left. A minute later, she heard the toilet flush and he was back. He placed the bucket in its corner. He leaned against the wall and folded his arms across his chest.

"Hot," he said.

She nodded.

"You can speak, woman."

"Yes, it's hot." Her voice was barely audible.

"*What?*"

She jumped. "Yes, it's hot."

"That's better. If I take you outside, will you promise to be good?"

Her heart skipped. *Outside!* Outside meant fresh air and sunshine and maybe, just maybe, the opportunity to escape.

"Well?"

"I would like that."

"And?"

"I promise to be good."

He pushed away from the wall and reached into his pocket. He removed a key and opened the lock. She whimpered when the shackle pulled away, ripping her skin where scabs had formed, binding the metal to her wrist.

He snarled at the sound of her pain and cocked his arm, ready to strike her.

Cheryl grasped her injured wrist, holding it against her stomach, and bent forward, cowering, keeping her eyes lowered. She stayed like that for several moments, too afraid to look away from the floor. She tensed, bracing for the expected blow. It never came.

"Get up."

She stood. "Can I have something to wear?"

"What you need clothes for? Ain't nobody around to see nothing. Besides, if you're good I may let you skinny-dip in the cove."

She hoped she did not look too anxious. If he let her go swimming, maybe she could escape—possibly swim out to sea. If a boat did not find her and she drowned, that would still be better than being here. Either way, she could not lose.

He gave her a hard look and repeated his warning. "Only if you're good."

"I promise to be good—you'll see."

He smiled at her. "It's good to see you're adjusting. Come on."

Cheryl gingerly followed him down the stairs. Days of confinement in the room's dim light had made her super-sensitive to the bright sunshine, and she paused at the door, shielding her eyes.

"Go on." He pushed her onto the porch.

16

Jimmy O'Leary sat at his desk, smoking a cigarette. "You hear what happened to Mike with the whore?" he asked Gordon Winter.

O'Leary chuckled. "Fucking idiot," he said.

Winter, too, had a laugh at Houston's expense and said, "Next time I see him, I'm not gonna let him live this one down."

"Yesterday afternoon I took him to Del Vecchio's place. Gordon, there's something weird going on. Hookers been disappearing all over the city."

"There ain't anything weird about that."

"This ain't the usual turnover, Gordon. Even the pimps are getting uptight."

"Do you think we got a turf war going on?"

"It doesn't feel that way. Women that been with their pimps for years have gone missing."

"And the cops don't care."

"To them it's no big deal. They couldn't really give a shit—less work for them." O'Leary ground his cigarette out in an ashtray. "For some reason, this has got me interested. Let's call a meeting."

"With who?"

"Mike and Anne need to talk to Shiloh Baines."

17

Houston hung up the phone. He had called every talent agent in New York, as well as an acquaintance on the NYPD. Nobody had seen nor heard of Cheryl Guerette or, for that matter, of Cheri. He scratched his head in frustration. Nobody could disappear as completely as she had. It was not possible.

The phone rang, and he snatched it up.

"Houston."

"Boy, you sound grumpy," Bouchard said.

"You would, too, if you'd just spent three hours with a cell phone stuck to your ear—and all for nothing. What have you learned?"

"Mike, something really scary is going on. Lisa and I have talked to seven women, and they're scared to death. The only thing they know is that every time a streetwalker goes missing, a truck from Maine is in the area. They can't put their fingers on anything, but he seems to be around every time there's a disappearance. The women call the driver the Fisherman."

"The Fisherman?"

"They say sometimes he drives a big truck, no trailer. The cargo box is built onto the back—sounds like a modified eighteen-wheeler to me. At other times he's in a van. They gave him the name because the insides of both his trucks smell like dead fish."

"Can anyone describe him for us? Maybe we can get a police sketch artist to do a drawing?"

"Mike, these women are not about to deal with the cops. They are truly terrified."

Houston recalled his encounter with the streetwalker. "I believe that."

"If we're going to meet with Jimmy and this pimp Shiloh Baines, we should get going."

O'Leary held the door for Houston and Bouchard and then followed them inside the bar. Once they were off the street, they paused for several seconds, waiting for their eyes to adjust to the diminished light, and then scanned the room. O'Leary spotted Shiloh Baines sitting at the bar. "There he is," he said.

Baines turned when the door opened and let in a bright shaft of light. O'Leary knew that the pimp was playing his street character. He sipped his drink and waited for them to approach. After a few seconds, O'Leary tapped on his shoulder. He turned and said, "Jimmy Fuckin' O'Leary! Hell, man, I ain't seen you in what—?"

"Knock off the phony splib crap, and join us at that table in the rear."

"Jimmy, Jimmy, man, you got to get with the times," Baines said, sliding off the barstool. "This is the twenty-first century. No one uses words like *splib* anymore."

"Right, and I guess you don't call me a cracker behind my back."

"That be the honest truth." Baines's eyes seemed to sparkle when he added, "We call you that *goddamned* mick cracker."

O'Leary smiled. "One thing I always liked about you, Shy. You like to push the envelope."

"An' you don't? You gotta be crazy to come waltzing in here with a cop."

O'Leary turned and gestured Houston and Bouchard forward. "This is Anne Bouchard and her partner Mike Houston. You're right, they were detectives but they ain't cops anymore. They've gone private and have some questions."

"Shit, cops always got questions."

Baines retrieved his drink and followed them to the table. Once seated, he turned to his visitors and said, "Okay, Jimmy, you knock off the tough guy shit, and I'll do the same with the ghetto rap."

"Works for me."

Baines looked at Bouchard and Houston, then asked, "How you doin'?"

"We're fine, thank you," Bouchard replied.

O'Leary said, "Anne and Mike are investigating the missing women."

"There isn't much I can tell you. One night they were working the streets—the next they were gone. It's as if they were snatched."

Houston said, "I don't know if *snatched* is the right word, but I'm in agreement that there's no way they just took off."

"One or two may have but not all of them. Let's be truthful here, shall we? Most of these women would be homeless, sleeping under bridges, addicted to heroin, and probably being raped on a daily basis if businessmen like me didn't give them a job and a place to stay. Even if they wanted to go, where would they run to? I learned a long time ago that you never run away from home until you have a place to which you can run. I won't insult you by trying to convince you that what I do benefits society because like any business, I don't care—I'm in it strictly for the profit."

Bouchard could not help but be impressed by the pimp's honest, straightforward attitude. "You sound . . ." she paused trying to think of the right word.

"Too educated for a lowlife pimp?" Baines chuckled. "Boston College, class of '95. I have a BS in Business Management. This time next year I'll have earned my MBA."

He grinned at Bouchard's look of astonishment.

"Yeah, I know a thing or two about running a business. The first rule is to maximize your resources. I don't beat my women, nor do I hook them on H or any other narcotic. If they're high, they can't earn. If they're addicted to smack, they'll steal to get it. I give them a decent place to live—usually no more than three to an apartment."

"And in return you ask for . . . ?" Bouchard said.

"Just like any other manager, I give my employees goals and objectives—hell, I even give them a form of profit-sharing. I receive a given percentage of their take to cover rent and various expenses. Anything they spend on clothes for the job, I reimburse, and anything they earn over quota, they get a twenty percent bonus—that's a better deal than you'd get as a salesperson for Microsoft. Hell, three of my younger women attend college during the day."

"Okay, I'll accept that you're an extraordinary pim— . . . manager. Is there anything else that you can you tell me about the missing women?"

Baines sat back, drank his whiskey, and then motioned to the bartender for a refill. "You guys want anything? It's on me . . ."

"In that case," Bouchard said, "I'll have a white wine—Chablis, preferably."

Baines looked at Houston and O'Leary; both ordered beer.

"Any particular brand?" the bartender asked.

"Whatever you got on tap."

"Got Sam Adams, that do you?"

O'Leary said, "Yup." Houston nodded.

The bartender placed Baines's drink on the table and said, "You got it, boss."

"You own this place?" Houston asked.

"I told you I'm a businessman, and it happens that I'm in the adult entertainment business. I own two clubs on Route 1 in Revere, three bars in Boston, and of course there're my escort services. Hell, if you knew everything I owned, you'd think I was a conglomerate. Now let's talk about the women. The first one I lost was three-and-a-half years ago in February. Her name was Victoria . . . on the street she used the name Ineeda Mann."

O'Leary chuckled, and Bouchard gave him a stern look. "Sorry," he said and then burst out laughing. "Ineeda Mann for Christ's sake! That's too much."

"Yeah," Baines said, "she thought it was hilarious, too. I really liked her. She had a great sense of humor and, when she wasn't using, had a good head on her shoulders. I was trying to get her into rehab, earning her GED, and then going to college. Hell, if I could have gotten her clean, I was considering taking her off the streets and having her manage the business. Then on one bastard of a cold night, she just up and disappeared."

The bartender returned and placed their drinks before them. He asked, "Can I get you anything else?" When Baines raised the fingers on his left hand, he nodded and returned to his post behind the bar.

"You've never heard anything from or about her?" Houston asked Baines.

"Nope, haven't heard a word or a rumor of her—not so much as a Christmas card in three years. She disappeared like a wizard in a fantasy novel. Since then, four more of my escorts have vanished—more than that, I can't tell you."

18

Houston followed Anne, carrying the first cup of precinct coffee he'd had in over a year. When they walked into Dysart's office, the captain was surprised by their sudden appearance and asked, "How the hell did you get up here? Nobody called up from the desk saying that I had visitors."

"Desk Sergeant remembers us from the old days," Bouchard said.

"Sometimes I think that if that sonuvabitch saw Whitey Bolger with a gun, he'd recognize him and just let him sashay up here, too."

Dysart turned his attention to Bouchard. "And how is my all-time favorite detective doing?" He pointed at Houston with his right thumb. "This degenerate treating you okay?"

Bouchard smiled. "I'm fine, Cap. How're you doing?"

"Broke my heart when they retired you on medical disability . . ." He again pointed to Houston. "Him, I don't miss so much." His craggy face broke out in a smile, and he motioned to the chairs that fronted his desk. "Sit down, guys. Christ, I wish I had you two back. You two were the best closers we had."

Houston sipped on his coffee and sat quiet while Dysart and Bouchard reminisced. After studying the oil slick that floated on the top of the cup for several seconds, he raised his eyes and stared at his old boss. Things had changed. In the past, Dysart would have performed his ritual of lighting a cigarette, taking one or two drags, and then tossing it out the window. He turned his attention to the windows and grinned when he realized that here at the new police headquarters the windows were sealed and could not be opened.

After several moments, Dysart sensed Houston's eyes on him and turned to him. "Jesus Christ, Mike, what's with you? You look like you're ready to kill something. You still suffering from your little mace exposure?"

Houston shrugged. "Nothing."

Dysart's smile belied his words when he said, "Nothing, my ass. I don't hear from you two for twelve months and then you're in my face unannounced. You want something all right. So cut to the chase, okay?"

Houston chuckled. "I guess I'm as conspicuous as a ten-dollar whore wearing a thousand-dollar dress."

"That's one way of saying it."

Houston placed his coffee on the edge of the desk and said, "Bill, talk to me about all the missing hookers."

"What the hell are you talking about?"

"Come on, don't yank my chain, okay? We go back too far for that."

Dysart glanced around the room as if trying to ensure they would not be overheard. "Okay, I'll tell you how things are. We've heard about the disappearances. However, to date, not a single whore has shown up, alive or dead, so nobody gives a shit. Come to think of it, the only hooker I've seen on Beacon Hill lately is the statue of General Hooker—of course, I can't speak for Government Center. You're likely to see anything there." He chuckled. "You know that's where the expression hooker came from, right?"

"No, I didn't," Bouchard said.

"Yeah, the whores who followed General Hooker's army around during the Revolutionary War were known as Hooker's Girls—hence, hookers."

"Thanks for the history lesson. . . . Now can we get back to the issue at hand? You're admitting to us that because you have no bodies, the problem gets swept under the table?" she said.

"Shit, Anne, nobody said that. We follow up when they file a missing persons report. I know you two been out of touch for a year, but nothing has changed around here. It's the same as when you worked for me—I don't have five or six detectives just sitting on their asses waiting for something to happen. Hell, right now we're working sixteen cases—half of them homicides. Just how much manpower do you think I'm going to spend looking for whores who go to the powder room and don't come back?"

"Bill, we're talking fifty women or more in a three or four year period," Anne said.

Dysart leaned back. His chair squeaked under his weight. "So call out the fucking National Guard—maybe they got the resources."

"Have you ever heard of a guy they call the Fisherman?" Houston asked.

"Nope, the waterfront's full of fishermen though."

"Very funny. . . . This guy's not local. We believe he's from Maine."

"Well, there you have it, then. Last time I checked, I don't have jurisdiction up there."

"That's it?" Houston said.

"Bring us a body—a Boston body—something for me to go on. Until then, I got enough shit piled up to keep me shoveling for the next six months. Have a good day, Mike."

Houston stood up and looked at his former boss. Dysart looked as if he were wearing down. The rigors of the job and age were taking more out of him than he had to left give. Still, Dysart's reaction to their visit irritated him, and he said, "Alright, Bill, we'll get you something. When we do get it, where do you want it? Is on your desk okay?"

Houston motioned to Anne that they should leave. When he turned, he could almost feel the heat of Dysart's glare burning into his back. He paused at the door. "Oh, by the way, Jimmy O'Leary is setting up a meet with most of the pimps working the hub. Call me if you want in on it—you never know, it might prove interesting."

"Who's to guarantee I'll get out alive?"

"If Jimmy sets it up, he'll protect you," Bouchard said.

"When did you and Jimmy O get so chummy?" Dysart asked her.

"He has his good points," she replied. "I think you should do it."

"Now that ought to do wonders for my reputation. Get the fuck outta here."

Dysart met Bouchard and Houston outside the warehouse, and they led him in. It looked as if a convention were taking place. The building was empty, and off to the left of center, the large open area was set up like a conference room; folding tables were butted end-to-end and side-to-side to form a six-foot-by-twelve-foot rectangular table. Around the edges sat a group of people the likes of which Houston thought he would never see congregated outside a courtroom or a precinct house.

"I can't fucking believe I'm doing this. I should have sent one of my sergeants," Dysart said. "If a reporter ever snapped our pic we'd be in front of a review board by eight tomorrow morning."

"You'll be alright. O'Leary set this up," Houston said.

"For five years now, I've let you talk me into situations like this, Mike."

"And I always get you through them. The fact that a captain showed up will cool things. These people are close to taking things into their own hands. You can rest assured that Jimmy has everything under control."

"Really? I can't believe anyone can control this bunch of frigging Apaches."

"You don't know Jimmy like I do. They all know that they either toe the line or Jimmy and his people will bust their asses. Let's get closer."

They walked through the room, ignoring the stares and malevolent looks from the gathered pimps. Satisfied that they had shown their distaste, the leaders of Boston's illegitimate sex trade turned their attention to O'Leary, who stood at the head of the table. The room and everyone in it seemed tense, and Houston thought the scene was macabre. Houston saw sweat on Dysart's brow and thought he looked as if he were wearing lead boots in a minefield—sure signs that the career cop felt uncomfortable if not threatened. Nevertheless, Dysart maintained his cool and otherwise seemed unaffected by the display of distrust and hatred. The three investigators found a convenient spot along the wall and settled back to watch the goings-on.

Houston folded his arms across his chest, stood between Dysart and Bouchard, and leaned against the wall. *This*, he thought, *should be more interesting than watching a monkey try to fuck a football.*

"Okay, okay," O'Leary said without a glance to acknowledge the presence of the three outsiders. "For the next hour or so, let's put all our differences aside and follow one of the guiding principles of AA. That means who you see here and what you hear here stays here." He paused, obviously wanting to add emphasis to his words. "Now we're all in agreement that there's some serious shit going down, are we not?"

The assembly nodded.

Houston watched the proceedings with renewed interest; he had never seen O'Leary act as a mediator, a facet of the man he would never have thought existed.

"I see the police department is here, too," O'Leary said. "If we're going to get to the bottom of this, we need to cooperate and work together."

"We're willing to work with you," Shiloh yelled, the sophisticated veneer of the previous day hidden by his pimp act, "but we ain't so sure about the five-oh over there."

Dysart spoke for the first time since he had entered the building. "The Boston Police Department is open to anything you have to say."

Houston thought he sounded defensive.

"That right?" Shiloh seemed unconvinced. "Then how come for three years we been reportin' that hoes been disappearing, an' you guys ain't done nothing?"

"Let's be realistic here," Dysart said, keeping his voice controlled. "The women who . . ." He paused to select the right phrase. ". . . work for you don't exactly have a stable lifestyle."

"That don't mean something ain't going on," a pimp in a flashy suit said. "I had four girls disappear, and two of them been in my stable a long time. I think some asshole either snatched them or they're dead."

"In three years, we've never found a single piece of evidence that leads us to believe anything happened other than they decided on a change of scenery."

"Change of scenery, my ass." The pimp leaned forward, his muscular arms folded on the table. "Them hoes disappeared," he snapped his fingers, "like that. I called people all up and down the East coast—ain't no one seen them."

Dysart leaned back. "Do you think if some pimp in New York or DC is working one of your runaway girls he'd tell you? Besides, it isn't as if you people have a nationwide network—or do you?"

"I know that I told you people about that fish dude in the freezer truck," Shiloh said. "You ever get a line on him? Seems like every time a hoe vanishes, that truck's been in the area."

"We're looking into the truck," Dysart said. "But even after we have a BOLO out for any truck meeting the description, our hands are tied without definitive evidence that a crime has occurred. Of one thing we are certain—if he's a fish wholesaler, he isn't anyone local."

O'Leary held his hands up, signaling for the discussion to stop. "Captain," he said, "it sounds to me as if you're sayin' that your department can't—or won't—do anything."

"Not at all. We're checking out as much as we can. Nevertheless, without an eyewitness or a body, there isn't a damned thing we can do. Every day, hundreds of trucks come and go on the waterfront—many of them fitting the description we've been given. We've even checked out the markets in Everett. Thus far, all we have is a vague description of the truck—one time it's a Peterbilt, the next a Ford. One of your women told us it was a Diamond Reo. Shit, there hasn't been one of them made in over thirty years. We've had reports that it's blue, yellow, red, and white. We don't have enough cops to check every truck that comes in and out of the city. I got to have something to go with—a license plate would be nice, but without that my frigging hands are tied."

"We understand your dilemma," O'Leary said. "But if you can't do something, we will."

"Jimmy, if bodies start turning up like they did in the Latisha Washington situation last year, I'll do everything in my power to bring you down."

"You do what you have to do, Captain, and we'll do what we have to."

With that, O'Leary closed the meeting.

Outside, Houston, Bouchard, and Dysart watched the pimps disappear into the night. Dysart leaned against his car and smoked a cigarette. The evening was warm, and Dysart rolled his shirt sleeves above his elbows. He waited until the flow of people tapered off, tossed his cigarette away, and said, "Mike, you got to put a muzzle on O'Leary. I can't have another of his vigilante deals."

The previous year, the mother of a young girl asked O'Leary to help her find the gang-bangers who had raped and killed her daughter. He resolved the situation with his own unique brand of justice; within days, the cops found the four rapists' bodies.

"Bill, I got no control over Jimmy. He always does what he wants. I'm sure he feels the BPD isn't responsive enough to problems in the neighborhood, so he takes things into his own hands. He's always been that way, and he always will be."

"I know that sometimes we don't do a good job in the neighborhoods . . ."

"That's because there's too much goddamned politics in the department, Bill. You know that as well as Jimmy and I do."

"That's life," Dysart said. "I don't like it any more than you, but I can't have guys like Jimmy holding court with a 9 mm judge presiding."

Dysart got into his car. He started the engine, rolled down the window, and said, "Mike, be careful, okay? Even though you two only been gone a year, things are different from what they were when you were cops. People are pretty anxious. You were right about one thing . . ." He nodded toward the warehouse. ". . . these people are more paranoid than most. Truthfully, if this meeting was an indicator, they're scared shitless." He waved as he drove away.

O'Leary and Winter walked out of the warehouse. O'Leary lit a cigarette and watched the cop drive away. "SOSDD," he said.

"What?" Bouchard asked.

"Same old shit, different day."

"Jimmy," Bouchard said, "Bill Dysart is possibly the most honest and straight cop I've ever known. But as he said, he can't investigate a crime until there's evidence of one. The powers that be would have him on the carpet within an hour of opening up an investigation."

"Well," O'Leary replied, "the powers that be got no hold on me ..." O'Leary walked away without saying anything else.

"Obviously," Houston said.

Winter grinned. "I wouldn't worry about it if I were you. He'll come around, if not in this lifetime, the next."

Houston grinned. "My money is on the next lifetime."

19

Cheryl sat on the porch and watched darkness settle over the Gulf of Maine. Every now and then out of the corner of her eye, she checked to see what he was doing. He was always the same—sitting in the old wooden kitchen chair, leaning back against the wall with his feet wrapped around the chair legs while he held the ever-present rifle in his lap. He looked peaceful and out of touch with his surroundings. However, she knew he was not. She recalled the lyrics to an old song her mother used to play—the one in which the singer lamented that there was a killer on the road. The gun was all the proof she needed to know he would have no reluctance to shoot her if she fled. It was very likely that her killer was not on the road; he sat beside her.

A cool, pleasant breeze blew in from the gulf, and Cheryl let it lull her. She recalled sitting on her grandparents' porch on evenings just like this waiting for some boy or another to stop by. They would sit and chat, maybe flirt a bit. The only difference was that now she sat naked beside a psycho who couldn't get an erection. She sobered; it was difficult for her to believe that those idyllic days of youth had been only one year ago.

His harsh voice suddenly broke the evening silence. "You're disgusting—you smell like roadkill."

His tone startled her. "I know," she said, taking care to keep any hint of defiance from her voice. "I'd love to take a bath."

"Go clean yourself."

She turned to the door.

"Not in there." He pointed to the ocean. "There."

Cheryl's heart skipped. Was she hearing him correctly? This was the third night he had let her out of her prison to sit in the cool night air. She could not believe that he was finally going to let her swim in the ocean. She fought the excitement she felt, not wanting to show it. She recalled a movie she'd seen as a child, how Br'er Rabbit goaded Br'er Bear and Br'er Fox by saying, "Please, don't throw me in that briar patch." She kept her hope under control and said, "But the Gulf is too cold—and public."

"The plumbing is fucked up," he said. "You got two choices, the ocean or nothin'."

Her heart hammered so fast she thought he would see it. Maybe she had a chance. Maybe—just maybe.

Cheryl stepped onto the unpaved walk. She used her toes to search the ground for pebbles before she placed her weight on bare feet. She concentrated on the path until she reached the grass, where she stopped and looked over her shoulder at her captor. She wondered if he was toying with her. Was this nothing more than another of his games? Her stomach in a knot, she saw that he still sat as before; however, she noticed that his hand seemed to have a firmer grip on the rifle.

"Go on." His smile and calm words belied the physical alertness of his body.

She turned and walked toward the water. Her shoulders tensed as she waited for a bullet's impact. She neared the water and forced herself to keep her pace under control and not to move too quickly. In seconds, she stood at the edge of the small cove that led to the sea. She turned and looked toward the house. He had not moved; still sitting like a silent sentinel, his eyes seemed to bore through her. She was certain that he would never let her into the water; this was just a ploy—an excuse to kill her.

Cheryl placed her left foot in the surf and quickly pulled it out. It was frigid. Even though it was late July, the temperature in the water of the

Gulf of Maine struggled to reach fifty degrees. She wrapped her arms across her breasts, slowly swishing her right foot back and forth, allowing it to become accustomed to the water. She stepped forward, shivering as the cold water reached her knees. When it was halfway between her knees and her waist, she stopped walking. Once again, she looked over her shoulder at the vigilant sentinel, who watched from his post.

The water lapped against her legs, and she shivered each time it touched a dry portion of her leg. She decided to get it over with and plunged in. The cold took her breath away, and then she felt a rush of exhilaration as the saltwater washed the filth, sweat, and grime of captivity from her body. Fighting off the urge to swim out to sea and get away, she realized that it was smarter to go slow and not arouse suspicion. She admonished herself, *Don't go too far or too fast*. She rolled over and began to back-stroke, all the while keeping her eyes on him.

The Fisherman was still on the porch, only now his chair was forward, and he leaned forward staring at the ocean.

She swam slowly, staying well within the confines of the cove and close to the shore, always watching him. She waved, feeling silly for doing it, but hoping it would put him at ease. She swam about ten yards then turned and swam back. With each lap, she allowed herself to drift a little farther and farther from the shore.

Cheryl was elated, suddenly feeling something she thought she would never feel again: hope. Even though she was still within his power, she felt free. She kept her eye on him. He stood, watching her every move; his hand seemed to be closer to the deadly rifle's trigger.

Cheryl looked away and then back, and her heart skipped. He had moved closer and stood at the top of the steps, his eyes seeming to bore through her, waiting for her to make one wrong move. Cheryl realized that this was a test, another of his endless games. She wondered how deep the water was. Would it be deep enough for her to dive, avoiding the bullets? She suddenly wished she knew anything about guns. How far can a rifle like that shoot? Three hundred yards, four hundred, more? She stopped swimming and tried to touch bottom. The water was deeper than she was tall. She waved at him. He hesitated for a second and then waved back. She could not make out his face, but she knew he was getting concerned. The question was if he was worried enough to shoot her. She rolled over and dove beneath the surface.

Cheryl turned and began to swim back to the shore. She wanted badly to turn out to sea, but he was too vigilant. A plan began to form in her mind. She knew, however, if it were to work, she needed one thing—his trust.

Cheryl stepped out of the cool water and looked toward the house. He stood on the ground, several paces from the porch, still holding the rifle and watching her as intently as a mother cat watching a litter of newborn kittens. She walked to the porch, all the while telling herself she was stupid for not trying to escape. When she stood before the warped stairs leading up to the door, he stood watching her.

"You're smarter than I thought," he said.

Cheryl avoided eye contact with him and returned to her chair.

He stared out to the sea, not taking his eyes from it, and said, "If you had tried running, I would have shot you." To prove his point he snapped the rifle into his shoulder and turned slightly to his right. "See that pine cone on the bottom branch on the big pine?"

Cheryl stared at the tree that stood at the very edge of the light from the porch's single bulb. After a moment, she identified the pine cone of which he spoke.

Without waiting for a response, he fired. The cone exploded. He smiled at her. The twisted smile was more of a grimace, and when coupled with his deformed head, he looked demonic. It made her shiver. Suddenly the smile vanished, and his eyes flashed with insanity. His hands began to twitch, and his face reddened. "Go to your room."

20

Cheryl woke to the sun beating through the window. Last night after her swim, he had locked her in her room but left her unshackled for the first time since he had brought her to the house. Not certain what had awakened her, she sat up, holding the sheet across her chest.

The Fisherman stood in the door while holding clothes in his arms. He threw clean underwear, a T-shirt, and jeans on the bed. "Get dressed, breakfast is ready."

Cheryl knew he had no patience and that when he told her to do something, she had better do it immediately. She leapt from the bed and grabbed the clothes. Everything seemed to be in good order except the underpants were boys' briefs. She slid the underwear on and dressed as fast as she could. All the while, she tried not to telegraph the pleasure and security she felt from being clothed for the first time since he had taken her to meet Mum. Once she was dressed, she followed him from the room.

He strode down the stairs, never looking to see if she followed. Cheryl paused briefly and looked at Mum's room. She passed by, wondering if Mum was still alive.

She was surprised when he said, "After breakfast, we're going out. I got a charter this afternoon, and you need to start learning the family business. It's time you started earning your keep."

―――――――

Cheryl stood on the deck, the skyline of Portland visible behind the charter boat. They had left the cove at his house, and the first thing that struck her was how conditions on the boat belied those inside the house. Where the house was cluttered and filthy, the boat was immaculate with everything in its assigned place.

The twenty-five-foot craft bobbed and rubbed against the old tires he used as bumpers to protect the sides from the pier. The Fisherman opened one of the boat's wet-wells and stirred the mess in it with a short paddle.

"What's that?" Cheryl asked.

"Chum. It's used to attract fish."

"I know what chum is. What are you using?"

"Blood, guts, bone meal . . . leftovers from the factory."

"Is that the building beside the house?" she asked.

"Yeah, my old man used it to make fishcakes. If people knew the shit he put in them, they'd never eat that crap again."

He glanced around to see if their charter had arrived. Seeing they had the dock to themselves, he said, "Do what you're told today. Don't be talking to the customers." He gave her a hard look. "One peep, and you'll be the next one into that wet-well."

It was then that Cheryl realized what he used for chum. Unable to keep her face from broadcasting her fear and revulsion, she turned away and stared at the pier. He saw where she was looking and turned that way. Two fat men descended the stairs onto the dock and walked to the boat.

One of them wore the loudest Hawaiian shirt Cheryl had ever seen, and his companion wore a sleeveless T-shirt through which she could see the box of fat that defined his stomach. Both wore Red Sox hats. She got the distinct feeling that it was going to be a long afternoon.

"Remember," he muttered, "not so much as one fucking word." He walked down the gangplank to greet his customers.

"Ahoy!" called one of the men. "Are you Captain Fischer?"

The fisherman held out his hand.

"Yeah, I'm Willard Fischer. Welcome aboard."

Hawaiian shirt thumped T-shirt on the arm, "I'll be goddamned . . . a fisherman named Fischer! I told you this was going to be a trip to remember. I'm Chester. This burnout is Matt."

The men stopped and looked Cheryl over. A wishful leer came over Matt's face. "This the mate?"

"Yeah," Fischer said, "she's the mate—and my wife. Let's get one thing straight right now. She ain't part of the charter package."

Matt's face reddened, and he tripped on the gangplank as he scrambled aboard the boat.

As they prepared to get underway, Cheryl knew that Fischer remained vigilant. In fact, he watched her so intently that she wondered if the clients would think that something was wrong; it had to be unusual for the mate on a charter not to say anything to the clients. Fortunately, she had grown up around boats and needed little or no instruction; she knew what to do to get a fishing boat ready for sea.

Cheryl avoided Chester and Matt as if they had a communicable disease. If they asked for something, she brought it quickly; wary lest Fischer would misinterpret her actions, she took care to avoid eye contact and conversation with either of the clients.

As soon as the engines died, the vessel gently rocked in the swells. Fischer stepped down from the cockpit. "We should get something here," he said. "Spread some of that chum around the boat."

Her heart sank, and she struggled to keep from vomiting as she dipped a small bucket into the wet-well. With great care not to get the foul mixture on her clothes or body, Cheryl poured the bait over the side. She avoided looking at the pieces of flesh and meat that the current churned around the surface. She wiped at the tears on her face and wondered if what she was spreading in the ocean had not so long ago been Monique. She glanced at Fischer and smiled a nervous smile. He nodded and turned his back to her.

She heard Chester ask, "What is that shit?"

"This and that," Fischer answered. "Leftover from when I grind up meat and fish."

"Nasty-looking stuff."

"Yeah, it's all of that . . . but the fish love it."

———

The afternoon crept slowly by, and Cheryl was running out of ways to avoid the fishermen. It was not easy on the cramped charter boat; the one named Matt had been undressing her with his eyes since they had cleared the harbor. To this point, Chester and Fischer had seemed unaware of his attention. She tried, as much as was possible on the charter boat, to keep a buffer zone between Matt and herself. Who knew how Fischer would react if the customer were to touch or make a pass at her?

She was coiling a line when the inevitable happened, and Matt grabbed her by the arm. "You know," he said, "for what we're paying, you could be friendlier."

"Let me go," she said in a low voice that she hoped Fischer could not hear. "I am not included in the cost."

"For what this charter cost me, I should get to mingle with the crew if I want."

"You have no idea how much trouble you're going to cause."

Before Matt could respond, Fischer loomed behind him. He grabbed the client by the shoulder and spun him around. "He will now."

Cheryl's heart leaped. In Fischer's left hand, he held a long shaft that had a pointed head with a hook several inches below the point—one of the gaffs they used to land big fish. His eyes were narrow, and his mouth was a taut straight line, and Cheryl knew things were about to escalate.

Matt stepped backward. "Hey, man, I didn't mean no harm."

Fischer turned as if he had already forgotten the incident, and she heard the client exhale in relief. Like a striking cobra, Fischer spun around and grabbed Matt's shirt with his free hand and drove him back against the rail. He pressed the metal point of the gaff to the bottom the fat man's chin and said, "You keep your fucking hands off my wife." The startled client made a futile attempt to ward off the menacing gaff.

Cheryl looked at Fischer; it was evident that he was volatile, and it would take little if anything to set him off. She scurried to Fischer's side and said, "It's all right, baby. He didn't hurt me." She saw sweat soaking Matt's face. His massive midsection seemed to sway in time with the swells, and he held his hands up in surrender.

Fischer lowered the gaff and turned to her. "Get in the cabin."

Certain that things might yet get violent, she darted across the deck. Fischer turned back to his client. "I allow everyone one mistake. You just had yours." He turned to Chester. "An' you been fuckin' warned. I told you guys before we left port that she ain't part of the deal."

Fischer walked to the cabin door. He looked to the east, stepped through the portal, and said, "Gonna be dark soon. Let's head in, honey."

She tensed when she heard the term of endearment and hesitated. "Step to," Fischer said. "There's work to be done."

———————

As they left Portland Harbor and turned toward his home, Fischer ordered Cheryl inside the boat's cabin. He followed her in and motioned for her to stand against the starboard bulkhead. "You did good," he said. "You seem to know your way around a boat."

"My grandfather taught me."

"Really, maybe I know him. What's his name?"

Cheryl hesitated; the last thing she wanted was for Fischer to know anything about her family. "You wouldn't know him. He lives in—" a brief pause as she tried to think of a place far enough away, "North Carolina."

He studied her for several moments and then turned back to the boat. "Go clean the deck. We have to get home. Mum's been alone all day."

Cheryl began coiling and securing the bowline, wondering if this would be a good time to make a break for it. She saw Fischer staring through the window at her. Even though she could not see his hands,

Cheryl knew he always kept a weapon close by. Finished with the lines, she picked up a mop and cleaned the deck. She put all of her tools away and returned to the cabin. When she walked inside, he met her at the door, grabbed her arm with a crushing grip, and slammed her against the wall. "Don't you ever again lie to me," he said. "I hate liars."

21

Houston walked through the Claddagh Pub and directly to Jimmy's office. He knocked on the door, and when he opened it, a cloud of smoke as thick as an early morning fog rolled out. He waved his hand in front of his face as if shooing flies, but the smoke just moved around. "Damn it, Jimmy, how can you breathe in this?"

"If it bothers you, stay the fuck out."

"We got to talk. I need your help."

Jimmy O appeared out of the smoke, much like Bela Lugosi's Dracula appearing from the mist. He shut the door behind him, walked past Houston, and entered the bar. He surveyed the room and pointed to an empty booth in the rear.

Once they were seated, Jimmy said, "Okay, talk."

"We keep hearing that this guy drives a fish truck. I want to check out the fish markets."

"You don't need me for that."

"There's too goddamned many of them for Anne and me to check alone. I need you to have your people canvass some for us."

"What do I look like, your personnel department? I got my own businesses to run. I know that finding this kid is a big deal for you and Anne, but I already spent more time on it than I should have."

THE FISHERMAN | 121

Houston sat back. "I know you're into all sorts of shit, Jimmy. But to the best of my knowledge, you've never been directly involved in the prostitution trade."

"Human trafficking was never my thing. You run whores, you gotta recruit kids . . . and you know how I feel about that."

"This guy doesn't discriminate, Jimmy. He's taken them in every race and age." He took an envelope from his back pocket and took out a bundle of photos, which he fanned across the desk. He studied them for a second and then selected two—one of a young woman barely older than a child. "This is Martha Kahn. Her street name was Tia Del Rio. She's believed to be one of his victims . . . and she was fourteen."

Jimmy leaned back. He stared at the ceiling for a few seconds, then sighed and said, "For someone who is on the other side of the fence, you sure as hell ask for a lot of favors. You do know, *brother-in-law*, that one day I'll be coming to you to return some of them?"

"We'll cross that bridge when we come to it."

"You can bet that we will. Okay, I'll do this much. I'll give you Gordon and five guys for two days, no more."

"Thanks, Jimmy."

Jimmy stared at Houston. "You been back in town how long now?"

"Three days."

"How's Susie?"

"Susie?"

"You remember your daughter, my niece, don't you?"

Houston's face fell. He'd completely overlooked contacting his daughter. "Aw, *shit* . . ."

"Exactly . . ."

Winter parked beside the loading dock of one of Boston's largest fish wholesalers. He had been questioning people all morning, asking if they knew of a truck fitting the description given by the hookers. Thus far, it had been an exercise in futility. He saw a man jump down from the dock and approach his Navigator.

"Sorry, pal, but you can't park here. You need to use one of the parking garages."

"I only need a minute. I'm trying to locate a guy, drives a big rig with a reefer box built on."

"Lots of guys drive trucks like that."

"This guy looks like he French kissed a brick wall at ninety miles an hour. The side of his head is fucked up."

"There's a guy with a fucked-up head who comes around from time to time."

"What color is his truck?"

"It varies."

Winter digested the information for a second. "It varies?" He parroted the man. "You mean he drives different trucks?"

"Nope, same truck—one time he'll come by and it's white. The next time it will be something else. Now that I think of it, I don't think it's ever been the same color on two consecutive trips."

"You got a name for this guy or the company he drives for?"

"You a cop?"

"No, I'm just looking for this guy. I hear he sells a quality product and my boss wants to place an order."

"His stuff is all right." He seemed to swell up with pride when he said, "We don't buy farm fish, only ocean caught."

"He catches the fish himself?"

"I think he owns a boat, does some charter stuff, too—up the coast of Maine someplace." The man started to look nervous. "Look, I'm not sure I should be telling you this."

Winter reached into his back pocket, removed his wallet, and took out a hundred dollar bill. He offered it to the man. "This should help overcome your reservations—and maybe get me a name."

The man glanced over each shoulder to see if anyone was around. When he was certain they were alone, he snatched the bill from Winter's hand. "Be right back."

The warehouseman returned in five minutes and handed Winter a piece of notepaper with a single name written on it. He turned, and before he could walk away, he looked back at Winter. "Looks like you wasted a hundred bucks." He pointed to a truck entering the yard. "I believe that's your guy right there."

––––––––––––

Fischer exited the O'Neil Tunnel at Purchase Street. He cursed the stopped traffic. Boston on a Friday afternoon was bad enough—throw in all the construction, and you had gridlock. He found himself thinking, *The old man was right. He always said there are only two seasons in Boston— winter and road construction.*

He turned into the loading dock of the fish market and parked the truck. He was wary but no more than usual; being in the city always made him nervous and suspicious of everything and everyone. He searched his surroundings, looking for anyone who paid him more attention than he felt was warranted. It did not take him long to spot the man: a big sonuvabitch wearing black jeans and a similar colored T-shirt. The fabric of his shirt stretched tight across his chest, conforming to the man's well-developed muscles.

Fischer climbed the steps to the loading dock, keeping the suspicious man in the corner of his eye. Like a feral cat at a picnic, he was curious about the man but still ready to bolt if he came too close. He stopped and stood on the edge of the dock, returning the man's stare.

The observer was dangerous, and Fischer sensed it. Something— maybe some form of innate kinship—told him that this was someone who would have no hesitation to kill. The nosy man seemed to transmit menace.

"What you got?"

Fischer turned to see the purchasing agent standing behind him.

"Pollack, some haddock."

"Fresh or farm?"

"Fresh."

The purchasing agent pointed to a portable chalkboard and said, "There's what we're paying today."

Fischer nodded and walked down the steps.

"Pull up to door twenty," the purchasing agent shouted. "Loose or palletized?"

"What?" Fischer's attention was still on the man across the parking lot.

"The load. Is it loose or on pallets?"

"Pallets."

"Great, we'll have you out of here in no time."

Fischer returned to the truck and backed up to the dock. When he stepped from the cab, the nosy man was beside the truck.

"You down from Maine?" the snoop asked.

"Yup."

"What part?"

Fischer did not like being questioned and felt his face heat with anger. "The coast. I don't see where it's any of your business."

"Hey, don't get upset. I got some frozen food I need to get to Portland, and a truck like yours is ideal. I figured if you were dead-heading back, you might like to make a few extra bucks."

"Well, you figured wrong."

"Okay, but if you change your mind, call me." He handed Fischer a business card.

Fischer glanced at the card. The only thing printed on it was *Gordon Winter* and a phone number. "I won't be changing my mind, now leave me alone." He flipped the card over his shoulder and turned on his heel. He did not look back before climbing the stairs and disappearing into the warehouse.

Fischer kept one eye on the mirror, watching the meddlesome guy in the shiny black SUV behind him. There was no way he could pick up a woman tonight. He would have to wait until his next trip into Boston. It was evident that someone was looking for him. He was going to have to change a few things. He decided he would use the van on the next run. It disturbed him to know that after all this time he seemed to have attracted the interest of at least one somebody in Boston. As to how they had finally caught on to him, he was clueless. He had always been careful to pick up whores only—women about whom no one cared. Had he slipped up and finally taken one who had somebody that still cared enough to send people looking? He thought about Cheryl saying her family were fishers. If, as she said, her grandfather lived in North Carolina, she might have relatives who lived close by. He would get more information out of her once he got home.

You fucked it up again, you damned idiot!

"Shut up old man, I ain't got time for you."

In his rear-view mirror, Fischer saw the black SUV turn off, and he breathed a sigh of relief. Still, he kept checking behind to see if any cars kept reappearing. If the guy watching the market had been a cop, there would be others—cops are like snakes, always traveling in pairs.

Fischer wanted to settle back and enjoy the drive, but the old man's incessant raving was bringing on a major headache.

If that friggin' Jesus freak had given me one more half-wit like you, I coulda opened my own school for simpletons.

Fischer slid into the right lane. He was upset because he did his best thinking while behind the wheel, and he wanted to plan how he was going to change things; the old man's constant badgering made it impossible.

Hey, dummy, how about first you do something with this truck?

Fischer snarled and tried to focus on the road. He slammed his fist on the console between the two seats; if anything pissed him off more than having the old man rave at him, it was when the bastard was right. He made a note to toss the truck's stolen plates as soon as he got home.

I told you that you had to stop. Now it seems you took one that somebody still gives a fuck about. They'll be closing in on you.

"Shut the fuck up, old man. I got enough to deal with without you ragging on me."

Have it your way, Willard. But it's only a matter of time now. I hope you don't have any delusions that the woman—

"Her name's Cheryl."

Whatever. Don't think for a second that she won't turn on you like a rabid dog.

Fischer drove in silence. He thought, *Maybe he's right . . . maybe it's time for me to deal with Cheryl and get another woman.*

22

Houston attacked his omelet while knowing that he'd regret it later. A large morning meal usually left him feeling sluggish all morning. The only reason he was in the diner was to meet with Gordon Winter, who sat across from him looking haggard and exhausted. "You look like crap," he said.

"Had some business to attend to," Winter answered.

"It must have kept you out late."

"You know how it is in my line of business."

"Not entirely. What I know is more than enough, though."

Winter sipped his coffee and watched a shapely waitress bend over a table. "You know," he said, "there is nothing I like better than a pair of legs rushing up to make an ass of themselves."

"You been with Jimmy so long that you're starting to talk like him." Houston followed his gaze and smiled. "I will admit that she's a looker, alright. Now, let's get down to business. You called and said you had a name."

Winter turned away from the woman and said, "Willard Fischer. He owns a fishing boat and charter service someplace on the coast of Maine."

Houston groaned. "Do you have any idea how much coastline there is in Maine? Not to mention the thousands of islands and inlets."

"A few ..."

"What else you know about him?"

"He sounds like a whacko. I've talked with several people who buy from him, and they say every time he comes to town his truck is painted a different color."

Houston put his fork down. "That could explain why the cops keep getting differing descriptions of the truck."

"Works for me," Winter said.

Houston parked in front of the Guerette home, and he and Bouchard got out. He opened the gate in the picket fence, and Betty appeared at the front door. He waved, and Bouchard said, "Morning, Betty, nice day isn't it?"

"Yup, 'twill be bettah if you have some news for us."

"Is Archie around?" Houston asked.

"He's in the back workin' on the boat. Come in. I'll fetch him." She held the door open and let him in. "I have fresh coffee in the kitchen."

She led them toward a cozy kitchen filled with the aroma of coffee and freshly baked bread. The inside of the house was as neat and clean as the yard. The primary feature of the living room was a huge marble fireplace with models of commercial fishing boats on the mantle. Houston stopped and studied the pictures that adorned the wall. Most were pictures of Cheryl as a child; several were of them with a young couple. Betty saw him looking at one of the pictures—the couple beside a fishing trawler—and said, "That's our son, Jeremy, and his wife."

"He was a good-looking man. I hope you don't mind my asking how he died," Bouchard asked.

"No, it's been long enough that I can talk about it. Archie still has a time of it, though. Jeremy worked with his father ... he was lost in a storm. They were fishing for swordfish off the Flemish Cap."

"The Flemish Cap?" Houston asked.

"It's about 350 miles east of Newfoundland, farther out than the Grand Banks."

"I'm sorry," Houston said, realizing how insufficient the comment was.

"It was over ten years ago. Laurel, Jeremy's wife, lost it after that. She got into drugs and just drifted away. We don't even know if she's alive or dead."

They followed her into the kitchen and sat at the table. Betty placed a steaming mug of coffee, cream, and sugar in front of them and said, "I'll get Archie."

A door led from the kitchen to the back yard, and Betty exited through it. Houston looked out the window at the most beautiful view he could recall. The water came up to within a hundred feet of the house, and he saw the same fishing trawler he had seen in the picture docked along a wooden pier with its aft facing the shore. On the stern, the name *Betty G* was painted in blue letters. The fishing boat was big but not big enough in Houston's estimation to go 350 miles out into the Atlantic. Obviously, not only was Archie strong, but he had more than one man's share of courage.

"We have to find Cheryl before it's too late," Bouchard said. "Everyone close to Archie and his wife has either died or fallen off the face of the Earth."

"We'll bring Cheryl home, even if for no other reason than they'll have at least one of their loved ones to mourn and a grave on which they can place Betty's beautiful flowers."

He watched Betty walk to the dock and heard her call out. Archie's head popped out of a window in the pilot's cabin. Betty said something more and then walked toward the house.

In minutes, she was back in the kitchen. "I been at him to sell the boat," she said as she sat at the table. "Archie's getting on a bit and can't crew it alone. But the sea is all he knows, and he can't seem to give it up."

Houston thought of his own situation. Being a cop was in his blood, but a year ago he had thought he could just walk away and never look back. However, of late he knew he never could—he would miss the adrenaline rush he got when he was on the chase.

Archie appeared through the back door, inhaling deeply. "Smells like you bin busy, old woman," he said. He pulled out the chair between

Houston and Betty, sat and spooned five teaspoons of sugar into his coffee. He saw Houston watching him and said, "Never could drink coffee with milk or cream, but I need my shugah. Have you learned anything?"

"It seems there is a man, Willard Fischer, who has been around each time a ..." Houston and Bouchard had agreed on the drive to Kittery that they would avoid using the phrase serial killer—afraid it would rob the Guerettes of all hope that Cheryl was still alive. He hesitated, trying to find the right words, "woman has disappeared."

"Seems to me I know that name," Archie said.

"Apparently he owns a fishing boat and does some chartering."

"Yuh, know who you mean now ... that'd be one of Hallet Fischer's boys. He was never the same after the accident."

"What accident?"

Houston realized that, like all Mainers, Archie would only tell a tale in his own way, so he sat back to listen.

"Hallet was a piece of work, mind you. He drove them boys like they was full-growed men. Had them working the boat and that stupid factory from the time they was old enough to walk. Was a time Hallet fished commercially—gave it up after the kid got hurt. They was out in the gulf one day, and a boom let go, and a turnbuckle slammed the kid in the head. God-awfullest thing I ever seen. Hit that boy so hard his eyes never straightened out—flattened one side of his head like it had been squeezed in a cider press.

"Hallet, now, he never let up on the kid. After getting smashed in the gourd, that poor little bugger was always a couple of sardines short of a full can. Of course, that don't surprise me none. A shot to the head like that youngster took would be enough to take the starch out of any man's pencil—"

"Archie," Betty admonished him, "there isn't any need to be crude."

Archie chuckled, making Houston believe he'd used the phrase for no reason other than to tease her. "Anyways, the old man kept him working the boat and making those fish cakes from sunup to sundown."

"Where was their place?" Houston bent forward as he spoke.

"Used to be north of here in Yarmouth, but twenty maybe twenty-five years ago, Hallet sold out and moved farther north somewhere—way north, could have been as far as Camden, ya know. I never saw him after that.

"His wife, Beatrice, now she was something else, too. Bible thumper—she could quote the good book better than any fundamentalist preacher I ever heard. Between Hallet's irreverence and her devotion to God's word, them boys never had a snowball's chance in hell. I r'collect the last time I seen Hallet. It was back in '93 . . ."

April 1993

Archie guided the boat in close to the dock and saw Hallet Fischer leaning against a post. When the boat was alongside the wharf, Archie idled the motors and looked out the window of the wheelhouse. Fischer strode down the pier and stopped beside the wooden gangplank. Hallet was not a trusting man, and he suspiciously eyed Archie's crewman. The sailor ignored Hallet, jumped off the trawler, and tied another line to the mooring. Like most Mainers, Hallet was tightfisted and squeezed a nickel so tight that Jefferson moved into Monticello. Rather than lose a piece of rope or a tool, he made a point of meeting every boat and staying on the dock until they were unloaded and on their way.

Fischer stepped aside as the boat thumped against the old tires strung along the pier as bumpers. He waited until the craft's motor died. The morning stillness seemed amplified in the absence of the rumble from the big diesel motor. A loon broke the silence, its call like a maniac's laugh.

Archie poked his head out of the cabin window and waved. "How you doin', Hallet?"

Fischer shielded his eyes. The morning was calm, and the sun reflected from the ocean's glassy surface. "Is that you, Guerette? Mite early to be heading in, ain't it?"

"We hit it lucky. We left Prince Pint at three this morning and hit a big school less than ten miles out. Got a bunch of mackerel if you're interested."

A cold wind blew in from the Gulf of Maine, and Hallet looked at the ice on the railing of the boat. "You suppose spring's ever going to get here?" he asked.

Guerette smiled. "Nope. But this is Maine, ain't it? We know what that means."

"That we do, Archie. Nine months of winter and three months of poor sleddin'." Fischer chuckled at the cliché.

Guerette walked out of the wheelhouse and down the gangplank. Although not a tall man, Archie possessed strength greater than one would expect from a man of his stature. He held out his hand and grasped Fischer's. "How's the family, Hallet?"

"The old woman ain't doing too well. Somethin' called alls-hiemer got her."

"Don't think I ever heard of that."

"From what I'm told, they might better call it the *can't remember shit* disease. Doc says t'won't be long b'fore she don't know anyone nor care about nothin'. I'll bet that won't keep her from caterwauling about the scriptures, though."

"Sorry to hear she's ailing."

"Yuh, well, that's the way it is. None of us gets out of this life alive, now do we?"

Archie pulled a pipe from his pocket and stuffed it full of tobacco. He paused, wondering how anyone could be so cold while discussing such a serious matter. He lit the tobacco and said, "That may be the case, Hallet, but nobody should have to go that way. Is she seeing a doctor?"

"Not no more."

Archie pulled the pipe from his mouth and stared at Fischer. "Not no more? Why the hell not? Those doctors in Portland can do miracles."

"I already had her down there. They said wasn't nothing they could do for her. So I said fuck it—I brung her home to die. It'd be just like her to hang on f'evah. Then agin, she might jist die outta spite."

"How's that?"

"She's gonna die an' stick me with slow-witted, cockeyed Willard. Woman only gave me two sons, and one had to be a friggin' dummy."

"He ain't such a bad boy. From what I see, he works hard."

"That he does. Does everything you tell him to do, too. You say, 'Willard, pick up the hammer', and he'll pick it up. Then you say, 'Take the hammer up to the shed and put it in the tool box,' an' he'll do it. Problem is you got to tell him every goddamned thing. He ain't got enough brains to look around and put away a ten-dollar hammer he sees sitting on the ground rusting. Hell, I got to either smack him in the head or give him a kick in the ass three, four times a day just to keep him from sitting around burning daylight. Fucking kid is dumah than a sack of assholes marked spoiled. He ain't like his older brother, Richard. That one has a head on his shoulders—I only wish he wasn't a goddamned sissy."

Just as Hallet finished his harangue, Willard stepped out of the small toolshed. Hallet's eyes narrowed when he saw his son. He yelled at the boy. "Get your worthless carcass on down here, shithead! Can't you see there's fish to be off-loaded?"

The boy's head snapped up at the sound of his father's voice. He stood still as if petrified.

"Come on, you fucking dummy," Hallet yelled. "Stop lollygagging, you dimwitted son of a whore! You know better than to stand around when there's work to be done."

Willard jogged toward the dock.

Archie felt for the boy and knew that one day Hallet was going to rue the way he treated his son. The youngster already had massive shoulders and arms, and he wasn't much over fifteen. "Boy's growing," Archie said.

"Yup but still stupid. Hell, time we was his age we'd already been down to Portland and Boston. When I was fifteen, I'd already had my first woman. Whore down in Scollay Square. My old man took me there when he sold a load of cod—said fifteen was time for a boy to learn the difference b'tween men and women. Willard though, he'd be like that Evangelist fellow down south . . . he'd just sit in a chair and watch."

Archie laughed in spite of himself. He bent over and tapped the pipe's bowl on the pier, knocking the fire into the water.

"Well, I suppose, we'd best get to it. That hold full of mackerel ain't getting any fresha."

Archie watched in amazement at how fast and strong Willard Fischer was. *God has a way of making up for things*, he thought. That boy may have been slow of mind, but he out-worked any two men Archie knew. In a little over two hours, the mackerel were off-loaded, and the *Betty G* had backed away from the dock. He gave the Fischers a farewell blast of his horn, turned into the channel, and sailed south for Prince Point.

Archie glanced back and saw Willard standing alone on the dock. The boy had a simple way about him, as if he were a little boy imprisoned in a man's body. But the thing that stayed in Archie's mind as he sailed away was the look in the boy's eyes. Archie recalled reading that people's eyes are like windows. If that was the case, Willard was home to an awesome rage.

Norwood Anders, who was responsible for loading and unloading ships on the Mystic River, sat before the desk, fidgeted in his seat, and tried to avoid Jimmy O'Leary's piercing gaze. "Relax, Norwood, I didn't have you brought here to bust your ass. What happened happened, and it's time to move on."

"Honest, Mr. O'Leary, I thought the Russian had paid his fees. I never would have unloaded that ship otherwise."

"Forget it. I'm more interested in what else he's carrying."

Anders looked like a kitten seeing a ball of twine for the first time. "I don't understand."

"That ship is carrying more than freight. There are jail cells in it."

"Well, I heard some rumors."

"Norwood, I'm getting tired of prying everything out of you. Tell me what you know."

"Well, it ain't like I got any proof or anything, but I hear they been smuggling in illegal immigrants."

"Mexicans?"

"No, that ship's home port is Odessa. I hear they been bringing in Russian women—young ones."

"Go on."

"They rendezvous with someone in international waters and transfer the women. I heard the women sign a deal with . . . I guess you could call it an agent in Russia."

"What's this deal?"

"Kind of like when the English first came here in colonial times, they get passage and once they're here, room and board. They work off what they owe . . . there's a word for what they were called . . ."

"Indentured servants," O'Leary interjected.

"Yeah, that's it. I heard some of them are mail-order brides—ain't that a kick?"

"Okay, I understand what you're saying," O'Leary studied the end of his cigarette for a few seconds, as if he were lost in thought, and then crushed it in an ashtray. He ignited another smoke and looked at Anders. "You better get over to the docks."

"Sure thing, Mr. O'Leary, and don't you worry, ain't going to be no more screw-ups."

"I'll take that as a promise, now beat it."

When the door closed behind Anders, Gordon Winter said, "I figured as much. Someone is importing young girls. Probably promising them the world and then making them do *around the world*."

"Get Shiloh. That sonuvabitch must know something about this."

23

Houston and Bouchard paused on the sidewalk, surveying the busy street. Portland, Maine's Old Port, was one of their favorite places. Houston enjoyed watching the boats come and go from the busy marinas, and she liked to spend hours poking around in the shops. The morning was warm and sunny, a perfect day for goofing off and playing tourist. Unfortunately, today he had no time—too much to do, too many people to see. He stepped out of the heat into the cool, dark interior of Two Dollar Louey's. As soon as he entered, Houston spotted Sam Fuchs. Fuchs was a homicide detective assigned to the Maine State Police Criminal Investigation Division I, known as CID One. They had become close friends when Houston was a cop, and they had once worked together on a case involving an interstate meth ring.

Houston slipped into the booth, and Fuchs grinned. "Christ, Mike, what's it been—almost two years since we last saw each other?"

"Give or take a couple of months."

Fuchs looked at Bouchard and said, "And who is this?" His look and tone were ample evidence that he found her more than a little bit attractive.

"Sam Fuchs, this is Anne Bouchard. Anne, Sam."

"So I finally get to meet the superwoman who can keep this reprobate in line." He offered her his hand.

Houston drank from his coffee mug and glanced out the window at Portland's bustling waterfront. "Seems like another planet compared to Oxford County."

Fuchs chuckled. "Shit, North Overshoe, Minnesota is more civilized than there. Okay, now we got the old times crap out of the way, what's up?"

"We got a problem," Houston said.

"So? Who doesn't?"

"We're talking serious trouble, Sam."

"How serious is this trouble, and how does it involve me?"

"How serious do you consider a serial killer?" Bouchard asked.

His eyes narrowed slightly. "Serial killer—what leads you to think we have a serial operating in Maine?"

"A few days back a couple from Kittery hired us to find their granddaughter, one Cheryl Guerette," Bouchard answered.

"And?"

"In the course of our investigation we've learned about missing women—a lot of missing women."

He sat back. "If there's a lot of missing women, why haven't I heard anything?"

"The guy doesn't make his contact here," Houston said. "He usually hunts Boston—more of his particular type of game available there."

"Exactly what does 'his particular type of game' mean?"

"He preys on hookers, drug addicts, and homeless women," Houston answered.

"So, why hasn't Boston PD sent out anything?"

"The brass doesn't care. BPD figures someone is cleaning up the streets for them, and they haven't found even a single body. You know how it goes with homicide cops—no body means no crime. No offense intended," Bouchard said.

Fuchs finished his coffee and motioned for the server to bring him another. "You still haven't told me why I should get involved."

"The women who have seen this guy say he drives a truck and that it smells like month-old fish guts," Bouchard answered.

"Lots of trucks like that in every seacoast town up and down the East coast."

"Well, this one has been reported to have Maine plates on it. I have a name for you to check out," Houston replied.

Fuchs leaned forward. "Now you got my attention. What's the name?"

"Willard Fischer, that's Fischer with S-C-H." He spent fifteen minutes relating everything he had learned in his investigation. When he finished, Houston sat back. "That's it, Sam. That's why we're here. We don't have the resources to handle this alone."

Fuchs's cell phone rang, and he flipped it open. "Fuchs." He was silent for a second. "Hold on. I need to write this down." He pulled a notebook from his back pocket and began jotting notes as he listened. "Okay, I'll be there in half an hour."

"Problems?"

"Yeah, there's been a homicide, I gotta go." He tossed a ten-dollar bill on the table. "Mike, can you send me what you got? I promise I'll look into this for you."

"Sure."

Houston gave him a business card. "Those are my current numbers." Fuchs left without another word.

Houston and Bouchard sat quiet, staring out the window, and watched Fuchs pull away with his emergency lights flashing. When he disappeared into the traffic, Houston said, "Now we get in touch with Luca Power, York County Sheriff."

He took out his cell phone and punched in a number.

After three rings it was answered. "Sheriff Power."

"My, aren't we formal."

"Hey, Mike, what's up?"

"I need a favor."

"You always need a favor."

"This one has to do with a possible homicide."

"Homicide? Outside of Portland and maybe Bangor, the state police usually handle them."

"Nevertheless, the victim may be a resident of Kittery—your county."

Houston heard Power's chair creak and knew his friend was leaning forward with interest. "Maybe you better fill me in."

It took less than ten minutes to update him, and in his usual manner, Luca got to the point. "What can I do for you?"

"Get me anything you can on Willard Fischer. I believe his father's name was Hallet. I can use anything you find on him and the family, and I need it soon. If that girl is alive, time is of the essence."

24

Shiloh appeared nonchalant, and O'Leary knew that his demeanor was a front. The pimp had never before been to the Claddagh Pub and had to be as anxious as a sewer rat in a bright light. O'Leary had not said a word since Shiloh shuffled into the office.

"Shy, how you doing?"

"Okay. We haven't seen each other this much in years, Jimmy."

"Yeah, ain't that the truth? I was over at the Chelsea docks a few nights back collecting some money owed to me."

"What's that got to do with me?"

"Probably nothing. However, I think you may have something I need."

"What could I have that you'd need?"

"Information."

"We been over this before. I don't know anything except what I told you about the missing whores."

"What do you know about illegal immigrants?"

"You need some landscaping done?"

"Don't fuck around, Shy. I was on a ship that looked like it was set up for more than cargo. Now, you being black and all, I would think you'd have some feelings about slavery."

"If it's white slavery, I'd say it's about time."

O'Leary slammed his fist on the top of his desk. "Don't yank my fucking chain, Shy. I've got word someone is importing women—the younger the better!"

Shiloh snapped back in his chair. He had never seen O'Leary this incensed. "This is too big even for you, Jimmy."

"Really? Enlighten me, please."

"This has been going on since the Soviet Union crashed. The economy over there was shit, and someone started recruiting girls—some as young as twelve and thirteen. They promise the young ones foster homes, the older ones jobs—husbands even. Anyway, here we are twenty years later, and it's still going on. Matter of fact, it's turned into big business for the Russian mob. They fly the girls into Mexico, and then they bring them in from there. If they're destined for here they bring them by ship. If they're going down South or out to LA, they use coyotes[1] to smuggle them over the border with the Mexicans. Don't you just love the shit out of NAFTA?"

"Only none of the promises are kept," O'Leary interjected.

O'Leary lit a cigarette as the pimp continued talking. "The one about jobs is—only they aren't secretaries to rich and powerful men as promised."

"Let me see if I can fill in the blanks here. They're forcing them to pay off their fare by being whores . . ."

"It wouldn't be bad if that was all. Now this is all hearsay, okay?"

"Okay."

"I heard they've even done some pornos and at least one snuff film."

"Snuff films are a myth—there's never been one that was proven to be real."

"Hey, you want to know what I heard, and that's one of the things going around."

"Are any of these girls being forced onto the streets?"

"Hell no. They keep them in special cribs around the country. We aren't talking fifty-buck blow jobs and no-tell-hotel quickies here. These girls, at least the lookers, are reserved for some powerful high-rollers."

---

[1] Coyote: Smuggler who brings illegal aliens from Mexico to the United States.

"Do you know if any of these places are local?"

"There aren't any in Boston itself—although I believe there's one close by, possibly on the Cape. They like them outside the city in remote areas. Like I said, the clientele ain't the type that wants to be seen coming and going at a whorehouse."

"Names, Shiloh. I need names if you got them."

"Man, you shouldn't stick your nose into this—like I said, it's too fucking big even for you."

"How big?"

"Nationally, they bring in about fourteen thousand girls a year—of that maybe five or six hundred a year will end up from New York north."

"No goddamned way they can be bringing in that much flesh and staying below the radar."

"If the people behind it control the radar, any number is possible."

"You saying the government is involved?"

"Not officially, but people in high places are making a shitload of money."

"Who's the local guy?"

"Again, this is all street talk. I don't know how reliable it is. But one name keeps coming up: D. Everette Halsey."

"Halsey?"

"Yup, the same guy you hired when you beat the rap on those gang-bangers that killed Latisha Washington."

O'Leary and Winter entered a plush office. It was three times larger than Jimmy's at the Claddagh Pub. Bookcases full of expensive matched-binding books lined two of the walls. Through the huge window behind D. Everette Halsey's desk, they saw an impressive view of the water traffic in Boston Harbor and planes landing and taking off at Logan Airport. Halsey sat behind his huge maple desk, looking as regal and puffed up as a French king at court. His suit probably cost more than the average worker made in six months, and even though Halsey was sitting, not a single wrinkle was visible in the fabric.

O'Leary dropped into one of the overstuffed armchairs that fronted the desk. "Nice view."

Winter moved beyond the desk and stood between the lawyer and his window.

Halsey cast an uncomfortable glance at Winter and then turned back to O'Leary. "I guess. I'm so busy that I don't get much chance to enjoy it."

O'Leary nodded even though he did not believe a word Halsey said. The man was vain if nothing else. If he were not the best criminal attorney in New England, he would not have a single friend in Boston. O'Leary thought he was an overpriced piece of fluff. Halsey was not a man to waste time unless it was billable time. His reputation was that he had never in his life pled a case out of court; there was not enough money in it.

"You want to have your boy move? He's blocking my light."

"Gonna look awfully fucking funny," Winter said.

Halsey spun around in his chair. "What is?"

"Your tombstone, when it reads, 'Here lies a fat fuck killed by a boy.'"

Halsey began to rise to his feet.

"I'd stay put if I was you," O'Leary said. He grinned as Winter stood his ground, glaring at Halsey, who dropped back into his chair.

Halsey tried to save face by staring Winter down for a few seconds. Once he felt that he had sufficiently regained his lordly image, he turned to O'Leary and said, "So, Jimmy, what brings you here? I doubt you came by to partake of the view."

"I need a favor."

Halsey looked surprised. "You surprise me. You're in the business of granting favors, not asking for them."

"Well, this time I'm the one in need."

"You name it, Jimmy. If I can help, I'll be glad to."

"I got some business men coming into town . . . people who could be instrumental in making a lot of money for me. You get my drift?"

Halsey leaned forward, placing his elbows on his desk. O'Leary knew he had just appealed to Halsey where he lived—in his wallet. No doubt, any favor the lawyer did for him would be, in the long term, expensive.

"If what you're about to ask is illegal, I can't be a part of it."

"Listen to what I need before you get all worked up, okay?"

"Alright, that's the least I can do."

"Fucking right," O'Leary said. "After all, I made several monthly payments on your yacht last year."

"Cheaper than twenty-five to life, and if I remember correctly, we were looking at multiple counts. Four or five wasn't it?"

"I'm not complaining about it—just reminding you that I paid you a pretty hefty fee."

Halsey smiled. "If I recall how it all turned out, I was worth every penny."

"Come on, Everette, let's stop the shit. I'm serious here."

"Alright, what is it you need?"

"From time to time, you and I deal with some pretty high rollers."

Halsey's pig eyes bored into O'Leary. He listened intently.

"The guys I got coming to town," O'Leary continued, "they like to be entertained. You understand where I'm coming from?"

"I think I know where you're going. I'm not a pimp. I would think you're in a better position to know them than I am."

"Everybody's a pimp if the price is right," Winter said.

Halsey snapped back in his chair as if slapped.

"Who is this gentleman?" Halsey asked O'Leary.

"Someone you don't want to fuck with. You'll get hurt bad no matter how much money, influence, and power you got."

"Really?"

"Really. See money and that other shit only works on people who got something to lose or people who want to live. Now Gordon here, he doesn't give a damn about anything. He'll come at you with a vengeance. He'll get you, too, because he has this unique quality—he ain't afraid of dying."

Throughout O'Leary's little speech, Winter remained stoic, giving Halsey as much attention as he would an ant on a sidewalk. O'Leary knew Halsey would come around the minute he saw Winter stare into the attorney's eyes with his face expressionless. He almost smiled when he saw uncertainty on the lawyer's face. He did smile when Halsey turned back to the front, avoiding Winter's cold stare.

"Now, back to the business at hand," O'Leary said. "I got a lot of contacts in this town, as you well know. My contacts tell me that you know ways that people with more money than morals can be entertained. My associates are interested."

"I may know some people," Halsey said, still trying to keep an eye on Winter without seeming obvious or showing how nervous he was.

O'Leary said, "See, Gordon, I told you ol' Everette would be the man with the plan. My business associates have specific tastes: young white girls, attractive, and willing to do anything. Price is no object."

Halsey looked suspicious. "You wired?"

"Me? Do I look like a fuckin' radio station—Gordon, am I wired?"

"Don't know, but you did have three cups of coffee this morning. That's usually enough."

O'Leary smiled like a used car salesman approaching a potential customer. "You want I should strip, Everette? I'll do it—right here, right now. But when you see I ain't wired, I'm gonna turn Gordon loose on your fat ass."

Halsey began to sweat. "I believe you. Jesus, Jimmy, I got to be careful, too."

"All bullshit aside, you gonna help me out?"

"I'll try, but I can't guarantee anything."

O'Leary stood up. "I'm looking at a high eight-figure deal here, Everette. It could be as much as eighty, ninety mill. It would be worth, say, ten percent—might go as high as fifteen if the service is exemplary."

O'Leary saw Halsey's greed take over. The fat bastard had a calculator for a mind, and he was no doubt computing fifteen percent—no way Halsey would settle for the lesser price—of eight or nine million, especially if all he had to do was give up a name. "It may take a few days."

"Well, don't screw around. My people are due in town next weekend, and I'd like something arranged for that Saturday."

"Where can I reach you?"

"You have my usual numbers."

O'Leary and Winter walked out of the high-rise office building and onto Atlantic Avenue. The bright sun hurt their eyes, and they put on sunglasses.

"Think he'll come through?" Winter asked.

"Halsey would sell his mother to a psycho for a shot at a million bucks. I got a hundred that says he's on the phone right now."

25

Houston and Bouchard were scanning the menu at a steakhouse when Sam Fuchs called. "Willard Fischer," he said, "lives on Northeast Cove about thirty miles north of Portland according to the DMV. I checked with the Department of Marine Resources, and they said that he does both charter and commercial fishing. I have a number."

Houston took a notebook out of his pocket and wrote down the number. "When you want to go fishing?" he asked Fuchs.

"Whenever you can arrange it."

Houston disconnected the call and put his phone on the table. "We found him," he said.

"Now what?"

"Now we go after the son of a bitch."

Fuchs met Houston and Bouchard in a coffee shop across from the public library in Portland's Monument Square. They sat at an outside table and watched a group of protesters standing along the sidewalk.

"What are they protesting?" Bouchard asked Fuchs.

"Probably the fact that they have nothing to protest about."

Houston grinned, took a drink of coffee, and said, "So any suggestions on how we should go about this?"

"I figure we call and make an appointment to see him and his boat. That way we have an excuse to go there and see the layout. Hopefully we'll see something that will get a judge to issue a search warrant."

"Who's the front man on this?"

"Don't look at me," Bouchard said.

"I'll call," Houston said. He turned to Anne and said, "I don't want him to get suspicious, so I want you to stay out of it."

She bristled. "You know I can take care of myself."

"Didn't say you couldn't, I just think you being there will interfere with my cover story."

"What's your story going to be?" Bouchard asked.

"We'll keep it simple. Two old buddies out for a day of drinking beer and fishing," Fuchs said.

"I'll make the call," Houston said.

———

Fischer placed the paint sprayer on the workbench. He stared at the truck, which was now a shade of light brown similar to that of split pea soup. He nodded, sure that no one would recognize it—not that it mattered that much. It was headed for retirement anyhow. He walked out of the barn and closed the door behind him.

He stood in the dark, smoked a cigarette, and stared at the window of Cheryl's room. She had been here for almost a month, and he still did not know if she was the one who would finally appeal to him. As much as he liked this one, she had not been able to excite him.

He heard the phone ringing and tossed the cigarette away before he entered the house. Once inside, he grabbed the phone from its cradle on the wall and said, "Fischer Charters."

"My name is Houston, Mike Houston, and a friend and I are interested in chartering your boat for a day of fishing."

"Okay."

"We'd like to visit you, see your boat—you know, stuff like that."

"When you want to come?"

"Would tomorrow morning be alright?"

"What time?"

"Well, we're driving from Portland, so how about ten o'clock?"

"Sure. You know the way?"

"I have a GPS." Houston read the address.

"See you tomorrow at ten." Fischer hung up. He looked at the staircase leading to the bedrooms upstairs. He popped a breath mint into his mouth. Mum would go ape shit if she smelled smoke on him. He climbed the stairs and turned toward her room. He would take care of Mum and then make sure the boat was shipshape for tomorrow's visitors.

26

"Good evening, I'm Ariana." Her native language accented her voice, and O'Leary guessed she came from somewhere in Eastern Europe.

The woman standing in the door of the expensive house was elegantly dressed. Her hair was done up in an intricate pattern of curls and waves that O'Leary was sure took hours in a beauty salon to perfect; then again, it could be a wig. The coiffure was too complex to be created every morning. The white evening gown she wore was top shelf. She looked like high society. All in all, he thought she dressed too expensively for a madam. A stocky man dressed in a tuxedo stood behind her. No matter how fashionable his attire, one look was all O'Leary needed to identify him as hired muscle. He looked past the woman and tried to see the interior; most likely Dapper Dan, the thug, would not be the only security in the colonial mansion.

O'Leary turned his attention to the madam. "I'm Jimmy O'Leary," He motioned to Winter. "This is my associate, Gordon Winter. Pleased to meet you, Ariana."

"Won't you come inside, Mr. O'Leary?" The woman stepped aside and motioned them inside with a refined sweep of her left hand.

O'Leary looked around the foyer. He had never been inside a home of a Fortune 500 CEO, but he had always visualized one as looking like this. The furnishings were top of the line, and the floor was of marble so highly glossed you could use it as a mirror to shave. He forced himself to remember that regardless of the plush, expensive surroundings, this was nothing more than a classy cat house. He followed the woman as she escorted them to a sitting room, where she motioned him to a well-used but comfortable leather chair.

"I understand you have need of some special services," she said.

"You might say that," he replied. "I have some business associates—men with particular tastes."

"Well, entertaining such people is our specialty," Ariana said. "When are you expecting them?"

"They'll be here late next week, Friday afternoon."

"I believe we should be able to accommodate your needs, but first I need some details."

"Okay."

"Will you be requiring us to make the evening a private affair?"

O'Leary made every effort to appear as if he were thinking about his answer. "That would be best, yes."

"How many clients will we be entertaining?"

"Five men . . . at the most six."

Ariana was all business; it was as if she were arranging a dinner reservation for a large group. "I'll need to know if they have any. . . . shall we say *special needs* . . . you'd like to have taken care of."

"I'm not sure, but I could get you that information by midweek."

"Of course. Depending on the nature of these special needs, there may be additional charges."

"That will be fine, in fact, I expected it would be so. I'd like to emphasize that it is imperative my clients be given whatever they want." O'Leary could not believe he had actually used a word like *imperative*; sometimes his ability to immerse himself in a role amazed even him.

"Would you like a tour of the manse?"

Tour the manse? O'Leary almost laughed aloud. No matter what she called the place, it was still a whorehouse. The degree people would go to delude themselves never ceased to amaze him. "Of course," he replied.

Ariana stood and led them from the sitting room and up a long curving staircase. "I think you'll find our facilities are well above the average," she said with as much pride as a wealthy old man showing off his twenty-year-old beauty-contest-winner wife. "We pride ourselves on providing our customers with a level of elegance and taste beyond anything they've ever experienced."

O'Leary doubted that carnal pleasures—even for an exorbitant fee—would look very elegant; screwing was still screwing, no matter how fancy the boudoir. He wondered if Ariana had a professional writer produce her sales pitch. As she climbed the stairs ahead of him, he studied her figure. Twenty years ago she had probably been beautiful with a body to die for. Her derriere swayed as she climbed, telling him more about her than any biography. He was certain Ariana had worked her way up through the ranks; every movement of her body exuded sexual invitation.

She paused at the top of the stairs and opened a door. The room was lavish; the decor and furnishings were eighteenth century with pleasing dark Persian rugs covering the floor and, in keeping with the décor, a portrait of a mostly undressed woman in colonial attire including a white curled wig.

He grunted and turned from the portrait. He knew nothing about art and couldn't care less.

The focal point of the room was a king-size canopied bed, covered with an expensive bedspread and huge pillows. The room looked more like a duchess's chamber than a prostitute's workplace.

O'Leary watched Winter drift over to the bed and glance up at the canopy's underside. He heard him chuckle and say, "Nice."

O'Leary walked to the bed and looked at what Winter had found so humorous. The underside of the covering was a mirror. O'Leary thought, *At last, something that looks like it belongs in a bordello.* He pushed up and down on the bed as if he were in a furniture store contemplating a mattress and box-spring purchase.

"All of our chambers are like this," Ariana said. "I'd show you more; however, the rest are occupied."

"Impressive," O'Leary said, turning from the bed.

"Would you like to meet some of our young ladies?"

"Sure," he answered, "why not?"

Ariana turned to the muscle-bound goon in the tux and said, "Richard, please have the girls who are not entertaining guests gather in the sitting room."

The muscle nodded and then left the room without a word. O'Leary wondered if this place were like a sultan's harem; all the males who worked there seemed mute . . . maybe, like the keepers of the sultan's harem, they were also eunuchs.

"Would you please follow me?" Ariana did not wait for their reply. She turned and exited the bedchamber.

"I will say this," O'Leary said to Winter, "it's a first-class joint."

Winter, on the other hand, did not seem as impressed as his boss did. "It's almost nice enough to make you forget that it's nothing more than an elegant prison—*almost.*"

"Yeah, that's the truth. Come on, we better follow her before she gets suspicious."

They walked into the hall and down the stairs. Ariana awaited them at the bottom. "Gentlemen, this way please."

They returned to the same room they had been ushered into when they arrived, and Ariana beckoned them to sit. "As you can see," she said, "we take great care and pride to ensure everything is top of the line."

"It's all of that," O'Leary said.

Before she could reply, six beautiful young women walked into the room. They were dressed as if they were going to their senior prom, and all looked young enough to attend one. All, that is, except the petite blond at the end of the line. O'Leary stared at her. He believed that she was no older than thirteen or fourteen, if that. Anger and indignation exploded within him. He strained to keep it from his face and his movements.

Ariana started at the right and introduced each woman, but he heard none of their names until she stopped beside the diminutive girl. "This is Inca," Ariana said, "our newest."

Each of the older girls had smiled and curtsied when introduced; Inca had not. "Inca, you've been shown how we greet gentlemen callers. Please do so." The girl looked awkward as she bent forward and lowered her head. Her eyes were wide with uncertainty and, O'Leary realized, fear of what would surely happen if she did not do it correctly. He thought she would not have a clue about how to act before strange men. Especially when they looked at her as if she were a horse they were considering purchasing.

Inca straightened up and tentatively looked at Ariana. She seemed to relax a bit when the madam smiled at her. Ariana turned her attention from Inca to O'Leary. "Would you like to spend some time with one of our ladies?"

O'Leary could not shake the idea that he was at a horse auction and wondered if he should check their teeth. Still, he was surprised when he realized that Ariana was a skilled salesperson. She was offering him a test ride on the horse of his choice. His first impulse was to request Inca. As the youngest and newest addition to Ariana's stable, it might be easier to pry information from her. He looked at Inca. She stood rigid, paralyzed with terror. He also noticed Ariana's gaze. Her body tensed; she gave him a scathing look. He knew choosing Inca would be stupid. The kid looked like a rodent in a python's den. Jimmy knew that even if she spoke English—he believed she must at least understand it—she would be too terrified to tell him what he needed to know. He decided not to put her at risk. He turned and faced the second girl in line, a shapely brunette. "I'd like her." He said.

He knew he'd made the right decision when Ariana relaxed, and Inca looked as if she would cry with relief.

"Tasha it is," Ariana said. She turned to the young woman. "Tasha, show Mr. O'Leary to your chambers."

He followed Tasha out of the room. As he mounted the stairs, he heard Winter say, "No, thank you, I'll wait here."

———

Tasha stopped before her door and smiled at O'Leary, and motioned him to enter first.

The room was the same one Ariana had shown him moments before. He dropped into one of the room's two easy chairs and placed his right index finger across his lips, signaling to Tasha to keep quiet. He took a small notebook and pen from his inside suit coat pocket and wrote, "Do they listen?"

Hoping the woman spoke English, he offered the note to Tasha, who quickly read it and nodded. She nodded toward the large mirror on the dresser. He got up and strolled around the room, making small talk. "This is a really nice place."

"Yes," Tasha said.

He stopped before the dresser and closely inspected the mirror. In the upper left corner, he saw a small dot and knew it was a listening device. *They make the goddamned things so small these days,* he thought. He pointed to the bathroom and walked into it, motioning for Tasha to follow him.

Once inside he walked to the whirlpool and turned it on. "These things really help me relax," he said. He twisted the handles until they reached their limit. When he thought that the sound of the jetting water would be loud enough to drown out their voices, he walked across the room and turned the shower on all the way.

He turned back to Tasha. She had shed her evening gown and stood before him wearing nothing but a petite bright-red bra and matching thong. She was breathtaking. So much so that he had to force himself to stay on task.

He pulled her tight against his chest and placed his mouth close to her ear. In a voice so low he wondered if she could hear over the rushing water, he said, "Don't be afraid, I'm here to help."

At first, Tasha was rigid; however, after a few seconds his words registered with her. She slumped into his arms and held him tight.

The feel of her body pressed tightly against his appealed to O'Leary's need to protect women. He clutched her snug against his chest and silently vowed he was going to get these women out of this mess—and he would kill anyone and everyone who tried to stop him.

27

Houston and Fuchs arrived at Fischer's place an hour before the appointed time. They parked on a dirt road about a half mile from their destination and entered the woods. "Pretty isolated," Fuchs said while they surveyed the pine and deciduous hardwood trees that covered the landscape.

"Very." They found a narrow footpath and followed it until they were on a promontory overlooking a small harbor. Two boats were moored alongside a wooden pier—one a charter boat and the other a small trawler. A multistory house was in the middle stages of decline and faced the harbor. "Looks like the Bates Hotel with outbuildings," Houston said. To the left of the house stood a barn with a sagging roof, and to the right was a rectangular building made of cinderblock. At the distance he was viewing it, Houston thought that it looked like a white shoe box.

Fuchs stood beside him and silently studied the layout. "When we come after him, we may need a friggin' battalion to cover these protective hills."

Houston scanned the high cliffs that protected the lot on two sides. "Only ways in and out are the driveway and the gulf."

Fuchs scanned the narrow drive that wound its way through the trees. "Gonna need SWAT . . . or the damned Marines."

Houston grinned. "That's why you got me."

Houston parked his Ford F-150 in front of the house. A man, whom Houston believed to be Fischer, stood on the porch as he and Fuchs disembarked.

Fischer nodded. "You the guys called yesterday?"

"That would be me," Houston said.

"Boat's at the dock." Fischer stepped off the porch before they could walk onto it. He led the way across the sandy lot toward the pier.

Houston followed, hoping he would get an opportunity to inspect the buildings closer. Fischer strode up the gangplank of the charter boat and stepped aside to allow the potential clients access. Houston was surprised. Based upon the appearance of the buildings, he'd expected to see a craft barely able to stay afloat. The opposite was true. The boat was neat and well-kempt; all gear was securely stowed, and the deck was spotless. "Nice vessel," he said.

Fischer nodded and moved his head at an angle that exposed the indentation Candy had described to Anne. His arms were folded across his chest, amplifying the size of his flexor muscles. He emanated raw power, and Houston decided not to get into a physical confrontation with him. There was a violent, evil aura surrounding Willard Fischer.

Bouchard watched Houston and Fuchs board the charter boat. She smiled when she visualized how Mike's face would look when he learned that she had decided to follow them and place Fischer's house under surveillance. She sat in the shade beneath the lower boughs of a towering pine, watching the house through binoculars. She scanned the boatyard and then turned her attention to the ramshackle house. She concentrated on the windows of the second floor and caught her breath when she saw a young woman in one. The figure was fleeting—there one second, gone the next. Nevertheless, she saw enough to know that the woman fit the description they had of Cheryl Guerette.

Bouchard took another glance and saw that the men had disappeared, probably touring the charter boat's interior. She decided to investigate and started down a narrow path that led to the bottom of the bluff. Reaching the bottom, she checked the area and saw no sign of the men— and more to the point, no sign of Fischer—and she dashed to the porch.

"When you want to go out?" Fischer asked.

"Well, we aren't sure," Houston said.

Fischer dropped his arms and turned toward the gangplank. "Then all you're doing is wasting my fucking time." He led them off the boat.

In an attempt to salvage the visit, Houston said. "If we were to charter you, could you pick us up in Portland?"

Fischer stopped walking and glared at them. "What is this anyway? Some kind of joke? You guys are about as interested in going fishing as I am in learning needlepoint."

"You're wrong," Fuchs said. "We are interested."

Fischer's eyes narrowed. "Well, I'm not. Get the fuck out of here."

He walked away and took a position on the porch, watching them as they got into the truck. As they drove up the tree-lined drive, Houston said, "I don't like that sonuvabitch."

"Either way, we blew that out of our asses."

Houston replied, "Yeah, but now I'm convinced that bastard is our man."

"The only way to prove it is to get inside that house," Fuchs said.

28

Bouchard tried the door and was surprised to find it unlocked. She entered the house and found herself in complete bedlam. The place looked like a supermarket after an earthquake; dishes, utensils, and trash were interspersed with sundry canned goods and processed foods. The sink overflowed, and she was certain that she saw the surface of several dishes move.

She turned right and entered a large room with a fireplace centered in the far wall. The furnishings were past due at the local landfill—the coverings torn, worn, and their insides open to the eye. She turned around and saw a staircase on the right.

Bouchard slowly climbed the stairs as she tried to avoid any creaking steps. She saw several doors and opened the first she came to. In a huge canopy bed that had once been elegant lay a diminutive old woman. Bouchard approached and said, "Hello." There was no response from the woman. She lay unmoving, her eyes open but seeing nothing. A thin line of spittle trickled down her chin. Without thought, Bouchard took a tissue from the box on the nightstand and wiped the old lady's chin. A quick inspection told her that the woman was alive, yet she was not alive.

"Advanced Alzheimer's," Bouchard whispered.

She turned, and through the old woman's door she saw another door across the hall—this one secured with a large padlock. She walked to it, lifted the lock, and looked at it. Her heart leapt when a voice from inside said, "Who's there?"

"Cheryl?"

"Who are you, and how do you know my name?"

"My name is Anne Bouchard. I'm a private investigator. Your grandparents hired me to find you."

"Anne or whoever you are, you need to get out of here *now*! He's crazy."

"I'm not going to go without you. I'll find something to get this lock off with."

She turned and inhaled sharply when she saw Fischer standing at the top of the stairs. "You ain't goin' nowhere," he said.

He punched Bouchard, driving her head into the doorjamb.

Willard stood in the doorway of her room. "I got a job for you."

She knew better than to ask questions. She got up from her bed and followed him out of the room. Cheryl had gained an appreciation for the smaller things in life—for instance, he had let her keep the clothes she had worn on the charter.

He stopped beside the room that had once been Monique's prison and took his ever-present key ring out of his pocket. Once the padlock on the door was open, he pushed her through. When Cheryl saw the condition of the naked woman that he had shackled to the bed in the same manner he had done to her, it brought back vivid images of her own first week in captivity. Then she remembered how Monique had said, "Now that he has you, he'll take me to the factory." Cheryl closed her eyes. Was he planning to replace her?

The woman tossed and groaned, reminding Cheryl of her struggle with addiction. This woman, however, was not in the thralls of drug withdrawal; she had been brutally beaten. "What am I supposed to do?"

"Nurse her until she's better."

Rather than scaring her, realizing the precariousness of her situation angered her. "What happens to me once I do that?"

He stepped back and looked at her with a furrowed brow. She was not sure if he was angry or surprised by her standing up to him.

Reluctant to give up her advantage over him, Cheryl pushed on. "Well? Answer me."

"Nothing."

"Does bringing her here mean that you are no longer interested in marrying me?" She turned on him, pushing her face toward his, her anger under control.

He gathered his composure and grabbed her by the arms. She felt tears well up in her eyes as he increased the power of his grip, hurting her.

"I said that nothing was going to happen to you!"

Cheryl tried another approach. "But you can only have one wife!"

"You don't know your Bible, do you? When Sarah couldn't give Abraham a son, she gave him her maid Hagar as a wife. So he had more than one wife, as did Isaac and Esau. King David and King Solomon each had more than one hundred. If God let them, why can't I?"

"What if I object?"

When he turned away from her, his tone didn't support the certainty in his words. "You won't. Now get to work."

Once he had walked out of the room, Cheryl walked to the bed and studied its repulsive condition. She realized that mere weeks—or was it months—before, she was just like this woman. She turned and started for the bathroom to get some towels, soap, a washcloth, and warm water but stopped short when she heard him talking in a low voice. "She shouldn't talk to me that way . . . only mums should talk like that."

She was surprised. He sounded like a small boy muttering under his breath after his mother had chastised him. *Was he intimidated by strong, assertive women?* If so, how could she use it as a weapon against him?

Suddenly his form filled the door. "Where you going?" He seemed to be back in his usual frame of mind.

"You said for me to nurse her. I need to wash the blood off her face and head."

He stepped aside, allowing her to pass. "You try anything, and you know what'll happen."

She turned and confronted him. "I'm reminded often enough."

He slapped her. The sound seemed explosive in the dark hall. As quickly as he had become enraged, he became timid; his head cocked as if he were listening for something. Cheryl stood before him, her hand against her cheek. She was still defiant and said, "Don't worry, *she* can't hear you. In fact, even if *she* could, she'd have no idea what it was."

He spun on her, his fist cocked. "You're going to regret your disrespectfulness! A woman should obey her husband. Now get what you need and go to work."

Cheryl filled a plastic basin with warm water and returned to the room. He stopped her at the door and lifted the towel and washcloth she had draped over her right forearm. He lifted the soap in the basin, and water dripped from his hand as he inspected it. She laughed at him. "What's the problem, *husband dear*? You afraid your wife may get her hands on a razor blade and cut your goddamned throat?"

He dropped the soap into the water, and his head snapped up. "You watch your mouth."

"And if I don't, you'll kill me? You're going to do that anyway . . . it's only a matter of when." Cheryl realized that as foolhardy as it was to confront him, it felt wonderful to stand her ground against her captor. "At this point, I might prefer death over a life with you."

29

Expecting to meet Bouchard in Boston, Houston returned there. He entered the hotel room and called out, "Anne, you here?" There was no answer. "Probably hit the shops on Newbury Street," he mused.

He took out his cell phone and accessed the directory. He highlighted the entry for his daughter Susie and hit talk. It was answered on the first ring. "Hi, Dad."

"Hey, I'm in town."

"I know. You and Anne have been here for four days now."

He felt his face redden. "I'm sorry."

He heard his daughter laugh. "I knew what was going on as soon as Anne told me you two were working a case. The two of you will never stop being cops."

"You got me there, kid. Want to have a late lunch or early dinner with your old man?"

"Sure. Where do you and Anne want to meet?"

Houston gave her the name of a favorite restaurant, and they arranged to meet in two hours. "Anne's out. She should be back by then, but I'll leave her a note just the same."

"Dad, it's the twenty-first century—just text her."

Houston was not about to admit to her that he had not a clue about how to text message. He opened the desk drawer and took out a sheet of hotel stationery.

Susie was already sitting at a table when Houston arrived. "No Anne?" she asked.

"I left a message at the front desk and a note in our room."

"You didn't text her?"

Houston felt his face redden. "No."

She laughed. "You don't know how to text, do you?"

"Hell, I'm still having a hard time making regular phone calls."

"Give me your phone."

He took his smartphone from his pocket and slid it across the table. Susie took less than a minute to send a text to Anne. "You could have called her."

"Oh no. I've had her isolated on that mountain for so long, the last thing I'm going to do is bother her while she's shopping."

"Dad . . ."

"Okay, I called, but she didn't answer."

The server approached and placed menus in front of them. "Would you care for a drink?" He eyed Susie, not certain that she was of legal age for alcohol.

"Iced tea, unsweetened with lemon," Susie said.

"I'll have the same," Houston said.

Once they were alone again, Houston said, "So tell me what my only offspring has been up to these days."

"I've been staying on campus mostly, although I do spend some weekends with Aunt Maureen. I don't suppose you've called her yet, have you?"

"Suze, this trip has been strictly business."

"Anyway, I changed my major."

"Oh? To what?"

"Criminal justice."

"Oh, lord, not another cop in the family."

"I intend to go to law school. I'd like to be a prosecutor."

"More money representing the other side."

Her face turned serious. "I'd rather put scum like Edwin Rosa away, not defend them."

"As a defense attorney you'd immediately get one client."

She giggled. "No way could I defend Uncle Jimmy—I'd know he was guilty."

"Not to mention the smoking. A visit to his office could be lethal."

It was after ten o'clock when Houston and Susie parted, and he returned to the hotel. He was disappointed and upset with Anne. She had not answered her phone nor replied to the text Susie had sent, and she knew that Susie would want to see her, too. Before entering the elevator, he checked his phone to see if he had missed a call or message from Anne—nothing. He stepped onto the elevator and punched the button for his floor. If she was in their room, he was going to chew her out but good.

He opened the door to the room, and as soon as he saw that the lights were off, his anger turned to worry. The room was as he'd left it, the note still on the desk apparently untouched.

30

Cheryl placed the tray on the small table beside the bed. She placed a finger over Anne's mouth to keep her from crying out. Bouchard's eyes were wide with confusion as she surveyed her surroundings. The room was austere with painted walls and minimal furniture. Bouchard sat up and stared at the fetter on her left wrist. Her eyes followed it to where the other end was hooked through a loop of heavy chain, which was in turn fastened to a beam in the ceiling.

"Keep your voice down," Cheryl said, her mouth close to the woman's ear.

The new arrival sat up and stared at her host. She saw Cheryl staring at the small circular scar on her left shoulder.

"Is that a bullet wound?"

"Yes. I'll tell you the story another time."

Cheryl kept her eyes averted and whispered. "He's probably listening . . . everything he does is some sort of stupid game or test."

The woman lowered her voice to a whisper. "Are you alright? Has he hurt you? Has he . . . ?"

"Raped me? Every time he's tried anything, he couldn't get it up—I think he's impotent."

"Impotent?"

"Yes. I guess I won't be here much longer now that you're here. There was another woman when I arrived—we talked through a hole in the wall. But then she wasn't there anymore."

She reached out and touched Cheryl's arm.

Cheryl panicked at the sound of the chains rattling.

"My name is Anne Bouchard. I'm a private investigator and will try to get you out. Your grandparents are looking for you."

Cheryl looked cynical. "You told me that—right before he caught you. I don't see how you're going to help me," she pointed at the chain, "considering you're in the same situation."

"I'll need your help. Can you get me something to remove this manacle?"

"Are you kidding? If I'm not locked in my room Willard doesn't let me out of his sight for two minutes."

Bouchard lifted the chain and manacle on her left wrist. "Does he still chain you?"

"No, I think he believes I've given up all hope. But he still locks me in my room at night."

They heard the sound of loud footsteps outside the room, and Cheryl spun around. "I got to go."

Cheryl stepped into the hall and stopped abruptly when she came face to face with him. "What took you so long? Only takes a minute to drop a tray and leave." He slapped her.

"I was telling her the rules." Cheryl rubbed the side of her face and fought to control the anger she felt. "You don't. You expect us to know what's going on." She clenched her fists, and her voice rose. "You're the one who told me to take care of her."

He flinched. "Keep your voice down." He cast a worried glance at Mum's door.

"Why? She can't hear anyone but you. You may have noticed that she's never said a single goddamned word to me!"

He regained his composure and grabbed her. "Get your ass back to your room. We'll talk about this later."

Back in her room, Cheryl sat in front of her window and stared out at the cove. She whispered, "My days are numbered. I've got to get out of here soon."

31

O'Leary walked into the warehouse and found Winter waiting for him. "Is everything all set?"

"Yup, got seven men. We'll go down two to a car. Jackie will drive alone in the bus. I figured that will give us enough room to bring the women back with us."

"Good."

"There's just one thing I ain't figured out, boss."

O'Leary lit a cigarette. Smoke drifted out of his mouth when he said, "What's that?"

"What in hell we going to do with these broads once we got them?"

"I'll figure that out when the time comes."

The drive to the Cape was uneventful. The cavalcade pulled into a public parking lot from which O'Leary could see the phosphorescent sparkle of the surf breaking on the beach. He stepped from the SUV, tossed his cigarette to the pavement, and watched the wind carry it away.

Winter got out of the second vehicle and walked over to him. He, too, studied the breaking surf for a few moments. "How you want to do this?" he asked.

"You and I go in the front. We'll tell them that we want to . . . I don't know. When the time comes, I'll make up something or other."

"Telling the madam we want to get laid might work," Winter said.

O'Leary chuckled. "You think?"

"Yeah, I think. Where you want the rest of the guys?"

The rest of the assault team gathered around their leaders.

"Chico, you and Dudley go around the back. When the shooting starts—and I'm sure it will—you come in. Dan, you and Scott stay out of sight and cover the front. We get too many people inside, we might end up shooting each other. Jackie, as soon as the shooting starts, you park that bus in front of the door."

The men nodded.

"We don't take anyone against their will," O'Leary said. "Although I doubt they'll want to stay and answer a bunch of questions when the cops arrive. If I got things figured out right, we'll find more leprechauns than green cards in there."

O'Leary and Winter waited while the men deployed to their assigned positions and then approached the front of the manse. O'Leary rang the bell.

"Away all boats," Winter said.

"What?"

"That's the last command troops hear before heading for the beach."

"Well, let's hope we have our beachhead established before they figure out what's going down."

The door opened, and Ariana appeared in the threshold. "Mr. O'Leary. This is an unexpected surprise." O'Leary detected suspicion in her demeanor.

"I enjoyed my last visit so much," he said, "I thought I'd come back for a more leisurely evening."

She seemed uncertain. "Usually we only entertain guests by appointment." She peered past his shoulder and studied the yard as if she were trying to see who else was there. She saw Winter and said, "Hello, Mr.

Winter." She peered into the darkness for a moment and then stepped back. "Come in, gentlemen."

They entered the expansive foyer. Ariana wasted no time expressing her displeasure. "Rarely," she said, "do we entertain on Sunday evenings . . . even my girls rate a night off."

"Hell, Ariana, I thought we got rid of blue laws in the Commonwealth of Massachusetts." O'Leary reached into the inside pocket of his suit coat. Behind Ariana, one of her security guards tensed, and O'Leary noticed their increased vigilance. "Settle down, boys," he said, his hand still concealed within his coat. "I'm just getting out my money." He removed his hand and held his wallet in plain sight. Turning his attention to Ariana, he said, "I fully intend to compensate you for any inconvenience." He removed several large denomination bills and offered them to her. "I assume you'll bill me for any services rendered?"

Greed overcame Ariana's suspicions. She took the money and said, "Oliver, tell Marcus and Willem that we must prepare for a couple of guests." Turning back to Jimmy, she said, "Will you want Tasha again?"

"I'd really like to look over your entire inventory. I'm certain you have several beauties I haven't had the pleasure of getting acquainted with."

"Very well, please have a seat in the sitting room. It may take a few minutes."

"Take your time," he said, "I'm in no hurry."

Ariana gave him a quizzical look. "I must say, Mr. O'Leary, you are full of surprises."

O'Leary flashed his best smile. "That I am, ma'am . . . you have no idea how full of surprises I am."

In less than ten minutes, Ariana had all the women lined up in the sitting room. O'Leary immediately looked for Inca. The child was not present.

"Where's Inca?" he asked.

"She's no longer with us," Ariana replied. "She didn't have the qualities we look for in our girls."

"Really?" his face turned hard. He looked to Winter and nodded.

Winter stood up and pulled his 9 mm pistol from the holster suspended from his belt. He turned to the security guard. Seeing the weapon, the guard reached under his coat, and Winter shot him in the chest.

Immediately, the women screamed and cowered, many with hands over their heads as if trying to ward off falling debris.

"Get down!" O'Leary cried as he removed a pistol from his belt and turned to the door.

Another guard ran through the foyer, a small assault gun in his hand. When he reached the threshold to the sitting room, O'Leary dropped him with a single shot.

Ariana cursed and ran at him, the fingers of her left hand extended like talons and a knife in her right hand. He had no idea where the knife had come from but saw that the blade was poised to strike. He stood his ground.

"Stop!" he warned.

The enraged madam ignored the terse warning and began shrieking as she ran at him. When she was within five feet and showed no sign of slowing, O'Leary fired. The bullet smashed through her chest. At such close range, it passed through her and slammed into the wall. She stepped back, looked at the spreading red smear on her chest and then at O'Leary. Then, like a circus tent collapsing, she dropped to her knees.

In the sudden silence, he heard two more shots ring out and knew Chico and Dudley had stormed through the back door. More shots rang out.

O'Leary squatted before Ariana, "Where's the kid?"

Ariana knelt on the floor, her expensive wig skewed to one side and blood soaked her elegant gown. She looked bewildered, as if she could not believe this unexpected turn of events.

O'Leary cupped her chin in his free hand. If not for the blood that trickled from her nose and the corner of her mouth, she would have looked comical with her lips puffed out from his grip.

"Who did you give her to?"

Ariana looked into his eyes.

He softened his tone. "Ariana, you got nothing to lose—you're dying. Please, stop this now. There's no fucking sense in letting another young girl suffer."

"The lawyer . . ."

"What lawyer?"

"Halsey, he took her early this morning."

O'Leary released Ariana's face, and she slumped over onto her side. When he got to his feet, he saw that Winter, Chico, and Dudley stood in the room. "Okay," he said to the women, "you got ten minutes to get what you want to take with you—keep it to the bare necessities, we ain't got a lot of room."

Tasha was the first to regain her composure. "You're taking us away?"

"Damn right."

"What will we do? We have no place to go."

"Just get your shit together. We'll have time to worry about the other stuff later. Now *move!*"

The women dashed out of the room.

"We may have taken a big bite out of a shit sandwich," Winter said.

"Not as big a bite as my former attorney," O'Leary replied. "Now, I want to know who's behind this operation. There has to be an office around here somewhere. You guys stay here, wait for the women, and keep watch. Gordon, you come with me."

The office was on the first floor near the kitchen. O'Leary circumvented the large teak desk and immediately went to a line of three filing cabinets. A quick look told him that Ariana kept them locked. He grabbed the edge of one and shook it. "Not too heavy," he said. "Get the guys to load these into the trucks."

While Winter went to get help, O'Leary began searching the office. He struck a bonanza within minutes. He found a laptop that Ariana must have been using when they had arrived. It was open to a file that was a ledger containing names and addresses and amounts of money spent. His heart stopped as he scrolled through the files and scanned entries; many of the names were those of well-known men in and around Boston. He opened the desk drawer and found a thumb drive. He quickly formatted the drive and copied the accounting files to it. He picked up the laptop and left.

When O'Leary re-entered the sitting room, Winter was still there. "Forget about the filing cabinets, I found all I need," O'Leary said.

"I gather we're going after the girl?"

"You bet your ass," O'Leary said, "my old friend Halsey is about to learn what it's like to be tried, convicted, and . . ."

The convoy raced over the Bourne Bridge. O'Leary looked at the parking lot of the state police barracks for signs of activity; there were none. He glanced to his right at Tasha's profile. "How long have you been here?"

Tasha turned to him, her beauty amplified in the ambient lights of the vehicle's instruments. "I'm not sure. I left Saint Petersburg in August . . . 2009. What is the date today?"

When he told her the date, she leaned her head back against the headrest. "I came to this house last Christmas. Before this, I was someplace else, not far from Chicago."

The implications of the size of the prostitution ring startled him. It could very well span the entire country. He recalled the names in the ledger and thought, *There's big money and power behind this. Maybe Gordon was right; this shit sandwich could turn into a footlong. . . .*

"Well, it's over now. You're going to be alright." He saw her smile as if she believed him. He, on the other hand, was not so sure.

32

Houston was frantic. It was eight in the morning and no sign of Anne. He began making phone calls to her friends that he knew. He tried Jimmy O several times but got no response, and then he called Dysart. Nobody had seen nor heard from her since he'd left her early yesterday. His final call was to Sam Fuchs.

"Sam, Anne is missing."

"What?"

"I think she's gone after Fischer."

"But we were there yesterday. There was no sign of her."

"Believe me, I know my woman. She isn't about to let us run with this. She probably followed us and was keeping him under surveillance."

"I'll get hold of someone to check it out."

"Under what pretense? We have no proof she's at his place."

"I don't know, goddamn it, but I'll sure as hell come up with something."

Bouchard heard the doorknob turn and sat up. When Cheryl slipped into the room and knelt beside the bed, she looked at the door and said, "What are you doing? What if he finds out you're in here?"

Cheryl placed an index finger across her lips. She leaned close and whispered, "We may have a golden opportunity tonight."

"How so?"

"I told you he can't get it up. He thinks it's because he hasn't yet found a woman who appeals to him."

"Sick bastard."

"Well, he's decided that maybe it's not a problem of quality . . . maybe it's one of quantity . . ."

"Are you saying . . . ?"

Cheryl nodded; the whites of her eyes seemed to glow in the dimly lit room. "Yeah, he wants a threesome—tonight."

Bouchard started to respond, her face red with anger and indignation.

Cheryl held up her hand, stopping her. "Let me handle the nasty stuff." Cheryl said. "*Cheri*, not Cheryl, will keep him occupied while you take care of him."

"How will I do that wearing this?" Bouchard held up her manacle.

"He won't do it in here or in my room. He has a king-sized bed—he'll want more room. He'll have to unshackle you if for no other reason than he'll be afraid you'll strangle him with his own chain."

"Now there's a thought to cherish. Nevertheless, it may work out to our benefit."

Cheryl stepped away and faced the door. She listened for a few seconds and then turned back to Bouchard. "You got to promise me one thing, though."

"What?"

"If you get the chance, you'll kill him."

Bouchard was searching the section of the room that her shackles allowed her to reach hoping to find anything she could use as a tool to free herself. She held the mattress up on edge and was studying the floor beneath the bed when she heard someone fumbling with the lock on her door. She dropped the mattress and sat on it just as he entered the room.

He stared at her for several seconds, saying nothing.

Bouchard turned to him and returned his stare.

"Who are you?" he asked.

"The worst thing that could possibly happen to you."

He paced around the room for several seconds and said, "You aren't in a position to do much."

"The authorities know about you."

He smirked. "They got shit. If they had anything they'd be all over this place."

"They'll find a reason to get a warrant."

He peered at her. "You talk like you know a lot about it."

Not wanting to alarm him by revealing what she did for a living, Bouchard decided to back off. "My brother is a cop in Boston."

"Boston . . . that explains the accent." He turned away. "I wouldn't get my hopes up that your brother can help you. This is Maine, not Boston." He stopped and turned back to look at her. "I can't help but wonder if the fact that you have a bunch of licenses as a private investigator, one of which is from Maine, in your purse has anything to do with it. What is it with you fucking women that you think you can lie to men and not get caught?"

Cheryl came into Bouchard's room shortly after nightfall. "He wants to see us."

"Listen," Bouchard said, "if the chance for you to get away presents itself, run. Don't worry about me . . . I can take care of myself."

Cheryl nodded. "Let's hope we can both get out of here." She leaned forward and pushed a key into the lock. Bouchard almost cried with relief when the manacles fell away from her chafed flesh. "Whatever you do," Cheryl warned, "don't make him suspicious. He's paranoid as hell."

Bouchard thought it was funny that Cheryl would be giving her advice on how to deal with a maniac. On the other hand, she listened because Cheryl had survived with this lunatic for several weeks. "I understand." She stood on wobbly legs and stretched her arms, reveling in her newfound freedom.

Cheryl turned to the door and motioned for her to follow.

"I suppose clothing is out of the question."

Cheryl did not answer. Bouchard followed her, taking small steps as her legs struggled to get used to walking and supporting her weight.

———————

Bouchard followed Cheryl down the stairs, memorizing the layout of the house. "I don't think *Better Homes and Gardens* will ever publish an article on his housekeeping abilities," Bouchard said.

Cheryl's eyes were wide, and she placed her hand against Bouchard's lips. "Shhhhh! If he hears you there will be hell to pay."

Bouchard had a thousand questions she wanted to ask Cheryl, but she refrained. She realized what Cheryl was trying to say; he could be lurking anywhere, spying and listening.

Bouchard stepped onto the porch, and immediately the cool night air chilled her. He sat in a chair, looking like a monarch on his throne. She watched Cheryl for clues as to how she should act. She noted that Cheryl kept her head tilted down, avoiding eye contact with their captor. Bouchard immediately recognized what Cheryl was doing; she was acting the role of a submissive lesser wolf in the presence of the alpha. She imitated her. Although with her eyes facing downward, she couldn't see their surroundings, she was able to discern objects—like the rifle that leaned against the wall beside his legs. The chair creaked as he shifted his weight. "It's going to be a great night . . ."

"It could be," Bouchard made a concerted effort to keep her anger out of her voice. She glanced wistfully at the weapon propped up beside his chair. If she could get her hands on the rifle it could be a terrific night; in fact, it would be wonderful.

"Sit," he said.

Bouchard sat in a wooden Adirondack chair beside him. She raised her head slightly and looked at him out of the corner of her eyes.

"Nice night," he announced as if they were cordial companions.

"Yes, it is," Cheryl said.

He turned to Bouchard, his eyes narrowed, and he said, "You don't agree?"

Bouchard saw his stern gaze and realized he had addressed her. "Yes," she replied.

"Yes it is or yes you don't agree?" His voice had a dangerous edge to it.

"Yes, I agree that it's a nice evening." She did not want to rile him. If they were to have a chance of escaping, they needed him calm.

He glanced at his watch. "Mum should be asleep by now."

He stood and picked up the rifle.

Bouchard noted that he scanned the water's surface. The ocean was calm like a shimmering sheet of glass in the moonlight.

"Looks like I got rid of the bastards," he said.

Bouchard couldn't resist the impulse to look at him. He returned her gaze and looked like he was talking to a child. "Seals," he explained. "Ain't nothin' I hate any more than them fuckers."

She glanced at Cheryl, who shook her head, warning her not to pursue the subject.

"Well, ladies, time for bed." He stood back waiting for them to precede him inside.

Cheryl took the lead and led them up the stairs. She paused before her door, waiting for him to tell her what he wanted.

"Keep going," he said, "to my room."

33

Cheryl led them down the hall and stopped before the last door on the left.

Willard shoved her aside. "Move away so I can unlock the door." Once the door was open, he stepped aside, keeping himself between them and the stairs. "Go in."

Bouchard followed Cheryl into the room.

He turned on a light, and Bouchard studied the room. A king-size bed sat in the center of the bedroom and dominated the floor. There was barely enough room to walk around it; the two miniscule end tables were crammed in so tight that they touched the walls on either side. The tables attracted Bouchard's attention. A tall lamp with what appeared to be a granite base sat on each.

He followed them in and locked the door behind him. He motioned the women to the bed but did not immediately join them. Instead, he put a finger across his lips and whispered, "We got to be quiet. If we wake Mum, she'll have a conniption. She won't approve of what we're doing. She thinks it ain't proper for married men and women to . . . do things with people they ain't married to."

Bouchard lay on the bed, keeping distance from Cheryl, and watched him prepare the room.

For several tense moments, she lay still, observing his psychotic behavior. He seemed to listen for sounds only he could hear. Satisfied all was well, he placed the rifle in the closet, closed the door, closed a hasp, and locked it with a combination lock.

Damn, Anne thought, *so much for the rifle.*

He turned off the overhead light and walked to the nightstand at the right side of the bed and turned on the lamp. She felt a light touch on her arm and glanced at Cheryl, who nodded as if to say, *"Don't worry."*

When Fischer climbed into the bed and settled between the women, Bouchard thought he looked like a man having his first extramarital sex. Cheryl immediately went to work on him. She turned on her side and stroked his chest.

Bouchard, on the other hand, struggled against her revulsion at having his naked body so close and wasn't sure what her role was to be in this threesome, so she laid still. She tried to block out the phony words of endearment Cheryl whispered to Fischer. She slowly moved her hand toward the nightstand. She hoped Cheryl could keep him distracted for a few more seconds. After what seemed an eternity, she gripped the lamp. It was heavy but not so heavy that she could not lift it with one hand. Bouchard heard Cheryl coaxing him, doing her best to keep his attention from their other bed partner. Slowly, so as not to alarm him, she lifted the lamp.

She glanced at Fischer and wondered how she could strike without hitting Cheryl. She saw her opportunity when Cheryl said, "Let's try this—maybe it will help," and slid down his torso.

Bouchard raised the lamp and for a second felt resistance. Suddenly, the plug pulled out of its socket, and it was free. When the room went dark, Fischer cried out in alarm. She raised the lamp as high as possible and smashed it into his head. As soon as she struck, she jumped from the bed and held the broken lamp up, poised to strike again if needed.

He grunted and then relaxed. Blood flowed from a nasty gash on his forehead. Cheryl popped up to a kneeling position. "Is he dead?"

"I doubt it. Come on, we have to get out of here before he comes around."

Cheryl's face shone in the moonlight that filtered into the room through a gap in the curtains. "Hit him again—*kill* the son of a bitch!"

He groaned and rolled over.

"Go on!" Cheryl said in a low voice. "Kill him!"

"No." Bouchard grabbed Cheryl's arm. "We'll send the cops after him."

Cheryl grabbed the fractured lamp from Anne's hand. "If you won't do it, I will."

Bouchard snatched the lamp back. No matter how heinous he was, she could not condone cold-blooded murder. "Come on, we don't have all night," she said.

Cheryl turned to the dresser and grabbed a photo of two people, one of whom struck a striking resemblance to the old woman in the next room. "Well," she said, "let's see how he likes this." She smashed the picture against a corner of the dresser and then did the same to three others.

Bouchard quickly rolled Fischer over and used the lamp's power cord to tie his hands. He moaned and his eyes fluttered as she bound him. She fought against her escalating panic; time was short, he would be regaining consciousness soon.

Once Fischer's hands were securely tied, she said, "Come on, let's get going."

Cheryl paused as if at a quandary. She punched Fischer in the groin and, when he grunted in pain, said, "If I had a knife, I'd cut that useless thing off."

"Let's go!" Bouchard grabbed Cheryl's arm and pulled her from the room. They bolted down the stairs and out into the night.

Bouchard turned toward the drive.

"This way," Cheryl said. "If we're on the road, he'll come after us with the truck." She pointed toward the gulf. "We'll swim along the shore until we're safe."

The women bolted from the house and ran along the shore. Bouchard wished she had shoes on as she stomped on pebbles and debris, the pain slowing her down. She ignored the agony of her weight landing on sharp stones and raced after Cheryl. Her heart skipped when she heard the sound of waves lapping against the shore.

They ran onto a pier and past three boats, a commercial trawler, a charter boat, and a small punt. *Damn*, Bouchard thought, *why didn't I look for keys? We could have used one of these!* Ahead of her, Cheryl did not hesitate; she vaulted off the end of the dock into the surf. Once she had swum away from the pier, she turned, paused, and beckoned for Anne to follow.

Bouchard gasped as she plunged into the fifty-degree water and knifed beneath the surface. She arched her back and, when her head broke the surface, gulped air. She kicked her legs and fought against the surf, using all of her strength to pull herself forward. She circumvented a large black rock and cautioned herself that she'd have to pay attention lest she smash into one. The current seemed to work against her. As she struggled to make progress, she wondered whether they'd made a mistake. They could travel faster on land and would put more distance between them and the Fisherman. She saw Cheryl swimming away from the shore out to sea and followed suit. In short time, her body acclimated to the temperature, and she swam with a renewed sense of urgency. Bouchard lengthened her strokes, knowing each one was taking her closer to freedom.

34

You goddamned moron. You fucked things up again!

Hallet! That language doesn't help matters. He'll make things right.

Fischer opened his eyes and lay dazed. It took a couple of seconds for him to remember what had happened.

Willard, get up.

"Yes, Mum." He felt a quick flash of guilt and fear. Mum was angry. He knew eventually she would find out what he had been doing with the women, and she would punish him severely.

You have to catch them. Mum's voice cut through him. *Do you think I haven't known what you're doing with the women you've brought here? If the new one gets away, she'll bring police. Now get after them! We'll deal with your lustful ways later.*

Fischer rolled over and tried to get up. He was unable to move his arms and realized they were tied. He flexed his arms, grunting with effort as he spread his hands. The electric cord bit into his wrists, but he felt it give ever so slightly. He screamed in frustration and rage. He looked around the room, wondering why Mum did not help him get free. He gathered his strength and spread his arms apart; the cord suddenly gave, and he was free.

He rolled from the bed with a curse. He staggered across the room, stepped on something sharp, and cursed. He snapped on the overhead light and then turned and glared at the broken glass and damaged photographs of his family. Rage burned through him when he saw the carnage on the floor. He knelt down, picked up the photo of his parents, and held it against his face. He sobbed. He swore that if it took him forever, he would make those bitches pay.

Something obscured his vision and made the room blurry. He wiped his eyes, and his hand came away covered with blood; he wiped it on his leg. He was going to kill them. He could get other women, just as he had done in the past. He wanted his rifle. He walked to the closet and spun the combination on the lock. His obscured vision made it impossible to see the numbers, and he slammed the lock in anger. He turned from the lock and saw a black lump on the floor—his pants lay in a pile where he had left them. He pulled them on and hissed in pain when they touched his battered genitals; he opened a dresser drawer and grabbed a black T-shirt. He slid it over his head and turned to the closet. He hissed, lifted his foot so he could see the arch, and plucked out a piece of glass. Standing on one foot to avoid the pain, it took him several tries before he was able to work the combination on the lock securing the closet door. He reached inside and grabbed his rifle, checked that it was loaded with cartridges, and ignored the pain in his foot as he ran from the room.

He bolted across the living room and stopped on the porch, looking for the women. He quickly scanned the sandy ground looking for any sign of which way they'd gone. He saw tracks in the sand, headed for the water. He knew he had time, calmly walked into the kitchen, and put on a pair of boots. Once his feet were protected, he opened a small cabinet and took the keys to the punt.

Willard, stop dallying!

"Yes, Mum."

Satisfied all was in order, he walked toward the dock.

———————

Fischer cursed loudly as he yanked the pull cord on the punt's outboard motor. It refused to start. He adjusted the choke and pulled again. This time the motor coughed and then began with a stutter. He readjusted the choke and gave it fuel until the sixty horsepower Johnson smoothed out. Fischer put the boat into gear and increased the throttle. The bow rose as the propeller churned water behind him. He sped out of the small harbor, and the boat bounced as it left the placid waters of the cove behind and encountered the two-foot swells rolling in off the Gulf of Maine. He wondered if maybe he should take the trawler but discarded the idea. While the trawler offered better visibility, the punt was faster. He turned out into the gulf, peering into the light of the rising full moon, searching for the telltale dark spot that would lead to his quarry.

Once again, the small craft bounced against the surf, and he saw something break the surface. He grabbed the rifle and stood up. He spread his legs for balance as the boat slowed and settled in the water. "Gotcha, bitch . . ."

He sighted until it looked as if the bobbing black spot sat on the sight blade and fired.

35

As she went under, Bouchard heard a dull *CRACK!* Something smacked the water beside her. She realized that he had shot at her. She dismissed all thoughts of stealth and swam.

A whirring noise filled the water. She surfaced and turned to look back. She saw the phosphorescent glow of the water rolling away from the bow of a small boat that raced toward her. She treaded water and gasped in deep breaths of air. What were they going to do now? Bouchard swiveled her body and saw that Cheryl, too, had stopped. Her face was illuminated by the moonlight, and Anne saw raw fear there. She cursed the brightness; in the dark, they had a chance. She motioned for Cheryl to dive and then inhaled deeply and jack-knifed, clawing at the water as she swam to the bottom. Her hands made contact with a slimy, elusive substance; she was as deep as she could go. She grabbed a handful of kelp, gripping it tightly to keep from drifting up.

The water suddenly roiled around her, and the whirring noise increased a thousand times. Above her, the moonlight made the surface look as white as the foam of a raging river. A shadow broke across her line of sight, and she felt a rapid current and saw the deadly propeller rip the water several feet above her. The water seemed to explode as the boat sped by.

Bouchard let go of her anchor and quickly surfaced into the swirling wake and gulped life-preserving air. The unlit skiff was drifting mere yards away, her captor sitting in the back with his body half turned toward her. He was looking forward, peering into the creeping darkness; obviously, he'd miscalculated how far she'd swum. She dove just as his head turned to check behind.

Cheryl resurfaced and treaded water. She used her hands as rudders and spun around, frantically looking for Bouchard. She saw the boat off to her right, and suddenly a dark spot appeared in its wake. Her heart hammered as she tried to decide what her next action should be. The boat's motor idled and slowly drifted as he tried to locate his quarry. She succumbed to desperation. If she stayed stationary, either he'd find her or she'd drown. She wondered how long it would be before the chilly water lowered her body temperature and overwhelmed her. She steeled herself, this was no time to panic—she was free now, and she intended to stay that way. She swam away from the boat, taking care not to make too much commotion or visibly disturb the water any more than she had to.

Suddenly he stood up in the boat and looked in her direction. She heard him curse. "Got you, bitch!" He snatched up the rifle and aimed it at Anne. In the dim light, the end of the rifle lit up like a lightning flash.

36

The caravan pulled deep into the warehouse. O'Leary got out of his SUV and watched the large overhead door slowly close. He lit a cigarette and waited for Winter to join him.

"Where are we going to put these women?" Winter asked.

"We'll set up something here—at least for tonight."

"This place ain't exactly set up for taking care of women."

"I know that. But, where else we got? This place has a bathroom and is only short-term. I'll work on it tomorrow. I got a couple of properties where we can put them until we figure out what's going on."

"We're going to catch some heavy heat over this."

O'Leary thought of the listing of names he'd seen on the laptop he'd taken from Ariana's office. "You got that right . . . it could very well turn out to be volcanic." He glanced at his watch. "Come on, we got to get things organized. I want to be at Halsey's place early in the morning. Before this is all over, I'm going to need a new lawyer."

"Are we going after the kid?"

"Bet your ass we are."

The women exited the bus and stood in the middle of the open space, staring at the dark interior. Winter chuckled. "About now they're probably wondering what the fuck is gonna happen. This place is a long way from what they had, and they're probably thinkin' that we're their new bosses."

"They'll settle down once they realize that they don't have to turn tricks and can leave whenever they want."

"I don't know about that, boss. Just because we'll let them go don't mean they can survive. They're illegal aliens, and if the names on that computer are any indication of the types of people that went to that house, there's going to be a lot of interest in finding them before they can open their mouths."

"I know. That's why we're going to make sure that anyone interested finds us before they find them."

37

The bullet smacked the water inches from Bouchard's head. She knew he had located her and that she had to do something to turn the situation around. She let out a loud grunt, rolled sideways, and then relaxed, letting her body float on the surface. She bobbed on the surf, hoping he would think she was dead. She shifted her arms slightly and let the surf roll her over onto her back. Through half-closed eyes, she watched the punt approach.

Fischer stood in the punt, set the rifle down, and then bent over and picked up a long gaff. The point and barb glistened in the moonlight. She heard him muttering. "Got one, now where's the other?"

The boat bumped against her arm, and Bouchard fought against her impulse to flinch. She opened her eyes in time to see the gaff coming toward her. She grabbed the end and rolled away from the boat. Her action took him by surprise, and he flew over her and splashed into the water, losing his grip on the fishing spear. She, on the other hand, kept hers and quickly reversed the lance so the spike pointed at him. She thrust forward. The lance struck him in the shoulder, driving him backward in the water.

He cried out in surprise and pain and pulled away from her. She lost her grasp on the wet wooden handle but knew she had hurt him. In the eerie moonlight, she thought he looked like a harpooned whale. With strength and agility she never before thought she had, Bouchard pulled herself over the side of the small boat and grabbed the throttle. She put the idling outboard motor in gear and twisted her wrist to increase the throttle and increase the flow of fuel to the pistons. The aft end of the punt dropped as the propeller bit into the water, and she turned the boat, aiming the bow at him.

Fischer rolled in the water to avoid the onrushing boat. He dove, clawing at the water as he fought to get below the spinning propeller. The prop grazed him, ripping a shallow gash across his back. The boat roared past, turned, and disappeared into the night.

Anne felt the boat shudder as its propeller hit something. She turned her attention to the water and looked for Cheryl. Unable to see her, she began circling, her eyes seeking any telltale black ball on the surface. She saw one about a hundred yards away and turned the punt toward it. As she closed with the object, she realized it was not Cheryl but rather the peak of a large rock. She barely missed the obstruction and slowed the boat. She studied the ocean for several minutes and then turned south, seeking a place to put ashore and get help.

Fischer surfaced, too dazed to think about anything but survival. It felt like a chainsaw had ripped across his left shoulder. For a second he panicked, worried the scent of fresh blood would attract sharks, then he got control of himself; there hadn't been a shark sighting in these waters in years—at least, he hadn't heard of any. Trying to swim while keeping his damaged arm immobile, he kicked toward shore.

It seemed like hours passed before he staggered from the sea, gasping and coughing brine. Staring out into the darkness, he cursed. He'd find

192 | VAUGHN C. HARDACKER

them. When he did, the new bitch was going to rue the day they had met. No one could fuck with him and not pay dearly for it. He turned his thoughts to the more urgent need for first aid; he turned north and trudged along the rocky beach. He recognized a rock formation and reckoned he was two or three miles from home.

38

Cheryl swam along the shoreline, keeping out of the surf. Her arms and lungs burned with fatigue, and her legs felt heavy. She knew it would only be a matter of time before she began to cramp, and she had to get ashore. She altered her course, turning toward the beach. She swam until exhaustion threatened to drag her under the surface. Just as she was about to succumb to the numbing weakness, her hands touched the bottom. It took the last of her reserves for her to climb to her feet and stagger out of the water. Once on solid ground, she scrambled to the security of the boulders that littered the rugged coastline and dropped to the ground. She leaned against the hard black rock for several minutes, inhaling deeply and watching the sea for signs of an approaching boat.

Finally, she felt strong enough to continue on and grabbed the hard black surface of the boulder and pulled herself erect. She stretched her aching muscles and wondered if Anne had gotten away. Over the sounds of the rolling waves, she heard the sound of a boat motor in the distance. Her heart began to pound. *No,* she thought, *I'm not going to let him get his hands on me again.* Frightened over the prospect that Fischer would be searching the shoreline from the still out-of-sight boat, she scanned the short span of beach, looking for anything that would give away her location. She gasped when she spied the line of footprints in the sand that told the world where she was. She had two options: run or try to wipe out the tracks. She chose the first and clambered up the steep bank that lined the shore.

———————

Fischer stomped into the house.

You didn't get them?

Of course he didn't get them. I bin tellin' you for years he'd fuck up a roll call in a one-man submarine!

Shut up, Hallet.

"I'm hurt, Mum."

That will be the least of your troubles if they get away. You're just like your father.

Woman, you watch your mouth!

You know you would have always been a clam digger if not for me. You had no head for thinking.

Beatrice, one of these days you're gonna go too far.

"But, Mum, one of them took the punt."

The other one didn't. She can only swim so far. Now go find her. Follow the coast road—she'll have to cross that eventually. Stop at every house along the road if you have to. She'll need clothes and help. We'll worry about the other one later. Son, sometimes you're a sore disappointment to me.

Sometimes?!

Hallet!

Fischer stood still, his head hanging and his damaged left arm limp along his side. "I . . . I'll try harder, Mum."

I know you will—after all, half your blood is mine. Now go, it'll be alright to leave me here with your father for a while.

Fischer spurred into action. He walked to his room and discarded his bloody, torn shirt by throwing it into a corner. He grabbed a denim one and slid it over his injured shoulder. He hissed in pain when the stiff fabric touched the deep gouge in his shoulder and the rip in his back. Leaving the shirt unbuttoned, he cursed and walked down the stairs through the kitchen and into the den and took his father's .45 caliber revolver from its place in the gun rack. Fischer opened the small drawer below the rack, took out a box of cartridges, and filled the gun with hollow-point bullets. He returned to the kitchen, grabbed the van keys from the key rack, and left. The door slammed behind him as he stepped into the night.

———————

Cheryl followed a hiking path along the edge of the cliff. She had no idea where she was, but she believed there had to be a road or houses nearby, as they littered the seacoast.

After what seemed like hours, she discovered a dirt parking lot and saw the shine of macadam. *A road!* Now all she had to do was find a house and get help.

Less than one hundred yards from the parking area, she spied a light shining through the trees and headed for it. She turned up a sand drive and paused just out of the light. Through the window of a rundown house, she saw an obese man wearing a filthy T-shirt standing over a cowering woman. He raised his arm and slapped her. Through the partially open window, Cheryl heard him screaming at the woman, and she backed away from the window into the safety of darkness. The last thing she wanted was to appear naked before yet another brutal man. She skirted the house and breathed a sigh of relief when she saw a clothesline filled with women's clothes. She grabbed a pullover blouse and pulled it on. Just as she stepped into a pair of faded blue jeans, the light mounted on the wall beside the door illuminated her. She froze, like an animal caught in the headlights of a runaway truck. The woman she had seen through the window stood in the door, silhouetted by the light behind her.

Cheryl slid the pants up and snapped them. The jeans were a size too large but were better than running around in the nude.

"What are you doing?" the woman asked.

"Please, I need help . . . I'm running from a man."

"Who isn't?"

"You don't understand how dangerous he is."

From the knowing look on her face, Cheryl realized the woman understood. "Show me one that ain't."

"Laurie, who's out there? Who the fuck you talking to?"

The woman glanced over her shoulder and said, "Take the clothes, and get out of here."

"Please, could I use your phone? Or maybe you could call the police for me."

"I wish I could, honey, but the rotten son of a whore ripped the phone off the wall last week."

"Goddamn it, woman! I asked you a question! Who the hell are you talking to?"

The man's dark bulk appeared behind the woman. She glanced over her shoulder and then turned back to Cheryl and said, "Go on, run. There're other houses down the road. *Go!*"

Cheryl bolted for the trees. Just as she entered their safety, she heard a loud slap. Scared and fatigued, she retreated into the darkness. Exhaustion overwhelmed her; she needed to rest for a while. Her strength and stamina depleted, she dropped down and rested her back against an ancient pine; the blouse stuck to the sappy bark and pulled it up her back. *I have to get up*, she thought. *I have to keep going.* But fatigue wouldn't let her. She rolled over and curled up in exhaustion.

39

The motor sputtered and stopped—out of fuel. Bouchard slumped forward, exhausted. Too drained to guide it, she let the tide push the punt slowly toward the rocky shore. She raised her head and saw a well-lit, sprawling building complex sitting on a point that jutted out into the gulf. She wondered how much money a place like that cost. She giggled. Of all the thoughts to have at a time like this, that was probably the most ridiculous . . .

A wave pushed the punt toward the shore, and she looked at the house and saw that a party or some sort of gathering was in process. The area between the house and the shore was lit brightly with spotlights. Another breaker pushed the boat yet closer to the lights, and Bouchard heard a voice shout that there was a boat approaching the beach.

Bouchard slumped forward, allowing the surf to carry her to the shore. A couple came to the edge of the water and peered into the darkness. It took all the energy Bouchard had left for her to say, "Help me."

"Harry, it's a woman," the female said.

Harry took off his shoes, rolled up the legs of his pants and started into the surf. "I'll come get you." He waded out, grabbed the bow of the punt, and pulled it toward the beach.

Harry looked at Bouchard and exclaimed, "She's naked!"

"Wait here," the young woman said to Harry, and she ran across the lawn to the house. In several minutes she returned with a blanket. When Harry stood in place she nudged him. "Turn around and face the house, Harry."

"What for? Oh ..." When Harry turned his back to the ocean, Bouchard rolled over the side of the boat and then stood on her feet and walked ashore. The woman wrapped her in the blanket and said to Harry, "You can turn around now."

Several other partygoers noticed the activity at the water's edge and started walking toward the beach. "We better take her to the old man," Harry said.

Bouchard, not sure what was going on, darted to the punt, held the blanket with her left hand, and grabbed the rifle with her right hand.

"Honey, you don't need that rifle," the woman said in a calm voice. "No one here will hurt you."

"I can't wait to hear her explain this to the old man," another male voice said.

Bouchard lowered the rifle and slumped with exhaustion. Harry's companion and another woman rushed forward and held her up. She was barely able to mutter, "Thank you."

"Lady," Harry said, "it looks like you've had one hell of a night."

Fischer drove along the road with his headlights on high beam. He was frustrated, and with each passing minute his rage grew; thus far, the only thing he had seen was a couple of deer.

He saw an unpaved parking lot and slowed to a crawl. He parked, got out, and studied the sandy ground looking for a sign. A skilled tracker he was not; after all, he was a fisherman, not a hunter. He surveyed the area and saw a light through the trees. He got back into the van and drove until he saw a driveway, where he turned in.

He parked the truck and got out, wondering if he should bring the revolver. The sight of a fat man and a bewildered-looking woman interrupted his thoughts.

"Who the hell are you?" the man asked.

"I'm looking for my wife."

"Why in hell would you do that?" The fat man grinned as if he'd just told the world's funniest joke.

"Don't ask me. Has she been here?"

Fischer saw the woman's eyes widen with fear. He knew then that one of the women had come through here. Maybe she was inside the house. "I got a picture," he said. He reached into the truck, his action hidden by the open door. He grabbed the revolver and stepped away from the van. He cocked the hammer on the single-action weapon and aimed it at the fat man's chest.

The obese comedian staggered back, raised his hands, and stared into the van's lights with surprise. Fischer cocked the hammer and said, "Now I don't want no trouble here. But I ain't gonna take no shit, either." He took one step forward and slammed the revolver's butt into the man's forehead. The fat man fell backward onto the ground.

Fischer glanced down at the body and said, "Big bastard, ain't he."

He stepped forward and took the woman by the arm, crushing it with his strong grip until she cried out. "One of them was here. Wasn't she?" He shook her so hard that she flopped like a fish on a line. "Is she inside?"

"No one is inside," she cried, eyes wild with fear.

"We'll soon find out, won't we?"

He pushed her ahead of him into the house. It only took him five minutes to search the small house. Feeling no need to be careful, he flipped beds over, threw furniture around, and tore clothes off their hangers. He ransacked the house. When he had exhausted himself and there were no more places to search, sweat soaked his face, and it mixed with the blood that covered the back of his shirt. The jagged puncture in his shoulder and the twelve-inch gash in his back stung when salt from his perspiration trickled into them. He stood in the middle of the small kitchen gasping for breath. The woman had not lied. The place was empty—if either of them had been here, they were gone. "Where'd she go?" he asked the woman. He grabbed her by the hair and slammed her head against the wall.

The woman staggered and blurted out, "The woods, she ran toward the woods!" She pointed toward the rear of the house.

He stormed outside, stepped over the body of the unconscious man without so much as a glance, and circled around to the back of the house. He spied a clothesline, and in the middle of it was an open space. He could not think of any reason why someone would leave a space in the middle—unless something had been removed. He squatted and studied the ground. He saw the tracks of someone running barefoot toward a line of trees. He straightened up and walked toward them.

Fischer was within ten feet of a huge pine when he saw a figure slumped against it. He stepped on a twig, and the loud snap spurred her into action. She leaped to her feet, recognized him, and bolted into the woods.

Fischer recognized Cheryl and ran after her. He believed that she would not get far; he was tired after the night's activities and knew she had to be near exhausted. He saw her dash through some small bushes and blasted his way through them, ignoring the pain as a thin lash-like branch whipped across his face. He fired the revolver into the air and shouted, "The next one is going through the back of your head!"

Cheryl pulled up and bent over, supporting herself by placing her hands on her thighs as she gasped. He grabbed her by the arm, spun her around, and slapped her. As quickly as he had attacked her he stopped, smiled, and said, "Hello, darlin'... you have a nice girls' night out?"

———

Bouchard staggered as the women helped her across the lawn. A statuesque man stood at the foot of a large stone patio. "What's happening?" he asked.

"Senator, I think we got a situation here," Harry said.

Anne stared into the bright lights that lined the private wharf. Her mouth fell open in surprise. The white-headed man was one of Maine's United States senators.

"Well, let's get her inside where it's warm and find out what's going on."

"Yes, sir."

As they led her to the huge seaside mansion, Bouchard felt as helpless as she had on her first day of kindergarten.

She was so emotionally drained that she barely saw the immaculate kitchen, large enough for a five-star hotel and populated with industrial strength stainless steel appliances, as they escorted her through it. Before she knew what had happened, she was sitting across from gigantic fireplace on the most expensive sofa she'd ever seen. She slumped back and closed her eyes while gripping the blanket tight and snug around her. After several tense moments, she heard people enter the room, and she opened her eyes. What she saw startled her into a heightened state of awareness. Over the fireplace hung three expensive-looking portraits: one was of the President of the United States, another of the senator, and third was of the woman who stood beside him.

A servant appeared, and the senator said, "Julia, get us some coffee." Once the maid departed he said, "I'm . . ."

"Sir," Bouchard said, surprised at the awe she felt, "I know who you are."

The senator's wife—at least Bouchard assumed she was—sat on the couch beside her, reached over, took her hand, and patted it gently. It comforted her. "Now dear," she said, "why don't you tell us how you came to be in a boat on the Gulf of Maine naked as the day you were born?"

Bouchard stared into the warmth of the crackling fire and started at the beginning. "My name," she gathered herself, "is Anne Bouchard." One of the people behind her reached across and held a glass of water before her. Bouchard took it and gulped down a large swallow. "Thank you. I'm a private investigator." She took another drink, noting that her hands shook, but whether from exhaustion or the deep chill she felt, she didn't know. "My partner and I have been searching for a young woman who's been abducted."

When she finished her tale, the senator turned to Harry, who by this time Bouchard knew to be his aide, and said, "Harry, call the FBI. You tell them that I want the closest SAC[2] to get over here, ASAP."

---

[2] Special Agent in Charge.

40

Houston's cell rang, and he looked at the display. Susie. "Hey."

"Any word from Anne?"

"Not yet. I'm really concerned."

Before he could say more, the room phone rang, its ringer so loud that he jumped. "Hold on, babe . . ." He lifted the handset. "Houston."

"Mike, Sam. We found her . . . she's shaken but alright."

"Thank God! Where is she?"

"Wells Point at Senator Griffeth's beach estate. I'll meet you in Wells and guide you in."

"Where?"

"Get off the 'pike at exit nineteen. Take Route 9 east. I'll meet you at the junction of 9 and US 1. Oh, she wants you to bring some of her clothes."

"What?"

"It's a long story. I'm sure she'll fill you in when you get here."

"I'm on my way." He hung up and put his cell to his ear.

"I heard," Susie said. "Take me with you."

"Are you in the dorm?"

"Yes." She gave him the address. "I'll be out front on the sidewalk."

Houston glanced at the digital clock. "Not at this hour you won't. Wait in the foyer, and I'll come for you."

"Dad, I'm not a little girl anymore." He heard the exasperation in her voice.

"I know. That's why you'll wait inside the building."

"Okay."

Houston and his daughter arrived at the rendezvous with Fuchs at two in the morning. They followed Fuchs for five miles until they came to a gated complex. A security guard checked Fuchs's credentials and then waved them through. In his headlights, Houston saw a stately coastal mansion.

"Wow," Susie commented when she saw the house. "So this is what it means to have money."

Houston's disdain for politicians came out. "Yeah, one of the perks of being a public servant. These people have set themselves up very well."

He saw Susie give him a quizzical look.

"Our elected officials have voted themselves a salary six times higher than the average personal salary. I don't want to get going on the other perks and benefits."

He saw the look on her face morph from quizzical to surprise. "I had no idea you felt so strongly about politics," she said.

"All my life I've been a victim of politics. You've heard the saying 'Them that can do. Them that can't teach'? Well, I think teachers get a raw deal. It should be: Them that can do. Them that can't become politicians and get in the way of them that can. Bottom line, I have no use for these people. In the *real* world, if anyone was as nonproductive as them, they'd be fired."

Without further discourse, he exited the pickup truck. Fuchs stood beside his state police car, and Houston noted him staring at Susie. "Sam Fuchs, this is my daughter. Susie, Sam Fuchs, Maine State Police."

Susie offered her hand and said, "Pleased to meet you."

"How is Anne?" Houston asked.

"I'm told all things considered, she's fine. The senator was throwing a party, and a couple of the attendees were doctors."

"She needed a doctor?" Houston replied, his brow furrowed with concern.

"Possible concussion. She has a nice shiner, too. That, my friend, is all I know." With that, he led them inside the house.

When she saw Houston walk into the room, Bouchard wanted to run to him, but professional decorum prevented her from doing so. She saw the concern on his face and that was sufficient for her.

Susie, however, had no such restrictions. She ran across the room and into Bouchard's arms. Anne held her close and gently stroked her hair. She knew that better than anyone in the room, Susie knew what was going on inside her head. Susie, too, had once been abducted.

"I'm fine, Suze."

Houston, too, fought back the impulse to take his partner into his arms. He watched as the two most important women in his life embraced each other and realized how close he'd come to losing each of them.

When the initial greetings and questions of concern were over, Houston got down to business. "How did he get you?"

Bouchard blushed, and he knew that she, too, was aware of how foolish her actions had been. Going after a perp alone was against everything they'd ever learned as police officers. "After you went onto the boat, I watched his place from the bluff overlooking it. I saw a woman in a window, and I went down. The door was unlocked, so I went inside. He had her—Cheryl. There's also an old woman in there. She's incapacitated. I believe she has either advanced dementia or Alzheimer's. Cheryl was locked inside an upstairs room. Once I was certain it was Cheryl, I turned to get something to break the lock—and he was there."

She completed the telling of her harrowing experience, omitting some of the racier aspects of her brief captivity.

"So," Fuchs said, "Cheryl escaped, too."

THE FISHERMAN | 205

"I don't know, we went into the water together but got separated. I tried to locate her but couldn't find any sign of her."

Fuchs looked at Houston. "I need to get this out. We already have people at Fischer's place, but the Coast Guard needs to search the water between here and there just in case ..." He refrained from saying what everyone knew was a possibility, that Cheryl had drowned.

"I want to go with you," Houston said.

Fuchs nodded, took his cell phone out of his pocket, and was already talking to someone as he walked out of the room.

"I'm going, too," Bouchard added.

"No." An elderly man stepped forward.

"Who are you?" Houston asked.

"Doctor Leland Hathaway. Ms. Bouchard needs to stay here ... at least for this evening. She has been concussed and needs to be under medical supervision."

Houston nodded reassuringly at his partner. "It's for the best, Anne. Susie, I need you to stay here with her."

Without further discussion, Houston followed in Fuchs's wake.

Sam Fuchs turned into the drive and saw a couple of uniformed state police officers talking with an obese man. He parked behind a couple of cruisers and got out. He recognized Jeff Littlefield, the Maine State Police officer assigned to this district, and motioned him over. Once he felt certain that they were out of hearing range, he asked, "What've we got, Jeff?"

"Hi, Sam. It appears to be an assault."

"This the vic?"

"Yes, George Blanchette and his wife, Mildred. He's a born loser. I busted him a couple times for DUI, and we've been here a few times on domestic abuse calls."

Fuchs studied the Blanchettes.

Fuchs stood up and looked toward the house. He turned to the local cop and said, "Secure this area, and don't screw the scene up any more than is necessary."

Fuchs motioned for Houston to join him and walked to Blanchette. He showed his badge and said, "Detective Fuchs, Maine State Police. What happened here, sir?"

"Some psycho drives in and wanted to know if we'd seen his fuckin' wife. When I said I ain't seen no friggin' woman, he whacked me with the butt end of a goddamned gun." He looked at his wife. "It seems she *was* here, hiding in the woods."

Fuchs turned to the wife and said, "You saw the woman?"

"Yes, she was as naked as the day she was born. I caught her trying to steal clothes from my line. I told her to take them and get out of here."

Fuchs showed her a picture of Cheryl Guerette. "Is this the woman?"

"Yes. He found her over there." She pointed to the line of trees about fifty feet from where they stood.

"Then what?"

"He took her and . . ." She cast a nervous look at her husband. "I ran to a neighbor's house and called 911."

41

Everette Halsey walked out of his house and stopped short. Jimmy O'Leary and Gordon Winter stood in his drive, leaning against Halsey's silver Mercedes. "What's the meaning of this?" Halsey demanded.

"Shut up, Everette. We got some business to do," O'Leary said. He motioned for Halsey to precede him to the black SUV parked at the curb. "We thought we'd give you a ride to work."

O'Leary took Halsey by the arm and guided him into the back seat. He stood beside the door, waited for Winter to get in with Halsey, and then walked around and got behind the wheel. He saw the fear in Halsey's face when Winter placed his arm around the lawyer's shoulders and grinned.

The lawyer tried to open the door. O'Leary said, "Ain't those child-proof locks wonderful, Ev?" He lit a cigarette and exhaled smoke in his face.

"Jimmy, you know I don't like smoking," Halsey complained. He tried to sound as if he were in control, but a nervous quiver gave him away.

"Would it surprise you to know that about now, I could give a fuck less what you do or don't like? I got some questions for you, and how you answer will determine whether or not I turn Gordon loose on your sorry ass."

Winter took his right hand off the lawyer's shoulder, placed it on his thigh, and began to squeeze. He smiled when Halsey began to squirm.

"What's this about, Jimmy?"

"A kid named Inca."

Halsey started, caught himself, and then tried to bluff his way out of what was obviously a bad situation. "I don't know anyone by that name."

"Bullshit," O'Leary said.

Winter increased the pressure of his grip until Halsey cried out in pain and leered at him as O'Leary pulled out of the driveway and drove down the street.

"Now, Everette, you've always been a no-nonsense type of guy, so I'm going to give it to you straight. You're a very, very well-paid pimp, Ev. Last night we took down your little amusement park on the Cape. I took the women—all but your fancy fucking madam. She was a dedicated employee, Ev—right to the end. Broad had infinitely more balls than you, I might add."

O'Leary blew another cloud of smoke into the confined area. "Seems that there was an item missing from the inventory though . . ."

Halsey said nothing.

O'Leary studied the lawyer through the rearview mirror. There was fear in the attorney's gaze, and O'Leary smiled. "I want that girl, Everette."

"Jimmy, you got no idea what you've done."

"That I do, bucko. I got all the accounting files, complete with names, addresses, and amounts. Ariana missed her calling; she'd have been one hell of a CPA."

"These people will crush you."

"That's been tried before. I'm still here—those that tried ain't." O'Leary stopped the SUV, turned around, and slapped Halsey on the side of his head. "Now are you going to take us to the girl or do I have to let Gordon take over this little interview? I got to warn you, his methods are a shitload more direct than mine."

Halsey was afraid to look at Winter directly, but from the corner of his eye, he tried to read his face. Winter was stoic, as emotional as an eighty-year-old nun.

"Where we going, boss?" Winter asked.

"To the warehouse in Chelsea . . . it's private there—and quiet. You could set off a bomb in there, and nobody would hear a thing."

"Jimmy," Halsey said, "I'll level with you. I don't have her."

"Oh? That ain't what Ariana said. I doubt that a dying woman would lie. Ain't that right, Gordon?"

"Yup, no reason I can think of for someone with a slug in her chest to lie."

"I did hear her right, didn't I, Gordon? Did she not say that she gave the girl to ol' Everette here?"

"That's the way I heard it, boss." Winter turned to Halsey. "If I was you, Ev ol' boy, I'd start telling the truth. The boss has been known to become unstable when he gets lied to."

"Alright," Halsey said, "I did have her."

O'Leary stared at the lawyer through the rearview mirror.

"It's not what you think, Jimmy. Jesus, I'm no pedophile."

"That remains to be seen," O'Leary said. "If you don't have her now, where is she?"

"I sold her—"

"You sold her?" Halsey flinched when O'Leary shouted in the confined space.

Halsey's shoulders slumped, and he bent his head forward. "Yes, I sold her."

O'Leary ground out his cigarette in the ashtray and hissed. "Before this is all over, Everette, I may sell your ass to a tribe of fudge-packing U-Bangies. You're lower than whale shit, you know that? Running around in your fucking thousand-dollar suits acting like a big shot. I've always wondered how cocksuckers like you last as long as you do. Killing you is going to be a public service."

Halsey began to sob softly.

42

Fuchs and Houston arrived at Fischer's house before dawn. They spent two hours sitting on the porch of the dilapidated house. It took all of their willpower to keep from barging inside the house, but discipline learned over the years made them wait until the search warrant arrived. A car pulled into the drive, and a uniformed state police officer got out.

"You get the warrant?" Fuchs asked.

The cop nodded and held up a folded piece of paper. "Judge gave us everything we asked for. We can tear this place down if we have to."

"Okay," Fuchs took the proffered paper, "let's get to it."

They entered the dark house, and the first thing they noticed was the stench. The place smelled like a landfill on a tropical day. They stepped into the kitchen, and Houston curled his face. "Jesus Christ. This guy hasn't washed a dish in ten years."

Filthy dishes, pots, and pans covered the sink and sideboards. Foodstuff had caked dry on the plates, and when Fuchs snapped on the lights, the surface of the counters seemed to move as thousands of roaches stampeded. Empty cans and paper wrappers littered the floor; newspapers and old magazines covered the table and were stacked everywhere. When they walked across the floor, the detectives' shoes stuck to the linoleum surface.

"How can anyone live like this?" Houston asked, more to himself than to Fuchs.

Fuchs chuckled. "You should spend some time patrolling the backwoods. There are places that make this look heavenly. At least this place has floors. I've been in places where the floors are packed dirt."

Houston shook his head. "I've been in some of Boston's worst slums, and I've never seen anything this bad." He kicked an empty can. "I'm going to look around upstairs."

Houston climbed the stairs and walked into the first room he came to. He took care not to touch anything as he slowly circumvented the bed, stepping over the ruins of several torn photographs. On the floor, by the bed, he saw the remnants of a broken lamp. He crouched down beside it, saw what appeared to be blood, and wondered if it had been the weapon Anne had used to subdue him. He turned and spied an open closet. He stuck his head through the door and saw that it contained women's clothes hanging above a cedar chest pushed against the wall. He used a handkerchief to keep from leaving fingerprints and looked at the clothes; it was obvious to him what the owners' profession had been; he squatted down and opened the chest. It was filled with women's purses. "Holy shit," he muttered. "There has to more than fifty in here . . ." Knowing that he had better leave the room for the crime scene technicians, Houston walked into the hall.

Houston spied three other doors and opened the one closest to him. Before entering the room, he stopped and clamped his hand over his mouth. The stink was horrible. He reached inside and felt along the wall until he found a light switch and flipped it, turning on the overhead light. The source of the smell was immediately apparent. An emaciated old woman lay on the bed. Waste covered the sheets under her, and her nightclothes were soiled. She stared at the ceiling through unseeing eyes. "Aw shit," he muttered. He walked to the old canopy bed and paused, unwilling to touch the filthy woman. Finally, he overcame his distaste and placed two fingers on her carotid artery. There was a pulse.

He backed out of the room, stood at the top of the stairs, and called out, "Sam."

Fuchs came out of the kitchen and looked up the stairs. "Yeah?"

"I found the woman Anne told us about. You'd better get up here . . . call the EMTs."

Banned from the house while the CSU team went through it, Houston walked toward the square cinderblock building that he and Fuchs assumed to be some sort of factory. He saw a side door open and turned in that direction. A state cop walked out of the door and bent over. He had a handkerchief over his face and was breathing deep. His face, in spite of his five o'clock shadow, was pallid. The trooper stood in the threshold of the door, blocking entry. He noticed Houston's shadow and straightened up. He inhaled and said, "You can't go in there. It's a crime scene."

A screen door slammed, and Houston saw Sam Fuchs walk out of the house. He glanced up and turned to the building. When he was beside Houston, Fuchs said, "What's up, Elton?"

"It ain't good, Sam. There are bodies in there."

"Bodies . . . plural?"

"There are three hanging in a reefer unit. It looks like this guy was disposing of them. He's got enough machinery in there to open his own meat packing plant."

Fuchs shook his head and turned to Houston. "Well, I guess we know why we haven't found any bodies."

He turned to the uniformed officer and motioned to Houston. "I'll take him in with me."

The cop stood aside. "I warn you, it isn't pretty."

The interior was dark, and Houston had to be wary so he did not bump into anything as he waited for his eyes to adjust. The room looked like the butcher shop in a slaughterhouse: machinery and stainless steel tables lined the walls. Most of it appeared unused, and dust coated it. He wondered how long it had been since anyone used it. They saw two officers standing beside an industrial-strength band saw and walked to them. A cursory look told Houston that this machine had been worked and often. The saw blade glistened in the harsh artificial light; what appeared to be dried blood and bits of meat and flesh stuck to the blade's teeth. Immediately to the saw's left were grinders—big ones with their outlets poised over plastic pails. "Jesus," Houston said. "He was cutting them up and grinding them into who knows what."

Fuchs turned and said, "I think we'd better leave this for the crime scene technicians." He took Houston by the arm and led him toward the back, where a walk-in reefer stood. When they opened the reefer's door, cold air rolled out creating an eerie fog that covered the floor to just below their knees. Houston thought it was like entering the scene of a 1930s horror movie. They walked into the fog and stopped immediately. The bodies of three women hung from meat hooks.

Houston shook his head in horror and disgust. "What the hell was he doing?"

"Based upon what we found in the bait wells of his boat," Fuchs said, "if I was a gambler, I'd bet he was making chum."

43

Fischer stood back in the trees and watched the activity at his home. There were six police cars in the yard, and people were scurrying around like ants after their mound was kicked and destroyed. Movement caught his eye, and he saw an ambulance drive into the yard. His heart jumped. *Was Mum alright?* A cold rage immediately replaced his concern. If anyone had hurt her, he would make them all pay for it.

He kept his vigil until he saw the EMTs wheel a gurney from the house, slide it into the back of an ambulance, and drive off. He spun on his heel and raced through the woods to his truck. He had to find out where they were taking her. Once he knew she was safe, there would be time for any reckoning that was in store.

Back in the van, he reached behind the passenger seat and raised one edge of the canvas that covered his cargo. Cheryl stared at him, her mouth sealed shut with duct tape. He checked her bonds to ensure she was secure. He slammed the side door, circled the truck, and got in. When the motor started, he put it in gear and drove down the tree-lined lane to the main road. He sighed with relief when he saw the ambulance disappear over a rise. He followed.

Fischer studied the hospital grounds, paying particular attention to the area near the emergency entrance. Vehicles from the local police, Sheriff's Department, and the Maine State Police were scattered around the parking lot. Several other cars were unmarked but bore government plates. "Shit." He wondered if the unmarked cars belonged to the FBI. Most likely they did not have to ask the Feds to interfere; he had crossed the borders of three states with his women, and that was all the Feds needed to stick their noses into the investigation.

He was sure that his identity was now common knowledge to the cops. If they had not figured out who he was, the damned woman would have told them. He should have killed that last bitch when he found her in the house; Cheryl was another issue—one he would deal with in time.

He turned his attention back to the building. There was no way he was going to get in using the door. He pounded the steering wheel in frustration.

If you don't calm down, you'll never get inside.

Fischer stared at the entrance to the building. "Shut up, old man."

That attitude is what's going to be your downfall, dummy. Get under control and scout the area.

Willard took several deep breaths, calming himself. Eventually, his heartbeat slowed.

Willard took the keys from the ignition, got out of the car, and tried to appear nonchalant as he walked toward the hospital. Fortunately, it was not a major facility; it was a single-story building intended for emergency and minor afflictions—major cases they sent to bigger hospitals, such as Southern Maine Medical Center in Portland. A row of mature fully bloomed rhododendron bushes created a dense hedge surrounding the building like castle walls. A closer inspection showed a two- or three-foot gap between the plants and the building—an ideal place for him to get close enough to search the rooms through the windows. Even though his thought processes were impaired from lack of sleep, he realized how big a risk he was taking. It was daylight, albeit early morning, and until he reached the cover afforded by the blooming rhododendrons, he would be exposed. Nevertheless, Mum was in there somewhere, and he was going to do his best to find her. He strolled up the walk that led to the emergency entrance and stopped beside the shrubbery. Fischer pulled the visor of his cap down to hide his face, looked around to ensure that he was unobserved, and then slipped inside the bushes.

He crouched as he scampered between the hedge and the brick wall and took care to remain unobserved as he stopped at each window and peered inside the rooms. The first seven windows had shades drawn, making it impossible to discern what was inside. He continued checking every window until he finally found her. He used a pocketknife to pry the window open and studied her for a few seconds. Lying in the uncomfortable-looking hospital bed, hooked up to several different machines and bottles, made her seem smaller and frailer than when he took care of her. Her eyes seemed to have sunken into her head, and her prominent hook nose pointed toward the ceiling. He surveyed the room. It was semi-private, and the second bed was unoccupied, although from the state of the bedding, it appeared to have been recently occupied. "Mum?" he kept his voice low so he would not be overheard.

So you finally got here? His mother admonished him.

"I got here as soon as I could. Cops were crawling all over the house."

Excuses always sound good to the person makin' them. Did you find the women?

"I got one of them."

Who got away?

He stared at his feet. "The new one. I got Cheryl."

His mother's voice was filled with resignation when she said, *Well, I guess all that we can do now is run. Get me out of here.*

"I can't, Mum. Where can I put you that's safe?"

You're useless, just like your father. What are you going to do, leave me here with a bunch of heathens? Look at me! Her voice changed, as if she had realized that he was right. It would be impossible for him to care for her while living out of his truck. *I guess you are right, son. Nevertheless, you need to find that woman before the police find you.*

"But, Mum, it won't matter because the cops already know who I am and where the house is."

Witnesses, you friggin' moron, those women are the only witnesses. Kill them, and they got nothing on you. His father reproached him.

His words stung. He turned to his mother for support. "Mum ..."

Don't "Mum" me. As much as I hate to admit it, your father is right. Now get on out of here—you got work to do.

"What good will it do to kill Cheryl? I'm sure that they already found the ones in the reefer. Besides, they can't make a wife testify against her husband."

When did you marry that slut? As for them bodies, they got no proof you put them there. They got to prove you took them harlots, and if the other two are gone, there ain't no one to link you to them. Now go on, do what needs doing. I'll be fine. You can come for me once the chore is done.

Fischer said, "Bye, Mum. I'll be back for you. I promise."

Get some rest, and then go find that woman.

He walked to the window, and as he exited, he heard his father's angry voice, *Useless! Woman, I oughta beat you silly ...*

Fischer tossed and turned. With every movement, the puncture in his shoulder and the gash across his back sent stabbing pain racing through him. He rolled over, taking his weight off the wounds, and cursed. He reached for the aspirin on the nightstand, shook five from the plastic container, and washed them down with a glass of water. Then he went into the bathroom, where he bent over the bathtub and checked Cheryl's bindings. He sat on the toilet and looked into her eyes. "I trusted you," he said, "and you were disloyal. Now we got to start at the beginning."

She muttered into the duct tape that covered her mouth, it sounded like a mumble. He ripped the tape from her mouth. "What?"

"I'll be good, I promise."

"You got to pay for going against your husband." He realigned her position in the tub and turned the shower on just enough for water to drip, hitting her on the forehead. "Your first punishment. You lay still until I say otherwise. Not a single movement!"

A slow flow of water dripped from the showerhead, hitting her forehead. Cheryl's eyes closed, and she flinched with each drop.

He replaced the tape over her swollen lips and left the bathroom door open when he exited. He paced back and forth, spanning the cheap hotel room in three strides. Wistfully, he thought of his own room. He sighed. Thinking of home made him think of Mum—and the horrible thing he had done. He was certain Mum had taught him that the Bible spoke against a son deserting his mother. He couldn't remember where it was; maybe it was in Revelations. Yes, he was sure—it had to be; that was her favorite book. He felt lost, alone, and adrift. For the first time in his life, he had no place to go and nobody to help him. He cursed the cops and Anne Bouchard for putting him in a position where he had to leave Mum in that hospital. Now, he was certainly doomed to spend eternity in Hell. Anger built. Anne Bouchard had made it so he would never feel the Lord's love.

44

O'Leary sat behind his desk, sucking on one of his endless
stream of cigarettes, and finished off the coffee he had been
nursing for the past ten minutes. "You take care of Halsey?"

Winter took a sip of soda and leaned back in his chair. "Yup, you want
to know how?"

"Nope, that's one less thing a prosecutor can try to get out of me."

"You won't have to worry about that."

O'Leary glanced at the television set that sat in the corner of his office.
The scene on the twenty-four hour news channel was of the manse.
"Well," he said, "the heat is about to be turned up."

"We can handle it."

"We always have, haven't we? You know, Gordon, there are days when
I feel like maybe I should scrap it all—drop everything except this place.
Today is one of those days."

Winter shrugged. "There's always tomorrow. The feeling will pass."

O'Leary ground out the cigarette. "Yeah," he replied, "there's always
tomorrow."

"Besides, you'd get bored if all you did was pour booze and listen to
every drunk in Southie's tale of woe."

"Yeah, you're right," O'Leary said. "You locate the ship yet?"

"Yeah, as you thought, Halsey sold the kid to Yuri. She's on his boat."

"Ship, Gordon. You and I may own a boat, but Yuri captains a ship."

"Either way, it's just a hole in the water you dump money into."

"Are you sure he's got her?"

"As they say on that millionaire show: Yes, final answer."

"You got everything set up?"

"As much as it can be."

"It could get nasty when we hit them. There ain't a lot of room for maneuvering on that thing."

"Yeah, but they won't have any more room than us."

"But it's their turf."

"We'll handle it."

"Yuri's crew looked as if they know one end of a gun from the other."

Winter stood up, drained his cola, and said, "Knowing how to shoot and doing it accurately with someone blasting away at you can be two different things."

"Okay, tell the boys it's a go."

"Around two in the morning should work best," Winter said.

"Really, what makes you say that?"

"Experience. When I was in the Army we'd always attack around then. Anyone on watch will be too busy thinking about a warm bed to pay attention to what's going on. Everyone else will be sound asleep then, and there should be less activity, fewer people about. I always hated the mid-watch myself."

"Any chance Yuri will sail before then?" O'Leary asked.

"Slim. They haven't even started preparations for getting underway."

"Have everyone here at twelve."

Gordon walked out of the office. O'Leary leaned back and stared at the news. He watched silently as EMTs carried gurneys bearing sheet-covered bodies from the manse. He opened one of the ledgers and looked up a name and number. He took out a cell phone he had bought for just this call, punched in the digits and sat back.

"Governor, I'm fairly certain that you don't know me, and my name isn't really important. I have some documentation in front of me that could really shake up the voters. What with this being an election year and all, I thought you'd appreciate a call ..."

He listened for a few seconds. "How'd I get your private number? Hell, Guv, all you need is a computer. No, not the internet—a laptop I got at a certain house on the Cape."

O'Leary's face cracked. "I see there's an investigation into some killings down there. Nope, not murders, killings. They were all self-defense. Still, you never know what might come out in an investigation. Do you know what I mean?"

O'Leary punched the off button and cackled. *Something tells me,* he thought, *this investigation will run into a dead end.*

———

"Why is it every time we come down here it's cold and foggy?"

O'Leary turned to the offender. "Shut your yap. You're getting paid good money for this job."

The man nodded. "Sure, boss."

As they walked across the parking lot, O'Leary muttered to Winter in a low voice. "He's right though."

"You just don't like docks and ships, boss."

"I'm not too crazy about the people who work on them, either. There's a funky smell about them, especially the sailors."

Winter wondered if O'Leary ever noticed the reek of cigarettes that hovered around him. He smiled and said nothing.

They gathered at the bottom of the gangplank.

"Everyone clear on what we're here for?" O'Leary asked.

He looked at each man in turn. Satisfied they knew their objective, he said, "Okay, let's do this."

The assault team screwed noise suppressors onto the muzzles of their semiautomatic pistols. They checked the action and magazines to ensure a round was in the chamber. Weapon in hand, O'Leary led them up the gangplank.

As he neared the top, a sailor appeared. "Is Yuri on board?" O'Leary asked.

The seaman noted the number of men climbing toward the ship's entrance. His eyes narrowed with suspicion, and he reached for his hip. O'Leary did not hesitate and shot him in the chest. "I'm going to take that as a yes," he said. He stepped onto the deck and turned left toward the door that led to the ship's interior. Winter followed him, and the three others turned right, heading toward the front of the ship.

O'Leary and Winter entered the hatch and into a narrow corridor leading to the bowels of the ship. They wasted no time, heading for the lower decks. At the bottom of the stairs another sailor confronted them. His eyes widened with surprise at the sight of armed men, and he, too, reached for a weapon. Winter took him out with a single shot and then turned to O'Leary. "I've never seen a commercial vessel where every son of a bitch is carrying. The cells are this way, boss." He opened a door and started down another metal stair.

"I'm not crazy about this, Gordon," O'Leary commented. "Not a lot of places to take cover."

"Yeah, if they catch us in one of these passageways, we'll be like fish in a barrel."

"There's going to be a change of plans, Gordon."

"Kind of late to improvise, isn't it?"

O'Leary shrugged. "Probably, but Yuri is going down. If he doesn't, he'll keep on doing this shit."

"You're the boss. You tell me what you want done, and I'll do it."

"Right."

They entered a hatch and scrambled down two flights of the metal stairs where Winter stopped beside yet another metal hatch. "If I remember correctly, this is the deck where the cells are," he said.

O'Leary nodded, and Winter opened the hatch and stepped through it. They saw the cells and looked into each one as they passed. They were all empty. "Maybe it isn't this ship," Winter said.

"Or that bastard Yuri is sampling the wares . . ."

"Captain's cabin is usually not far from the bridge and the radio room."

They ran down the passageway and up the stairs. At the top, they walked into the ship's communications center. Winter pushed the door open and leaped through. O'Leary watched the corridor behind them until he heard the muffled sounds of shots. He entered the small room.

Winter stood beside a radio console. The radio operator lay across the desk with one side of his head bloody.

"Which way you figure to the captain's quarters?" O'Leary asked.

Winter pointed to a door at the rear of the room. "I believe that that door leads to the captain's quarters. He walked to the door and turned the knob. "It's not locked, but I'll lay you even money Yuri is in there."

Jimmy studied the metal door. "And he's probably armed . . . I know I would be."

"Follow me," Winter said. He pushed the door open and then burst through it. A second later, O'Leary jumped through the open door and found Winter pointing his pistol at a cowering Yuri.

The captain's back was against the wall. He looked comical, clad in nothing but a pair of dingy boxer shorts with his hands in the air. "Don't shoot!" Yuri yelled.

"Shut up," O'Leary said.

He studied the room. Compared to the other rooms on the ship it was large. *Rank has its privileges*, he thought.

Inca cowered in a corner, her hands in front of her face. O'Leary said, "Keep him covered," and went to the girl. He squatted before her. "You okay?"

Unable to speak the terrified girl nodded.

"Did he . . . ?" He fumbled for the right words.

She shook her head.

O'Leary stood up and faced Yuri. "Gorky, I can forgive you for trying to beat me out of my money. But this," he pointed to Inca, "I can't abide."

Gorky suddenly lunged for a nightstand and pulled open a drawer. He grabbed a gun, and O'Leary shot him in the forehead.

He reached out a hand to Inca. "Come on, honey. No one is going to hurt you now. It's over."

As if on cue, several shots rang out. The loud pops were immediately followed by the dull sounds of silenced weapons. Winter rose to his feet and said, "Easy for you to say. We better get out of here. After those shots, this ship's going to be crawling with cops and who knows who else."

Jimmy O'Leary leaned against the edge of his desk with his legs crossed. His right arm bent upward, he spun a lit cigarette back and forth between his forefinger and thumb. He was deep in thought and staring at the wall but seeing nothing. He puffed on the cigarette, held the smoke in his lungs for a few seconds, and then expelled it with an explosive burst. He thought about Ariana's ledgers, filled with the names of affluent and politically powerful people—none of whom were going to accept having someone know of their involvement in a prostitution and white slavery ring. There were going to be repercussions for his attacks on the manse and the ship.

Winter walked into the office and dropped into a chair. "We're as ready as we can be."

"They're going to come at us hard."

"Yup."

"The question is how."

"I doubt," Winter said, "it will be through the cops. The last thing these people want is publicity."

"That's how I figure it, too."

"I got the guys scattered in a few safe houses around town."

"Good," Jimmy ground out his cigarette.

"They'll hit here, too," Gordon said as calmly as if he were recounting the score of yesterday's Red Sox game.

"Can't be helped."

"Still, it doesn't make sense you sitting here waiting for them."

Jimmy shrugged. "If I disappear it will look as if I'm scared. Then how long will I be in business?"

"Okay, but I got a few of the guys spread around the neighborhood in case they do try something here."

"Best bet is after hours. They'd have to be nuts to hit while the bar is full."

Winter shifted in his seat. "People as powerful as these may not give a damn. They may even think they're untouchable."

"No one is untouchable. Not you, not me, and not them."

Uncomfortable in the smoky room, Winter stood. "It's your call, boss. I think I'll roam around a bit, sort of check out the area."

"You do that."

———

Winter strolled into the Charlestown Pub and sat at the bar. Before he got settled, the bartender placed a Maker's Mark and ginger ale in front of him. He nodded at the bartender, threw a twenty-dollar bill on the bar, and asked, "How's things, Larry?"

"Not bad, Gordon. How's with you? You haven't been around in a while."

"Yeah, I been busy."

"So I've heard. Come to think of it, I been hearing a lot about you and Jimmy of late."

This piqued Winter's interest. "What have you heard?"

"Just that you guys have pissed off some heavy hitters, and they're planning on squaring the books."

"You got names?"

"Nah, you know how it is . . . more bullshit flies around this place than at the Chicago stockyards. I do know one thing, though: most of the names I'm hearing are Russian."

Winter sipped his drink. "You hear any more, I want to know about it."

"Sure, Gordon," Larry began wiping the bar. He glanced around to ensure no one was close enough to hear. "I did hear one thing though. Jimmy needs to engage his brain before he runs his mouth. Word is he went so far as to call the governor—if he did that, it was about as fucking stupid as you can get. There's a big contract out on Jimmy."

"That's been tried before, and Jimmy's still around—the shooters aren't."

"Yeah, only this time I hear the shooters won't have to worry about repercussions."

"There are always repercussions."

"Not if the shooters know that cops been told to stay out of it . . . there's only one person with the firepower to do that."

Winter looked up from his drink and smiled. "In that case, the governor better watch his ass because I'll be the repercussion . . ."

45

L uca Power called Houston. "I got something you may find interesting."

"Lay it on me."

"Your boy Fischer has three siblings: a brother, killed in an accident about twenty years ago, and two sisters—one's dead, and the other lives up north in Aroostook County."

"Aroostook County. . . . I hope you have a phone number."

"Nope, but I got in touch with the Sheriff up there. He knows her and says she's one of those back-to-nature types—no phone, no television . . . hell, he's surprised she owns a truck. He said he'd be more than happy to have one of his deputies take you out there. Either way, it looks as if you got a drive ahead of you."

Houston grimaced at the thought of driving three hundred miles one way. "You got a name for me?"

"She's either an old maid or divorced and took back her maiden name. First name is Ernestine."

"Ernestine?"

"Hey, I didn't name her, and I've heard worse. A friend of mine's last name is Hazzard. His old man must have been drunk when he was born—named him Rhode."

"Where do I meet this deputy?"

"County jail in Houlton. They're expecting your call."

Houston glanced at the time on his phone; it was eight in the morning. He could be in Houlton by two or three and maybe he would be able to talk with Ernestine Fischer today.

He hung up the phone and turned to Bouchard. "I have to go up north."

"Not alone you don't."

"Anne, you should rest." He crossed the room and sat on the bed beside her. "I heard you last night."

She gave him a surprised look. "Oh."

He pulled her tightly against his chest and in a soft voice said, "You don't need to hide in the bathroom to cry. I do have a shoulder you can use."

"Mike . . . never before have I felt so embarrassed and humiliated."

"What about the big H?"

She pushed back and gave him a questioning look.

"Helpless. You and I are cops. We're accustomed to always being in control. He took that away from you."

Her voice was muffled when she said, "What really bothers me is . . ."

"What?"

She wiped at the tears that trickled down her cheeks and said, "When we had him unconscious, Cheryl wanted to kill him, and I wouldn't let her. If I had, she wouldn't be in his hands right now, and this whole mess would be over."

"You did what you thought was right. All your life you've dedicated yourself to saving people. Killing anyone—especially someone who is defenseless—is against everything you've worked for."

"Would you have done it?" she asked.

"Killed him? I don't know. That's one of those questions that in order to answer truthfully, you'd have to be there."

"I tried to kill him with the boat. If I'm ever given another chance, I will."

He gently pulled her to him and took her in his arms again.

"If we're going north, we should get started," she said.

He chuckled. "Would you please let me be the macho one? Just for a while?"

She smiled and once again wiped at the tears that soaked her cheek. "Only if you promise not to listen to sports talk radio all the way up there."

Houston pulled off exit 302 on I-95 and turned right, following his GPS to School Street in downtown Houlton. He pulled into a visitor parking spot and entered the building. Houston approached the counter and saw a fit officer standing before it talking to a seated man, whom Houston assumed was the dispatcher. In spite of the gray in the man's hair, he looked as if he could still pass the most stringent military workout. Houston paused and waited until the two officers finished their discussion. The officer sitting behind the counter had sergeant's emblems on his shirt, and Houston addressed him. "I'm Michael Houston, and this is my partner, Anne Bouchard. Sheriff Power of York County called."

The athletic officer held his hand out. "Glad to meet you. I'm Sheriff Gendreau. I spoke with Luca this morning. Why don't we talk in my office?" He turned to the desk sergeant and said, "Get hold of Wera, and ask her to come in."

Once they were in Gendreau's office, a deputy walked in and stood beside Bouchard and the Sheriff. "This is Wera Eklund, she'll be taking you to see the Fischer woman. Wera, this is Mike Houston and his partner, Anne Bouchard. They're the investigators from downstate that Sam Fuchs called about." Gendreau motioned for them to sit and leaned against his desk. "Before you go, Sheriff Power didn't give me a lot of specifics—only that he was checking some stuff out. Is there something we should worry about here?"

"Truthfully, Sheriff, we don't know. We've been hired to look for a missing young woman. To make a long story short, she was a student in Boston who got involved with drugs and ended up working the streets.

In the course of our investigation, we've learned that there have been a number of disappearances of prostitutes in Boston."

"What does this have to do with Ernestine Fischer?"

"Her younger brother, Willard, is believed to be our perp, and he's disappeared. We're hoping that she can shed some light on things."

Gendreau straightened up. "Well, she lives in what was once Howe Brook Village on the shore of Lake St. Croix."

"Is it that far?"

"On good roads," Eklund said, "a couple of hours. However, the last thirty miles will be on logging roads, and with all the rain we've had this summer it could be rough going. What are you driving?"

"A Ford F-150."

"If it isn't a four-by-four, you might have a problem getting there in that," Gendreau said. "It's been a wet summer, and those woods roads can become impassable without four-wheel drive. You'd better to go in Eklund's SUV."

Eklund checked her watch. "It's 2:45 . . . it doesn't get dark until eight, so we should be able to get over there."

Eklund drove south on I-95. The speed limit between Stillwater Avenue north of Bangor to Houlton was seventy-five, and she took advantage of the fact that she drove a sheriff's car and did ninety. They left the interstate at the exit for Oakfield and Smyrna Mills, where they picked up US 2. From there they followed State Route 212 to Knowles Corner and the intersection of State Route 11. "In twenty miles we'll turn off. We're still an hour from Ernestine's farm."

"She farms?" Houston looked at the endless expanse of woods. "In the middle of the woods?"

"Ernestine is a bit of an eccentric. She's into organic everything. Her farm isn't much more than a clearing along Howe Brook. There used to be a village there back in the fifties and sixties. The logging companies built a store, train station, and hotel of sorts. They had a saw mill in there, but once they'd cut all the spruce and pine they could, they tore down the mill and their buildings and then burned what they didn't want. After that, it became a weekend getaway and sort of hippie haven. There isn't much left now—just some camps and Ernie Fischer living there."

"The logging company just decided to close down and destroyed an entire village?"

"It was different back then. There was an infestation of a parasite called the spruce budworm, and they took out all the trees they could before the worm destroyed them. It did help to end the problem."

"It must take a particular type of person to live out here," Bouchard said. "I thought where we live is remote, but this is miles away from anything."

Eklund laughed. "This is the only place I know of where you first head to nowhere and then turn left to get to it. Still, the lifestyle is simple—and in a way inexpensive, seeing as there's no place to spend money. These last ten years or so, the Amish have discovered the county. There are settlements in Sherman, Smyrna Mills, and farther north between Easton and Fort Fairfield."

"Actually, that doesn't surprise me. This area looks to be a couple of centuries behind the times," Houston said.

Eklund smiled at him. "Truthfully, I talk like I hate it here, but I'd take this over the craziness of a big city like Portland any day."

Houston had to admit that she might have something there. "I can understand why you'd feel like that."

They came upon a sign that said St. Croix Road and turned onto the road.

"Are we getting close?" Bouchard asked.

"That depends on what you call close. In a straight line we're about ten miles away, but by road its closer to twenty. We'll follow St. Croix Road until we come to Harvey Siding Road, which will take us down to where Howe Brook Village was. If you think this is remote, wait until we get there."

"How do you keep track of these backwoods roads? There has to be hundreds of them!"

"It's a joint effort between the State Police, the Department of Inland Fisheries and Wildlife, the logging companies, and us. Whenever one of us finds something, we notify the appropriate authorities, and they disseminate it."

At 4:30 they left St. Croix Road and turned onto Harvey Siding Road. "When do we get to St. Croix?" Bouchard asked.

"We've been in it for the last fifteen minutes." Eklund smiled. "What? Were you expecting a town or something?"

"Or something."

At five o'clock, they came to railroad tracks, and the road took a ninety-degree turn along them. Houston laughed when he saw a street sign that said North Main Street.

Eklund said, "Welcome to Lake St. Croix and what's left of Howe Brook Village."

They followed the narrow lane past a wash where water from a beaver dam flowed across North Main, and Houston saw a bunch of buildings, three of which were on the opposite side of the tracks. The buildings were backed by a barrier of scrub brush and immature trees so dense that he could only see brief glimpses of the lake. On their side of the tracks, the road turned right and climbed a small knoll upon which stood two more structures. Eklund followed the road and stopped beside the first set of buildings: a rustic shingled cabin and what Houston believed to be a storage building. The road continued past the buildings then narrowed into two ruts and disappeared into the woods. Behind the shingled house was a small garden in which a woman, who Bouchard thought to be in her mid-fifties, hoed a row of green plants. The long flowered dress and huge sunhat she wore made Houston think that she looked like the pioneer woman depicted in the Western movies of his youth. She heard the SUV and stood up straight, placing her left hand in the small of her back. Her eyes narrowed, and Houston easily saw she was not happy about the intrusion.

"Let me do the talking," Eklund said.

They got out of the truck, and Eklund waved to the old woman, "Afternoon, Ms. Fischer."

Fischer squinted her eyes as the deputy approached, holding the hoe like a soldier at port arms. "That you, Wera?"

"Yes."

Fischer kept approaching, and even though Eklund had identified herself, the old woman kept her guard up. "Who's that with you?"

"This is Mr. Michael Houston and his partner, Ms. Anne Bouchard. They're investigators from downstate."

Fischer stopped and scrutinized him then snorted and spit off to the side. "Ain't no intelligent life south of Millinocket."

Houston found himself smiling in spite of the slur. "How do you do, Ms. Fischer?" He held out his hand. When the old woman gripped his, he felt the grip of someone half her age and twice her size, as well as the calluses of someone who did manual labor on a daily basis.

She abruptly dropped his hand and said, "Got coffee in the house." She turned and walked up the path toward the front door of a log cabin home.

Houston looked at the workmanship and turned to Eklund. "Something tells me that's not a prefabricated cabin."

"Nope, she and some local people cut the logs and hauled them down with horses. It was kind of like an Amish barn raising."

"Local people?" Bouchard asked. She scanned the area and, although there were five houses within a couple hundred yards of her, saw not a single soul.

"The summer people who own the other camps—there are five or six more along the lake about a half mile south. Ernestine is the only year-round resident."

Houston stepped up onto the wooden porch that ran the width of the cabin. He found himself admiring this unique, independent woman. Fischer had lit a kerosene lantern; it was apparent that she had no electricity—nor had he seen any power or phone lines along the unpaved forest roads they had used to get here. He saw that the inside of the cabin consisted of a single room. A bed and dresser sat in one corner, and the rest of the room was partitioned with throw rugs in such a manner that one could determine the living area from the kitchen. A huge wood-burning cooking stove, which also served to heat the cabin, sat along the far wall, and the aroma of coffee permeated the air.

"Sit yourselves down," Fischer said, gathering some coffee mugs from one of the cupboards that lined the walls adjoining the stove. Houston sat and noted that even the furniture appeared to be handmade, rustic, and sturdy.

"I really like your home," Bouchard said.

"I doubt you're from *House Beautiful Magazine*," Fischer said. She turned to Eklund. "They still publishing that one?"

"They are."

Fischer seemed to ignore the deputy's response and said, "So, what brings you to Howe Brook? You didn't come all this way to see my home."

"No, ma'am, the truth is that we're trying to find your brother."

Fischer sat and poured coffee into each of their cups. "Only brother I got would be Willard, an' he ain't right . . ." She touched the side of her gray-haired head. "That one is a couple of logs shy of a bonfire."

"Can you explain?" Bouchard asked.

"He's nuts. Been that way ever since he was hit in the head by that block and tackle."

"Excuse me?" Houston said. "I'm confused . . ."

"Willard got smashed on the side of his head when he was eighteen, and if that wasn't enough, he's manic as hell."

"He's bipolar?" Eklund asked.

"It is also called manic depression." Fischer smiled at the look of surprise on Bouchard's face. "When you live without radio or television, you get lots of time to read. Whenever the train goes by, Charley Dodge throws me a bundle of newspapers."

"Which reminds me," Eklund interrupted. "There's a box of books for you in my truck."

"Hope you brought some mysteries and thrillers . . . ain't nothing I like better than scarin' the hell out of myself on a long winter's night."

Houston took a drink of coffee and asked, "Do you know where we can find Willard?"

"At the homestead, I would imagine. Back in '88, when our father died . . ." She looked at the ceiling. "May that one rot in hell . . . Willard would have gotten everything. Maddie—that's Madeleine, my departed sister. She's buried under that oak on the hill over yonder. She and I left as soon as we were able. After Richard killed himself, that left only Willard for the old man to abuse. What's my crazy brother gone and done?"

"He's a suspect in a number of murders. We need to talk with him."

"I don't think he's living at the old place. I heard that the old man sold that and moved north . . . where they moved, I haven't a clue."

"We've been to his home," Houston said with a quick glance at Bouchard.

"I haven't had anything to do with my family in better than thirty years," Fischer said. "All I know is that it was between Bath and Brunswick." Fischer slurped a mouthful of coffee and smacked her lips, exposing a mouth that was missing a few teeth. "You wanting to talk with him about a murder don't surprise me either. Maddie and I always knew that one day he'd go over the edge. Who's he supposed to have killed? Besides my father, that is."

46

Fischer parked near the back of the lot. As he had done on his last visit to the hospital, he studied the building and the surrounding grounds. A security guard with a German shepherd on a leash appeared around the corner of the building. Fischer muttered. He felt certain that he could avoid the guard; the dog, however, was another matter. He put the transmission in drive and coasted out of his parking spot. He followed the pavement to the rear of the building where the emergency room was located. He found a vacant spot, parked the truck, and reached for the door handle.

You nuts, boy? All these years, I knowed I raised a fool. Now I learn you're a babblin' idjut . . .

Fischer cocked his head to better hear the voice only he could hear. "What the hell you want, old man?"

What was you gonna do, shit-for-brains, just stroll in there like it was friggin' Kmart or something? Every cop in three states is huntin' you, moron.

"Ain't nothin' I can do about that. I got to see Mum. She'll tell me what to do next."

Like that Bible-totin' ol' bitch has a clue. Now listen to me, retard. You only got one choice, and gettin' your ass caught visitin' that looney toon ain't it. Your problem is them women. You got to fix them—one way or th'other.

"You ain't as damned smart as you think you are, old man. I heard on the news that the bitch that got away is some kind of fucking cop . . . I'll never get close enough to fix 'er."

Nobody said nothin' about doin' it right now. What you got to do is lay low for a while, get the fuck out of Dodge.

"Dodge? I ain't in no place called Dodge, I'm in Brunswick."

Then get the fuck out of Brunswick—way out. Go up to Aroostook County, the place your uncle left you on Square Lake—it ain't been used in years. Only way in is on loggin' roads. Ain't never been a cop in there.

"I remember it. How long do I got to stay?"

How in hell do I know—as long as it takes, you friggin' idjut. For once, stop being like your nutcase mother and listen to me. You stay around here, they gonna get'cha sure as there's a tide tomorrow. Go to a gas station or a bookstore and get one of them map books—one that shows the back roads. Stay off the turnpike and interstates, the cops watch 'em.

"Who'll take care of Mum?"

Who cares? She sure as hell don't—she ain't been aware of shit for ten years, maybe longer.

"You lie, you ol' bastard—she's aware of things. She talks to me all the time."

So do I, dummy—an' you killed me almost twenty years ago.

Fischer sat in his van and watched the hospital for several minutes. He ignored the old man's cursing tirade. He touched his shoulder where the gaff had gored him; the wound had gotten infected. He reached under his shirt and squeezed the puncture wound. When the scab over the laceration split open, he ground his teeth against the pain—one more debt for which the bitch would have to pay. A small stream of pus flowed out of the open sore, covered his fingers, and made them sticky. He turned back and wiped the noxious stuff on Cheryl's shirt. A slow sinister smile looked back at him from the rearview mirror, and he felt excitement cause a strange tickling sensation in his stomach. He was going to enjoy getting even with her—no one could hurt him and get away with it.

Satisfied that Cheryl was still secure, he drove US 1 north on his way to Aroostook County.

47

O'Leary looked around the small kitchen for a second and then turned his attention to Tasha. She, being the most fluent in English, had become the official spokesperson for the Russian women. "Are you ladies being taken care of?" he asked.

"Yes," Tasha answered, "we have all we need."

"I didn't ask if you had all that you need. There are always little things we want that we don't really need, and I know this place ain't the most luxurious, especially when compared to the house on the Cape."

"We are fine. This warehouse has everything we need and is many times nicer than what most of us grew up in. Besides we don't have to . . . how do you say it? Fuck for our supper."

He ground out his smoke and sipped from the coffee mug that he held and studied her for several seconds. "Tasha, I'm a pretty good judge of when something is bothering people, and I can see that you got something on your mind. I hope that by now you realize I'm here to help you, not use you like Adriana did."

"We know, Jimmy. But . . ." she was hesitant to say more.

"Tasha, in this country we have a custom. It ain't anything unusual, but what it boils down to is if you don't tell me what's buggin' you, I can't do anything about it."

She reached over and took a cigarette from the pack Jimmy had placed on the table when he arrived. Once she had lit it, she arched her head back and exhaled a stream of smoke at the ceiling. "What will happen to us?"

O'Leary, too, lit a cigarette. He stared at the fiery end as he thought about his answer. After several moments, he used his right index finger to tap the cigarette, dropping ash into the ashtray, and sat back. "I ain't exactly sure—not yet. However, I can say this, there are several avenues available to us. Two of which I'm not about to let happen: you ain't goin' back to Russia, and you ain't goin' back to no place like that fancy whorehouse on Cape Cod—at least not as long as Gordon and I are alive."

Tasha looked away from him as she, too, tapped ash from her cigarette. She rolled the burning end around the ashtray until the fire was a perfect dome. She looked at Jimmy. "I hear things."

"We all hear things."

"I hear there are people who are determined to kill you."

"Is that what's bothering you?"

She smiled. "Jimmy, no one is indestructible."

"Didn't say I was. I'm just awfully careful."

"I have also heard," she said, "that some of the people who want to harm you are in positions of power."

He reached over and gently lifted her chin with the side of a curled index finger. He looked into her large brown eyes. "I'm starting to think that your interests are more than you're saying."

She blushed. O'Leary found it charming. Considering all she had been through and had been forced to do, blushing did not come easy. She smiled—he thought it a sad one. "You are very special to all of us . . ."

He grinned, more than a little pleased that a woman as beautiful as Tasha could have strong feelings for him. "All of you . . . or you?" He pulled his hand back and gazed into her eyes.

"Both but especially to me."

Winter walked into the room and stopped short when O'Leary glared at him. "Am I interrupting something?"

"Of course not," Tasha said.

"Give me five minutes, will you, Gordon?" O'Leary said.

When Winter left, he turned back to Tasha. He ground out his cigarette and said, "Tasha, you're one gorgeous woman, you truly are. But you just been through some heavy shit . . ." Her quizzical look made him pause. "You've been through some tough times." Her face showed that she now understood what he was saying, so he continued. "So let's take things slow, okay? If after this is all over you still feel the same way . . . well, we'll deal with it then."

She nodded. "I understand."

"Do you *really* understand?"

"Yes." She looked forlorn when she stared at the floor. "I cannot blame you. No man would want a woman who has done the things I have done . . ."

"Stop right there. That thought has never crossed my mind. What I'm trying to say is that you're one of the most beautiful women I've ever known—and I ain't exactly eye candy. I don't want you to confuse gratitude for something else. Am I making myself clear on this?"

"I think so . . ."

"The last thing I want you to do is change from one form of slavery to another. I've done many things that are, let's say, illegal. Things far worse than anything you have ever done. Let's wait until all this shit settles down, then we'll see what happens. I don't want you to say or do anything now that you'll later regret."

She nodded, took a final drag on her cigarette, and ground it out.

"There is nothing I'd like better than to go around Boston with you on my arm—and woe to any son of a bitch who said anything about you. But I want you to be sure that an old beat-up hoodlum like me is what you want."

She smiled. "Jimmy, you will always be my knight. Your armor may be tarnished, but it will always shine for me."

O'Leary got up from the table, walked around, and placed a hand on her elbow. He urged her to stand and then took her in his arms. He kissed her and felt his heart increase its beat when she responded. After several intense moments, their lips separated, and she tilted her head back to better see him. "Woman, you have no idea how you make me feel . . . and even less of an idea of how big a problem you would be taking on."

"Problem? I see no problem."

He laughed. "When you have a few minutes, you need to have a long talk with Gordon—he knows me better than anyone else."

As if on cue, Winter reappeared. "Boss, we got to go . . ."

48

Fischer got out of the van and studied the crude cabin. It was small and showed the effects of being vacant. Jonah Churchill had been dead for more than fifteen years. A lifelong bachelor, he'd had no heirs and had left the cabin to Willard, his closest relative. Fischer had not visited since that long ago summer.

Fischer circled the building and stood on the lakeshore, staring at the placid water. He watched as several small boats trolled for fish about a hundred yards off the shore. On his first visit to his Uncle Jonah's lakeshore getaway, he had heard many of the local stories of Square Lake and the way it could change in the blink of an eye. "One minute the water's as smooth as a baby's ass, the next a squall will come up and swamp a boat. There's been many a fisherman lost on this lake." The old man had pointed to a spot directly across from the camp. "That's the thoroughfare from Cross Lake," he said, "'bout halfway acrost there's a sandbar, and the water is only four foot deep. A hundred yards straight out from where we stand it's over 120 feet deep. The reason I'm tellin' you all this, Willard, is b'cause this ain't a lake you want to take for granted."

Fischer snorted and turned away from the water. He was not there to fish. He was there because of all the lakes in the Fish River Chain, Square was the most undeveloped. Unlike Long, Cross, and Eagle Lakes, which were lined with houses called camps by the locals, there were only a few miles of them on the shores of Square Lake . . . and they were unoccupied for most of the year. He knew that he would only be able to stay for a short time; winter came to Aroostook County in November, and the downside to the lack of human presence was that the roads were not plowed. To stay after that was foolhardy—asking to die of starvation or exposure.

Spiderwebs hung from every outcrop on the building. He saw a spider twice the size of his thumb sitting in the center of a web that sealed the steps leading to the door. He picked up a fallen branch and used it to sweep the snare away. The arachnid scrambled across the gray wood and Fischer stomped on it.

"It's going to take a lot of work to make this habitable."

Willard spun and was surprised to see Cheryl standing behind him. He had untied her and allowed her to ride beside him during the six-hour drive north. "I told you to stay in the truck."

"You afraid I'll run away again?" She gazed at the forest around them and the placid surface of the big lake. "Where would I run to?"

Willard stared at her for several seconds. "You planning on helping clean up?"

"If I don't this place will be as filthy as the house on the coast."

"I don't need any of your lip."

Willard dug in his pocket for the key his uncle's lawyer had sent and hoped that after fifteen years the lock would still be functional. He inserted the key into the rusted lock and cursed when it twisted and broke off in the plug. He threw the useless piece into the woods and walked to his truck, where he opened up an old toolbox and found a small crowbar. He returned to the door and pried the hasp from the door frame.

The condition inside was no better than the outside. Spider and cobwebs hung down from the rafters and dust coated everything. He surveyed the furniture, which consisted of an old Formica-topped table, chairs on which the vinyl covers had cracked and split, a couch that had outlived its usefulness twenty years ago, and a rusty woodstove.

He crossed to the opening that led into the bedroom. An antiquated metal bed with a decrepit striped mattress was against the wall; the stuffing showed through tears in the ticking. Rodent droppings covered every horizontal surface in the building.

He left the ramshackle interior and began to unload the van. He carried several boxes inside and hoped he had everything he needed for their stay. If they had need of anything, it was about twenty miles by road to the nearest store, and that was really a bait shop that sold beer and a few canned goods. The nearest town of any size was Fort Kent, and it was more than thirty road miles to the northwest. The towns in northern Aroostook County were, for the most part, small, and he was unsure how much he'd stand out.

He found an old broom propped in a corner, brushed the spider- and cobwebs from it, and then threw it to Cheryl. "Don't just stand there, clean this place up."

49

Ernestine Fischer had spent a great deal of time thinking about her brother, Willard. She had been away from the craziness in which her overly pious mother and rednecked father had raised them. It was obvious from what she'd learned from Wera Eklund and the people from away that Willard had been affected by the dysfunctional upbringing more than any of his siblings. She quickly amended that thought. Willard had always been slow-minded, and having his head smashed by that heavy block and tackle only made him slower. But Richard had definitely suffered the most. As he'd grown, his homosexuality had shown, and their father had made a crusade out of getting his oldest son to suppress it and become a *normal* man. The verbal and physical abuse had gotten so bad that one night Richard went into the bathroom and slashed both of his wrists to the bone.

If I were Willard and I wanted to hide, she wondered, *where would I go?* The answer came to her, and it was so obvious that she couldn't believe she hadn't thought of it sooner. She needed to talk to Wera. She was due to make a run for supplies, and it wasn't much farther to Houlton than it was to Presque Isle. She closed up her house and held her breath as she cranked the old truck motor. She let out an involuntary, "Yes!" when the truck started.

Deputy Sheriff Wera Eklund was surprised when Ernestine Fischer walked into the Aroostook County Sheriff's Office. "What's the problem, Ernestine? You haven't come to Houlton in years."

"When you brought them folks from away out to Howe Brook, you said Willard was on the run and wondered if there was someplace he might go."

"That's right," Eklund said. "Come in, I just made a fresh pot of coffee." She led Fischer into the large room the deputies used as their office. Once they were settled, Eklund said, "Since we talked, we've learned that it's a hell of a lot worse than we told you. They found three bodies on the property. At this time, no one has a clue as to how many victims he's had. But the state police found a trunk with about fifty purses and wallets in it. Apparently, he's been at this for several years."

"Lord, help us."

"Ernestine, he's gone underground and dropped completely out of sight. Do you have any idea where he might be?"

Fischer drank her coffee. "As you know, I usually get my supplies at that big Walmart in Presque Isle, but I've been thinking about that last visit and wanted to talk to you, so I came to Houlton instead. There is a place . . . and it's not very far from here . . ."

"Where would that be?"

"We had an uncle, Jonah. He's been gone for years. He had a camp on the western shore of Square Lake."

"Our Square Lake?" Eklund asked. "There may be more than one in Maine."

"Yes, our Square Lake, just north of here in the Fish River chain of lakes."

"Can you help me narrow the search a bit?"

"Lord, it's been years since I was up there. I don't even know if the cabin is still standing. I do recall one thing, though: once you get to the lake road, the camp was the fourth on the right . . . maybe the fifth. It was a log cabin on the west shore, I recollect that."

Eklund called Houston. "We may be on to something," she said and passed on what she'd learned.

"Ernestine thinks he may be staying at the cabin on Square Lake?" Houston asked.

"We'll know in a couple of hours—it'll take me that long to get there," Eklund said.

"Do you want us to head up there?"

"Not yet. The only way into the lake is by logging and private woods roads. Let me check it out first. If there's any reason for you to come up here, I'll call."

"Wera, be careful."

"Not to worry, if I see any indication that he's up here I'll call in everyone I can—including the National Guard."

"Okay. Anne and I will be at our place." He gave her the number. "Call us the minute you know something or if they show up."

"I will."

Fischer listened to the rain hitting the roof and was surprised to learn that there were no leaks in it. He opened the cupboard and shook his head. It was as bare as the one in the nursery rhymes. He would have to risk a trip to a store. They'd have to go to either Stockholm, where there was a general store, or to a supermarket in Fort Kent or Caribou.

"Come on."

Cheryl had been cleaning the small bedroom. She walked out into the common room and asked, "Where we going?"

"We need food."

"I'll wait here."

"The fuck you will. You'd bust out of here as soon as I was out of sight. Come on."

He took her arm and pulled her outside the cabin. He latched the door behind him, and when he tried to lock it, he realized that he also had to stop by a hardware store to get a lock and hasp to replace the one he had destroyed. They got into the van, sat for a few seconds waiting for the engine to smooth out, and then backed into the narrow gravel lane that was the only road in or out of the small collection of camps. He came to the top of a long hill and had to pull to the side to allow another vehicle to pass. He tried not to stare at the oncoming driver. A chill ran through his spine when he saw the gold-and-white logo of an Aroostook County Sheriff vehicle painted on the side of the SUV.

"You make a move to signal this cop and you're dead," he warned Cheryl.

He smiled at the cop as the SUV drove past.

The driver waved as she passed, and Fischer returned the greeting. He watched her drive by, obviously headed for the camps on Square Lake. He felt his heart beat faster, and he panicked. He turned around to follow the SUV. *What in hell are you doing, dummy?*

"That cop saw me."

She's probably seen a lot of people as she drove around these woods roads.

"But she's headed for the lake . . ."

She also could be headed for the lodge on Eagle Lake to check fishing licenses. You turn around and follow her, and she's going to think that you want to talk with her.

"If you're so smart, old man, what should I do?"

Go about your business. Chances are you'll never see her again.

Fischer ignored Cheryl as she stared at him during the conversation with the old man. He gave her no explanation as he executed a tight K-turn and continued on.

Eklund passed the van and raised her hand to wave at the driver. The van's side windows were covered with dirt, and it was difficult to see the driver's face through the tinted glass. In the tradition of the area, they exchanged waves and passed by each other.

Twenty minutes later, she was parked in front of the Square Lake Camp. She got out of her truck, adjusted her pistol, and studied the area for a few seconds. The drive was empty, so she decided to take a look around. She circled the building, peering through the filthy windows, and it was evident someone had recently been staying in the small cabin. She walked to the lake's edge and saw large footprints in the soft dirt on the water's edge. She walked back to her truck and backed out of the camp's drive. As she started back the way she had come in, she picked up her radio, contacted her dispatcher in Houlton, and asked them to relay a message to Sam Fuchs for her.

———

Fischer returned to the cabin and immediately noticed the small boot prints in the soft ground. Someone had been to the cabin. He remembered the Deputy Sheriff and cursed. He grabbed Cheryl, dragged her into the bedroom, and began throwing their few belongings into a backpack.

They know where you are.

"I know that, old man."

Then get your thumbs out of your ass and get out of here. It's been four hours since you saw that cop—by now she'll have called for help. They'll be here before you know it, an' they's only one road in and out of here.

"I'll get a boat."

Then what, you idjut? You gonna hitchhike south?

"Leave me be." Fischer ignored his father's curses and began gathering his belongings.

———

Wera Eklund stopped her SUV in a large open area that had once been Blackstone Siding, a railroad stop where loggers loaded their timber onto railroad cars. But the Bangor and Aroostook Railroad went bankrupt, and the siding had not been used for more than forty years. The right of way through the woods from Presque Isle to Van Buren was abandoned in the 1970s and turned into an ATV and snowmobile trail in 1980. As a result, the siding was now a several-acre grass-covered parking area.

She exited the vehicle and waited for the rest of the assault team. Within twenty minutes she was joined by two other Aroostook County Sheriff's Department Deputies, three members of the Department of Inland Fisheries and Wildlife Warden Service[3], and two members of the Maine State Police Tactical Team[4]. She gathered them into a circle and briefed them on what they faced.

"This guy is extremely dangerous, very likely armed, and we know he has a hostage. He's a suspected serial killer and will have no reservation about killing any one of us who gets in the way of his escape."

One of the Tactical Team members was a Maine State Police Sergeant, and he took charge of the impromptu meeting. "The subject has only a few escape routes: this road, the lake—if he has access to a boat—and the woods, but he'll have to go by foot. We don't have enough people to completely blanket the area, so we'll have to use surprise as our primary tool." He turned to the three wardens. "You folks know these woods better than I, is there anything we should be careful of?"

The oldest warden spoke up. "We have to keep him off the lake. If he gets out there, he can go in several directions. There are thoroughfares between this lake and Cross and Eagle Lakes. The entrance to the Cross Lake thoroughfare is shallow and, when the water is as low as it is now, could be impassable for some boats. Bottom line, he could disappear very quickly if he gets afloat. We have a plane from our Eagle Lake station on location. He'll try and keep a visual on him if it comes to that, but . . . well, you get my drift. It'd make things a whole lot easier if we take him here."

---

[3] Members of the Maine Department of Inland Fisheries and Wildlife Warden Service are law enforcement officers.

[4] The Maine State Police Tactical Team works in conjunction with the Maine State Police Crisis Negotiation Team to safely resolve critical incidents, which include barricaded subjects, wanted felons, high-risk K-9 tracks, hostage situations, and high-risk warrant services.

The team spent several minutes dividing up responsibilities and establishing methods of communication. Finally Wera said, "Okay, let's get this done."

The task force drove ten miles on rough, unpaved woods roads and stopped a quarter mile from Square Lake. They left their vehicles and closed in on the camp on foot. Wera took the middle position, as she knew the precise location of the building. She stopped across from the camp, staying concealed in a dense copse of alder bushes, and saw the same van she'd passed earlier that day parked beside the cabin. When she was certain that everyone was in position, she darted across the narrow dirt road and stopped against the front wall. She raised her service pistol and called out, "Aroostook County Sheriff's Department!"

———

Fischer happened to glance up and see the cop in the tan uniform dash across the narrow lane. He grabbed his rifle and hissed at Cheryl, "Get down and keep your mouth shut."

A female voice called out, "Aroostook County Sheriff's Department! Is anyone in there?"

Fischer estimated the location from which the voice came and fired a round through the window. He raised his head and saw other cops, some in the green uniform of the warden service and others wearing camouflage. He fired at one of the wardens.

———

The bullet missed Eklund's head by inches. She dropped to the ground and crawled on her belly to a new location. She saw members of the task force moving through the brush and trees that bordered the rudimentary camp road. A warden broke from cover, and another shot erupted from the interior. The warden dropped in her tracks and rolled into the drainage ditch that ran along the road's thin shoulder. Eklund wanted to call out and see how badly the warden was hurt but dared not give away her position.

"Holmquist, are you all right?" It was the voice of the State Police Sergeant.

"Yeah, it's just a scratch."

"Well keep your ass low!"

Another shot came from the camp.

Cheryl heard Fischer fire a third shot and then saw him scramble over to the bedroom, where she was curled up against an interior wall as far from the exterior as she could get. He glanced at her. "We got to make a break for it," he said.

"Leave me, Willard. If they find me it will slow them up enough for you to escape." Cheryl hoped he would fall for her ruse and she would be free.

"I didn't chase you all over the fucking coast to just let you go. You'll go where I go."

Cheryl's heart sank. Death was going to be her only escape.

He popped up, looked through the window, and said, "Come on." He grabbed her arm and pulled her from her haven. He led her through the common room to the porch that faced the lake. Through the windows that enclosed the veranda, she was unable to see any of the members of the law enforcement team that was assaulting the camp. He paused before the glass door and cautioned her. "Run as fast as you can to the woods!" He pointed to the left of the cabin.

He opened the door and tugged her arm, "Run, goddamn you, run."

Cheryl bolted from the enclosure, vaulting over the three wooden steps, and raced for the safety of the trees. A shot rang out, and for the briefest of moments, she thought that they had shot him. But she knew her prayer had gone unanswered when he came running up alongside her. He grabbed her arm and dragged her into the trees. When they were at the forest's edge, she almost lost her balance, but he lifted her, and suddenly they were out of the brilliant late morning sun and into the cool shade of the woods.

He dropped to one knee, forcing her to squat beside him. When he looked at her she was surprised—something she had heretofore thought he could no longer do. Instead of looking panicked and desperate,

Willard looked cool as if he were in his element. He released her arm and gripped the rifle with both hands. He reached into his pocket and took out several cartridges. He replaced the spent ammunition with new rounds as he searched the immediate area for any sign of pursuit.

When he motioned for her to move to her right along the lakeshore, he seemed happy, almost euphoric, as if he believed himself to be indestructible. She realized he was high on the adrenaline of the situation.

"There's a camp about a hundred yards this way. They have a boat. Stay low, and don't make any more noise than is necessary," he said.

As she crept through the brush and trees, Cheryl heard a loud snap as someone stepped on a piece of deadfall. She looked at Fischer. He placed his finger across his lips and motioned for her to lie down. She dropped to her stomach, and he did likewise. He crawled beside her, and when she looked into his eyes, she knew not to make any sound.

After a few seconds, she heard footsteps off to her left. She ventured a peek through the brush and waist-high ferns. One of the wardens, alongside one of the camouflaged men, were creeping through the woods. They spoke in hushed voices. "We're going to need to get some dogs in here," the camouflaged sniper—by now Cheryl had decided that the men dressed like Marines were police snipers—said.

"By that time he'll be halfway to Timbuktu," the warden commented. Without further words, they passed by.

It seemed like hours passed before Fischer nudged her. He raised up slowly, surveying the woods around them. "Come on," he whispered.

They trotted in a low crouch to the edge of the lake and in minutes were at his neighbor's camp. They stopped just inside the trees and waited for several moments. Fischer's caution paid off. Two of the tan uniforms were slowly walking around the building with their pistols drawn. Cheryl watched Fischer, expecting him to open fire on the unsuspecting officers at any second. Although he held his rifle on his shoulder, prepared to shoot, he waited until the cops circled the building and disappeared. She could hear the low murmur of their voices as they moved away toward the next camp in the line.

Fischer waited until it was quiet and the only sounds were the breeze in the trees, the squealing of blue jays, and the gentle sound of the water hitting the shore. He crept toward the dock, where a small boat was suspended above the water by some sort of framework. They crept across the dock, and Fischer used the hand crank on the frame to lower the boat into the water. He motioned for her to get in and then followed her. He lifted the gas can and cursed. "Stay here, and keep the boat close to the dock." He held his rifle as he darted off the dock to a small shed. He used the rifle's barrel to wedge the hasp free. It came loose with a loud screeching sound. Fischer looked paranoid as he checked to see if anyone had heard the sound, and then he disappeared inside. In seconds he reappeared carrying a red plastic gas can. Cheryl saw the way he held the rifle up with his left arm and knew he was using it as a counterbalance; the can was heavy.

Once on the boat, Fischer filled the fuel tank and secured it and the gas can. He squeezed the bulb in the fuel line several times and said, "Get behind the wheel." When she was seated, he opened the plastic battery case that sat beside the fuel tank and connected the cables.

"I hope there's juice in this battery," he said. "Start it."

Cheryl flipped the toggle switch labeled choke, turned the key, and the motor cranked several times before it began idling. Before the motor smoothed out, Fischer grabbed his rifle and jumped into the front seat beside her. "Get us the fuck out of here."

She pulled the transmission handle back, felt the motor engage, and then slowly backed away from the dock. When they were about fifty feet from shore, she reduced throttle, shifted the transmission forward, and then gave the motor some fuel. As they started forward, there were shouts from the shore, and several members of the police assault force appeared. They opened fire. Cheryl increased the throttle, and the boat's nose rose as they sped away. Fischer stood up and fired several useless shots at the cops.

In minutes they were well beyond the range of the cops' weapons, and Cheryl asked, "Where to?"

He pointed to the northwest. "We'll head out by way of Eagle Lake."

50

O'Leary stood in the unlit hall that led to his office and watched as Winter began to close the bar. Two men strode through the door, and they did not have to wear signs for him to know what they were—either cops or hired muscle. He stood still and watched them until they took seats at the bar. The older of the two—at least his gray hair indicated he was oldest—flashed a badge at Winter. "O'Leary in the back?" he asked.

"Nope."

"Mind if we take a look?"

"You got a warrant?" Winter asked.

"No, but we can get one."

"Then you better get it."

"You are aware that he's up to his ass in alligators—and they're snapping?"

"I'll be sure to tell him that when I see him. You guys drinking or bullshitting?"

The younger cop gave him a hard look. When his partner nudged him on the arm, they slid off the bar stools. "We'll be back with a warrant."

"I'll be waiting with unbridled anticipation."

Once the cops were gone, O'Leary walked out of the darkness.

"You heard?" Winter asked.

"Yeah, they'll be back."

"You think they got probable cause for a warrant?"

"Nope. But it won't matter. There're at least six judges listed in that ledger—they'll have a warrant in an hour."

"So what we gonna do?"

O'Leary lit a cigarette.

"Smokin' in a public place is against the law," Winter said, knowing his boss couldn't care less.

"Then lock the door. As of now this is a private club."

"You didn't answer my question."

A cloud of smoke surrounded O'Leary's head. "We go on the offensive."

"I wondered when you were gonna start kicking ass and taking names."

"We already got the names," O'Leary said with a sardonic smile. "Now we're gonna kick some ass."

O'Leary had just finished locking the door as he turned away from the building and Winter said, "We got company."

Three men walked out of the darkness and into the glow of the street-lights. O'Leary immediately took a pistol from within his jacket. Winter already had his out and pointed in the direction of the men. When they were a quarter of the way down the block, the three split, making it difficult for two guns to cover them. When the one who had remained on the sidewalk stopped walking and raised his hands, showing he had no weapon, O'Leary recognized him. "What brings you to Southie, Carl?"

"Take it easy," Carl Konovalov answered, "we're here to talk." He spoke with a heavy Russian accent.

"It takes three of you to talk?"

"Jimmy, Jimmy, your reputation precedes you. They're merely a precaution—not much different than your man." He half-turned and said something in Russian. His two companions stopped their approach, one standing on the empty street and the other on the opposite sidewalk.

"You okay, boss?" Winter asked.

"Yeah, I can handle this guy if it comes down to that."

"I'll be right over there." Winter stepped back several paces and then positioned himself between two parked cars, where he could watch the gunmen in the street and on the sidewalk.

O'Leary motioned for Konovalov to approach. "When I learned that Gorky was involved in this, I knew you were too," O'Leary said.

"That is part of what we must speak about."

"I don't think we should discuss business on the street." O'Leary put his pistol away, turned, and unlocked the door to the Claddagh Pub. "You can bring your muscle in with you . . . or you can come in alone."

Konovalov motioned for his companions to follow them inside.

Once inside, Winter deactivated the alarm system, walked behind the bar, and carefully placed his pistol on it. O'Leary nodded at him and then turned to the Russian mobster. "You want to sit at a table or will the bar do?"

Konovalov seated himself on a bar stool, and his henchmen separated once again—one standing by the door and the other to his right about twenty feet away.

O'Leary took a seat on Konovalov's immediate left, keeping the Russian between him and his men. "You want a drink, Carl? It's on me."

The Russian turned his head and said to Winter, "Vodka."

"Neat?" Winter asked.

"What is this . . . *neat?*"

"Straight up, no ice, no chaser."

Konovalov nodded.

Winter turned and took a bottle from the bar back.

"None of your American swill—the good vodka."

O'Leary nodded his approval, and Winter replaced the bottle of bar brand, picked up a bottle of Stolichnaya, and poured a shot. He pushed the glass toward the Russian. "This do?" he asked.

Konovalov nodded again.

"Okay, Carl," O'Leary said, "you called this meeting. What's on your mind?"

"You have caused a major disruption in our revenue stream."

"Revenue stream? You an accountant now?"

"Every business needs a good accountant."

"Okay, suppose you get to the point? If you haven't noticed, it's getting late."

"You have taken our property and . . . taken away two of my valued employees—"

"Cut the bullshit, Carl. This place ain't bugged. I gather that you're upset because I killed Halsey, Gorky, and Adriana."

"Replacing the women will be easy, Gorky not so easy, but we have other vessels to carry our cargo. The madam is a minor inconvenience, and the lawyer was no loss—them I can buy for . . . how is that American saying? A dime a dozen? Yes, that's the expression. I can get lawyers for a dime a dozen."

"Still," O'Leary said, "it's the cargo you're after."

"I said it was easy to replace the women, I didn't say it was cheap. I have a considerable amount of money invested in them."

"I get the feeling that isn't all you want."

"What else is there?"

"The laptop."

The Russian waved his hand in front of his face as if he were shooing a fly away, and O'Leary was surprised by his answer. "Pshh, that's of no consequence, merely a client list."

"You sayin' that the names on that computer aren't part of running this business?"

"Other than I have to pay them for certain services, no."

O'Leary thought about what he had heard. It made sense; the Russian mob had a long history of infiltrating and using corrupt government officials in their kryshas. "But," O'Leary said, "they're still covered by your krysha?"

"Yes."

"Well, here's the problem I got with this, Carl. I don't like the fact that you've brought kids—virtual babies—and placed them in your fancy whorehouses. Adults who understand what they may be getting into are one thing . . . kids are another."

Konovalov's expression turned hard. "Since we are being blunt, I want my property back."

"There's a problem with that, I don't have them," O'Leary said.

"Who's bullshitting now?" Konovalov stood, picked up the shot glass, drank the vodka in a single mouthful, and banged the glass down. He wiped his lips with the back of his hand and said, "One day—that's all I will give you to return my property to me. One day, not a minute more." He nodded to his men, and they left the bar.

Once the door closed after the mobsters, Winter picked up the shot glass and threw it in the trash. "You gonna do it?" he asked.

"Fuck no! How long you think we'd last if we gave in to a bunch of foreign goons?"

"That your only reason?"

"You know better. There's no way I'll ever return those women to him."

Winter nodded. "Okay, I'll make sure the boys are ready. What in hell is a krysha?"

"It's Russian for roof. All their businesses and corrupt officials are sheltered under the krysha—it's like a mafia family."

"Okay, how we gonna handle this?"

"We got to make them come after us. . . . Is Chaney still in town?"

Winter looked at O'Leary. "Are you sure you want him involved in this?"

"As much as I hate it, he's got some special skills we can use. After all, he owes me, and who else is there?"

"Mike."

"Naw, he's got his hands full chasing that psycho up in Butt Fuck, Maine. Besides, there's still a lot of cop left in Mike. We'll go with Chaney."

51

Houston chopped the last piece of firewood and threw it on the pile beside the cabin. He wiped sweat from his forehead and entered the house. He looked around the living room, saw no sign of Anne, and crossed the room to the bedroom. He heard the shower running and smiled. He decided he'd surprise her, and they could take a long hot romantic shower. He turned the knob and was surprised: the door was locked—something she'd never done before. Then he heard her sobs. He knocked lightly on the door. "Anne, are you all right?" He waited several moments for her to reply and then knocked again. Again she failed to respond. Houston walked into the kitchen to find a long thin tool that he could poke into the hole in the knob that unlocked the bathroom door from the outside in the event of an emergency. He found what he needed and returned to the bedroom. He saw that the bathroom door was open a crack and pushed the door open and walked inside.

Anne sat on the toilet, wrapped in a towel and staring out the window at the valley below. He could see tears running down the sides of her face. "You alright, hon?" he asked.

She quickly wiped at the drops, and replied, "I'm fine."

Houston walked over and squatted beside her. "Bullshit."

"Mike, I'm alright—"

"Anne, this is me you're talking to. Just like you know me better than anyone else, I know you. On many occasions you've told me to let my feelings out—that although I was a cop, I was still human. Well, now I'm telling you the same thing."

She looked at him, and he noticed how red her eyes were, especially when contrasted with the pallor of her skin.

"I don't know what's wrong," she said. "He didn't . . . Cheryl . . ."

"Anne, honey, you're suffering from PTSD—you've been through a harrowing experience. Don't try to hold back. Let it out. Trust me, I know something about this. I went through it after Somalia, again last year after the Rosa situation, and several times as a cop."

She forced a smile, and then her face twisted, and her composure broke like glass after being hit by a rock on a frigid day. Sobs racked her body; Houston wrapped his arms around her and held her securely while she cried. Feeling her body tremble against his made him feel awkward. On one hand he felt helpless—as much as he wanted to make her hurt and fear go away, he had no idea of what he should do; on the other, he maintained his protective posture, cursing Fischer for hurting his woman this way. For the first time in his life, he wanted to inflict pain on another human being. He wanted to kill Willard Fischer . . . and do it slowly.

"You're sure he's gone?" Houston asked.

"I went back this afternoon with a tactical team," Eklund said. "We ended up in a firefight, and he got away."

"Firefight. Was anyone hurt?"

"I got the shit scared out of me, and one warden received a superficial wound. I underestimated him—I think he knew we'd found him. Somehow or another he knew that we were onto his location—maybe something as simple as him seeing my tracks when I investigated the camp this morning. When we got inside, all their things were packed. He was getting ready to take off."

"Damn."

"We have a BOLO out on him, but there are any number of ways he could have gone. All we know at this point is that he stole a boat from a nearby camp. They took the thoroughfare to Eagle Lake. We lost him—there's more boat traffic on Eagle than Square and a number of trailerable launches where he could steal a car. That's not taking into consideration that he could have put ashore at a private camp or residence. After that it's a short trip to Route 11. He could take Route 11 north to Fort Kent or south to Bangor. If he got on the American Reality Road, he could go all the way to Quebec and never hit a public highway. We've got every law enforcement agency in Aroostook, Penobscot, and Piscataquis Counties, as well as the Warden Service and the RCMP[5] looking for him."

Houston could hear the frustration in her voice and tried to ease it. "It's probably for the best," he said. "I wasn't too crazy about you taking him on alone."

"I can take care of myself. Besides, I wasn't alone. I had a team of three deputies, three wardens, and two members of the state police tactical team."

"I'm glad to know that, Wera. This guy is extremely dangerous, and going there by yourself wasn't wise. I wouldn't want to take him on alone."

"I understand. But up here deputies are used to working alone."

"Okay, okay. Let me know if you learn anything else."

"In the event he tries for Quebec, we've notified the gatehouses on the private woods roads to watch for him, as well as immigration and customs enforcement, although ICE doesn't have the manpower to watch every point where he could cross the border on foot. There's places up here where he could abandon whatever he's driving, walk across the border, and steal something over there. In the meantime, we're searching the camp for anything that may give us a clue as to where he went."

"Thanks, Wera. You be careful. Okay?"

---

[5] Royal Canadian Mounted Police, colloquially known as the Mounties and internally as the Force, is both a federal and a national police force of Canada.

She laughed. "Always. I'll call if we find anything of value in there."

Houston broke the connection and said, "The bastard got away again."

"How can anyone be this lucky?" Bouchard asked.

As much as he wanted to jump in his truck and drive north, Houston knew that it would be foolhardy—at least until they had a fix on Fischer's location . . . if they ever did.

52

Burton Chaney walked out of the elevator and saw Gordon Winter sitting in one of several easy chairs that were in the lobby. He crossed the room and sat across from him. "What are you doing here, Gordon?"

"The boss sent me, Burt."

"What does he need?"

"Your expertise."

"What?"

"We got a situation."

"Gordon, I won't do it. I'm not in that life any longer."

Winter stood and said, "Jimmy ain't gonna be happy about this. He feels you owe him."

"I do. I just don't want to go back to that."

"I'll tell him."

Winter walked toward the exit, and Chaney said, "Gordon."

Winter turned. "Yeah?"

"Tell Jimmy that if he wants my help, he can come ask for it personally. No offense intended."

"Gotcha," Winter said, "I'll pass it along."

It took less than twenty minutes for the call. "Meet me at the Claddagh Pub." The tone of voice told Chaney that O'Leary was not happy about the way things were turning out. "Be here in an hour."

"It's nice to hear from you, too," Chaney replied, making no effort to hide his sarcasm.

"Just be here."

———————

Southie had not changed much since Chaney had last been there. But then, that was only a year ago; it had not changed much in the last fifty years, so it was unrealistic to expect anything drastic to have taken place. The streets felt claustrophobic when compared to the wide-open land around Chaney's New Hampshire home. The triple-deckers were crammed together, separated by narrow alleys that were barely wide enough to allow a car to pass. Everything seemed in need of a good washing. Chaney thought flushing would be a more appropriate term. Cars lined both sides of the street, which was more suited to having parking restricted to a single side. He recalled the first time he drove these streets and how worried he was that he would sideswipe the cars that limited the thoroughfare. He saw the only open spots on the block were directly in front of Jimmy O'Leary's Claddagh Pub. No one in Southie would dare to park in one of the three slots, which were reserved for O'Leary and his personal guests. Chaney parked in one of them.

The interior of the bar was dark and smelled of spilled beer and liquor; even though O'Leary spent lavishly to make the place look upscale, it was still nothing more than a neighborhood watering hole. Once his eyes adjusted to the dim interior, Chaney saw Winter backing the bar. Gordon said nothing, just tipped his head in the direction of the corridor that led to O'Leary's office. Chaney gave him a casual wave and entered the hallway.

He knocked once on the office door and then entered, not waiting for permission. O'Leary sat behind a broad desk on which not a single piece of paper resided. He was smoking one of his ever-present cigarettes. O'Leary watched Chaney through narrowed eyes and said nothing until his childhood friend sat in one of the two easy chairs that fronted the desk.

O'Leary ground out his cigarette and said, "You're lookin' good. That country air must agree with you."

"More so than the fog in here."

O'Leary ignored the comment and said, "I suppose you're wondering why I sent . . ." He amended his words. ". . . asked you here."

"Yup."

"I'll get to it then. I know you don't want to have any more to do with me than I do you."

"It's your meeting—do what you will."

"First, let me clear the air . . ."

Chaney looked at the layers of tobacco smoke that hung in the air. "It'd be nice. This place smells like a full ashtray."

O'Leary ignored the comment, which told Chaney that whatever the favor was that Jimmy wanted, it was big.

"I need you to cover my ass . . . for old time's sake."

"Old time's sake? As I recall in those *old times*, I was a soldier, and you were a hood."

"I'm talking about when we were kids—the old times before those old times, Burt. You know what I mean."

Chaney glared at his former friend. "Yeah, unfortunately, I do."

"A little less attitude would help."

"Last time we talked, I was recuperating from a gunshot wound, and you informed me that our truce was over, and it was business as usual."

"Yeah, I know. But it boils down to this: back then, you needed my help, now I need yours."

"I'm not a hit man anymore."

"Never said you were. You gonna listen to what I have to say, or are we gonna sit here and hiss and spit at each other like two tomcats?"

"Okay. What's got you so nervous that you're willing to lower yourself to the point you'll ask me for help?"

"The Russian mob."

Chaney was silent for a few seconds and then said, "Thank God, for a few minutes there I thought it was something big."

O'Leary stood up. "C'mon, let's take a ride."

"Don't know if I like that choice of words."

"Okay, how about, *I need you to see something?*"

"On one condition."

"Which is?"

"No smoking in the damned car."

"You know, Burt, you can be a real ball buster sometimes."

"I learned it from an old friend . . . he's a master at it."

O'Leary grinned. "That I am—"

Chaney sat in the back and only spoke when O'Leary asked something that required an answer. When Winter turned off 1A and onto Chelsea Street, he knew where they were going. "Should I be concerned?" he asked.

"What?" O'Leary asked.

"We're headed for your warehouse, aren't we?"

"Yeah."

"People you take there don't usually come out alive."

"For fuck's sake, Burt, give it a rest."

"You're slipping, Jimmy."

O'Leary turned and looked at him. "How so?"

"No one has frisked me. For all you know I could be carrying."

"That tell you anything?"

"Yeah, it makes me think that I may live through this after all."

O'Leary turned to the front, blew through his lips, and said, "Jesus Kee-rist. You can be a real nag when you get a mind to."

Winter pulled up beside a warehouse and said, "End of the line."

"You know," Chaney said, "I could have gone all day without hearing that."

Winter grinned. "How about 'we're here'?"

"That's better."

O'Leary led him to a side door and stepped aside to allow him to enter first. Chaney stepped inside and immediately stopped. One side of the warehouse was arranged like a huge dormitory. Women—many of whom stopped and, at first, stared at them with fear—occupied the area. "Since when did you start pimping, Jimmy?"

"Ever since we were kids, you always thought that you had all the answers," O'Leary said. "Now how about just once you shut up and learn the question."

"Okay, what's this?"

O'Leary led him to a small dining area, and they sat at the table. Immediately, two women were at the table asking if they could get them anything. Their accents were Slavic, most likely Russian, and Chaney saw respect, not fear, when they spoke to O'Leary. A frail child raced forward and sat on Jimmy's lap. "Meet Inca. Inca, this is a friend of mine. His name is Burton."

The girl, who looked to be no more than eleven or twelve, said in faltering English, "Pleased to meet you, Burr-ton."

Chaney smiled at her. "The pleasure is all mine."

O'Leary slid her from his lap and said, "Now run along, Burt and I have business to do."

Chaney watched the girl dash away and then turned to O'Leary. "I guess that at this point I should ask *what the fuck is goin' on?*"

O'Leary told him the entire story.

"So," Chaney asked, "what is it you want from me?"

"I'm gonna force the issue with Konovalov. He'll come with a damned army. I need you and your sniper rifle to even the odds a bit."

"I don't have a sniper rifle anymore."

"I'll get one for you—same one Mike Houston used to bring down that sniper last year."

"As I recall," Chaney said, "that weapon was damaged."

"I had it fixed."

Chaney was reluctant to get involved in a gangland war, but O'Leary was right about one thing: he owed him. He looked at the young women as they moved about, straightening and cleaning their living quarters. He saw Inca, sitting off by herself, watching Jimmy much like the owner of a new Bugatti Veyron looks at his or her car. "The kid seems devoted to you. What's her story?"

"She's been taken away from everything she knew and was almost forced into being a whore."

"Almost?"

"Yeah, *almost*. I got wind of it and stopped it."

Chaney stood and said, "Introduce me to some of the women."

Twenty minutes later, Chaney turned to O'Leary and said, "Okay, I'll help you."

53

The truck shifted, and Cheryl woke up. Fischer got out of the truck and slammed the door. He leaned in through the open window, glared at Cheryl, and said, "Not one fucking sound." He turned and watched the attendant approach.

"Good afternoon, what'll it be?"

"What time is it? The damned clock radio in this heap doesn't work."

"Four o'clock. What can I do for you?"

"Fill it up."

"Been driving far?"

"Far enough," Fischer answered.

"Hey, mister, no need to get touchy, I'm just trying to be friendly."

"Then shut up and fill the goddamned tank. You got a toilet?"

"Inside."

Fischer turned to walk to the restroom, and Cheryl started when the attendant looked through the driver side window and said, "Morning, ma'am." She turned away from him, stared forward, and ignored him, as she remembered the charter boat trip and knew that any action on her behalf could set Fischer off.

Fischer suddenly appeared behind the attendant. "Hey," he said, "talkin' to my wife ain't gonna help you get that fucking tank filled."

The young man spun around and held his hands up in an apologetic pose. "I didn't mean nothin', man. I was just being sociable, that's all."

"What is this—a gas station or a social club?"

"Hey, I didn't mean any harm . . ."

Fischer stood beside the truck as the kid removed the gas cap, activated the pump, and began to fill the tank. He turned to Cheryl and said, "You need the toilet?"

"Not right now."

"Do it anyway." He gave the attendant a hard look.

Cheryl saw how close Fischer was to becoming violent, slid across the seat, and opened the truck door. She circled the truck and said, "I really wish you hadn't broken the door handle on my side."

"I bet you do." He guided her to the ladies' room.

The gas station attendant returned to the station's office and wrote down the license number of the four-by-four pickup. He thought there was something odd about the couple in it. An hour later he was watching the early evening news on the TV that was mounted on the wall across from the desk. The anchor told of a shootout between law enforcement personnel and a suspected serial murderer on Square Lake. When the announcer read the description of the suspects and added that it was suspected they had stolen a truck in Eagle Lake, the attendant thought about the asshole whose truck he'd filled up an hour before. When the license number appeared on the screen, he compared it to the one he'd jotted down. His heart raced as he dialed the phone number for Troop F of the Maine State Police that appeared on the screen.

Fischer stopped a hundred yards short of the border station in Fort Kent. Normally vehicles exiting the United States stopped on the Canadian side; however, he wanted to assess the situation first. If he did a U-turn in front of the customs window, it would raise alarms from Ottawa to Washington, DC. He watched as armed Border Patrol officers stopped and searched a truck before allowing it to cross. It was evident to him who they were looking for. He backed up and turned around. This necessitated a change in plans. Instead of crossing into Canada here, he would have to follow Route 11 south.

Fischer glanced at his watch. An hour had elapsed since he had stopped for gas, and he needed to get some rest. It had been more than eighteen hours since he'd last slept, and his eyes burned with fatigue. He realized that he should have known the cops would close the border; he could have saved precious time. Now he would have to drive a hundred miles of woods and nothing to get to I-95 and on to Bangor, adding three hours to the drive. He did not like it when things changed.

Houston and Anne were preparing for bed when the phone rang. When Houston answered, Wera Eklund informed him that Fischer had reappeared. The stolen truck had been seen at a gas station in Fort Kent and again in Ashland.

Anne listened while Houston spoke with Wera and, after he broke the connection, said, "Where's he going?"

"He probably tried to cross the border at Fort Kent but got scared away."

Houston walked into the living room and grabbed his copy of DeLorme's *The Maine Atlas and Gazetteer* from the bookcase. He flipped through the pages until he found the one he sought. "From Fort Kent he could go south on a couple of roads to Route 1. I doubt he'd go west because once he gets past Dickey there are no public roads." He pointed at the map. "Route 11."

"What's on Route 11?" Anne asked.

"He'd pass through Ashland again, then at Masardis he could leave the highway and go to Howe Brook . . ."

"His sister's place."

"I doubt he's had any sleep in a while. He's probably exhausted. I think he's headed to Ernestine. It's possible that he thinks he'll be safe there."

274 | VAUGHN C. HARDACKER

Anne leaped from the bed, took off her nightgown, and started putting on a pair of jeans. "Call Wera and tell her to put together another tactical team," she said. "If we split the driving we can be there in the morning."

"Anne, are you sure you're up to this?"

"When a kid falls off a bike what's the first thing you do?" She didn't wait for his answer. "You make them get right back on it."

"This is not the same—"

"Oh, you bet your life it is. Now make the damn call."

Houston saw he was not going to dissuade her and dialed the number. He spoke to Wera as he opened the closet door, removed a Remington 700 bolt-action rifle equipped with a high-power scope, and placed it on the bed. Anne heard him tell Wera, "I'm coming equipped this time . . ."

54

They came during the afternoon, only not the way O'Leary thought they would. Instead of Russian mobsters, the first assault was from the Commonwealth of Massachusetts in the form of the Health Inspector, who went through the Claddagh as if he were looking for the missing key to his girlfriend's chastity belt. O'Leary leered at him when he resentfully gave him a pass on the inspection. Once he was out the door, Winter said, "I suppose we better start carding everyone we serve."

"Yeah, I imagine the Alcoholic Beverage Control will be in here next."

"You know, boss, they'll keep hounding you until you die."

"Or until I do something about it."

O'Leary entered the warehouse by the side door and slowly walked toward the corner, where his men had erected small cubicles with crates as walls and drapes for doors. One of the compartments had the curtain pushed to one side, and he looked inside. The room was furnished with a single bed, a dresser with mirror, a small nightstand with lamp, and a chair. He was impressed with how ingenious and versatile his men had turned out to be. They had even found ways to provide electricity to each of the rooms and had used a mixture of tarps and canvas to enclose the ceilings, giving the women total privacy.

He turned his attention upward, scanning the catwalks that criss-crossed the ceiling, and nodded with satisfaction. He saw several of his men strategically located along the metal walkways and knew that, even though he was not visible, Chaney was up there, camouflaged and on guard. He turned down a makeshift corridor, and the center of the complex opened into a large common area with tables, couches, and everything that was required for a rudimentary degree of comfort.

Tasha sat in an easy chair that she had placed strategically beneath a skylight; he thought she looked angelic sitting in the shaft of sunlight. She looked up from her book, smiled, and stood when she saw him. As O'Leary closed with her, she placed the book on the table and greeted him. "How are you, Jimmy?"

"Just fine. What are you reading?" he asked.

She picked up the thick volume, showed him the cover, and said, "*Doctor Zhivago.*"

He took the heavy book from her and glanced at the cover. The words all seemed alien; while he recognized a few letters, most made him wonder if the author suffered from dyslexia.

"It's in Cyrillic," Tasha said. "Russian."

"I wondered what language that was. I never read it," he said. "But the movie was pretty good."

"The Soviets would not allow it in Russia, Pasternak had to . . ." She seemed to struggle to think of the correct English words, " . . . smuggle the manuscript into Italy for it to be printed."

O'Leary looked at her with a newfound interest. There was obviously a lot more to this woman that he had thought. "You know a lot about it."

"Before all this," she said, "I was student of literature at university."

O'Leary led her to one of the couches and motioned for her to sit. Once they had settled, he turned to her with a solemn look. "Tasha, I need you to take charge of the women."

She gave him a questioning look. "Take charge . . . what means take charge?"

"I need you to be a . . ." He, too, fumbled for the correct word, ". . . their commissar."

Her brows arched, and she said, "Commissar is a military position of communists."

O'Leary thought for a minute and then recalled a title he had heard used when one of Carl Konovalov's men had addressed him. "I need you to be *pakhan*[6] . . . a boss."

"You mean like a brigadier?"

O'Leary had heard of brigadiers. They were the Russian mob's equivalent to the Italian mob's Capo régime. "Yes, a brigadier. There is a chance that Carl Konovalov will be coming for you."

O'Leary immediately sensed her fear and tried to overcome it. "You don't have to worry. I have more than enough men here to protect you."

"What is it you want me to do?"

"If and when things get crazy, you need to gather all of the women and get them to someplace out of the line of fire. I'll have my guys look into building some sort of shelter where you can get out of danger." He hoped she did not realize that there would most likely be no place where they were truly out of danger. He stood up and looked down at her. She had raised her face, and her brown eyes seemed wide with trust. He touched her cheek and said, "It's going to be okay, Tasha, we'll keep you safe."

"I know, but who will keep you safe?"

O'Leary smiled, exuding a confidence he was not sure of, and kissed her on the forehead. "Gordon and Burt Chaney are all the safety net I need."

O'Leary left the small community and stopped in the center of the warehouse's open area. He took out his cell phone and punched in a number. While he waited for the phone to be answered, he scanned the catwalks. Chaney stepped out of a secluded corner holding his phone to his ear and waved to him. "Meet me outside," O'Leary said.

---

[6] Similar to a Godfather in the Italian mob.

In less than five minutes, Chaney walked out into the sunlight and blinked as his eyes adjusted from the dim interior of the warehouse. "What's up?" he asked.

"It's time to hit Carl Konovalov is what's up."

"Won't be easy . . . he'll have an entourage with him."

"Just do what you do best, and I'll make it worth your while."

"Okay, where do I start looking?"

"He owns a club on Comm Ave, not far from Harvard Street. You'll find him there most nights."

"Consider it done."

Chaney peered through the rangefinder, centering the rear window of the Cadillac in the square box. The number three hundred appeared in the block where the device displayed the distance to the target. He placed the instrument in its case and searched the area between him and the car while looking for flags, pennants, or anything that would give him an indication of wind direction and speed. Not that three hundred yards was that long of a shot—hell, he had scored hits as far out as 650 yards. Usually, under five hundred yards the wind did not become a factor unless it was blowing hard or gusting. He saw a flagpole in front of an official-looking building. The flag barely moved in the soft summer breeze. This shot was going to be routine. He settled in to wait . . . and watch.

It was two in the morning when Konovalov and his entourage of bodyguards appeared. Thankful that streetlights had made the use of a starlight scope unnecessary, Chaney centered the crosshairs of the scope on the Russian's chest, then moved the reticule left, scarcely enough for the untrained eye to notice. He inhaled, let his breath out slowly until he had a steady sight picture, held his breath, and squeezed the trigger. The rifle's angry bark broke the stillness of the night. The pakhan was dead before his guards heard the rifle's sharp crack.

Chaney crouched behind the building's parapet, fully aware that the Russians had no idea where he was. They hunched down, weapons drawn as they looked in every direction, confused and scared, and awaiting the next bullet, which would never come.

Chaney took a cell phone from his pocket and punched in a text message. The message was succinct and to the point. "It's done. Who's next?"

55

In the primordial darkness, the truck's headlights bored a tunnel through the never-ending ocean of trees. To Cheryl, it seemed as if they were lightyears from civilization. Even the roads had long since ceased being paved and had names like St. Croix Road instead of route numbers. She stared through the windshield, trying to ignore the smears left by flying insects smashing against the glass and splotches of mud from driving through huge puddles at too high a speed. As Fischer drove, Cheryl's spirits sank lower and lower. She tried to remember how long it had been since she had seen another vehicle. Even if she were to escape, she would be who knew how deep into the wilderness and would surely starve or be attacked by a wild animal.

They rumbled across a narrow wooden bridge and turned along the small stream they had just crossed. They followed the road around a sharp turn and immediately stopped. In the middle of the road, looking as if he had been disturbed, was the largest moose she had ever seen. Its huge flat antlers were majestic; its eyes shone brightly in the headlamps, and it towered over the truck. The animal seemed to resent their presence and stood in the middle of the gravel and hard-pan lane as if he owned it. "What do we do now?" she whispered as if she were afraid it would overhear her and take umbrage with their presence.

"I guess we wait for him to move on. Hell, I don't know. I'm a fisherman, not a hunter."

They sat staring through the dirty glass until the moose decided they were not a threat or of interest and sauntered away into the darkness.

"I don't think I've ever seen an animal so large—" Cheryl said, her voice still hushed, "at least not outside of a zoo."

Fischer ignored her comment and started down the road. "We should be there in an hour."

"Where is there?"

He looked at her in such a manner that she felt as if she were a child. "Where we're going, that's where . . . now shut up and enjoy the ride, or I'll gag you, tie you up, and throw you in the back."

The moon had come out, illuminating the openings between the trees, and shadows seemed to be in command of the woods. As they drove, shafts of light would rip through gaps in the foliage where the trees had been thinned, allowing Cheryl to see little more than if it were still a moonless night. They crossed yet another bridge—this one looked like a large metal culvert. She saw a shaft of moonlight illuminate the road and in the headlights she saw a sign announcing they were turning onto Main Street. Suddenly they turned along some railroad tracks. Across the rail bed she saw several buildings that appeared to be vacant. "Where are we?" she asked.

"Howe Brook."

"That's it, Howe Brook?"

"Look at it. Do you see anything worth talking about?"

"You have family living here?"

"Two sisters—they're throwbacks to the hippies. They won't eat nothing that ain't organic, and they try to live off the land. Last time I was here, they didn't even have indoor plumbing, let alone electricity. Couple of crazy fuckin' women . . ."

Cheryl stared at him and wondered just how eccentric his sisters were—especially if *he* considered them to be crazy.

He turned onto a narrow track and followed the ruts until several cabins came into sight. The first lodge on the right was the only one with lights on inside, and he stopped the truck in front, got out, and walked around to open Cheryl's door. He led her to the porch that ran across the front of the rustic structure and banged on the threshold.

A voice from inside called, "Who's there?"

"Willard," he answered.

The door opened, and a gray-haired woman appeared in the threshold with a shotgun in her left hand. The stock rested across her forearm and was wedged into her armpit. She stared into the darkness, squinting her eyes as she tried to identify the visitor. She stared at him. "My brother, Willard?"

"Hey, Ernestine."

She lowered the shotgun and stepped back. "I been hearing all sorts of stuff about you. What you been up to?" She noticed Cheryl standing beside him. "Who's she?"

"That's Cheryl, my wife."

"The hell you say . . . ?"

"Where's Maddie?"

The old woman pointed into the bright moonlight toward a massive oak tree. "There. She's been dead for more than five years."

56

O'Leary and Chaney sat across from each other. The bar had been closed for over an hour, and Winter was finishing up closing.

"Thanks, Burt. As usual, you did good work."

"You got any more problems that I can fix?"

"I'll know in the next day or two. By the way, your expenses and hotel have been covered."

"Thanks." Chaney stood and stretched. "Speaking of which, I think I'll get some sleep. Call me when you know whether or not you're finished with my services." He paused, turned back to O'Leary, and said, "You watch your backs. This is probably only the beginning. These guys won't take this quietly . . . they're gonna hit back."

"You got it."

Once Chaney was gone, O'Leary walked to the bar. He placed the glasses he and Chaney had used on the surface and slid onto a stool.

"What's up, boss?"

"You ever think of going into business, Gordon?"

"Every now and then I do. Why, you got something in mind?"

"I've been thinking about retiring. I figure that you could take over the business for say . . . forty-five percent of the profits from current business and all of any new business you drum up."

"I ain't got much dough in the bank, boss."

"Like I said, you wouldn't need it. Every month you send me my share of the profits, and any new business you generate is all yours."

Winter folded the towel he held and draped it over the sink. He circled the bar and sat beside O'Leary. "What you going to do?"

"I been thinking about moving to a warmer climate . . . like Florida."

"Does a certain little Russian lady have a role in this new life?"

O'Leary stood up. "There's a very strong possibility." He slid off his stool and walked away.

Winter watched O'Leary walk to his office, smiled, and shook his head. "Mr. and Mrs. Jimmy O'Leary . . . who would have known?"

At eleven in the morning, O'Leary was back in his office and on a conference call with several of the men whose names he had found on Ariana's laptop. "So gentlemen, there you have it. I have taken care of the local pakhan who was extorting each of you for your indiscretions. I, however, am still in possession of the laptop and its contents and can ensure that it will never be used again—unless someone decides to interrupt my pending retirement. Do I hear any objections?"

There was silence from all of the other parties. "Then I consider our business concluded. Gentlemen, in the future you might want to do a bit more investigation before you decide to let your hair hang down."

"How can we be sure that you'll uphold your end of the bargain?" It was the unmistakable voice of the governor.

"I have nothing to gain from destroying your good names and reputations, Governor. You mind yourselves, and you'll never hear from me again. If you think you can eliminate the risk by hitting me, I'll make a call, and the same party that solved your previous problem with a three-hundred-yard shot . . . well, I think you get the point. If there isn't anything else, good day, gentlemen."

He broke the connection and stood up. He opened the door to the safe in his office and handed the laptop to Winter. "Keep this safe, Gordon. It may be the only thing that keeps us alive."

"I'll guard it with my life, boss."

"I'm not your boss anymore, Gordon. For the time being, let's just say we're partners—only I'm going to be a silent one." He lit a fresh cigarette. "Gordon, keep your eyes open."

"For?"

O'Leary pointed at the phone. "I don't give a fuck what promises the Governor made, this ain't over."

"Shit, boss, I know that," Winter answered. "He's a politician. They're experts at tellin' you what they think you want to hear then doing what they want."

"You can always tell when they're lying to you," O'Leary said.

"Yeah, their lips are moving."

57

Houston and Bouchard sped up I-95 north. Shortly after two in the morning, they reached the Stillwater Avenue exit north of Bangor. When they drove past the speed limit sign that announced an increase in allowable speed to seventy-five miles per hour, Houston stepped on the accelerator. Bouchard glanced at the speedometer and commented, "You're going to get a ticket."

Houston glanced at the indicator, which said that he was doing a steady eighty-five. "They'll give you ten over," he said. "Besides, if we meet more than five other cars, I'll be surprised."

Bouchard sat back, crossed her arms, and said, "Suit yourself. It's your license."

Houston glanced at her. "How're you doing?"

"I'm okay."

The road raced beneath their tires, and Houston peered into the windshield, trying to see beyond the range of his high beams. He saw a yellow sign appear, and as it neared, he saw it was a warning to watch for moose in the road. Bouchard must have seen it, too, because she said, "At this speed we'll be roadkill if we hit one of those things."

"We'll be fine."

"Mike ..."

"What, babe?"

"If he gets his hands on me, don't let him take me with him—even if it means you have to kill me."

He glanced at her, and her face looked pallid in the blue aura of the dash lights. "He's not going to get his hands on you ... and we're going to bring Cheryl back alive."

From the corner of his eye he saw her looking at him. "Promise me, Mike."

"Anne—"

"Promise me."

"All right, hon. I promise."

She turned back to the front. "Where do we turn off?"

"In about fifty miles, exit 264, Sherman. From there we take Route 11 north to St. Croix Road, where we'll meet Wera and the rest of the team. Then we have a ten or fifteen mile ride through the woods."

———

Houston and Anne reached the rendezvous point at 4:30. They saw several vehicles parked along the entrance to the gravel woods road known as St. Croix Road. The first vehicle in line was a white SUV with the markings of the Aroostook County Sheriff's Department. His headlights lit up Wera Eklund standing amidst seven other law enforcement people. He recognized the uniforms of the game wardens and assumed the two men wearing camouflage were members of the state police tactical team. Houston stopped in the middle of the road and rolled his window down.

Eklund approached his truck and shined a flashlight at his face. "Mike?"

"Looks like you really called out the troops," he said.

She walked to the window and bent over, looking past Houston at Bouchard. "Hey, Anne, how you doing?"

"I'm fine, Wera."

Eklund smiled. "I would imagine you're hearing it a lot lately."

Eklund turned to business. "This is the team that was at Square Lake. They want to take him down as much as anyone after that goat rope."

Houston and Bouchard got out of their truck, and Eklund introduced them to the others. Eklund stepped forward and handed Bouchard and Houston each a cup of coffee. In the early morning chill, steam rose from the foam takeout cups and drifted through the beams of Houston's truck lights. "What's the plan?" Houston asked.

Eklund placed an enlarged satellite photo on the hood of her truck. "This is what was once Howe Brook Village. All it is now is a cluster of seasonal camps except for . . ." she placed her finger on one building, ". . . this place. That's where Howe Brook's only year-round resident lives. It's the home of our perp's sister, Ernestine." She let everyone study the photo for a few moments and then continued. "Ernie knows Anne, Mike, and me . . . maybe you wardens, too." Holmquist nodded. "We'll approach the cabin. I want the rest of the team to set up a perimeter around the house. If he gets into the woods behind it, we'll play hell trying to find him. Everyone ready?" She waited for a few moments, and when no one spoke up she said, "Let's roll. It's between three quarters of an hour and an hour drive in there."

Houston and Bouchard's was the second vehicle in the convoy. It had been a dry summer, and the woods company had recently graded the road but had not gotten around to oiling the surface; the result was a cloud of dust so thick that the five-vehicle procession had spread out until it was almost two miles long.

Since all the law enforcement vehicles were equipped with two-way radios and Houston's had none, they felt lost and isolated. "I hope no one runs into us," he said as he backed off the accelerator, opening the distance between his truck and Eklund's SUV.

"Give me your cell phone," Bouchard said.

Houston tossed the phone in her lap. "Wera should be the first number in the recent call log." He listened as Bouchard spoke to either Eklund or the deputy riding with her.

As soon as Bouchard closed the call, she placed the phone in the console, and she reached into the back of the extended cab for her backpack. She extricated a pair of L. L. Bean Maine hunting boots, removed her walking shoes, and replaced them with the boots. "If he gets into the woods, I'm going after him," she said. "I put your boots in the back, too." She laced the leather uppers and sat back. "Looks like it's getting light," she said, sounding as if they were on a Sunday excursion.

Houston noticed that she was correct—the truck's headlights had less effect on the billowing cloud of dust, but he was still able to see. Eklund's SUV suddenly appeared off to the side, and he stopped. He rolled to a stop and opened his window. The air was chalky and smelled of dust. "Problem?" he asked when Eklund appeared.

"Nope. This is Harvey Siding Road. From here we walk."

Houston and Bouchard exited their truck and studied their surroundings. The dust had settled, and they saw the trees that lined the road seemed to be suffocating in the powdery dirt that coated them, forcing their limbs to droop with the weight. "Come the next rain," Eklund commented, "this place is going to be one huge mud pie."

"Never mind that," Houston said, "a good wind and there'll be a sandstorm of Olympic proportions."

58

Ernestine was already awake and sitting at the table when Fischer woke up. He rolled out of the bed and saw her. "There's coffee on the stove," she said.

"Gotta go," he said.

"Privy is out back."

She sat at the table until Willard returned from the outhouse. He poured a cup of coffee and sat across from her. "Who is she, Willard?" The woman he had brought with him was asleep on the old sofa that sat in front of the fireplace.

"I told you, she's my wife."

"Where and when were you married?"

"In Portland, last year. You can ask the old woman and the old man. They were there."

Ernestine stared at him. "Willard . . ."

He sighed in frustration. "What?"

"Dad has been dead for over twenty years."

Willard looked confused, almost bewildered. "That can't be. I talk to him all the time."

"You and Mother talk with each other, too . . ."

His face flushed, and he began to fidget like a schoolboy enduring a boring math lesson on a warm spring day. "Why shouldn't I talk with her? She's my mother."

"Because I've been told that Mother is in an advanced stage of Alzheimer's. She doesn't know where she is, let alone have the ability to talk."

He suddenly became suspicious. "Who told you that? Who's been here?"

"Calm down, Willard."

Willard leapt to his feet and knocked his chair over. "You're just like the rest of them! Always questioning, never believing a thing I say!"

"Willard, please sit down."

He slapped the table and pushed his face toward hers. His eyes seemed to light with a demonic fire, and he snarled, "I don't want to." She realized how dangerous her brother was and tried to calm him.

"Willard . . ."

"What?"

"I'm sorry that I doubted you. Sit down . . . please?"

He picked up the chair and placed it by the table.

"Willard."

He dropped into the chair, folded his arms across his chest, and turned his face away from her.

"Look at me, Willard."

When he faced her, the rage was gone and a calm, reasonable man smiled at her. "Hey, how about you give me a break, okay? After all this time, you don't know me." He glanced around the room. "You haven't had to bust your ass trying to keep the business going and take care of the old homestead. After I got rid of the old man . . ."

"I always thought that Father drowned at sea."

A wicked leer covered his face. "He drowned with a gaff in his back." He stood up. "I need some fresh air."

"If you're going for a walk, stay on the roads, there are millions of acres of woods out there. You could get lost forever. And take your rifle, it's getting on toward fall, and there's been some bears hanging around."

Fischer picked up his rifle and walked outside.

As soon as the door closed, Ernestine darted to the sofa and woke Cheryl up. "We have to get out you of here."

Cheryl sat up and looked startled as she took in the interior of the single room cabin. "Where's Willard?"

"He's gone out for a bit. How long has he had you?"

"Truthfully, I'm not sure. What's the date?"

"September 10th."

"A month, give or take a few days."

"Are you and he married?"

"Only in his twisted mind."

"Has he . . .?"

"Had sex with me? No, he's impotent. He's been kidnapping women for a long time trying to find one who will help him—and give him an heir."

"I was told that he's been getting away with this for several years? Why haven't one of the women's bodies been discovered before this?"

Cheryl looked at her and said, "They won't find them. He disposes of the bodies."

59

Once the state police and wardens were in place surrounding the cabin, Houston, Bouchard, and Eklund walked up the drive. When they turned the corner around a line of dense bushes, they spotted the stolen truck. Houston said, "He's here."

Eklund took her service revolver out. "You carrying?"

"Yes." Houston took a 9 mm pistol from his holster and checked the magazine. He racked the receiver and loaded a round in the chamber.

"What's our plan?" Houston asked.

"All we can do is play it by ear."

"Wera, don't fool with this guy. If he as much as looks at us cross-eyed, shoot him."

Bouchard also drew her weapon, and they spread out until they were separated by about twenty feet. She checked her Glock, ensured there was a live round in the chamber, and slowly approached the cabin, watching for any sign of movement.

They were thirty feet from the cabin when the door opened. All three dropped to one knee, their weapons pointed at the open door. When Ernestine Fischer led Cheryl Guerette through the door, they relaxed but kept their pistols ready.

The sight of three armed strangers rattled Cheryl, and she stepped behind Ernestine. "Who are these people?" she asked.

"The woman on the left is Deputy Sheriff Wera Eklund. I only met the other two the other day. It seems your folks hired them to find you."

Cheryl stepped to one side and studied the three people. "Anne?"

"Yes, Cheryl, it's me."

Bouchard lowered her Glock when Cheryl ran forward and leaped into her arms. The two former captives hugged each other and began to cry. "You were right," Bouchard whispered in Cheryl's ear.

Cheryl pulled her head back, looked into Anne's face, and asked, "When was that?"

"That night in his room when you wanted me to kill him—I should have listened."

"Where is he?" Houston asked, watching the front of the cabin.

"I don't know," Ernestine answered. "He went for a walk."

Houston turned his attention to Cheryl. "Are you alright?"

"Yes, bruised and scared, but other than that I'm fine."

A shot was fired in the woods behind the cabin; within seconds it was followed by two more.

Fischer strolled along the old logging road, which was really two tracks with a grass median in the middle. The wind had picked up and created enough noise that it drowned out the sounds of birds; occasionally he heard a tree creaking as it swayed back and forth. Suddenly a figure in a green uniform appeared to his right.

Fischer spun, dropped to one knee, and shot the game warden. The morning calm was ripped apart by people shouting and calling. Fischer's heart pounded. *They're everywhere.* He ran straight down the road, deeper into the wilderness. He heard something snap by his head followed by the immediate report of a weapon being fired.

Fischer ran as hard as he'd ever run in his life, vaulting over downed trees, skirting brush and large rocks, and blasting through ferns. After five minutes, he slowed and listened. At first it was difficult to hear over his own rasping breath, but his breathing soon slowed. He saw a game trail that meandered up and down a series of small hills and ridges and listened for the sound of pursuit. Hearing none, he turned his back to Howe Brook and ventured deeper into the woods.

Houston ran to his truck and drove it to Ernestine Fischer's cabin. He took out his Remington 700 and a box of ammunition. He placed the ammo, extra magazines, and some food supplies in a rucksack. He felt a presence and turned to see Guy Boudreau, the MSP Sergeant, standing nearby. The cop said, "I'm going with you. I can take him into custody and, should he be killed, back you up in any inquest."

"Someone needs to stay here with Cheryl," Houston said.

"I'll stay here," Eklund said. "Someone needs to coordinate things when the reinforcements arrive."

"Okay, I'll be ready in a few seconds." Houston opened the rifle's bolt and, one at a time, pressed four .308 caliber rounds into the weapon's internal magazine. He engaged the safety with his thumb.

One of the game wardens stepped forward. "I'll be with you, too." She held out her hand. "Allison Försberg, this is my district. I know these woods and have tracking skills."

"Glad to have you." Houston slipped the rucksack onto his shoulders, adjusted the straps, and turned to Bouchard. "I'm ready."

The four-person party set off following the narrow lane that Fischer had taken. Once inside the protection of the trees, Försberg took the lead. The warden's face was grim when she stopped alongside the trail. She pointed at a small pool of blood. "This is where he shot Nick Holmquist. When Nick gets back to duty, he'll catch hell. It isn't everyday a warden gets shot twice by the same perp . . . not to mention with the same rifle."

"So he's going to be all right?"

"Should be—he was hit in the thigh, but it missed all the major blood vessels. Wera is arranging for a helicopter to get him out."

They moved on, each of them looking at the spot where one of their party had been shot. After she'd walked about ten yards, Försberg led them off the lane into the brush and ferns. The sun shined through openings in the canopy, making the woods come alive in a kaleidoscope of color. Ferns and shade plants grew alongside the brilliant colors of sundry blooming flowers. The small squad ignored the aesthetics of nature and concentrated on the area, expecting Fischer to attack at any moment.

Försberg pointed at the top of a dead fallen tree; someone or something had leaped over it, scraping the moss that covered its surface in the process. "He's headed this way." She pointed to the northwest. "It's about ten miles in that direction before he'll hit a road of any size. These woods are littered with old tote roads, most of which are impassable unless you have an ATV or are on foot. But they'll make walking a lot easier."

Bouchard stood beside the warden. "How will we ever find him in here?"

Försberg touched her on the arm. "Believe me, he's leaving me a trail a blind woman could read." She walked in the direction she had earlier indicated.

Bouchard watched her walk away and turned to Houston and Boudreau. "Is that so?" she muttered, "Well, I'm not blind, and I can't see it."

Houston kept his voice low and said, "Let's get this bastard."

Fischer stopped and wiped his forehead. He had been trying to make a looping left circle that would lead him back to the railroad tracks that passed through Howe Brook. He came upon them as the sun was making its presence felt. He realized that he was not in the best of situations. He'd been forced to flee with no provisions and only had the four rounds that were loaded into his rifle. More than anything else, he needed transportation. Once he found the rail bed, he would be able to find the St. Croix Stream, which would lead him to St. Croix Road. Once he was on the road, he could hopefully steal a ride. Worst case, he'd have to follow the road to Route 11 and follow it until he came to a house or business where he could find assistance.

He quickly glanced at the sky. By now they would have put out calls for backup. There would be eyes on all of the major thoroughfares and in the sky. Fischer wondered how far behind him the ground troops were—at best he had an hour's head start. He dashed across the railroad tracks and into the woods on the far side.

"He's heading for the tracks," Försberg said.

"What?" Houston asked.

"The railroad," Boudreau answered. "It's the old Bangor and Aroostook right of way, the same one that runs through Howe Brook belongs to the Montreal, Maine & Atlantic Railway for now—after that derailment in Lake Mégantic, they'll probably be bankrupt soon. He won't be stupid enough to stay on them, though. He'd have to be a complete idiot not to realize there's an air search going on."

"But," Försberg said, "if he crosses over, he could follow the stream to the road."

"And," Bouchard said, "he's been known to steal a car or two."

"Shit," Houston added, "if there are still trains running through here, he could hop one, then who knows where in hell he could end up."

"We can't be concerned about that. From the looks of his trail, he's headed north along the stream. I think we can get ahead of him." Försberg said, "Guy and I will stay on his trail." She turned to Houston and Bouchard. "You guys can walk the tracks, and when you hit the road, turn left to the bridge over the stream . . . he'll come there sooner or later."

60

O'Leary guided Tasha into a seat in the back booth of the Claddagh Pub. After the waitress had dropped off menus and took their drink order, Tasha said, "This is nice place. Do you own it?"

"Until yesterday I did—now I'm a partner."

Their drinks came, and O'Leary said, "Tasha, I'm leaving Boston."

Her smile dropped.

"I'm heading down to Florida. I bought a place on the gulf coast south of Fort Meyers."

"When will you leave?"

"I'll be around for a while yet. I want to get you and the others settled in someplace where you'll be safe from assholes like the late Carl Konovalov and his people."

"You shouldn't worry about us. We'll get along alright."

The waitress returned, and they ordered meals. Once they were alone again, O'Leary said, "I was thinking about taking Inca. I'll enroll her in school . . . I've never had a child of my own."

Tasha sipped her drink. "What do you know about raising a girl on the verge of womanhood?"

"Not a lot, that's certain."

"Then I better come with you."

O'Leary's acne-scarred face broke into a jagged smile. "Christ, I thought you'd never offer."

Winter suddenly appeared beside their table with a bottle of champagne wrapped in a towel. "Compliments of the new management," he announced as the waitress placed two long-stemmed glasses on the table. Winter began to pour. "So are we pouring a farewell drink or toasting a budding relationship?"

———————

The Samovar Restaurant was empty, an uncommon occurrence for a Friday. However, the ownership was not concerned. The entire restaurant had been reserved for a meeting between Zinovy Istomin, Athanasius Aliyev, Vyacheslav Evseyev, and Yaropolk Kryukov—the recently deceased Carl Konovalov's brigadiers. The men—similar to caporegimes in the Italian mob—each were in charge of one of the organization's businesses.

Once all were in attendance and bottles of chilled Stolichnaya had been opened, they got down to the matter at hand. Since all were Russian speakers, the meeting was conducted in their native tongue. "What," Istomin asked, "is to be done about this O'Leary?"

"I am taking care of that," Evseyev answered. "He will not be a problem much longer."

Istomin gave Aliyev a quick look. Evseyev's way of dealing with matters was well known. He was reputed to have killed so many people in Russia that the krysha there had shipped him to New York. The Brighton Beach krysha had in turn sent him to Boston. "Vyacheslav," Istomin said, "we cannot have a blood bath in the streets. This O'Leary has information that if it becomes known could ruin any number of our benefactors."

"Da, I understand. Nevertheless, I also understand that if we allow the killing of our pakhan to go unpunished, we will lose a great deal of influence."

There was general consent that he was correct. They seemed willing to allow him a free rein when he said, "Trust me, I will not jeopardize our business."

"Now," Istomin said, "what is to be done about the . . . product we lost on the Cape?"

"Nothing," said Aliyev. "We look at it as a loss. The leverage O'Leary has on our benefactors is dependent upon us leaving those whores alone."

"I believe," Evseyev said, "that brings us to the most pressing issue before us: who is to be pakhan?"

The conversation dropped to an uneasy silence. The assembled brigadiers wondered who Evseyev would try to kill first.

61

Fischer followed the stream, circumventing several swampy bogs and weaving a path through mud and ferns for hours. Twice he'd heard the sound of an airplane motor and had been forced to take cover in the waist-high weeds and brush. Flies and mosquitoes, attracted by the blood and pus that seeped from his wounds, flew around his head, and he blew through his lips trying to keep them away from his eyes. His exposed flesh itched from more insect bites than he could count, and he wondered how many blood-sucking ticks and leeches had infiltrated his clothing. From his knees down, he was soaked from the water he'd splashed through, and from the knees up, he was wet with sweat and blood. He cursed and pushed onward.

The sun was directly west and dropping toward the horizon when he saw the bridge where the St. Croix Road spanned the stream of the same name. He breathed a deep sigh of relief. Now all he had to do was wait for a vehicle to come along. He paused, wiped his forehead with his sleeve, and wondered what Cheryl was doing. His *wife* would remain at Ernestine's and wait for him to come for her. He squatted down in a stand of bulrushes and cattails, the cottony fluff filling the air around him. He saw someone walk onto the bridge, and he squatted lower, peering intently at the figure. She was familiar. He flushed with a mixture of anger and satisfaction when he realized that here, in the middle of fucking nowhere, stood the woman who had taken Cheryl away and forced him to flee his home. He hissed with pain as he raised the rifle to his shoulder. *Maybe there is justice in life after all.*

Bouchard half walked, half slid down the bank to the eddy beside the bridge. She dipped her hand into the water and dabbed it on her forehead and the back of her neck. Suddenly she heard the thud of a bullet hitting one of the bridge's wooden supports—the last thing she heard as she dove into the oily water and cattails was the report of a weapon firing. She pulled her 9 mm pistol out of the waistband of her jeans and stared through the branches of the rushes, looking for the source of the attack.

"Anne, are you alright?"

"Yeah."

"Where'd the shot come from?" Houston asked.

"Downstream."

"Stay where you are and stay low."

"Can you see him?" Bouchard asked. There was no response, and she knew that by now Houston had gone into sniper mode and was stalking the shooter.

Fischer heard the woman talking to someone else—a man. He turned and began to follow his own trail south. The stream, which only a short time ago had been his guide, was now a hindrance. He had no idea how deep it was, and it was too wide for him to cross without exposing himself. He recalled a spot where a series of large rocks spread across the waterway's breadth. He could use those rocks as stepping stones to ford the river and disappear into the woods.

Fischer realized that he needed to move quickly, and that meant he'd have to move away from the stream and the swampy marshes along its bank. He turned to his left and out of the corner of his eye spied two figures moving north alongside the St. Croix. He recognized the green uniform of a game warden and one of the camouflaged cops. *He was caught in the middle.* There was, he surmised, one positive to the situation; maybe he could get the two groups shooting at each other. He scrambled through an area of thick bushes and into the dense pine forest and crouched low enough that the undergrowth hid him from view. He heard voices behind him shout but no gunfire. He ran due east and, after a hundred yards or so, spun left into an area of boggy moss and dead trees. His feet sank into the soft ground, and he surprised a cow moose that was foraging in the marshy vegetation. The large clumsy-looking animal bounded over some deadfall and disappeared into the wilderness.

Boudreau was the first to recognize Houston. He waved, and when Houston returned the signal, the two snipers slowly advanced until they met in the shade of a huge pine.

Houston was on one knee studying a scuffmark in the pine needles. "Looks like he went that way." He pointed into the darkness created by the dense trees.

"Who fired the shot?" Boudreau asked.

"He did."

Försberg appeared through the bushes and tall grass. "Where's Anne?"

"By the bridge. She's the one he shot at." As if on cue, a pistol shot rang out, and Houston forgot his training and started running toward the source.

Fischer made a loop turning toward the bridge. He hoped that he could circumvent the two parties, and once past them, he could dash across the bridge and get away. He broke out of the woods about two hundred yards from the bridge and crouched in the waist-high grass that bordered the road. He crept forward, keeping his rifle in a position where he could quickly fire. He halved the distance between him and the bridge and saw no sign of pursuit or ambush. He fought back the impulse to leave the grass and run down the road. He continued his cautious approach.

The wind gusted, and the sounds of it coursing through the trees covered any sound he made. When he estimated that he was within twenty-five yards of the bridge, he exploded from the cover of the bulrushes and dashed for the bridge. He was a quarter of the way across when the woman appeared, partially hidden in a stand of bushes. She held a pistol and fired at him. He fired from the waist as he ran, and she went down. He kept running and disappeared on the western side of the stream.

―――――――――

Houston sprinted through the cattails, ignoring the explosion of down as he blasted a path through them. He stopped abruptly when he saw Bouchard standing on the road and aiming her pistol across the stream. He was in the throes of an extreme adrenaline rush but still paused in relief when he saw that she appeared to be okay.

"Did he hit you?"

"No."

"Did you hit him?"

"If I did, it didn't slow him down any."

―――――――――

Cheryl sat at the table in Ernestine's kitchen, staring off into some destination only she could see. Wera Eklund pulled out a chair and sat across from her. "You'll be out of here soon," she said. "And this will be over."

Cheryl looked at the Deputy Sheriff and appreciated her caring words, but she wasn't sure whether or not to believe them. "Over? I don't think I'll ever get over this."

"With time and help, you will."

Ernestine brought over a pot of freshly brewed coffee and three mugs. She sat beside Wera. "This must have been a very harrowing month for you."

"You know what's ironic about all this?" Cheryl said.

"What?" Wera asked.

"In spite of everything, Willard may have saved my life."

The two women looked at her, and she saw the disbelief in their faces.

"When he took me, I was addicted to heroin—strung out bad. When he had me shackled to that bed, he nursed me through a cold turkey withdrawal."

Ernestine poured her a mug of coffee and slid it across the table. Cheryl added cream and sugar and said, "If he hadn't taken me, I'd most likely be dead from an overdose or possibly HIV positive by now from unsafe sex or a dirty needle."

"All that matters," Eklund said, "is that you're safe now."

"Safe? Is anyone ever truly safe? I'm sure that those people out there are going to put an end to Willard one way or another, but who's ever safe from themselves? What will keep me off the smack or off the streets?"

"You have a couple of things going for you," Ernestine said.

"Really?"

"You have a support group now. Look at what these people have done to save you. They have risked their lives and even when it seemed there was no hope of ever finding you, Mike and Anne—and your grandparents—refused to give up. They kept looking."

"My grandparents? How will I ever explain all this to them?"

"I'm sure they'll forgive and forget," Eklund said.

"I'll settle for forgive—I don't want anyone to ever forget."

Eklund reached across the table and took Cheryl's hand. "No, don't forget, but don't dwell on it or let it drive you."

"If it gets to be too much for you," Ernestine said, "you can come up here for a while. You can't get much further away from *it* than here."

Cheryl felt a wave of emotion, and she began sobbing. The two older women circled the table like mother bears protecting their cubs and wrapped their arms around her. For the first time in what seemed like eternity, Cheryl Guerette felt safe. They stayed that way until the sound of a landing helicopter made them part.

"Well," Eklund said, "looks as if your ride to the hospital is here."

"I'm fine," Cheryl protested, "I don't need . . ."

Ernestine placed a finger against Cheryl's lips. "The first step in getting over this is to listen to the people who care about what happens to you."

62

"Did you see where he entered the woods?" Houston asked.

"By that dead tree," Bouchard said.

Houston looked at the stumps and trunks of thousands of cut trees that the loggers had discarded along the periphery of the road.

"The one with the red paint on it," she added.

Houston saw Boudreau and Försberg appear on the road. They waited for them and then spent a few seconds updating them. The foursome set off in pursuit. Boudreau looked at Bouchard and said, "You really should have a long gun."

"Why? It wouldn't have made a difference. Besides, every time I've seen this perp, he was well within the range of my Glock."

They crossed the bridge and left the road. Without saying, they all knew better than to offer Fischer any easy targets of opportunity. "We'll go in here. You're a better tracker," Houston said to Försberg. "You guys follow his tracks."

Fischer bolted away from the road and into the trees. A large grouse exploded out of a pine tree, and he started, his rifle aimed in its direction. In seconds, the bird disappeared into the deep woods. Realizing that he was in an agitated state, Fischer forced himself to stop, get his breathing under control, and calm down. He sank to the ground and leaned against a tree. He studied his surroundings and verified what he already knew—he had no goddamned idea where he was.

Well, you got yourself into a fine fucking mess this time.

Fischer sighed in frustration. The last thing he needed now was to listen to a harangue from his old man. "Go away."

Go away? You need me more than ever, dummy. What do you know about surviving in the woods?

"I'll learn."

If you get a chance. What you think those cops are doing right now? I'll tell you one thing they ain't doin'... they ain't sittin' on their asses like you. Get up and get movin'.

"I don't know where I am."

Doesn't fuckin' matter where you are. You're still free. There'll be time to worry about where you are once you ditch those assholes chasin' you.

As much as it pained him, Fischer knew the old man was right. He struggled to his feet and moved deeper into the trees.

Houston glanced at his watch: three o'clock. At best they had four-and-a-half hours of daylight left. If they didn't catch Fischer soon, they had a decision to make; they were not equipped to spend the night in the forest. Truthfully, they weren't carrying even the rudimentary equipment for a day in the woods—no food or canteens. He knelt beside a small brook and scooped a handful of water into his mouth. At first Bouchard had refused to drink that way, but as the chase wore on, thirst overcame her objections, and she, too, drank whenever they found a moving source.

Bouchard sat on a boulder, wiped her brow, and stared up the ridge they had been climbing. She looked to her left and saw Försberg and Boudreau to their right. The pairs had regrouped after they were several hundred yards off the road and had spaced themselves so they could keep Fischer's trail in sight. He had led them deeper and deeper into the forest. Bouchard wondered how long it had been since human beings had ventured into these woods—if ever.

Suddenly Houston dropped to one knee and shouted, "Stop!"

Bouchard and the others looked at him and saw that he aimed his rifle toward the top of the ridge. They turned in that direction and saw a figure at the crest. Houston fired, and the figure disappeared. They scrambled for cover, expecting return fire. It didn't come.

Houston raced upward, and they fell in behind him.

Fischer felt the bullet pass through his side, propelling him forward. He crashed through a copse of alder bushes and tumbled down a slope he had heretofore not seen. He slid downslope in the detritus of years' worth of dead leaves and humus. Too shocked to do anything but keep a tight grip on his rifle, he let gravity propel him down. He hit several broken limbs and came to rest amidst the branches of a downed pine. He scrambled to a shooting position. A quick glance upward told him that he had to move. The trail he'd left while sliding down the grade was so evident a cub scout would have no problem following it. He crawled out the back side and scrambled away.

"Did you hit him?" Boudreau asked when they joined Houston on the ridge top.

"Not good enough. He turned at the last second. If anything, the wound's superficial." He pointed at the line of disturbed leaves. "We know where he went, though."

The four hunters slowly descended, their bodies at an angle so that their forward legs acted as brakes to keep them from entering an uncontrolled slide. They reached the downed pine and saw a blood trail. "You hit him," Försberg said. "Don't know how badly, but he's bleeding."

"I hope he bleeds out," Bouchard spat.

Fischer didn't think the bullet had hit any vital organs, but he felt his strength flowing out of his body with his blood. He slowly walked along the footpath that followed the cliff's edge. He looked over the promontory and saw the beaver pond about twenty-five feet below. He heard a sound behind him and spun around. . . .

———————

Fischer was less than twenty yards away when they broke out of the woods along the periphery of the ledge. The man in the lead carried a lethal-looking rifle with a scope. He dropped to one knee, but before he could get a shot off, the bitch who'd caused all this skidded to a halt and had her pistol out. She screamed, "Bastard!" and fired twice.

———————

Houston saw the first bullet hit Fischer in the left shoulder. He watched in silence as the Fisherman rotated and then fell over the precipice. He followed the killer's descent until he disappeared into the water. The four manhunters stood watching the surface for several minutes, waiting for his body to reappear.

It did not.

———————

At seven, the sun was sinking below the trees and Eklund, Houston, Bouchard, and Försberg stood on the shore of the abandoned beaver dam watching bubbles break the surface where three warden service divers searched the pond for Fischer's body.

Eklund looked at her watch and said, "They'll have to come up soon. It'll be dark in a half hour, and they'll never find anything."

"No sign of his having gotten out?" Houston asked.

"Do you really believe he could have survived being shot twice and then falling from up there?" Eklund pointed at the promontory from which Fischer had tumbled.

"No offense to my partner," Houston said, "but I saw him get hit in the shoulder. Unless the bullet hit bone and ricocheted into his heart or lungs, there isn't anything there vital enough to kill him. At least he won't be using that arm anytime soon."

One of the divers broke the surface and swam toward them; when he was able, he stood and staggered through the deep mud until he was beside them.

"Anything?" Försberg asked.

"A shit load of old stumps and downed trees. One entrance into an abandoned old beaver hut, but it's too dark for us to get in there and check it. Looks like the entrance had caved in—there was debris all around it, so I doubt he would have fit in there."

"Well," Eklund said, "if the weather holds, we'll check it out tomorrow. We may as well put a wrap on it for today."

"I'll have a couple of wardens stay in the area," Försberg said. "Just in case he's still around."

63

He woke up lying with his torso on wet dirt and his lower extremities submerged in water. Wherever he was, it was pitch black and smelled of dead wood, mud, and something musty. His shoulder throbbed with pain, and he felt hot. He pushed back into the water and almost cried when the pain from his multiple wounds ripped through his body. He lowered his head below the surface, it felt cool and refreshed him. *Where the hell am I?*

He pushed himself out of the water and onto the muddy shelf. He lay back and remembered the bitch shooting him then the plunge into the water. He sank to the bottom and saw the dark mound. He clawed his way inside and remembered gasping for air and then feeling around until he felt the muddy shelf. With the memory came the knowledge of his location. He was inside the beaver lodge—the musty stink he smelled was probably beaver shit.

Fischer knew that as much as he'd like to stay where he was, he had to get out of there. He rolled back into the water and found the short tunnel that led to the entrance. It took his last reserve of strength to stretch his ravaged torso. He was unable to raise his left arm, so he swam with his right hand in front and, for a brief moment, panicked when he encountered an obstruction. With strength he didn't think he had,

Fischer clawed at the obstacle, all the while fighting back the terror every fisherman had of death by drowning. He wedged his feet into the soft mud bottom and surged forward, kicking hard, and the blockage fell away.

Fischer pulled himself out of the narrow opening and swam to the surface. He broke out of the grasp of the inky water and swam to the dam. He crawled out of the pond, collapsing on the narrow path that fishermen had made along the dam top.

He was unaware of how long he lay on the top of the barrier. But when he felt he had recovered sufficiently, he crawled to the swamp that surrounded the downstream side. He grabbed the trunk of a tree and pulled himself to his feet and stood beside the pond. After the primordial darkness of the beaver hut, the silhouette of which he could see clearly, the night seemed brilliant. The moon had yet to elevate over the trees, but there was enough light for him to walk. He found a one-inch-round stick that would serve as a staff and hobbled away from the dam to the base of the short cliff from which he'd tumbled.

Several times he wrenched his damaged shoulder as he scaled the ledge. He knew that the cops had most likely left someone in the area, and he stifled the desire to cry in agony. When he reached the summit, he laid on the ground. Both of his shoulders were fucked—one with the infected wound from the gaff and the other from the bullet—and he was sure that blood and pus seeped from them, as well as from the wounds in his back and side. He wasn't sure where he was, but he knew in which direction the road lay. Once he was there, he knew how to get back to Howe Brook, where his wife surely awaited his return. As he started the trek to his sister's, he thought of the bitch who had done so much damage to him. He pushed his pain aside by planning and visualizing the ways he was going to punish her once he had her.

He was also aware that it was suicidal to remain where he was; he had to put as much distance as possible between himself and the beaver pond. Moving slowly so he wouldn't draw the attention of any cops in the area, it took most of his remaining strength to walk back to the road.

It was daylight when Fischer arrived at Howe Brook. He hid in the forest and saw a strange vehicle in the yard. He sat against a tree and fought against his desire to sleep. His ravaged body screamed for rest, but he couldn't allow it.

He burned with a fiery fever and had no idea how long he remained in a semi-comatose state beneath the tree before Ernestine came out of her cabin. He tried to call out, but all he could manage was a hoarse croaking sound that was immediately lost in the sound of the wind through the trees.

His first thought was to make his sister pay for betraying him. Then he realized that he was too weak to confront her. He needed to find someplace where he could hide . . . and heal. There would come a day when he could get even with them all: Ernestine, the bitch, and his unfaithful wife.

64

Cheryl lay in bed, staring listlessly out the window. She heard people enter the room and turned toward them. At first, she seemed scared when she saw her grandmother. Then she smiled as tears ran down her face. "Gram . . ."

Betty Guerette darted across the hospital room and hugged her granddaughter. Archie followed and looked more than a bit awkward as he stood beside the bed waiting for them to finish their embrace.

Sam Fuchs stood back, silently observing as the family spent a few moments consoling each other. After a tearful few minutes, Cheryl looked over her grandmother's shoulder and saw Fuchs.

"Hello, Lieutenant."

"Do you two know each other?" Betty asked.

"We met last night when they brought me here," Cheryl replied.

Fuchs smiled. "How are you?"

"Better. Have they found him?"

"No, but they're searching every inch of the woods up there and have alerted the rest of the state, New Hampshire, and Massachusetts, as well. They'll find him; it's only a matter of time."

Fuchs took charge of the meeting. The state policeman took a small recorder out of his pocket and placed it on the stand beside her bed. "I'd like to tape this conversation if you don't mind. Cheryl, we need to know everything you can tell us about this guy." He looked at her grandparents. "You folks might want to step outside . . . this could be hard to hear."

"If Cheryl is going to get past this, we need to know what we're dealing with," Betty said. "We'll stay."

Fuchs wondered how Cheryl felt about them hearing her story. When she said, "I want them here. I have to tell them what happened eventually," she gave Fuchs an intent look.

Fuchs nodded his head and then started his recorder and told everyone to find chairs and take a seat. Once everyone was settled, he sat back, perched on the unoccupied bed. He looked at Cheryl and said, "Why don't you start? It may be best if you start at the beginning when he abducted you."

Cheryl glanced at her grandmother. Her lower lip trembled. "I was looking for a fix, working around Traveler Street and the Public Garden . . ." She looked at her grandmother, uncertain of the reception she would get when she confessed to being a drug addict and prostitute.

Betty wrapped her arms around her granddaughter. "Don't worry, just tell your story."

Archie sat on the foot of the bed and softly patted Cheryl's leg. "Ain't no judges or juries here, Cheryl—just your family and friends."

She inhaled and stiffened like a condemned woman who'd just decided to get her execution over and done with. "Gram, Gramp . . . can you ever forgive me?"

Elizabeth patted her hand. "Don't you worry, baby, there's nothing to forgive. I know what you were doing." Trying to ease the tension, she glanced at Archie. "You don't live with a sailor all your life and not know of such things."

Archie reddened and said, "Now, Betty, that was before I married you . . ."

Betty shut him up with a wave of her hand. "Go on, Cheryl, tell these people what they need to know to find this man."

65

Houston and Bouchard sat on the front porch of their cabin. The sun hung low in the sky, and an early fall chill hung in the air. "You think they'll ever find his body?" Bouchard asked.

"It's hard to say. If his body ever comes up, there's any number of predators out there."

"Body would be pretty wasted anyhow."

"That depends. It gets awfully cold in those woods. That pond will have a couple of feet of ice on it. He's not in there, anyway. The divers didn't find anything but a bunch of old trees." Houston sipped from his mug of hot cider.

"Do you think he's still alive?"

"Well, the chances are slim—you put a nine in him, and then he fell twenty-five feet into that pond." He sipped the cider. "Still, I wouldn't put it past that sonuvabitch to have survived and still be out there."

"What," Bouchard asked, "is that saying that Jimmy used?"

"The one where he says he'll live forever because God doesn't want him, and the devil's afraid he'll take over?"

"That's the one."

"Almost seems to fit doesn't it?"

"How is Cheryl handling this?"

"When last I spoke with her, she'd taken an NRA handgun course and got a license to carry a concealed weapon. If Fischer comes after her, he may get more than he expects. She's not the same woman she was." Houston changed the subject. "How was your trip into Boston?"

Bouchard was quiet for a second. She'd gone to Boston under the guise of doing some early Christmas shopping, although she was sure Houston knew there was more to it. The truth of the matter was that she'd gone to see an old friend, who happened to be a psychologist who worked closely with police officers who'd been involved in traumatic situations. "It was fine."

"Lisa Enright still on a campaign to legalize prostitution?"

"As far as I know she is, and I heard that Jimmy O'Leary left."

"Left?"

"Yeah, he and some Russian woman got married and went to Florida with her teenaged daughter."

"Willard's mother?"

"Dead from complications related to Alzheimer's."

"So," Houston picked up a large thermos and offered it to Bouchard. When she nodded, he replenished the cider in both of their mugs. "Looks as if it's a wrap."

He walked into the cabin and sensed her behind him. She kicked the door shut and said, "Living up here in the willy-wags isn't so bad after all."

Houston turned, placed his mug on the table beside the door, and took her into his arms. He felt her resist his touch then loosen and return it. He inhaled the scent of her hair and sighed. He knew everything was going to be alright.

SIX MONTHS LATER

66

Ernestine Fischer tossed the shovelful of heavy wet spring snow to the side and straightened up. She stared at the early morning sun and wiped sweat from her forehead. She was pushing fifty-five, getting too damned old for all this manual labor. She heard the sound of a large truck braking and wondered who it could be. It was April, and no one hauled timber during mud season. She heard the vehicle splash through the large puddles left by the early melt and saw its nose appear along the track of unpaved road that was called Main Street. The truck ground to a halt, and the door opened and slammed. With the rising sun in her eyes, she was unable to identify the driver when he rounded the nose of the large eighteen-wheeler, though it was easy to see that it was a man, and his walk and demeanor seemed familiar. She pushed her shovel into the snow beside the narrow path she'd been digging out and splashed through the flowing water that coursed down to the cabin. As she walked, she took great care not to rush or appear frightened.

She stepped onto the porch and looked back before entering the house; the figure had waded through the thigh-deep snow and had reached her path. Ernestine reached inside the door and grabbed her bolt-action .308 rifle. She opened and closed the bolt, loading a round into the chamber and then took the safety off. She waited until the man closed to within twenty yards. He wore filthy, worn clothes, and his face was obscured by a heavy black beard. His hair was long, stringy, and in need of both cutting and washing.

Trying to keep a calm tone of voice, Ernestine asked, "Can I help you?"

"Ernestine . . . don't you recognize me?"

The voice was familiar, and her stomach sank. "Willard?"

He smiled, and she saw that he had lost at least one tooth in the months since he had disappeared into the northern Maine woods. "Yeah, surprised to see me, sister?"

"Willard, it's not safe for you to be here. The police are still looking for you."

The smile left his face, and he looked every bit the killer that she knew he was. She knew that she had to do something; at the very least she had to notify the authorities of her brother's reappearance, but how could she? She lived in a house so far away from the benefits of society that her only electricity came from the gas-powered generator she used sparingly, and there was no way the phone company was going to run a line in for one permanent resident.

"So, big sister, are you going to let me in or not? After all, it's been six months since we last talked."

Houston was dozing, an open book on his lap and the Red Sox Patriot's Day broadcast playing at a low volume on the radio, when the phone rang. He answered on the second ring. "Houston."

"Mike? Wera Eklund."

"Hey, how are you, Deputy?" Houston was surprised. "What's up?"

"Ernestine Fischer just left my office."

"How is she?"

"Willard showed up on her doorstep on the eighth . . ."

Houston was on his feet before he realized it. "So he's alive. Is Ernestine alright?"

"He beat her quite severely. She believes that being his sister was the only thing that saved her life."

"Why did she wait so long to go to you?"

"He left her place this morning. You know how she lives—no electricity and no phone, just whatever she needs to survive. Once he left, she got in her old truck and drove here. I don't know how she did it. She's one tough old lady, that's for certain. She's over at the hospital now. I'm going to try and get her to stay a few days. At least until we get a fix on his location."

"Does she know where he went?"

"He didn't say anything, but he did go on a rant about getting even with someone."

"Cheryl?"

"Eventually . . ."

"Anne."

"Mike, you two need to watch yourselves. Somehow or another he found out where you live."

"Shit," he swore. "You know, last summer when he had her, we never did recover her wallet or her credentials and driver's license."

"There's a BOLO out on him. He was last seen driving an eighteen-wheeler log truck."

"Thanks for the call, Wera. We'll do what we have to. He's personal."

"Okay, but if you end up chasing him into my jurisdiction, I want to know about it."

Houston hung up the phone and heard a noise in the kitchen. Anne Bouchard entered the room and asked, "Who was that, hon?"

"We need to get ready. We got company coming."

67

Fischer left the eighteen-wheeler at the bottom of the grade and jumped out of the cab. He zipped his coat up, trying to ward off the predawn chill. True spring came late to Maine, and here in the high country the cold and ice hung on longer than it did at his home on the coast.

He reached inside his coat pocket and gripped the knife that he wore on his right hip, cursing at Ernestine. She'd hidden her rifle and he was unable to find it—even slapping her around did no good. The best he could do was the Bowie knife he'd been carrying since he became a fugitive. Thinking of the ordeal brought on a spasm of the memory of the pain from the sundry wounds that the bitch had inflicted on him. He fingered the handle of the knife and smiled when he thought of the pain and carnage the twenty-four inch blade was going to inflict on her.

He walked up the gravel lane, the frozen surface crunching under the heavy soles of his boots. He avoided frozen mud puddles and stayed in the worn, packed tire lanes—even though he felt certain that his quarry had not a clue about the imminent danger she was in. He hoped the man, the shooter with the long gun, was there, too. He'd kill that one first, a quick slash across his throat. If things went as he hoped, the son of a whore wouldn't die too quick—he wanted him to live just long enough to see what was in store for his bitch.

The night slowly gave way to the dull gray of early dawn, and he stood in the yard staring at the house. A trail of smoke drifted from the chimney, and the smell of wood smoke hung heavy in the air. He stepped onto the porch and gently touched the door knob. He applied a gentle pressure and was surprised when the door opened.

Fischer crept through the door and found himself in a spacious, rustic living room. A small fire burned in the fireplace, and he heard the sound of water running in the room to the right rear. Someone was in the shower—the perfect place to attack. He passed by the first of two easy chairs that faced the fire and slowly approached the door that he assumed led to the bedroom. He pulled the knife and reached for the doorknob.

"If Cheryl was here, she'd tell you that your father was right, Willard. You are a fucking idiot. You brought a knife to a gunfight."

He spun around, and the woman stood between the chairs, holding a pistol that didn't waver as she aimed it at him.

Bouchard held the 9 mm Glock with both hands. "Willard, I've knocked you senseless with a lamp, stabbed you with a gaff, tried to run you over with a boat, and shot you—this will be twice. I guess you're one of those people who just never learns."

His shoulders seemed to drop for a split second, and then he bolted. She fired at him, not sure that she scored a hit. Fischer dashed through the front door and headed for safety.

She heard the crack and thud of a rifle firing and a bullet hitting home. A spray of dark liquid splattered on the window and slowly turned from black to red in the early morning sunlight. She heard a thump, and through the door she saw a hand holding a Bowie knife flop down. Then blood slowly flowed across the porch.

She held her pistol at the ready and walked to the door. Standing in the threshold, she saw where Houston's bullet had entered the crazed killer's head . . . directly in the center of the deformed flat spot. She nudged the body with her foot, and when she was certain he was dead, she looked away and watched Houston climb down from the tree stand across the road. She smiled at him as he approached with his sniper rifle braced on his right hip and pointed at the sky. *Maybe,* she thought, *I'll get the first good night's sleep I've had since this scumbag grabbed me.*

Anne stepped over Willard Fischer and ran from the porch. She met Mike in the middle of the yard, and neither of them said anything as they held each other tight and watched the Fisherman's body go still.

ACKNOWLEDGMENTS

O f all my work, *The Fisherman* took me the longest to write, just over eleven years. I owe thanks to many people. To list a few: The two Connies: my late wife and soul-mate, Connie Hardacker, as this story was her idea. People ask where do ideas come from? This one came when my biggest fan walked into my den and showed me the website where I learned of the case upon which this novel is loosely (very loosely) based. Cancer took her before she could read the finished manuscript, and after eight years, I still miss her terribly. At the same time that Connie was my most devoted fan, she was also my most valuable critic—she was always willing to tell me what I needed to hear, not what I wanted to hear. On those occasions where I wanted to give up writing, she was the one person who gave me the strength of purpose to struggle onward.

The second Connie, my editor Constance Renfrow, who liked the manuscript from the first time she read it . . . then sent me four single-spaced pages of recommendations. Every writer looks upon their work as if it were their firstborn child, but like children, it can always be improved . . . she was right. The net result was a better, stronger story.

This brings me to my partner and new first reader, Jane Hartley. She read this manuscript at least four times and found who knows how many mistakes, typos, and inconsistencies. I knew what I meant to say, but she was quick to say, "This doesn't make sense."

To be successful, a writer needs a strong critique group of writers who are willing to read the bad stuff and to be strong enough to give him (or her) constructive, honest criticism. I have been fortunate to be involved with two such groups. First is The Monday Murder Club group where I truly learned *how* to write. Thanks Paula Munier, Steve Rogers, Andy McAleer, Margaret McLean, and Jim Shannon. Second, The Breathe Group in Maine. Thanks are also due to Wendy Koenig, Heather Hunt, Vince Michaud, and Larry Bubar for their invaluable feedback and input.

Thanks are owed to Jay Cassell and the staff at Skyhorse Publishing; without them none of this matters.

Finally, my friend and agent, Paula Munier, who has had faith in my work since we first met in 2002.

This book is a work of fiction, and any mistakes and/or inaccuracies within are entirely the fault of the writer.

Vaughn C. Hardacker
June, 2015

THE AUTHOR

Vaughn C. Hardacker has completed seven novels and numerous short stories. He is a member of the New England Chapter of the Mystery Writers of America and has published short stories in several anthologies. *The Fisherman* is his second novel to be published by Skyhorse Publishing. His thriller, *Sniper*, was released on February 4, 2014.

He is a veteran of the US Marines and served in Vietnam. He holds degrees from Northern Maine Community College, the University of Maine, and Southern New Hampshire University.

He lives in Maine and, at this time, is working on his next mystery thriller.